D0391505

In the cities of the South, there were perhaps a hundred Maggies flowering in any given year, girls planted, tended, and grown like prize roses, to be cut and massed and shown at debutant balls and cotillions. Nevertheless, the technique of creation varied only in small details and circumstances. It was a process of rules, subtle, shaded, iron bylaws that were tacitly drafted sometime during the Reconstruction. The formula lasted through a world war and a depression and another world war, and its end product, the young women of a certain caste of the South, were, on the main, as uniformly bright, hard, shining, and true as bullets from identical molds.

There was certainly no reason to think that The Rules would fail to hold, certainly no omens of mechanical malfunctions, when the life of Maggie Deloach began.

Praise for
HEARTBREAK HOTEL

"An absolute gem . . . a rare and wonderful book."
—*Richmond News Leader*

"Too real for comfort. Anne Siddons has truly captured the unwritten unspoken rules of the 'Southern society' game."
—*Charlotte Observer*

"A disturbing poignancy . . . Anne Rivers Siddons chronicles the everyday 1950s Deep South with a polished and disarming prose."
—*The Washington Star*

"Lots of colorful touches about growing up in the '50s. . . . . Bound to bring some smiles and, to the very soft-hearted, some tears."
—*Houston Chronicle*

Books by Anne Rivers Siddons

John Chancellor Makes Me Cry
Heartbreak Hotel
The House Next Door
Fox's Earth
Homeplace
Peachtree Road
King's Oak
Outer Banks
Colony
Hill Towns
Downtown
Fault Lines
Up Island
Low Country
Nora, Nora
Islands
Sweetwater Creek

HEARTBREAK HOTEL

ANNE RIVERS SIDDONS

POCKET BOOKS
New York   London   Toronto   Sydney

Pocket Books
A Division of Simon & Schuster, Inc.
1230 Avenue of the Americas
New York, NY 10020

This book is a work of fiction. Names, characters, places,
and incidents either are products of the author's imagination
or are used fictitiously. Any resemblance to actual events or
locales or persons, living or dead, is entirely coincidental.

Copyright © 1976 by Anne Rivers Siddons
Copyright renewed © 2004 by Anne Rivers Siddons

All rights reserved, including the right to reproduce
this book or portions thereof in any form whatsoever.
For information address Pocket Books Subsidiary Rights
Department, 1230 Avenue of the Americas, New York, NY 10020

First Pocket Books trade paperback edition July 2007

POCKET and colophon are registered trademarks
of Simon & Schuster, Inc.

For information about special discounts for bulk
purchases, please contact Simon & Schuster Special Sales
at 1-800-456-6798 or business@simonandschuster.com

Manufactured in the United States of America

10 9 8 7 6 5 4 3 2 1

ISBN-13: 978-1-4165-5350-2
ISBN-10:   1-4165-5350-9

For Heyward

BEFORE MAGGIE DELOACH went back for her senior year at college there had been a Benevolent Order of Elks parade, a water ballet at the municipal swimming pool in which she had starred with a flimsy backstroke and a water-lily face, a rhinestone tiara loaned from a gift and jewelry chain store in Atlanta, a speech by the governor, and a tattered monkey on the end of a leash held by a Jaycee.

It had been the Centennial celebration of her town, a small, heat-stunned town named Lytton, strung out on both sides of the Atlanta and West Point Railroad south of Atlanta, and Maggie had been the queen, largely because she had a yard of tanned, spectacular legs, slanted, odd brown eyes, an apple-green organdy hoopskirted dress with a hat to match, an attorney father who knew the governor from their fraternity days in law school, and a letter from the governor that would have gotten her, at the time, into any graduate school in the South. Her grades and antecedents, both the product of no effort whatsoever on her part, had gotten her as far as she had gone at her undergraduate school, for it took less to get further in the South of the middle fifties.

Maggie, tiaraed and sloe-eyed and itching for whatever, sweated the governor's pats and the monkey's probings equally and docilely. They were both part of The Rules. If she had thought about it consciously, Maggie would have liked the monkey a bit better than the governor. The monkey had one choice: to bite the Jaycee or the governor or whoever annoyed him, or not to bite. It was inconceivable that Margaret Hamilton Deloach should bite the governor. Rather, she smiled.

On the last night of the Centennial celebration, Maggie was crowned with the loaned crown at a ceremony in the Veterans of Foreign Wars lodge, and given an armful of red roses by the mayor of Lytton, and danced the first dance with her father, as if she were bowing to society. But she had, in fact, bowed to Lytton's small society twenty-one years earlier, when a tasteful card, inscribed with her name, date and time of birth, length, weight, and her parents' names—Frances Hamilton and Comer Hutchinson Deloach—went out in a January snowstorm to most of Lytton and a few people in Atlanta. There had never been another birth announcement after Maggie's to come from the tall old house with the stone gateposts on Coleman Street. It was as though Maggie was stamped Sufficient at her birth, and any other child would have been extraneous, an afterthought.

It was a good night crowning a good week for Frances and Comer Deloach, and they have the Centennial scrapbook still. Maggie has a small, star-shaped scar from a monkey bite.

After that, two days later, she went back to school. She drove the two-toned green Plymouth coupe her parents had given her when she graduated from high school, and it was full of crinolines and starched cotton skirts and blouses, ironed to blooming, sheened perfection a week earlier by loving black Carrie and hung from a broomstick sawed off and fitted over the back seat.

It was the first quarter of her last year at school, and she was going to summer school because she had done so for the past two years. There was little waiting for her at her east Alabama university except graduation, but there was less in Lytton.

When she drove into Randolph, Alabama, it was 2:00 P.M. Central Standard Time on Friday, June the fifteenth, 1956.

1

THE MAKING OF MAGGIE DELOACH was a process as indigenous to her part of the South as the making of cotton textiles in the fortress-bricked mills that crouched over the muddy, fast-moving rivers of the Georgia and Alabama plateau country. But it was a process far more narrowly applied. In the cities of the South—in Atlanta and Birmingham and Charlotte and Mobile and Charleston—there were perhaps a hundred Maggies flowering in any given year, girls planted, tended, and grown like prize roses, to be cut and massed and shown at debutant balls and cotillions in their eighteenth year. Unlike roses, they did not die after the showing; instead, they moved gently into colleges and universities and Junior League chapters, and were then pressed between the leaves of substantial marriages to be dried and preserved.

In the smaller towns, there were always perhaps three or four current Maggies. And in the smallest, like Lytton, there was only a Maggie. Nevertheless, the technique of creation varied only in small details and circumstances. It was a process of rules, subtle, shaded, iron bylaws that were tacitly drafted in burned and torn households sometime during the Reconstruction by frail, reeling gentlewomen throughout the exploded South, laws for the shaping of new women who would be, forever after, impervious to casual, impersonal chaos. The formula lasted, with only those modifications that were a nod to the times, through a world war and a depression and another world war, and its end product, the young women of a certain caste of the South, were, on the main, as uniformly bright, hard, shining, and true as bullets from identical molds. There was no reason to think that The Rules would fail to hold, certainly no omens of mechanical malfunction, when the life of Maggie Deloach began.

And so it was that Maggie's making began far earlier than the April night of her conception in the mahogany bed with pineapple finials that stood in a high-ceilinged bedroom of the house that had belonged to four generations of Deloaches. Comer Deloach, just out of the University of Georgia law school, had brought Frances Hamilton there as a bride of twenty, a tall, unworldly, drooping farm girl fresh from a north Georgia female academy. For the first four years of their marriage, Frances and Comer had shared the house with Comer's mother, a still-pretty woman of such relentless Christian charity that she had driven Comer's father, a stout, flushed dentist, to increasingly frequent all-night fox and possum hunts with what she called his Cronies, in

Lytton's surrounding pine woods. On one of those nights of drinking sour mash and following the baying speckled hounds, Big Comer had stumbled into an abandoned well on the deserted old Macintosh homeplace, covered only by tangled kudzu vines, and had broken his neck. By the time the fuddled Cronies had summoned old Dr. Clayton and the Lytton constabulary, with flashlights and ropes, Comer was dead.

For two years after his death, Elvira Deloach had lived comfortably alone on insurance and the considerable rentals from Deloach properties, largely in the black section of Lytton called Lightning, and had dispensed her charity to the less fortunate of Lytton and its environs via the funnel of the First Methodist Church of Lytton. And when Comer and Frances moved into the old Deloach place on Coleman Street, she leveled it at the young couple; chiefly at Frances, since Comer's proud new association with an Atlanta law firm meant an hour's train ride to the city, nine hours in the firm's library, and another chuffing hour's ride home. Frances Hamilton Deloach, conventional and biddable from her curly crown to her long, narrow feet, soon learned to fear, loathe, and obey her mother-in-law, and to ferment with tightly capped resentment even while she sat smiling with Elvira's missionary circle in the cool afternoon cave of her living room, studying Elvira's endless tracts and sewing awkwardly for the newly-come-to-Jesus in darkest Africa. Always, when as the junior member of the circle she was dispatched to the cavernous kitchen to bring in the tray of coconut cake and iced tea, prepared by muttering Theopal, she would hear the bee-drone of conversation drop to the level of a sweetly malignant litany, and she knew Elvira was sighing to a breath-held circle of Christian ladies about her daughter-in-law's ineptitude at the kitchen range and the lacy iron Singer sewing machine, her lack of initiative in the Work of the Church, and her inferior Hamilton antecedents. ("She tries, I suppose, but everybody knows they sharecropped until the twenties, at least, and the Good Lord only knows where they got money enough to send that child to Brenau. Jess MacLaren told me for a fact that there's no Hamilton money in *his* bank. Blood tells.")

By the time Maggie was conceived, Frances Deloach was unalterably a cowed and silently angry woman, but a confirmed standard-bearer of The Rules. They had, after all, gotten her off a sharecropper's red acres and into a lawyer's house.

Maggie's conception was accomplished in dead silence under cover of a spring thunderstorm and with the barest possible minimum of bedspring squeaking. Sanctified joy under her own roof was something Elvira Deloach effectively discouraged by calling softly to her son, through their connecting bedroom doors, that she thought she'd heard an intruding animal in the chicken coop, or that she'd heard an odd noise, almost like a moan; was Comer or Frances feeling ill? Or that she was "feeling her bad old stomach again" and would he please bring her a glass of Sal Hepatica, as she'd left her glasses on the sun porch again, silly woman that she was. She varied the timing of her nocturnal requests; a mutely furious Frances and a resigned Comer could not predict them. She died of a stroke—quite possibly an undissipated clot of Christian charity—before Frances's pregnancy was obvious even to her stiletto-sharp, tilted, cola-brown eyes. Frances Deloach was shocked and frightened when Maggie's baby eyes lost their unfocused blue and those same eyes stared at her from Maggie's small face.

From that moment on, as if to exorcise the ghost of old Elvira that, from time to time, looked at her out of those eyes, Frances drilled Maggie, tended her, groomed her, cherished her. Toward what, she could not have said, specifically. The Best for Maggie, she and Comer agreed when they discussed their child. Marriage ultimately, of course, a good one, but that was only a part of The Best. Safety, Frances meant, absolute, insular safety from the pain of an Elvira and all other pains ethereal and corporeal. But she did not know that this was what she meant.

There was never any doubt in the minds of Frances and Comer Deloach that the love they lavished on Maggie was honest love, nor was there in Maggie's mind, and Maggie still does not doubt it. Fierce, fathomless love is seldom wise love, but as Maggie told her therapist only a year ago, it is infinitely better than no love or cool, constructed affection.

Maggie was taken early and often to doctors, dentists, piano and art and dancing teachers, the better children's ready-to-wear departments, always in Atlanta. Sunday school and church services never began without Maggie Deloach, in that year's blue or burgundy velvet coat, leggings and bonnet to match. Piano and dancing recitals were never without her plodding, competent small fingers and feet and her grave face. Maggie was, for all her cadet training, a quiet child whose reticence looked sometimes like an oddly lovely sullenness, and sometimes was.

Maggie had the only Shetland pony in Lytton, and the only professional permanent wave given to a child.

She went, with only a few minor lapses, from Gerber babyhood into winsome toddlerhood into exemplary prepuberty. She was a bright child, and an increasingly and disturbingly pretty one. "Storm cuttin' up behind them eyes," Carrie would say, and a small surf of unease would wash over Frances. Maggie read early, and this made Frances inexplicably uneasy, also. Comer was charmed and amused when his small daughter ignored the carefully chosen books from Lytton's branch of the Carnegie Library and buried herself in his leather-bound volumes of Shakespeare, Arthur Conan Doyle, and Walt Whitman. De Maupassant was regularly taken away from her.

"Comer, I don't mind her reading when she's resting or the weather's bad, but she's always got her nose in a book. She reads under the covers with a flashlight. She told me the other night that Harry Hotspur plays in the sandbox with her and she *talks* to him, and I've *seen* her out there, right by herself, talking to *nobody* for hours. Comer, it's just not *right* for a child to lose touch with . . . with . . . *real* things like that." Frances Deloach talked mainly in italics; it was always one of her greatest charms for her husband, and kept her a girl to him always.

"Let her read," he said. "She's smart as a whip, and it isn't trash she's reading, Frannie."

And so reading remained one of Maggie's small and constant rebellions.

Maggie spelled impeccably, and wrote small poems about her dogs and her pony on Blue Horse school tablets. She drew with an early and mechanical facility, though little imagination, an endless succession of rearing horses with flowing manes. And she had playmates, the handful of children her age who lived in Lytton proper. Most of Lytton's young lived on outlying farms and helped with the chores at an age when Maggie was still not allowed to cross the street, and Maggie knew little of their existence, except to see them in overalls and bare feet, spilling out of pickup trucks and going into Lytton's feed and hardware and grocery stores with their parents on Saturday afternoons. It was not that Frances and Comer Deloach considered them inferior to Maggie; indeed, Frances was fond of saying that her own childhood on a farm had been healthful and happy in the extreme. It was only that they had so little in common with her. This was true. Maggie would have found little to say to those tough, laconic children in whose worlds a Shetland pony was a ridiculous toy of an animal that wasn't worth spit in front of a plow.

Frequently, on those Saturday afternoons, the farmers with the crosshatched, red backs-of-necks would lift a straw hat to her father. "Evening, Marcus," her father would say, and, "Evening, Mr. Deloach," the farmer would say in return.

"Why does he call you 'Mister' and you don't him?" Maggie asked once, after a sidewalk encounter.

"He's a client of mine, honey," her father said.

"You mean he owes you money," said Frances.

"Hush, Frannie. Marcus will pay me when he can. The Clevelands pay their bills."

Frances never mentioned the money those spare, quiet men owed Comer again in Maggie's hearing. She was, essentially and superstitiously, a charitable woman, and an obedient one. And until she began high school, Maggie never saw much of those oddly faded, Saturday-afternoon children. Once in a while there would be a still, bleached small face in the pickups and red-dusted Fords that pulled into the Deloach driveway in the evenings, and the small face would stare impassively into her own while the father and her own father talked their business, each man with a foot propped on a running board. The eyes of the children met in middle distance and clashed and dropped, and there was no ken in either pair.

So Maggie skated on her roller skates, went to

birthday parties, rode her bicycle, jumped rope, cut out *Gone With the Wind* paper dolls, colored in *Snow White* coloring books, and was driven into Atlanta in the Deloach Chrysler for Children's Symphony and Walt Disney matinees with the sons and daughters of Lytton's druggist, physician, Methodist minister, schoolteachers. She played seldom, by choice, with the small boys, who intimidated her and were deliberately rough with her in their games, smelling some essential, alien Maggie-ness instinctively, like wild young animals. And after Frances discovered her and the seven-year-old son of the hardware dealer playing doctor in the Deloach Cape jessamines, and spoke tearfully to her child of Jesus and cleanliness, Maggie's intimidation slid over into real fear, and she played largely with a narrowed field of little girls.

But she much preferred the company of adults, and since she was a precocious and mannerly child, and charming to look at, the people who came to play bridge and have cake and coffee with Frances and Comer suffered her presence with grace and even interest. She was in the habit of curling up with her cheek pressed against the warm, round, wood-fretted vent hole of the big floor-model Magnavox in the Deloach living room, so quiet, so still, that it was easy to lose her in the lamplit room. By the time she was ten, Frances had quite forgotten to admonish, "Little pitchers have big ears," and Maggie absorbed the talk of Lytton's select adulthood like a hardy, hidden flower in a spring rain.

*   *   *

High school was, for Maggie, a walk-through. Frances's Rules, absorbed as by osmosis through Maggie's faultless olive skin, proved to be workable, and augmented by her flashing, if unoiled, intelligence. They obtained for her all that Frances and Comer could have asked. Lytton's high school was a consolidated county school; in a student body comprised largely of rangy, rough-knuckled teen-agers ferried in every day by the orange Blue Bird county buses from the outlying farms and returned in time for a good three hours' chores, Maggie shone like a Staffordshire shepherdess. Those students, the bleached Saturday children of her childhood, were not Maggie's friends, but they prized her as the Cretans did Ariadne, without aspiration or rancor, and the votes that elected her cheerleader, Homecoming Queen, president of the Student Council and the Beta Club, editor of the student newspaper and the yearbook, Best All-Round in her graduating class, were offerings, homages, sheaves of wheat laid at her feet. Even her best friends—for she had two of those, daughters of Lytton's doctor and Methodist minister, respectively—could not call Maggie stuck-up. With them Maggie giggled, slept overnight, rode in their family cars to the Varsity in Atlanta in order to ignore the Georgia Tech students, listened to lugubrious 45 records, swapped angora sweaters, sneaked Pall Malls, double-dated the four or five "townies," whom they swapped amicably among themselves for four years.

With the others, the bus kids, she chatted in halls and homerooms, and learned their names by the second week in September. She went steady, her senior year, with one of them, a large, exquisitely wrought young man who was captain of the football team, and she wore his letter sweater, and she necked proficiently and dispassionately with him on the bus that carried the football team and the cheerleaders to and from the out-of-town games. Frances did not worry about that; Maggie drifted away from him in May, while the other girls of her senior class drifted toward marriages to their fullbacks and shortstops, as Frances had known she would. Maggie was the only one of her class to go to college.

On the night of her graduation, Frances and Comer gave a party for Maggie's entire senior class in the vast backyard of the Coleman Street house. All her teachers were invited, too, and came; there was ginger ale and lime-sherbert punch and sandwiches, and Japanese lanterns in the old oaks, and a band engaged from Atlanta to play for dancing on the brick terrace. Maggie was radiant, animated, tense in yellow tulle. "You should be very proud of her," said all Maggie's teachers to Frances and Comer, and, "Well, she's a sweet girl, and we *are* proud of her," said Frances and Comer.

Black Carrie, carrying out another tray of the party sandwiches she had made over the past two days, stopped to talk to the next-door maid who had been recruited for extra help. "She look like a princess, don't she?" said Carrie. "That chile always has been too good to be true."

In a shadowy corner of the yard, under a mimosa tree spilling its benediction of fragrance over Maggie's party, a young English teacher from Ohio, whose first teaching job after graduation had been Maggie's senior English class, poured a tot of gin from a pint bottle in his pocket into his punch cup and regarded Maggie, who had won, under his tutelage, a national essay contest on "Traditional Values in a Changing World." No Lytton student had ever done such a thing; the young teacher's tenure was assured.

"That," he said to the assistant football coach, who was sharing the gin, "is the most anonymous girl I have ever seen."

Three weeks later, Frances drove Maggie and a snowstorm of new summer clothes to Randolph University. Comer followed in Maggie's new graduation Plymouth. Randolph had been Frances's and Comer's first choice; it had a good but not frightening academic standing, a good but not *outré* English department (Maggie's major), and strict rules governing its women students. They had visited, the fall before, a small number of carefully winnowed southern schools, and came to Randolph on a bronze October Saturday. Maggie had been captivated and oddly, nervously, excited by its ersatz Georgian brick buildings and rows of sprawling sorority and fraternity houses and by the shoals of tweeded and plaided students spilling toward the stadium for the Randolph-Tulane game. The Dean of Women had been met, and had offered coffee and a sweetly worldly little talk on what Randolph strove to give to its young women, and a handful of literature.

Later, after Maggie had applied and been accepted and her roommate assigned, the roommate had been written, and had visited the Deloach house, and had been adjudged a nice girl. Maggie had liked her and she Maggie (Comer remarked later to Frances that the girls rather resembled each other), and they had driven around Lytton to smoke illicit Pall Malls and talk about Randolph. Both girls opted for summer school, and that too had been parent-approved. "Far less of a strain for her, don't you think, Comer, than fall, with everybody pouring in all at once?" Frances said. Comer thought it would be, undoubtedly.

After they had met her housemother in Marian Creighton Hall and hung her curtains and made her bed with an orange-and-blue plaid bedspread and plugged in her record player and student lamp and hung her clothes in her closet and found a parking place close to the dormitory for Maggie's Plymouth, Frances and Comer kissed Maggie, and Frances wept, and they drove away.

Maggie sat down on her bed and fished her covertly purchased ashtray and Pall Malls out of her purse. She lit a cigarette and looked out her window over the Women's Quadrangle and waited for her roommate and for other things.

"Now," said pretty Maggie, through smoke. "Now."

2

RANDOLPH, ALABAMA, in June 1956, looked much as it had for the past thirty years. It was a town born of its child eighty-four years earlier, and though both town and college had grown larger, it was as though they had both been magnified, rather than matured.

Town and school had grown out of the east Alabama plains as if from the same taproot. Indeed, if there had not been a rather grandiose main gate across from Mooney's Drugstore on the corner of Main and College streets, whose chiseled arch proclaimed, "Randolph University. A Land Grant School. Est. 1872," it would have been difficult to tell where town left off and school began. Except for the Victorian hulk of Semmes Hall, the oldest building on campus, which served as the school's administration building and scowled redly over the landscape for miles around, Randolph's commercial and academic edifices blurred into each other in a uniform smear of red brick, white concrete, stained, turn-of-the-century wooden gingerbread, and great, obliterating old trees.

Randolph University took its name from the farm
trading community where it sprang up, which in turn
had been named for the one affluent planter in the
county. It had flourished fitfully on its plain, steeped
in undulating wet heat in summer and blasted with
cheek-chapping winds, howling an unbroken hundred miles from the west, in winter, since its incep-
tion. It grew with utilitarian, bramble-bush tenacity,
if not much languid grace. Such academic grace as
Alabama had to offer was the province of the older
state university to the west, in white, neoclassic Tuscaloosa, where the progeny of Alabama's cotton and
peanut aristocracy had always been sent to be prepared to take up the guttering torch of agricultural
patriarchy.

Randolph was pragmatically and paternally designed some years later to accommodate the next
echelon, the future engineers, veterinarians, high
school teachers, and agricultural artisans of the New
South. It had been named, in the beginning, Randolph Polytechnic Institute, and kept its practical,
bucolic tenor until the late forties, when it found itself inundated in a tidal wave of solemn young men
on the GI Bill and a following wash of young women,
many of whom did not wish to be engineers, veterinarians, home economists, or county demonstration
agents.

So Randolph alumni were importuned, endow-
ments solicited, the Board of Regents wooed, and
applications accepted by the thousands. The School

of Science and Literature was hastily fleshed out with courses designed to prepare the newly sober young for the Business of Business. A handful of professors of some real academic note were lured to the campus to dispense such exotica as Contemporary Poetry, Philosophy, Ethics, Dance, Drama, Fine and Applied Art, largely to a swelling stream of girls like Maggie and a few young men thought to be fruity by the boys on Ag Hill.

Classrooms and dormitories were erected in searing new red brick to match the school's older, neo-Georgian buildings; Quonset huts and unabashed barracks were put up for temporary classrooms and housing for married students, and remained; one or two glaring new glass-and-concrete buildings soared to three-story height, and a vaguely Mies van der Rohe, air-conditioned Student Union building was added. Someone thought to apply for university status in 1950; the laconic football team mushroomed into a powerful machine made up of feral farm youngsters and a few savage young Pittsburgh Poles, and was feared throughout the Southeast. And Randolph came stumbling into tentative, MGM maturity as a "real" university.

But most of the change was internal, and the external changes dribbled west to be hidden by the Alabama pine woods, and Randolph town and Randolph University still had, in the mid-1950s, a dreaming, Brigadoon-like physical quality. At the time Maggie entered, you could still provoke a fine donnybrook with any Randolph student by calling it a cow college. And you still can today.

Randolph's business district consisted of four streets in a grid, four traffic lights, a railroad passenger depot for the fey train that shambled from Montgomery to Atlanta, a Greyhound Bus station-cum-post office, five service stations, and a Western Union office with a derelict franchise dance studio upstairs. Such businesses as lined the four streets were geared to the university trade. There were two book and college supply stores, a record shop, three self-conscious campus wear emporiums, two drug-stores with a full line of Revlon and Helena Rubinstein and a brisk under-the-counter trade in Trojans, five cafes and Snack Shoppes with booths and jukeboxes, a self-service laundromat, a portrait photography studio, a bank for the cashing of checks from home, a scabrous florist's shop, and an elderly, cream-brick hotel with a stygian lobby and fourteen chaste cells to let. Nothing in downtown Randolph was taller than two stories. Vaulting old trees lined the sidewalks and gave an oddly luminous, John Constable air to what was essentially a stark and unlovely smalltown commercial district. This canopy of misted green bewitched alumni and visiting parents into remembering Randolph as an idyllic, movie-set college town, and the tree roots cracked and humped sidewalks and wrenched black-suede Cuban heels askew by the hundreds.

Townspeople needing hardware, groceries, clothing for children and adults, liquor from the state ABC store, medical and dental care, and most other services drove twelve miles east to larger, uglier, and far more efficient Opelika.

On the fringes of downtown Randolph, where businesses slid into old wooden frame houses, boarding houses offered home-cooked meals or tickets for meals by the week to male students who scorned the dormitory dining halls and were not Greek affiliated. Women students dined, perforce, at the Women's Dining Hall in the Women's Quadrangle, or at their sorority houses.

Well-kept faculty homes lay in a secluded green wedge of Randolph to the east of the business district, along with the homes of the town tradespeople and the three or four professionals and the really lovely, white antebellum home of the original Randolph, who had deeded it to the school to house generations of presidents.

Farther out, on the Montgomery and Opelika and Birmingham highways, there was a sprinkling of peeling wooden cubes where students could dance, drink beer, and play pinball machines, from which women students were barred and to which they went in droves. Still farther out, toward Montgomery, was a state park with a lake, where students swam and had picnics and cooked hot dogs and necked on blankets and got pinned, drunk, and/or pregnant. And farthest out of all, into farm country, was a corrugated tin shack weeping rust and called "Pop's," which served the unrestricted male students as a gin mill and bawdy house.

And to the southeast, on the Alabama side of the Chattahoochee River, across from Columbus, Georgia, lay Phenix City, smeared and sooty citadel of strip shows, glass-brick and neon bar-and-lounges, whorehouses, organized crime, and Life. So Sodom-and-Gomorrahed was Phenix City that any woman student known to have visited there faced instant expulsion, and most of the popular girls had gone there with dates by the time they were juniors.

When Randolph had been a small college, constrained in a neat rectangle on the west perimeter of the business district, deans and department heads and one or two merchant princes had built sprawling, ersatz antebellum and Georgian homes along its four borders, and as the school had swollen and broken its boundaries and spilled west onto the forested plain, the educators and princes had moved to the eastern fringe of Randolph, and their homes had become sorority and fraternity houses.

It was to one of these old houses, a vast, square, whitebrick dowager on Van Lear Street across from Van Lear Hall, that Maggie Deloach came on a blinding, swimming hot midafternoon in June.

"Maggie! Mag-gie-e-e-e!" An ecstatic fluting squeal from an open upstairs window of the Kappa house caught Maggie, laden chin-high with crinoline and trailing extension cords, halfway up the weed-choked flagstone walk. A white-blond head helmeted with pin curls followed the squeal out the window: Delia June Curry, from Prattville. She met Maggie on the veranda, hugging Maggie and crinolines alike.

"*God,* I'm glad to see you! There's but nobody in this whole place! Look at your *tan!* Let me have some of that stuff; oh, *look,* that's *darling,* it's *new!*"

Later, after seven sweating trips up the curving staircase from the Kappa foyer, they sat on the bare mattress of Maggie's still unmade twin bed in her upstairs rear bedroom and lit cigarettes. Beaded Coca-Colas from the rusted machine in the basement laundry room were already tepid in the swaddling heat, stirred but unmitigated by Maggie's electric fan. It was very quiet and still and hot and no time at all.

"What are you doing back so early?" asked Delia through a double-nostriled plume of Kent smoke. She was startlingly, Botticelli pretty, even in pin curls and baby doll pajamas and Cuticura dots.

"Oh, Freshman Orientation," Maggie groaned. "I told Dean Fisher I'd be on the pre-planning committee way last spring and forgot about it till she wrote me last week. We don't meet till tomorrow, but I thought I'd get here a day early and get the good closet before Sister does, for once. It *is* a tomb, isn't it? Who else is here?"

Tactfully, Maggie didn't ask Delia why she was in Randolph five days before the summer quarter started. Seeing a shoo-in for every campus queenhood that didn't involve scholastic merit when they had rushed her two autumns before, the Kappas had pledged Delia before she could bat her indigo Jane Powell eyes, and had spent the time since trying to keep her off academic probation. She had, Maggie knew, flunked sophomore English again last spring; this summer was her last chance. She'd stayed on at the Kappa house between quarters to be tutored by a young English instructor named Tucker; looking at the delicate blue stains under Delia's eyes and the fading strawberry hickey on her fragile neck, Maggie knew who had been tutoring whom in what, and sighed. The Kappas would have to put her on inactive if she didn't make her grades this summer, which meant she couldn't be run for Homecoming Queen next fall. Delia was pinned to Jenks Foley, who was Randolph's head cheerleader; she'd have had Homecoming Queen made in the shade. *Maybe* Cornelia Quin could pull it off, but her acne flared in cold weather, and as for that nerd in Animal Husbandry she insisted on dating, in the face of concerted Kappa disapproval . . .

The matter had been put to Cornelia by an unofficial committee of three sisters, including Maggie, the winter before, when Cornelia had come in from the Randolph Independent Organization Ball and announced coolly that she would probably marry Leon after graduation.

"How *can* you?" M.A. Appleton, Kappa president, Religious Emphasis Week chairman, and self-appointed spiritual advisor to the Sisterhood, had almost wept. "How can you *marry* him if you can't even be *pinned* to him? He's an Independent."

"Why?" Jean Lochridge had asked levelly in her best Student Judiciary Committee voice.

"*Because* he's an Independent," flashed Cornelia, who was dean's list in third-year Architecture but was forgiven because she was dark and chic, a Birmingham Quin, and had an MG. "And because he's *independent.* Do any of you even understand the difference?"

Maggie had said nothing; she did not, really, understand the difference, but the words gave her an eye-flicker of unease, as if they had been in a foreign language she should have known, and didn't.

No way for Cornelia, she thought now, and sighed again, and pushed the ashtray to Delia, and repeated, "Who's here?"

"Oh, M.A., who came back a week early so the Burb wouldn't be by herself and burn the house down, and so she could hug me goodnight when I came in from studying with Tuck and see if I'd been drinking. And the dummies like me who have to study and the wheels like you who have to plan stuff for the freshmen. *God,* I'm glad you're here, or M.A. would rat on me to the WSGA for smelling like beer last night and I'd get kicked out instead of just flunking out. And then the Burb's here. Of course. And still 'asleep.' Her iced tea smelled like a Jack Daniel's distillery at lunch."

"Oh, no," Maggie giggled, clapping a hand to her forehead. "Tonight she'll have a migraine."

"No, a hot flash!"

"No, heat prostration!"

"No, she'll be worn out from the carpet men coming this morning and have to take a catnap."

"Catnap, catnip . . . catshit!" Maggie collapsed backward in helpless laughter, bumped her elbow on her white plastic Arthur Godfrey ukulele, and caught it up. She strummed, ineptly. They sang, convulsed, to the tune of "Ja-da":

"Catshit, catshit, c-a-t-s-h-i-t.

"Catshit, catshit, c-a-t-s-h-i-t.

"You can smell it in the corner, you can smell it in the hall.

"You can wipe it on the ceiling, you can wipe it on the wall.

"*Oh,* catshit, catshit, c-a-t-s-h-i-t!"

And fell into a huddle of laughter at nothing at all but heat and liberation and Maggie and Delia.

"It's Bourbon you can smell in the hall," choked Delia, wiping tears and Maybelline from her cheeks. "And all over the whole damned house. Whatever, she's going to be out like a light by eight o'clock. What I was going to tell you, Tuck and I are going to Phenix City tonight. Come go. She'll never know."

"Delia, I *can't!* And you'll be out on your butt if M.A. finds out. And what's this Tuck business, anyway? Jenks would have a hissy."

"Oh—Tuck." Delia dismissed the Randolph faculty from instructor to president with a wave of her hand. "Besides, what can M. A. do, tell the WSGA? You're the *president!* Come on, Maggie, there's nobody on campus to see you, and that freshman stuff isn't until tomorrow, and Boots isn't back yet. . . . " She looked quickly at Maggie's sleeveless blouse for the diamond Kappa Alpha pin that should be there, just below and to the left of Maggie's Kappa pin. It was. "So you couldn't have a date anyway. The picture show on College is still closed, and the Roxy's got *Above and Beyond,* again, and we're going to Ma Beechie's. Tuck says there's a woman there that can pick up a Dixie Cup with her you-know-what. Come on, Maggie, you're going to end up just as square as M.A. if you don't do something just a *little* awful once in a while. And I've got a key to the sun porch door. Come on, hear?"

Maggie looked out her window over the line of neat Kappa garbage cans in the backyard; over the privet hedge that separated the Kappa house from the backyards of the boarding houses beyond; over the parking lot that held only her Plymouth, M.A.'s brown-and-tan Chevrolet, and the Burb's battered Dodge. Heat uncoiled from the black asphalt, eddied and swayed, cobralike, blurring the privet hedge. The afternoon seemed stuck at three forty-five; shadows had not lengthened, nor sounds seeped through the wall of shimmering heat. There was no one in sight.

"Sure," said Maggie, stumping her Pall Mall. "Why not?"

3

I T WAS A RADIO that woke Mrs. Myra Cutler Kidd
at five that afternoon, reached deep and hurtingly
into a dead, sweated sleep, and nagged her eyes open.
The radio was in an upstairs room toward the back of
the house, away from her own suite just off the foyer
of the Kappa house.

Her rooms had been carved in plasterboard from
the huge drawing room of the old house when the
sorority had bought it: the Housemother's Suite. A
cubicle of a bedroom, in which Mrs. Kidd had in-
stalled her narrow, heirloom tester bed and a hot
plate and little else; a minuscule bathroom; and a private sitting room full of graceful old French pieces,
which she had brought from her own home in Elba,
Alabama, when the Judge had died and a Kappa
niece at Randolph had persuaded the sisterhood
that her aunt, a gentlewoman in suddenly reduced
circumstances and left with no close, encumbering
family, would be a perfect substitute for the sweetly
senile old lady who'd just had to be retired.

"She's a lady," Carol Ann had told the Kappas
simply in her tired, ancestral Kidd voice. The soror-

ity was still smarting from the defunct Mama Lee's
last official appearance as Kappa housemother. She
had appeared to preside over the Georgian silver
coffee service at the Kappa Preferential Rush party
in black suede pumps, stockings, her good jet jewelry,
and a black satin slip, dripping dewlaps of white-
crepe flesh around her various cinching straps; had
given the stricken sisterhood and Preferred Rush-
ees alike a wide, wild blue stare, said, "I must be out
of my fucking mind," and left the room slowly and
magisterially.

The Dean of Women had come and sat that
night with Mama Lee, and a daughter had come the
next morning to take her away to a rest home in
Tuscaloosa, where a Kappa delegate dutifully called
once a quarter and came back to report that the old
woman was as crazy as a bedbug. Meanwhile, the
house had had to be closed and the girls moved into
overcrowded dormitories until a new housemother
could be found, and the Kappas lost their top four
rush choices. A lady sounded wonderful—it was the
"fucking" that had appalled everyone, not the sudden
dementia; most Kappas came from small southern
towns where gentlewomen of a certain age went ba-
roquely crazy with some regularity.

And so Mrs. Myra Cutler Kidd had come, and removed the Naugahyde furniture that went with the
quarters to the Kappa basement, and arranged her
sitting room into a little salon where her girls might
come to have coffee or iced tea and listen to her clas-

sical records and be counseled in connection with their troubles and their identities and their hopes for womanhood.

That had been seven years ago. The troubles that were aired in the salon during her first year of residency had little to do with the symmetrical, childless world of camellia shows and porcelain collections and official dinners in Montgomery that the Judge's Lady had just lost; they shocked and frightened her, and it showed, and the girls gradually quit trickling into her sitting room in dusters and pin curls and settled things among themselves; Elvis Presley and Kitty Kallen overpowered her Beethoven, and she drank her coffee and tea increasingly alone, liberally laced with Jack Daniel's.

It was Elvis Presley who clove into her brain now and set the familiar point of pain behind her eyes pulsing even before she opened them.

> *Since my baby left me,*
> *Found a new place to dwell.*
> *Down at the end of Lonely Street*
> *At Heartbreak Hotel . . .*

Obscene, she thought, waiting to let the queer, hot, faraway room settle back around her before opening her eyes to the shaft of sunlight that would smite them shut again. Ugly, dirty, wriggling, obscene thing, grunting, thumping, *indecent* . . .

The radio went silent suddenly; a silver giggle

replaced it. Delia. Sorry, witless little thing. Little tramp. And then a clearer, rounder voice whose words she couldn't hear, whose owner she couldn't place for a moment. Not Margaret Anne Appleton, not Virginia Crewes, not Catherine Barnes. Who else was in the house? Dear God, it couldn't be that she had lost another day, the quarter couldn't have started, not another of those terrifying holes in time and space . . .

". . . have a key in the first place unless you stole it, and you'll have to put it back in the morning or I *will* tell M.A.," said the clear, round voice with a rich hill of laughter in it, into the sudden, airless rush of silence. Maggie Deloach.

Mrs. Kidd sat up, sinuses dried and pounding, heart skidding sickly with the palpable, wet heat and the noon's liquor. Oily, cold sweat beaded between her heavy breasts and thighs, making a paste of the Cashmere Bouquet she floured herself with, futilely, against the fiery heat-and-girdle rash. Her little diamond Bulova swam into focus. Five-fifteen. The bars of sun through the Venetian blinds were still savage. Friday. What for dinner, the tuna-fish salad? Had she told Estelle about the salad? How many for dinner? Four . . . no, five now, with Maggie back. Well, Estelle could stretch the salad. And the bread order had come, and there was plenty of iced tea left from lunch.

She thought about the iced tea, cold and infinitely, richly wet. Her mouth and throat were so dry that there were hurting edges. An hour at least until she had to bathe and dress for dinner. Delia and Maggie would probably giggle and chatter for another hour, giggle at her, most likely. They called her the Burb, because of the Bourbon, she supposed, and she hated them for it, but dully, with no heat. They all called her that. Her own niece, Carol Ann, had come to call her that. Bitches. Spoiled little fornicating bitches, who came in with Bourbon on their own grassy-fresh breaths, steaming from the back seats of cars, their cottons wrinkled over their smooth young, young bodies, smiling at her, gusting waves of Bourbon-disguising Juicy Fruit in her face: "Night-night, Mama Kidd." "Oh, don't hug me, Mama Kidd. I'm all hot and sweaty. The library was *murder.*" That blanket at the lake, that was what was murder, wasn't it, honey? And murder is what that doctor over at Tuskegee will do when he rips out that baby. Oh, yes, I know about that doctor, and murder is what . . .

There is time, she thought, jerking her mind back to the hot orange now, for me to just slip on my wrapper and run back and get some iced tea before anybody shows up for dinner.

She met them coming blindly back from the kitchen, her wrapper askew around her, slaked and heavy with the iced tea, wild-haired, carrying the trembling cut glass pitcher. She hadn't heard their feet on the stairs; the runner had just been replaced after the semiannual cleaning. Her own feet were bare on the wide old boards. They stood frozen on the landing, two furtive fawns, one tawny, one gilt. They were starched and crinolined, strawbagged, earringed. The inevitable, toe-showing Capezio shells were replaced with patent leather pumps on bare brown feet. White chalk pop pearls shone eerily from Delia's throat in the stained glass gloom. Maggie, in wide-skirted, scoop-necked white, wore no jewelry.

You tell me library and you're lying, she thought, and she said, highly and falsely, "Well, chickies, you caught me raiding the fridge. Hey, Maggie, darling, I didn't know you were coming back so early. How are your mama and daddy? Goodness, I must look a sight, it's *bad* trying to nap in this heat . . ."

"Hi, Mama Kidd. I'm sorry we woke you up, isn't it awful, this heat? We thought we'd run out to the Holiday Inn and get a Coke or something, I told Estelle not to count on us for dinner. . . . " Delia, flustered, was bleating like a sheep.

"We might drop by and see Dean Fisher," said Maggie, still-faced with the lie. "I've got to do that Freshman Orientation thing. Don't wait up for us, Mama Kidd. Mama and Daddy said tell you hey."

After they had fled pattering through the foyer and across the tiles of the veranda, Mrs. Kidd took the pitcher of iced tea into her bedroom and sat down in the path of her fan. She flicked the cord of her blinds slightly, just enough to get a narrow, slitted glimpse of Maggie and Delia shimmering into the front seat of a blue Ford. She knew the car. Tucker, that young instructor who was tutoring Delia. Tutoring, my foot. Delia wasn't even fair game; she would inevitably flunk out of school or marry that young loud-mouth idiot cheerleader or be pregnant by winter quarter and the house would be rid of all that gum-snapping gilt whorishness. Pregnant. She would have an abortion, she would die. Tragic, a cruel thing. Mrs. Kidd could, though, make a little lesson of it, a gentle talk with her girls around her on her Oriental, in flannel robes and fuzzy slippers, while she sat on her love seat and poured the coffee. No, hot chocolate. At Christmas. She would put out the little Florentine crèche. And put some carols on her old mahogany Capehart . . . no, perhaps a *little* too much, in light of the circumstances. Beethoven, of course, the Fifth . . .

"Girls, Delia would be the last one to object if we thought about her at this time, and talked a little about . . . "

Oh, my God, forgive me for what I think and help me help my girls, said Mrs. Kidd into the heat. Delia really doesn't know any better.

Maggie Deloach, though, that was different. Maggie was lying, she was sure of it. Lying and sneaking off, Phenix City, undoubtedly. Maggie, with everything. With her grades, with her campus offices, with her popularity, with her fine family and that young man she was pinned to . . . money there, she knew. His family had practically settled the Mississippi Delta. The Judge had known the family, spoken often of Courtney Claiborne, the boy's father, also a judge.

Cotton and farmland and a law practice now, and a great deal of money . . .

I cannot let Maggie slide, she thought. Maggie has to be taught. Maggie has too much to lose. Maggie has everything. Maggie has eyes the color of iced tea, of Coca-Cola, of Bourbon . . .

She had been planning to stay up tonight, to wash out some things and write some letters, to listen to her records. To catch them in their lie. She went to her bookshelf and took down the boxed set of Kahlil Gibran they had given her for her birthday and took out a pint bottle of Jack Daniel's and poured it into the pitcher of iced tea.

Estelle can manage dinner, she thought, but I cannot manage this heat. Maybe, if I can just get to sleep early, it will rain in the night, and tomorrow will be cooler, and things will be better. . . .

After a while she did sleep.

4

ON THE TINY STAGE, a ripened and burst woman in a G-string and a lei of plastic cherry blossoms was doing incredible things with a maraschino cherry impaled on a swizzle stick. She was got up, so far as it went, in varying shades of red and pink. Her clear plastic Springolator sandals, slapping tiredly against her calloused heels, were tinted pink. Her long gloves were deep red. Her hair was the precise color and texture of cotton candy. There was a clump of artificial cherries bobbling insanely at the point where the G-string disappeared between her loose white thighs, and another clump poised on the nipple of each long breast. Her breasts slapped against the cuff of flesh that encircled her waist, bisected by the G-string, which disappeared into her waist at her sides and emerged again over her puckered buttocks. Standing still, she looked like a grimy snow-woman hastily made of loose, wet snow. In motion, she was stunningly obscene. Her face, above all the wildly bouncing flesh, was heavy and Balkan and pitted with acne scars, and should have been stupidly, stolidly impassive. Instead, she closed her eyes in ersatz ecstasy, pursed her mouth as if blowing bubbles underwater, punctuated the climactic forward thrusts of her pelvis with breathy small grunts. Her professional name was Miss Cherry Delight, and she did her act to the sliding, insinuating strains of "Cherry Pink and Apple Blossom White." Since the song had hit the top ten the previous year, she had been the ten o'clock featured attraction at Ma Beechie's, and the take from the soldiers stationed at Fort Benning in Columbus, Georgia, just across the river, had tripled.

Maggie, chewing the plastic straw in her tom collins, watched Miss Cherry Delight from under her eyelashes, her face slightly averted, a skewed smile of fabricated worldly amusement pinned rigidly on her mouth. She had worn the same expression when Rhett Butler had carried Scarlett O'Hara up the endless stairs into the pulsing red, bed-concealing darkness when she had gone to see a revival of *Gone With the Wind* with a date in high school.

Maggie was sincerely and deeply embarrassed by Miss Cherry Delight and her spotlit, sagging nakedness and what she was doing to the maraschino cherry. A dull-fuchsia wave of heat, partly gin but mostly mortification, stained her skin from the neck of her dress to the roots of her hair. The heat flooded her entire body. She could feel it all the way to her waist, flushing her own neat, small breasts and pounding at her cheekbones and forehead. It made her uneasily aware of all her taut skin and sweetly fitting flesh, and of the slender, precise bones under them. She knew if she looked down, her chest would be mottled with magenta just below her collarbones. On Maggie, liquor and emotion could never be concealed. They were spelled out in scarlet letters on her chest.

Tuck, owlish and thickly precise from a succession of neat Bourbons chased with beer, was propped in his chair by the silver-painted wall at his back and Delia's bare brown shoulder on his right. Charles Peyton Tucker had thick, horn-rimmed glasses and a shock of dark hair that slid limply into his eyes. He wore it—and the glasses—so as not to be confused with the crewcut and back-buckled young men he flogged earnestly through sophomore literature. Tuck was twenty-six, but looked younger, with a blind, vulnerable face. He was a graduate of Boston University. He had thought to bury himself gratefully in the gentle bog of a good, small New England college, where he would brew Earl Grey tea for small groups of students in front of a grate fire in some dim, bayed, book-lined room overlooking a quadrangle. He would publish a little—the Russians were his specialty—and he would marry, eventually, one of the shetlanded, intense young women who knew how to pour tea as well as appreciate Gogol. He would eschew the delicately murderous politics of academe and espouse the dreaming, underwater life of the scholar, and retire in love and honor somewhere on the fringes of an elmy green campus, where he would be visited by a steady

stream of former students seeking counsel and an afternoon of radiant peace. Tuck had never gotten over
Robert Donat in *Goodbye Mr. Chips.*

Instead, he had found himself at Randolph, with
vast, shuffling classes full of bored young southerners who retained just enough of *Bleak House* to squeak
through his carefully wrought finals, could not read
Henry James aloud, and thought perhaps Gogol was
a freshman fullback from Gary, Indiana. His tweed
jacket acquired a permanent gamy stink from the
winter radiators and savage spring heat in his peeling
classroom in the university's oldest building; his landlady at the boarding house would allow no visitors to
his Sears Roebuck Swedish Modern room, which had
no grate fireplace and no bookshelves and overlooked
the Adult Education wing of the Randolph Baptist
Church; the blurred drawls and semiliterate mono-
syllables of his students irritated his eastern ears,
and they laughed at his pipe. The bulk of the faculty,
southerners themselves, thought him snobbish and
pretentious. The heat overwhelmed and disoriented
him. He thought often that he was growing decadent
in it, languid and rotted, like a character in a Somer-
set Maugham novel. He blamed his helpless involve-
ment with Delia Curry on the heat, but in truth he
was a sitting target for Delia. As perfect, ruthless,
simple, and impersonal a consuming organism as a
young shark, Delia had devoured his frail, tentative
complexity in a single bite on the first night of their
tutoring, without compunction or even thought.

Delia was not embarrassed by Miss Cherry De-light. Neither was she entertained. In a corner of the smoke-soured room, by the cash register, was a juke-box for playing between the performers' acts, and a minuscule space for dancing had been clawed out of the jumble of tables. After her first technical interest in the several talents of the stars—the tassel woman, the lady with the fluorescent hands painted on her body that glowed when black-light spots hit her, the woman with the tattered and drugged-looking boa constrictor—had waned, Delia had dismissed them all as fat, tacky old cows.

Delia wanted to dance.

The room was jammed with lean, prowling-eyed young soldiers, cool and mean and languid, in droves, whistling and stamping and calling out matter-of-fact obscenities to the uninterested strippers. They were drinking hard. No beer now, not at Ma's. Just the house hard stuff. Ma's kept a few token bottles of call brands, but they were dusty and unused. Ma's prices were prohibitive. No one was mean drunk, fight drunk, yet, but the chemistry of an evening is a delicate and unpredictable thing.

The manager of Ma Beechie's—if there had ever been a Ma, no one currently employed there knew who she was—ran a practiced eye over the house. Ma Beechie's was strictly off limits to the soldiers, but Ma's and the MPs from Benning had a long-stand-ing gentleman's agreement: no raids unless things got so bad they had to be called. There was enough along

Phenix City's main strip to keep the MPs busy without going looking for trouble. In a way, Ma's kept the boys off the streets.

In return, Ma's kept its girls clean and its whiskey watered enough so that serious, bloody, attention-provoking brawls were rare. In this heat, though, things could deteriorate very fast. The manager was never at ease on truly hot nights. And when Randolph was in summer session, he was distinctly apprehensive. Goddamn little college girls, switching in all tricked up and prissy on the outside, little bitches in heat inside their long full skirts and starched blouses, little bitches come to get their jollies watching the dirty stuff. That dancing they did, that dirty bop thing, was twice as filthy as anything his tired whores could master. And their music. The words, if you listened to them, were gutter stuff . . . "I'll let you keep it tonight, if you'll hold it real tight, but, baby, don't break it." "Work with me, Annie." "Git it, git it, git it, aw-w-w, *baby!*" As for that Presley punk, he sounded like he was screwing the microphone. Looked it, too. And didn't they just love it, though?

He looked over at the table in the corner, where the little blonde was. She had come in about eight, with the booky-looking cat and the tall, quiet girl in white. The manager's eyes kept going to the girl in white; she was oddly, hypnotically beautiful in the fetid gloom, with her lovely, restless hands and averted topaz eyes and her embarrassment. She was so obviously out of her element, so stiffly cool, so

not-to-be-touched that there was an intense pro-
vocativeness about her. But every other eye in the
house was on the little blonde. She had danced once
with the guy in glasses; he was awkward and a little
drunk, and it was easy to see that the humping, sexual rhythm was distasteful to him. But the blonde . . .
God, thought the manager, that's not decent even
in this place. They had sat down at the end of the
record, but not before all the eyes had been slowly,
palpably and explicitly over the blonde's body. She
had given them back the look, in a slow, violet sweep
around the room, and from then on, the manager
had known that the night could go any way at all. He
hoped the guy with glasses would get so drunk they
would have to leave soon.

But no. A tall, tight-faced, red-haired corporal
got up, put a coin into the box, pressed a button. The
velvet Presley smirk uncoiled into the room: "Well-
ah, since my baby left me, found a new place to dwell,
UH. Down at the end of Lonely Street at Heartbreak
Hotel . . . . " Weaving a little, never taking his eyes off
her, jeered brashly by his companions and then the
whole room, the corporal walked to the table in the
corner. He held out his hand to the blonde, silently.
Silently, she rose and followed him onto the dance
floor.

Tuck regarded Delia and the corporal morosely.

"'La Belle Dame sans Merci,'" he said carefully,
draining the melted ice in his glass. "Look at them,
Maggie. Two fossils. Two perfect throwbacks. Bron-

tosauruses at play. No, brontosaurus and tyrannosaurus, whooping it up in the land of Hogarth. They're extinct, but they don't know it. Let's have another drink, Maggie, and talk of shoes and ships and sealing wax."

Tuck made Maggie uncomfortable. She could not pin him down. She had read Lewis Carroll, but no one she knew quoted him conversationally. Furthermore, she had never had social intercourse with a Randolph faculty member, and she could not forget that Tuck was one of them, even though he was only an assistant instructor and obviously besotted both with Delia and Bourbon. She thought him romantic and a bit exotic, in the Heathcliff manner, with his fine-drawn eastern face and his literary allusions, but she also felt a small and shamed contempt at the way he allowed Delia to superimpose her bright shallowness over his depths. In Maggie's world, poetic, deep young men did not tag after the Delias, and professors did not take students to strip joints, and men coped with marauding corporals with curly-lipped, James Dean cool. Tuck was not playing by Maggie's rules, and she did not know what to say to him.

So she said, "I really shouldn't. If Mama Kidd caught me, I'd be out of school in a minute, and that would look just great for the president of the WSGA, wouldn't it?"

Then she thought, I sound like I'm bragging, and she said, "Did you follow Grace Kelly's wedding? I thought that picture of her in *Life* was the most gorgeous thing I've ever seen. I just love the cool, aristocratic look she has. She really does look like a princess, doesn't she? I mean a born one. . . . "

Why don't I just shut up? thought Maggie miserably. I don't care about Grace Kelly and neither does he. Tuck was laughing, snapping his fingers for the waiter and laughing at her.

"Do you want to be a princess, Maggie? I thought you *were* a princess, Maggie. A real southern princess, the new aristocracy of the Bozart. H. L. Mencken."

"That was Sahara of the Bozart," Maggie said meekly but with unconscious ice in her voice. There was a rising edge to Tuck's voice that she did not like.

He looked at her, not laughing any more. "So it was," he said. "So it was. A southern princess who reads Mencken, yet. What else have you got there behind your brown, brown eyes, Maggie the cat? That's . . . "

"Tennessee Williams, *I* know," said Maggie in exasperation. She wished he would stop, yet the talk was strangely titillating.

Tuck's drink came, and he took a deep swallow. He leaned closer toward her across the table, reached out and touched her cheek with the dripping tip of his swizzle stick. He was noticeably drunk. Maggie turned desperately to look over her shoulder at Delia and the corporal; they were swaying, glued together, their feet not moving, to "The Great Pretender." Delia's eyes were closed, and the corporal's red chin was resting on the yellow-white crown of her head.

Maggie saw suddenly that he had been right about them. They did look like superb, healthy animals from another age, savage innocence mating in sunlight, surrounded by a melting, corrupted civilization. I must be getting drunk, she thought. I want to go home.

"Actually, I know more about you than you think I do." Tuck was confiding, leaning far over into her face. "I know that Claiborne kid you go around with. I had him in a class a couple of years ago. He's a toad, Maggie the cat. A tall, blond, beautiful, spoiled, rich Mississippi toad with a toad's brain, Maggie the cat. I flunked him. I suppose you'll marry him and go live with Big Mama and Big Daddy on the Dayulta, won't you? Then you really *will* be Maggie the cat. You're a fool, Maggie. He's meat for Miss Delia June Curry there, she of the great big blue eyes and tiny little mind. That's James Thurber."

"Boots is not stupid," Maggie flared. "If he flunked your class, it makes me wonder what kind of a teacher you are. I think I want to go now."

"He's stupid. And you're a fool. Ah, shit." Tuck drew back and gulped his drink. She thought he had tired of baiting her, but he went on.

"I read an article you wrote last winter for the *Senator,* that thing you did after Autherine Lucy enrolled at the university. It was a surprise, Maggie. It was a piece of simplistic manure, but it was the only positive thing I read in all the yellow journalism that came out about that poor, stupid Negro. Maggie the nigger-lover. What did your good Kappa sisters say about that article, Maggie? What did your barefoot Mississippi boy say? I'll bet it made Big Mama and Big Daddy beat their feet in the Mississippi mud, and not in down-home joy, either. You better not let the sun set on your head in Yoknapatawpha County, Maggie."

Maggie flushed redder. The article had been one of her weekly columns for the student newspaper; she had been a feature writer for the *Senator* since her sophomore year, and was made feature editor at the beginning of her junior year. The columns were fun for Maggie, and easy for her. They were facile, flowing, amusing small things, their uniform innocuousness effectively masking Maggie's one real gift: a rich, glinting virtuosity with words.

Since her gift was accompanied with no perceptible profundity, originality of thought, or insight, Maggie did not know she had it. She would not have acknowledged it if she had known. Writing was simply too easy. It was a part of the inevitable bounty that flowed when one followed The Rules; it was almost a trick she pulled on the world. Subconsciously, Maggie assessed all her credits in this manner. She learned the drill, she applied it, *ergo,* she was rewarded. Maggie was a Kappa and the *Senator*'s editor-in-chief was a close friend; it was therefore meet and right that she be an editor. She was, moreover, an English major and a dean's list student.

Maggie thought, vaguely, when she thought about

it at all, that she would "do something in advertising" when she graduated. Meanwhile, she wrote her columns much as she rolled her socks and bought Bass Weejuns. One did.

She wrote them, usually, in a scant half-hour on the day they were due, neat little weekly essays on the honor system, the successful basketball team, or late coed permission for pep rallies. Once in a while, out of boredom or a vestigial sense of duty, she ventured into world affairs. Maggie was as effectively insulated from the world outside Randolph as her peers; these columns were not successful. She had done a heated and chauvinistic piece on an Egyptian border ambush at Gaza once, and the *Senator* had received an irate letter from an Egyptian student in Chemical Engineering, pointing out that "Your hotheaded little feature editor has grievously misplaced the Suez Canal and misspelled Nasser."

The Autherine Lucy column fell into the latter category. It was not a political column, nor a moral one; Maggie had not been aware of the politics or the morality of the situation. Her ideas about Negroes had never been examined. She thought about them seldom and without curiosity. She loved a few of them and knew none of them. The column had been a hasty, quixotic trifle praising the Randolph student body for not rushing over to Tuscaloosa and joining the fray surrounding the entrance of the university's first Negro student. Maggie had not been talking about civil rights, only about student reaction. There had been none of that, either to the event or to the article.

"The Claibornes didn't say anything about it," she told Tuck sullenly. "I've never even met the Claibornes. And the Kappas didn't either, and neither did anybody else. I don't think anybody even read it."

"I read it," he said. And then, suddenly, "Maggie, you ought to get out of here."

"I'm ready whenever you all are."

"No. Out of Randolph. There's nothing in that southern-fried playpen for you."

No one had ever told Maggie she should get out of anything; only into things. The world that had seemed to fit her like her sleek skin took a slight, queer skew. She wanted to probe, to nibble at this alien insight as you do an ulcer on the inside of your mouth, but she wanted far more not to.

"I don't know what you mean," she said.

Whatever he might have replied was lost in a scuffle of feet and chairs from the dance floor, and a following glissando of outrage. They swiveled.

The red-haired corporal was swaying like a white pine in a high gale. His feet were planted apart. His face was furious, blind, contorted. One enormous hand was closed around the biceps of a smaller, swarthy soldier whose legs were bent in a feral crouch, whose free arm was drawn back and ended in a sunburned fist. The corporal's other hand was snapped to Delia's upper arm so tightly that his fingers dug white pits into her flesh. Delia was scrabbling at his hand with both of hers, pulling away from the two men, whimpering in fear. Black Maybelline streaked her cheeks.

"Tuck, please, go get her, they're going to fight, please, let's go home, please. . . . " Maggie pushed at him frantically, terrified, embarrassed, angry at him. He jerked away from her hands, overturning his drink, which flooded across the Formica into her lap. He turned in his chair and lit a cigarette, looking frozenly onto the empty stage.

"I don't give a good goddamn if they pull her apart."

The dark soldier's arm arced into the red face. The corporal staggered back. Blood flowered suddenly from his nose. A chair went over, a glass broke, Delia screamed, a high, thin, kitten's cry. Men half rose or sprang from their chairs, lunging back from the fluid circle of the fight. The dark man crouched, bent and coiled, bouncing slightly on the balls of his feet, his lips pulled away from his teeth. "Come on, come on you sonfabitch, come on you mothuhfuckin' bastard, come on . . . "

A wordless, atavistic, savage sound swelled in the room, rose, burst into killing words. The crowd was forming camps, choosing sides. A sobbing, murderous sound came from the corporal. He sprang at the crouched dark man, blinded and runaway with rage, dragging Delia stumbling and mewling after him. The smaller man hit him again, and he spun and slid, overturning a table and fetching up on hands and knees half under it, head hanging, like a spent and bleeding bull in an arena. Delia went flying into the teeming darkness beyond the jukebox's green fox-fire.

Maggie was on her feet, Bourbon plastering white piqué and sodden crinoline to her legs, plucking at Tuck's seersucker back with witless hands, moaning wordlessly. He did not turn, did not move.

The crowd, which had swarmed back before the corporal's impetus, flowed forward in an amorphous mass as he stumbled to his feet. Blood sheeted his lower face; it was soaking his khaki shirt, and he gar-gled through it. He was bellowing terrible high word-less things, and his right fist held a broken bottle. The dark man shrank back against the jukebox.

Another man was there suddenly, a short, thick man in bagging blue pants and a white short-sleeved nylon shirt. He was powerfully built. His chest and shoulders were massive and his arms were very long. He was dark, by nature or with sun; even in the boil-ing murk of the room, Maggie could see the brown of his chest through the wash of white nylon. His eyes were the white-blue of opaque ice, and there was a ring of white around their irises that flashed in the dark, giving him a look of tightly capped intensity, of trancelike purpose, or of madness. His hair was dark and rough and would have been very curly if it had been longer. He moved quickly between the dark sol-dier and the corporal.

"Drop the bottle, Jack," he said to the corporal,

and the corporal stopped in mid-lunge, looking stupidly at him.

"Somebody better get him out of here," the thick man said to the room at large, into a sudden deadness of silence. "The manager called the MPs." He turned to the dark man, who was uncoiling from the jukebox and knotting his hands into fists again, growling low in his throat.

"Don't be an asshole. Get the hell out of here or you'll spend the rest of the summer in the stockade. Go on. You got about three minutes."

The room came alive again. Two soldiers materialized beside the corporal, each taking a slack arm. One of them removed the bottle from his unresisting fingers and set it down on a table. They dragged him, reeling, toward the door.

"Come on, Virgil," one of them said. "You be in that hole the rest of your life, do they catch you again."

Muttering, the stumbling corporal disappeared into the surf of khaki that broke against the door and burst out into the thick night. The dark soldier, surrounded by his own supporting coterie of khaki, followed. In a muted scramble and scuffling of feet and chairs, they were gone. The room was dead and empty and stale and quiet; an incurious stripper in a cotton wrapper looked briefly from between the drawn curtains on the stage and let them drift together again. The manager had vanished into his tiny office. A frail feather of sound curled into the room from the street: sirens.

The civilian loomed abruptly beside Maggie, who was still on her feet: He had Delia by her wrist. She was disheveled and blank with shock. Her mouth was drawn into the square rictus of a crying child, but she made no sound. Her blouse had been jerked askew at the neck; white straps were visible against her tan, and blood speckled the front of her like confetti. Her mouth was puffed and worn clean of lipstick; around it, a ring of smeared Persian Melon and beard abrasion bloomed feverishly.

"Come on out of here," said the civilian to Maggie. "Get her purse. What's the matter with that guy, is he drunk? Come on, move it, Mac. The cops'll be right behind the MPs. There's a door back there to the alley. My car's out there."

"I . . . we have a car . . . is she hurt . . . who are you?" Maggie felt as though she were trying to move underwater. The sirens grew louder.

"WILL YOU MOVE!"

He shoved Delia into Maggie's arms and hauled Tuck to his feet. Supporting him by the collar of his jacket, he herded them before him through a black, cluttered corridor smelling evilly of sour sweat. A door hung crazily ajar off the corridor, revealing a tiny, incredibly filthy toilet and washstand, and stacked rolls of toilet paper. The odor of disinfectant and stale vomit brought saliva flooding into Maggie's throat. Delia began to go bonelessly limp; Maggie clutched her fiercely, clenched her teeth, and gave her an unloving shove. They burst out into the heavy night air, stumbled down a weed-nested concrete block that served as a step, and fell heavily against the fender of a Thunderbird. The short man followed, half carrying Tuck, who was giggling. He had gotten abruptly and totally, soddenly drunk.

Tucker, you're faking, Maggie thought suddenly and clearly. It made her lucidly, whitely furious. Strength and control returned to her arms and legs. She wheeled on the stranger, who had draped Tuck over the hood of the Thunderbird and was jerking at the door.

"What do you think you're doing? I don't know you. I'm not getting into any car—"

He gave her a violent shove and she fell into the back seat of the Thunderbird. Another shove and Delia came flying into the car, beginning to sob audibly. The short man slammed the door, dragged Tuck around the front of the car, opened the door opposite the driver's seat and half threw half pushed him in. Another slam. In the dark of the alley, he was a luminous nylon blur as he rounded the hood, shrugged into the driver's seat, and turned the key. The engine came alive and headlights flared, picking out garbage cans, slicks of spilled oil, and piled cardboard boxes. At the end of the alley, streetlights threw a wedge of empty street and blind, scabbed buildings into black-and-white relief.

"Where are we going? What do you want with us?" Maggie's voice was high and fragile with anger

and fear. Delia sprawled across her, crying monotonously.

"We're going away from here," the man tossed
back at her over his shoulder. His voice was flat and
harsh and angry also, southern but with something
else in it. "I'm trying to keep the stupid bunch of you
out of trouble. What did you think I wanted with
you, your warm white body? Now shut up until I can
get us out of this frigging alley."

The Thunderbird roared, lurched down the narrow alley, screeched insanely out onto the street on
two wheels. In front of Ma Beechie's, a tan military
sedan was pulled up. MPs were spilling out of it. Another siren cried out a few blocks away, wailed closer.
The Thunderbird took off in the opposite direction,
squealing down the deserted, neon-dancing street.
One MP looked after it, half started for the military
car, then turned back into Ma Beechie's.

"Oh, wait!"

"What the hell for?"

"We forgot to pay!"

The short man laughed. It was a curiously gay,
young sound. He was still laughing as he turned
the Thunderbird into the red-and-blue-and-green
freshet of Phenix City's main street.

5

"YOU GO TO RANDOLPH."

It was a statement, not a question. They were drinking coffee in a back booth at an all-night truck stop on the road to Randolph, well past the fringes of Phenix City. They had driven in silence punctuated only by an occasional snorting giggle from Tuck and hiccuping sobs from Delia. He had passed two or three hamburger and pizza places, all with cars pulled up to them. By the time he had found the truck stop, its parking lot innocent of traffic, Delia had stopped crying and begun to prod Maggie and whisper, "Who's he? Where are we going?" Maggie had ignored her. Tuck had fallen against the door and slept, snoring.

"Yes. I'm Margaret Deloach"—she wondered why she had not said Maggie—"and this is Delia Curry."

Delia had borrowed Maggie's purse and gone to the rest room. She had washed most of the corporal's blood off her blouse and the Maybelline off her face; combed her gilt hair and applied a ripe layer of Maggie's Fire and Ice. She looked just-born and guileless as water. She gave the dark man a radiant smile.

"You are a *hero!* I declare, I think they would have killed me. I never thought . . . "

"Yes, you did."

"Well, I did *not!* He just asked me to dance like anybody would. . . . "

"I saw you. I was watching you all night. You're lucky somebody isn't dead, like that poor son of a bitch in the car out there. What in God's name were you doing in that place?" He was looking at Maggie.

"I don't know that it's any of your business, Mr.—?" The adrenaline had subsided and Maggie was dully, grumpily, endlessly tired. She wondered how they would get home.

"Cunningham. Hoyt Cunningham. And I reckon it's a little of my business, seeing as how I just saved your precious behinds from the whole damned paratroopers' school. Pleased to meet you, Miss Deloach, Miss Curry."

He flashed a grin of knowing wolfishness at Delia. He had very white teeth and his eyes were dark-lashed and beautiful in his heavy face. The ring of white still encircled his irises. It made him look as though he were paying very close attention.

"You're not being very cordial to somebody who just kept you from being kicked out of school. Am I right?"

Maggie smiled, unwillingly.

"To put it mildly. Thanks, Mr. Cunningham. Hoyt. We had no business in Phenix City, and we're going to be mighty lucky if we can get back in the house without somebody finding out. Got any more bright ideas, Delia?"

Delia dimpled. She was back on firm footing. The dark man was not handsome, but he had a palpable aura of being in charge, and she liked the dark skin showing through the damp white shirt, and the blunt, black-haired hands.

"You're an awful square, Maggie." She looked at Hoyt through the tangle of newly blackened eye-lashes. "She's president of the WSGA, the Women's Student Government Association, yet. We're safe as bugs in a rug. Maggie just doesn't have any spirit of adventure. I can tell you've got a real spirit of adventure, Hoyt."

He didn't answer her. He looked at Maggie, a level, unfriendly look.

"Well, Madame President, I hope your little foray into the wild side of life was worth it. That was stupid, that was really dumb. Those horny bastards could have killed one of you. That's a really crummy place, you know. A dose of clap is about the mildest thing you can get out of there with. You little college girls, honest to God, you don't know your asses from first base."

Maggie was suddenly very angry again. Two men in one evening had looked at her with alien eyes, and she had read less than the accustomed approbation in them. Tuck had jeered at her. And now this squat, froggy creature was turning her madcap, Richard

Halliburton adventure into something smeared and squalid and contemptible.

"If it's that bad, what were you doing there?"

"Believe it or not, I was working."

"Oh, sure. You're studying to be a bouncer."

"I work for the AP." They looked blank. "The Associated Press. The southeastern bureau, out of Atlanta. There's been some trouble at Benning lately with the Negroes. Started after Nat King Cole was over there in a concert last month. The whites booed him pretty bad, and there was one hell of a fight. Things have been pretty tense ever since. I'm doing a kind of in-depth piece on race relations around the southeastern bases. Benning's a good place to start. I mean, it ain't exactly West Point. Paratroopers are a mean bunch of bastards."

"I saw King Cole in Birmingham last spring," said Delia. "He was fabulous. I just *love* 'Blue Velvet.'"

"I covered that concert," he said. "Were you there when the trouble started?"

"You mean that kind of scuffle while he was doing 'Little Girl'? Yeah, but I didn't see much. I mean, they played 'America,' and then the police came right then and took those people out. And everybody clapped like crazy when he came back on the stage. I think they were just, you know, kids kind of picking on him."

"Those kids had two rifles and a blackjack and brass knuckles out in their car."

"Well, it didn't amount to anything after all, did

it? I mean, people down here *love* Nat King Cole. The whole crowd was white. I didn't see a single nigra."

"Jesus, they couldn't get *in* the place. There's a city ordinance against mixed audiences in the most holy Birmingham Municipal Auditorium. Where have you been, under a rock? There's something really big and bad piling up right under your nose, something that's going to last a long, long time. Open your eyes."

"If you mean that bus thing in Montgomery, that thing that Dr.—what's his name, King? . . . the nigra preacher—that's not anything. They don't do anything but sing and not ride the buses, and who cares if they don't? It's white people and newspaper people from up north that are stirring it all up, anyway. And Communists. They'll get tired and go home before long."

"You think it's going to blow over?"

"Well, Daddy says it is."

Delia was bored with the conversation and uneasy, both at his messianic blue stare and the implicit criticism in his words. The affairs of the black race, save their music, were as alien to her as the comings and goings of aborigines, or ants, or hartebeests. She sought to bring the talk back to the personal present, and to shift its emphasis away from herself.

"Maggie did a piece on the nigras," she said. "She wrote her column on that nigra girl who tried to get in the university last winter—she's feature editor of the Randolph *Senator,* too. Hey, you're both newspaper reporters. Look what all you've got in common!"

"What did your piece say?" His eyes were intent on Maggie's face.

"Just that it was good that no Randolph students went over there and got in the middle of things. It wasn't much of a piece. Nobody noticed it." She remembered Tuck, and added, "Much."

"What do you think about Autherine Lucy going to Alabama, Maggie?"

"Nothing. I don't think anything. I'm sick of the whole thing. What *is* there to think? I mean, she was expelled about two months later. I believe the Negroes have the right to go to school wherever they want to. I just don't understand why anybody would want to go somewhere where everybody . . . *hated* them so much. There are *good* Negro colleges—Tuskegee and the Atlanta University complex. What kind of life could she have had in Tuscaloosa?"

Her voice faltered and fell. He was laughing at her again.

"What kind of life, indeed? You really don't understand, do you?"

"No. Maybe you'll tell me, since you obviously know so much."

He drank coffee and got a cigarette from Maggie's frayed, damp pack. He blew smoke and looked bluely into middle distance over her head.

"I'm talking about revolution, Maggie. Pure revolution, like they had in Russia in 1917. With riots and shooting and burning and killing. The whole social structure of this country is going to be torn to pieces and rebuilt. Negroes are not going to be oppressed much longer, they're going to fight in the streets if they have to—and they'll have to. Good God, look at Eastland, look at Big Jim Folsom, look at Earl Long—do you think those bastards are going to listen to reason? Just sit there and grin and say, sure, come on into our schools and our churches and our lives? Come marry our girls? It's going to be a long, bloody goddamn fight, and you're right in the middle of the vanguard. You're living with history."

"But it's just the schools—just school things. Nobody's *shooting*, for goodness sake! Anyway, isn't it supposed to be a nonviolent thing, isn't that what this Dr. King is talking about? Nonviolence?"

"King is a good man, but he's just one man. No, the southern whites will fight to keep somebody lower than they are, and that's the Negroes, and the Negroes will fight back. I've seen their mood, the young ones, over at Benning. There's nothing nonviolent about it. It's mean and mad and ugly as hell. There was nothing nonviolent about those hoods in Birmingham. We'll force them to fight, and we'll wish we'd never seen the day we did it. There's a whole new generation of them coming, Maggie, and one behind them, and they're not like the older ones, not like the ones who've ridden at the back of the bus all their lives, and gone to shack schools if they went at all, and been glad to work as washwomen or maids or yardmen. They're overdue, they're two hundred years overdue. This whole thing is . . . is a great idea whose time has come. Voltaire or somebody said that about the French Revolution, and I say it about this one. I say it while the rest of you say 'Let 'em eat corn pone' and worry about the stupid Communists and watch Ed Sullivan."

Maggie stared at him. The ring of white was wider. His face was deep red-brown and full-looking. She thought perhaps he was drunk and she had not noticed before.

"You sound like you *like* the idea."

"It doesn't matter whether I do or don't. Or whether you or anybody else does. It's *right*. It's the purest example of abstract, Marxian revolution we'll see in our lifetimes. It's really beautiful."

Delia said suddenly, "Are you a Communist?"

His laugh exploded through his nose, through twin streams of Pall Mall smoke.

"Sweet God!"

"Well, you keep talking about Russia and Marx and revolutions. And you don't sound like a southerner. And you work for a newspaper."

"I work for a wire service. And I was born in and raised in the South. In Greenville, Mississippi, right in the middle of God's little acre. You can't get any more southern than that. If I sound like a Yankee, it's because I went to school at Columbia and worked in the North for a year or two. And I spent a little time at Harvard."

"Oh, well, Harvard," said Delia vaguely. "No wonder."

"It was just a few months. I was a Nieman Fellow."

"A what?"

"It doesn't matter."

Delia brightened. "Greenville. I bet you know Maggie's boyfriend. Boots Claiborne? Everybody from Mississippi knows the Claibornes. Boots's daddy is just everything in the Delta, and they've got *tons* of money. Maggie's going to be a rich lady."

Hoyt gave Maggie another long look. The blue, vision-seeing distance was gone out of his eyes. They were opaque and shuttered.

"Sure, I know Boots," he said. "I went to school with him. He's a little younger than I am."

"He went to Castle Heights. It's a military school. It's in Tennessee," she said.

"No, grammar school. He left for the playing fields of Tennessee about the time I was in high school. *Public* high school. Good old Andrew Johnson High. Not exactly the thing for old Courtney Claiborne's only son and heir. You going to marry him, Miss Maggie?"

"I'm just pinned to him. I'm not . . . I don't know if we'll get married or not."

"Why, Maggie Deloach!" Delia was sincerely shocked. "Of *course* you and Boots will get married!

You've been pinned for over a year. Everybody knows you'll get married."

"Well, I don't know it," Maggie snapped. But she had known it, vaguely, hadn't she? She had thought they would probably get married eventually, after she had worked awhile in Atlanta in advertising and he had settled into a place in his father's affairs. She realized that she did not know precisely what those affairs were, and that she had looked no further than the flower-banked altar of the Lytton First Methodist Church. She felt stampeded and obdurate, and the skewed, out-of-focus strangeness was back.

"I haven't decided what I'm going to do yet," she said.

"Well, you're really spastic," Delia chirped. "If you don't want him, I know about a thousand people who do. Me, for one. I think he's gorgeous."

"I think he's rich," said Hoyt. "He'll be one of the richest men in the Delta when the old man kicks off. Think about it, Maggie. You'd have an honest-to-God antebellum plantation, complete with an army of loyal retainers. The Claibornes haven't gotten the word about the Emancipation Proclamation yet. You could sit on the veranda and fan and drink mint juleps and never have to lift a finger again. Of course, I'd advise you to give up integrationist journalism."

"The Claibornes are wonderful to their help," said Maggie stiffly. "Boots told me there are several of the old ones who can't work any more, and his father lets them have their cabins—their houses—free, and gives them money to live on. He's sent two of the younger ones through Tuskegee. Boots's family is probably better to the Negroes than anybody you've ever met."

"Have you ever heard of old Senator Vardaman? He said, 'I'm just as much against Booker T. Washington as a voter as the little coon who shines my shoes every morning,' or words to that effect. Did you know he's supposed to be kin to the Claibornes on Boots's mother's side, Maggie?"

"Well, so what! That was a long time ago. Boots doesn't feel that way."

"How do you know? Have you asked him?"

"Yes." But she hadn't.

"Well, well, old Boots. You'll be a real ornament to Greenville society, Maggie. I'll drop by when I'm in the neighborhood, if you'll give me house room by then. Is Boots coming back for summer school?"

"He'll be back tomorrow."

"Well, sure. I forgot. Boots is a regular on the summer school circuit, isn't he? Maybe I'll drop by the KA house and see him when I'm through over at Benning. See if he's still the same old rich, beautiful Boots I remember."

Maggie slammed her empty cup on the oilcloth.

"You were very nice to get us out of there. We owe you for that. But I don't have to sit here and listen to you knock my . . . my fiancé, and my *mind* and the way I think about . . . about things. I didn't ask for your opinion. I don't know you from Adam's housecat, and I don't want to know you any better, and if you would be so kind as to drive us back to that place, we'll get Tuck's car and go home. We must be boring you to death."

"Did anybody ever tell you you're very pretty when you're mad, as the man said? When you're not mad, too." He was laughing again, the bright, child's laugh.

"Oh, shut up!"

He flipped some coins onto the table and followed her out of the truck stop. Delia trotted after them, patting her hair regretfully. He had seemed so forceful and masculine. But he certainly did run on about the Negroes. And he had really been awfully mean to Maggie. And even worse, ignored her own efforts to be friendly. Delia thought he was probably common.

When they reached the Thunderbird, Tuck was supine, dead-looking against the door. When Hoyt shook him, he did not rouse.

"No sense even trying to wake him up. Come on, I'll drive you back to Randolph. We're almost halfway there now. He can get somebody to bring him back for his car tomorrow."

"Don't bother," said Maggie.

"It'll be my pleasure."

They drove the night miles back to Randolph in another silence. Delia fell asleep like a small animal, her head bent awkwardly against Maggie's shoulder.

Maggie listened to the faint music from an all-night New Orleans station swimming out of the green-lit dashboard, fading in and out in the low places. She let the feeling of queerness roll over her like ground fog, but she did not examine it. When they pulled up into the back parking lot of the Kappa house it was 3:00 A.M. No lights burned.

Maggie shook Delia awake and pushed her out of the back seat, shushing her automatically when she whimpered with sleep and protest.

"Thank you," she said briefly to Hoyt. He did not get out of the car.

"You're welcome. Maybe I'll see you again. We can start from scratch. We sort of got off on the wrong foot."

"I doubt it."

She was halfway up the path to the sun porch when she stopped and looked back. He had not started the car; he looked at her whitely from the lowered window.

"What *were* you doing in that place?" she said.

His laugh came up the path to meet her.

"Why, I went to see the burlyque. Just like you."

They were nearly to their adjoining rooms in the upper hallway when a door opened. M.A. Appleton stood in the door, light from her bedside lamp limning her square body through her pink duster. She was blinking like a pale cave creature unused to the light.

Her nose was twitching tinily, rabbitlike. There was a puckered nylon cap over her pin curls.

"Maggie, honey, Mama Kidd said you were back! Where have y'all been so long? Come give me a big hug."

"M.A.," said Maggie, "if you kiss me, I swear I'll smack your face."

6

THE BACK PATIO of the Kappa Alpha house—or the veranda, as the brothers called it—looked out over a rectangle of heat-blanched lawn, a Cape jessamine hedge, and into the formal rose garden of the President's Mansion beyond. It was the only fraternity house in Randolph to enjoy such proximity to the green corridors of power on the east side of the town. Randolph's Kappa Alpha order was the oldest Greek brotherhood on campus, but the house was fairly new. It was a mirror image of the columned antebellum house the first Randolph had deeded to the school to house its presidents, but its bricks were pristine and red and sharply square, instead of old and white and mellowed with age and Alabama sun.

When the KAs had an alfresco affair on their veranda, as they did almost every spring and summer Saturday night, the presidential chandelier rattled in the medallioned dining-room ceiling, and the presidential Irish setters howled dismally from the old slave quarters that had become their kennel, and the presidential couple retired to an upstairs back den and turned their window air-conditioning unit and Jackie Gleason up as high as they would go. No protests were ever registered, however. The president was a Kappa Alpha himself.

It was nine-thirty on the first Saturday night of the summer session, and the Kappa Alpha veranda pulsed and boomed and keened and squalled with the amplified efforts of The Crewcuts rendering "Sh-Boom." Girls in wilting butterfly cottons jerked stiffly at the ends of arms of sweating brothers in chinos and Bermuda shorts. The bulk of the chapter and their dates were dovetailed onto the patio. The president, peering down upon the veranda from the besieged Olympus of his front bedroom, remarked sourly to his wife that they looked like Pygmies preparing to murder a missionary or undertake a mass mating.

"They're good boys," she said vaguely. "But that Negro music really is dreadful. I think I'll make up the beds in the guest room."

Flaring torches burning exotically tinted insect repellent stood at each corner of the veranda, and the tired and sullen houseboy had been driven up a ladder in the afternoon to string a few perfunctory colored lights in the lowest branches of the closest trees. Someone had tossed aged, artificial water lilies into the fish pond that sat in the center of the veranda, and someone else had pulled the inevitable jock strap over the chaste fig leaf of the stone David who posed showily in its middle.

Beyond the veranda the lawn was dark, illumined in the blackest pockets with the chalk smears of white shirts and the red periods of cigarettes. A keg of beer sweated and leaked to one side of the French doors that opened onto the veranda from the dining room. A galvanized washtub full of grape juice punch with lemon wheels floating torpidly on its surface rested on a card table on the other side. The Kappa Alpha social chairman had dumped two fifths of gin into it before the party began, and others of the brotherhood had contributed slugs of their private stock whenever the bite seemed to be fading. By nine o'clock the punch was as noxious as Macbeth's witches' brew and as paralytic as curare.

Mrs. Eulalie McClesky, the Kappa Alpha housemother, ostentatiously avoided the veranda and received the bevies of fluttering coeds in the drawing room. What she did not see she could not be chastised for by the Dean of Women. Mother Mac knew when she was beaten. The rout had been accomplished early in her first quarter with the Kappa Alphas.

In the farthest corner of the backyard, on a stone bench beside the Cape jessamine hedge, Maggie pushed Boots away from her slightly and sat up straighter.

"Don't, Boots. It's too hot, and I'm all smeared."

He laughed lazily. He had a soft, deep laugh that rarely rose above a chuckle or showed his teeth. All the Kappas considered Boots very sexy. He had been lounging and cool and sleepy-eyed long before *Rebel Without a Cause.*

"I'm the one that's smeared. You're costing me a damned fortune in laundry bills. But I'd rather have good lovin' than clean shirts any day of the week."

He slurred "shirts" slightly. He had been drinking since late afternoon. He pulled her against him again and slid his hand down the neck of her dress, under the rigid cup of the strapless brassiere.

"*Don't,* Boots!"

"What have you got under that damned padded thing that's so goddamn priceless? For Crissake, I've been pinned to you for a year and you've never even let me touch 'em. Every one of your precious Kappa sisters that's pinned over here has gone all the way at least once. But not Miss Iceberg of 1956. Not even one little feel. I don't think you got any."

He flung away from her sullenly and pulled a cigarette out of his pocket and lit it.

Until he had met Maggie, Boots Claiborne had not been accustomed to feminine rebuffs. His sexual prowess with the languid girls of the Delta had been a legend that preceded him to Randolph, and his career since arriving was even more storied. He had played the field until he met Maggie, pledging the diamond Kappa Alpha badge to a dizzying succession of groomed and glossy sorority girls on an endless succession of nights in the Forestry Plot or at the lake, in the cramped front seat and, once, the jump seat of his cobalt-blue Jaguar. Groans were groaned and moans moaned and scores scored, but the pin remained firmly affixed to his cashmere chest. Rumor had it that he had knocked up more than one early-ripening sharecropper's daughter back in Mississippi, and a Chi Omega with whom he had kept company his freshman year had fainted in an economics class one winter morning and left school abruptly soon after.

His reputation had frightened Maggie when she met him at the Kappa Alphas' Old South Ball at the end of her sophomore year. But she had been dazzled by his long-boned leonine grace and his cat's movements; in his gray Confederate officer's uniform, he looked like Leslie Howard as Ashley Wilkes. He had bowed over her hand and kissed it, and said she was a picture in her centennial hooped organdy and hat, and that he'd love to see her, just like she was, standing on the steps of Groveland, his home back in Mississippi. Maggie's world in Lytton, though comfortable, did not include houses with names; she envisioned columns and arcades and cool tiles and long, magnolia-canopied drives, and photographs he showed her later proved she was right. His slow, green eyes titillated her, and from the first, he treated her with an air of grave, protective, exaggerated courtesy that charmed and soothed her.

Almost from the first, too, Maggie realized that Boots was a totally conventional creature. He might bed with glee any number of girls whom he could not quite envision on the dazzling white steps of Groveland. The girl who wore his pin would, in the last analysis and despite the damp fumblings and ritual sulks, be saved for a carved bed in some upstairs Mississippi bedroom off a wrought-iron-guarded gallery. He was, moreover, usually passed out cold behind the Kappa Alpha house or in the party room by ten-thirty of a weekend evening. Maggie's virtue was safe.

Boots's conventionality was not a disappointment to Maggie. It was, in some obscure and unexamined way, reassuring. Only once, and then briefly, did she wonder if he would have parted with the pin if she hadn't had a green organdy hoopskirt with a hat to match.

"I met somebody who knows you," she said, more to coax the discontent off his face than to impart information. Boots's face in a pout slackened into a caricatured pudding of a spoiled three-year-old and lost its high-planed, cheetah-like purity; the sheaf of wheat-colored hair became disheveled and damp-looking, as if after a breath-held tantrum, instead of rakehell and piratical. The sulks exasperated Maggie, as if a loved, bright child were behaving unattractively.

"Who?" He blew smoke and looked restlessly toward the punch tub.

"Hoyt Cunningham. He said he went to grammar school with you."

"Yeah, he did. I haven't seen him in five or six years. Where'd you meet him?"

"Well, I let Delia talk me into going over to Ma

Beechie's last week when I came back for Freshman Orientation, and she got herself right in the middle of a fight between two soldiers, you know Delia . . . and he was there and broke it up and got us out of there. We had some coffee later and talked, and then he brought us back to the house. It was nice of him, but I don't like him, Boots. He's . . . funny."

"He always was. What the hell were you doing at Ma's? What was he doing there?"

"He was doing a story for the AP on the soldiers over at Benning—something about the Negroes after a King Cole concert, and he was just there, drinking beer. And I went with Delia and Charles Tucker, that poor instructor who's trying to pass her in English. Don't look so snotty, Boots, everybody goes over there. You were going to take me yourself this summer. Nobody found out about it, and nothing really bad happened."

"Well, it could have. Delia ought to have her little ass kicked. Jenks ought to know better than let her run around like that; she's started more fights than the Randolph-Alabama game, and I swear to God she likes it. I had one of that Tucker guy's classes couple of years ago; what'd he do, hit those guys with his purse? Somebody ought to tell Jenks. Only he's as dumb as Delia is. Well, I guess it's a good thing Cunningham was there; he's funny but he's no fruit like Tucker. He almost tore up an old boy after a football game back home once, I remember it. You say he's working for a newspaper?"

"No, it's a wire service. You should have heard him, Boots. He started talking about the Negroes, and how this stuff with the schools and the bus boycott over in Montgomery was just the ... the vanguard of a real revolution, and how there'd be fighting in the streets, and how the Negroes weren't going to be oppressed any longer. He was really *rude* to me. He almost scared me."

"He make a pass at you?"

"Oh, no, I mean he just seemed to think all of us down here were stupid and wouldn't recognize that there was even a problem with the Negroes, and he talked like we still beat the slaves every night after supper, and ... oh, I don't know what all. He sounded like he *wanted* a revolution, like it would be a really good thing. But, no, he didn't make a pass at me."

"Well, he wouldn't if he knew you were my girl," Boots said comfortably. "He may be full of shit; there's not going to be any revolution, not in Mississippi. Our Negroes have got it good. They don't want to go to school with us any more than we want 'em to, and they sure to God aren't going to fight any of us. Too scared of the Klan. Hoyt always did have his head full of liberal shit and his nose in a book. But he's pretty much a good old boy; his folks aren't *real* quality, but they sure aren't poor white trash, either. He wouldn't bird-dog my girl."

Well, don't be too sure about that, Maggie thought, remembering the intense, white-ringed eyes on her, and the remark he had made about seeing her again.

Boots's bland assumption that no one would challenge his hold on her stung her; it smacked of ownership and complacency, which had always made her feel secure and cherished but now, somehow, rankled.

"He's not quite the Mississippi gentleman you think he is," she said perversely. "He said some pretty sarcastic things about your family. You too, for that matter."

He wouldn't be baited. "Well, I never said he was a gentleman. Hoyt's daddy runs one of my daddy's sawmills. His mother's a schoolteacher. They never did have a pot to piss in. It was Daddy that arranged for him to go to that school up North, got Ed Copeland over at the bank in Leland to lend him the money when nobody else would. Mississippi folks don't like to be beholden. He owes the Claibornes, and he knows it, and it frosts him. He was just blowing off."

"He as much as said you were spoiled rotten and your folks still kept slaves."

"He's full of shit, and I'm tired of all this nigger talk. It's a drag. Come on, let's go get a drink."

Maggie was mulishly reluctant to drop it.

"He says he's going to come over and see you this summer."

"Let him. Come on, there's your song."

The overripe voice of Gogi Grant sobbed into "The Wayward Wind," and they got up from the bench and moved into the light of the veranda.

*   *   *

When Boots got drunk, it was with a sweet abrupt-
ness, like a good child sliding suddenly and wholly
into sleep. One moment he would be, for him, animated and expansive, slapping his passing fraternity
brothers on their buttocks and giving their girls ex-
travagant, double entendre compliments and long,
undressing looks. He would dance tirelessly and fluidly and with a grace that flirted on the edge of femi-
ninity, saved by his long, heavy bones and palpable
sensuality. He was rarely without a Dixie Cup of
whatever the KAs were featuring that evening, even
while he danced. He would drink steadily and with
only a modicum of slurring in his speech, one arm
draped around Maggie's shoulders, and when he had
passed some interior landmark in his yellow head, he
would excuse himself gravely and go upstairs, osten-
sibly to the bathroom but in actuality to sprawl head-
long onto his bed. Later in the evening, his roommate
would come up and turn him over and take off his
shoes and throw a sheet over him, and later still, the
stupor would drift into deep and healing sleep. Boots
never had the hangovers so loudly cherished by the
other KAs.

This would occur about ten in the evening, and a
pledge designated for the purpose early in the afternoon by Boots would appear at Maggie's elbow and
tell her respectfully that Boots wasn't feeling well
and he would be happy to take her back to the Kappa
house. Maggie did not complain, publicly at any rate,
since it ill became a pinned girl to linger escortless at

a fraternity party and flirt with the brothers. The first time she had chided Boots for passing out and leaving her alone, he had told her that all Mississippi boys heard the click early on in the evening—Maggie had once read him parts of *Cat on a Hot Tin Roof*, thinking he would find it absorbingly like his own world, but it was so blatant a case of art imitating life that he had shrugged it off and remembered only Brick's interior click. Moreover, he had said she ought to count her blessings. Few people, save Mississippians, could drink like gentlemen. Maggie had to agree; Boots never became truculent or embarrassed her, or threw up behind the fraternity house or in the stadium, as did others of her acquaintance.

The pledge didn't complain, either. He got to drive a campus beauty and wheel home in a blue Jaguar, and could lie casually and knowingly to his fellow freshmen about what a hot number Maggie Deloach was under her cool exterior, and what she had said to him on the dark drive back to her sorority house, and how sweetly the Jag handled. Sometimes, if the night was moon-silvered and tender, Maggie would slip away and walk home alone, the heartbreaking smell of the presidential roses aching in her nostrils and heart. And sometimes she would ride with a Kappa sister whose curfew was earlier than her own, and her date. But mostly she rode in Boots's Jaguar with the pledge.

The Kappa house was usually empty at ten o'clock on weekend evenings. Mama Kidd would be sunk into her own sweating Bourbon dreams, the kitchen staff would have long since left. Especially in the summer, with fewer Kappas in the house, it was very still and quiet. Even the girls who had flunked courses and were back to make them up were liberated until eleven on weekends and would be out on dates. There were few Kappa dogs, and those were legacies. Maggie liked the stillness and the big, dim old rooms downstairs, with odd-shaped shadows dancing where nothing was, and only the Tigress and Woodhue and Chantilly ghosts of the fleshly Kappas walked. She would peel off her damp clothes and take a long shower and get into shorty pajamas, and curl up on her bed and read until midnight, when the flood tide of chatter and girl-squeals rose up the stairs and brought the house back to hivelike life. Knots and cliques of girls would swarm into various rooms, pajamaed and dustered and creamed and medicated and pin-curled; Cokes would be brought up from the machine in the basement, and Baby Ruths and cheese crackers, or evil instant coffee brewed from the scalding Kappa tap water if it was winter, and cigarettes would come out, and the stylized ritual of coming of age in Alabama would be brought forth for another Saturday night's anthropological examination.

Her own roommate was first in on this night.

"What are you doing back so early?" said Maggie, raising her head from *Marjorie Morningstar*. "I thought y'all were going to Columbus for a pizza."

Sister Vaughan was petite, red-haired, and volatile. She was Kappa social chairman, a cheerleader, Superintendent of Student Spirit, and held a number of other campus offices for which personality and "peppiness" were requisite. She was also between steadies, having received what the Kappas considered an ignominious shaft from a Phi Delta Theta in Industrial Management, who had unaccountably decided to become a minister the quarter before and defected to an Episcopal seminary in the East. Kappas were not habitually shafted; to lose out to the Church was a particularly stinging personal and collective affront, and Sister had come to summer school to Forget. She was breaking in a rather promising SAE, and the chapter thought summer school by far the best course for Sister. By fall, when the bulk of the student body was back, Sister would probably be safely pinned again, and the shame of the thing could be buried in a whirl of pep rallies and pledge swaps. At least, they hoped so. An unattached social chairman would be a disaster.

Sister was angry. Her pale blue eyes, so engaging when crinkled along with her pert nose when she grinned, watered with fury. When she was angry, Sister no longer looked like Piper Laurie, and was given to throwing things.

"Pizza, my *foot!*" screeched Sister, and she threw her straw purse across the room onto her twin bed, knocking a superannuated stuffed dog with ΦΔΘ on its floppy ears off onto the floor. Her white dangle earrings followed, and her patent leather pumps, one after another.

"What's the matter?" Maggie knew that Sister would tell her eventually, but probably not until she had run through her Susan-Hayward-in-a-spirited-huff routine. Sister was a member of the Randolph Players and had Temperament. Maggie hoped to stanch the tirade this evening and get back to *Marjorie Morningstar*.

"He's a damned *octopus!* We never went *near* Columbus! We went to some cruddy hole of an apartment one of his precious fraternity brothers has . . . he told me they were having a party, but of course there was nobody there, and he practically crawled all over me all night. He's got the fastest hands in America! He ripped my *dress!* Oh, he was really smooth about it . . . when we got there he said he knew he shouldn't have fooled me, but he had something important to ask me and he wanted us to be alone. And he put on "Something Cool," and he had a bottle of Bourbon and made us a drink, and lit this drippy old candle in a Chianti bottle . . . it just *happened* to be there on a table . . . and then he just plain *jumped* me!"

"What did you do?"

"I slapped him. And then I asked him what he wanted to ask me that was so damned important he had to lie to me, and he had the *nerve* to ask me to do the Black Act! The Dirty Deed! He just came right out and *asked* me!"

"Oh, Sister, what did you say?"

"Well, hell, Maggie, what do you *think* I said? I said what kind of girl did he think I was, and who did he think *he* was, and then I said to take me home."

"And then what?"

"And then he jumped on me again like a damned bull, and I told him if he didn't stop it I'd yell 'Rape' as loud as I could, and he said, 'It ain't rape when it's willing.' Oh, Maggie, you *know* I don't tease!"

Sister collapsed in a crumpled drift of blue polished cotton and wailed. She did look awful. Her circle-stitched, padded Peter Pan bra leered rigidly out of the neckline of her dress, which was indeed torn. Her mouth was swollen and pulpy like bruised fruit, and there were red marks, going to blue, on her neck and shoulders. Maggie wet a washcloth and handed it to her, and she mopped at her face, sniveling.

"The worst thing is, he'll tell all his stupid brothers that I'm a . . . I'm a . . . oh, Maggie, he called me a cockteaser!"

"Sister, you know he won't do that. You're not a . . . not that. He was just worked up and blowing off steam."

"He *said* he would."

Sister got undressed, kicking out of crinolines and dropping the Peter Pan waist cincher that reduced her already slim waist to painful waspness to the floor, still crying loudly. She wriggled, wailing, into seersucker shorty pajamas, but she allowed Maggie to put a lit Pall Mall into her fingers, and she sat down on Maggie's bed. High heels clattered in the hall

then, and girls' voices chimed, and Maggie started for
the door to close it. But M.A. Appleton stood there,
peering nearsightedly past Maggie at Sister. Two
other Kappas stood behind her, smelling trouble like
a brace of nervously elated young beagles.

"What's the matter with Sister? Did something
happen? I could hear her crying all the way down in
the foyer. Did . . . ?"

"Sister's got the cramps," said Maggie firmly,
pushing the door shut in M.A.'s twitching face.

"Let me in, Maggie, I've got something that will
help."

"I gave her some of my prescription stuff, M.A.
She's fine now. She's going to sleep. '*Night,* M.A."

"Damned nosy ghoul," she said to Sister. "Listen,
I don't want to butt in, but what on earth gave him
the idea you'd do *that?* You've only been dating him a
month. That's not long enough to . . . I mean, that's
still just necking. If he starts shooting his mouth off
in the fraternity, we'll put the word out he's a sex
maniac and you're going to drop the SAEs from the
fall swap list. M.A. can just have a little talk with the
SAE president—I know, she's a bitch, but she's good
at that kind of thing—and there's not going to be any
more trouble with him. I'll talk to her myself in the
morning if you don't want to."

"No!" The tears started again, a runnel of anguish.

"Why on earth not? We can't have that nerd
spreading stuff like that around campus. You're the

social chairman! That would be *awful!* That could ruin us in rush this fall!"

She looked at the bent red head.

"Sister, you didn't. You haven't."

"Not the bad thing, Maggie, just ... you know, just ... feelio boobio and things like that. Just a little bit."

"Oh, Sister, *why?*"

She raised her stricken face, wet and not pretty, not pert, not engaging. Maggie thought suddenly that Sister would not be a pretty woman for very long.

"Oh, Maggie, I thought he was going to ask me to wear his *pin.* I want to be pinned, Maggie!"

Maggie lay awake for a long time after Sister had cried herself to sleep, listening to "Moonglow with Martin" on her ghostly radio. It was still very hot. Her bedspread and sheet were flung back, and her fan made whispering trips across her body, drying the faint dew of perspiration on her arms and legs but not touching the damp under the short pajamas. After a while, she sat up and peeled them off. But the fan's fingers on her breasts felt sly and violating, and she pulled the sheet back up. She lay under the weight of the moon.

"Something is wrong with all this," Maggie thought, but she did not know if she meant the night or the moon or the girl whimpering in her sleep in the other bed, or the world, or herself, and so she turned off the radio and went to sleep.

7

"Miss Deloach, since you insist upon polluting the rarefied atmosphere of my classroom with the noxious weed, I insist that you pass me that pack so that I may do the same."

Professor Bennet G. Flournoy, whose specialties were contemporary poetry and fiction, rarely had large classes, and so they tended to the informal. These courses were electives to upperclassmen; Maggie's Contemporary Poetry class, at 11:00 A.M. in the Semmes Hall, was composed of six junior and senior girls and one pale, silent boy in Library Science. Ben Flournoy remembered one bumper crop of fourteen students, but he could not account for it and reflected that he had flunked five of them. He liked his smaller classes of upperclassmen girls; they tended to absorb his proffered Frost and Yeats and Pound with rapt faces and a few sentimental tears, and if their essays were longer on passion than logic or wit, at least he reached them.

This was a good class. The pale youth, whose handwriting was illegible and whose name seemed to be Coolidge, had turned in a rather fine piece of sat-ire on "Felix Randal," and the Deloach girl was coming alive like a parched vine in a showery April. She was going to be a weeper, though; her eyes had filled when he read them Hardy's "Afterward," and she had raised to him a face of pure, misted joy when he had taken the class out onto the grass under the trees and run extension cords out the open window and played his recording of Dylan Thomas reading "A Child's Christmas in Wales" and "Do Not Go Gentle into That Good Night." Dylan Thomas was his own tacit test of a class. Most of them could not follow the singing Welsh voice and doodled or nodded. The ones who could and did, he felt, would work at submerging themselves into poetry.

He did not want Margaret Deloach to lose the first green shoots of order and insight that he glimpsed among the florid tangle of her mind. A few tears would water them; many would rot the roots. She had, he knew from reading her column in the *Senator,* a rich facility with words but few perceptions. So he needled her when she wept.

He was in the habit of crouching on the top of his desk, rocking on his heels and chain-smoking and stabbing the air with a nicotine-stained finger when he wished to make a point. He was small and simian, with bright, malicious dark eyes and a brush cut that stood wildly on end. His clothes were invariably covered with a fine gray effluvium of ash.

It had been Yeats today. He had been reading aloud. He did not often do this, feeling that the quick and ardent responses were too facile, too fragile, not earned and apt to blow away. He preferred to assign a poem, circle it, dissect it, worry and nag it, see what marrow they could crack from its bones. Often they came to no conclusions except that it was a lovely poem, and often that was the conclusion that he wished them to reach. But often, too, they found strange and glinting things in the deeps, things seen through the scrim of their own time and place in the world, and these charmed him. Today, however, was a languid day when currents ran idly, and he loved the aloudness of Yeats, and so he indulged himself. He had read them "An Irish Airman Foresees His Death," and "The Song of Wandering Aengus," and "The Lake Isle of Innisfree," and finished up with "When You Are Old." When he had finished, letting "Murmur a little sadly, how Love fled and paced upon the mountains overhead, And hid his face amid a crown of stars" curl out into their silence, he had seen the quick tears start in Maggie Deloach's brown eyes again. And so he snatched a Pall Mall from her and lit it and drew deeply on it, and closed his eyes and chanted rapidly from memory:

"Lord, confound this surly sister,
Blight her brow with blotch and blister,
Cramp her larynx, lung, and liver,
In her guts a galling give her.
Let her live to earn her dinner
In Mountjoy with seedy sinners:

Lord, this judgment quickly bring
And I'm your servant, J. M. Synge."

Maggie started, and then she smiled, and then she laughed aloud, a clear rich sound. Lord, she's a pretty child, he thought.

"Well, Miss Deloach, and who might the dyspeptic Mr. Synge be?"

"He wrote *Playboy of the Western World* and *Riders to the Sea,*" said Maggie. "But I didn't know he wrote poetry."

"In God's truth, he didn't," Ben Flournoy said. "That liverish little limerick was written to the sister of an enemy of his, who, I gather, disapproved of *Playboy*. All is not passion and sea mist and leering God with the Irish, you see, though far too much is. Well. It is now five till noon, and you are all no doubt eager to seek shade and sustenance in the company of some muscle-bound young Clydesdale. Tomorrow we will move on into Gerard Manley Hopkins, so see that you fast and pray this evening and mortify your nubile flesh. He was an exceedingly God-struck man, though a fine poet."

There is some difference in her, he thought, watching Maggie drift out with a tall girl from New Jersey named Aiken Reed. I don't know what it is yet, but I hope I can find it before the summer is out. It would be fine to help her use it. Otherwise, I think it could destroy her. And this thought surprised him so that, instead of going home to lunch, he went to the hotel coffee shop and had a sandwich with the elderly professor who dispensed Greek plays in modern translation, and they talked about the Philadelphia Phillies and Robin Roberts.

"I think Professor Flournoy has a letch for you, Maggie," said Aiken Reed as they walked across the campus toward the main gate and town, in the three weeks that they had had Contemporary Poetry together, Maggie and Aiken had fallen into the habit of having a hamburger and Coke at the Snack Shack instead of going back to their sorority houses. Both walks were too long in the heat, and they both had one o'clock classes far away from their houses. Maggie did not meet Boots for lunch this summer, as she usually did; he was at the opposite end of the campus at noon, incarcerated in a makeup trigonometry class. Aiken was not pinned.

"Don't be silly. He's as old as my father," said Maggie. Professor Flournoy roused a confusing welter of feelings in her; from them she could isolate an obscure gratitude and a simple one-faceted hero worship, but there was also an undefined and prowling uneasiness among them, and Aiken's words brought it bubbling nearly to the surface. It had something to do with being singled out, and something to do with tacit expectations she could not fathom but struggled to meet. But it was neither. There was a watchfulness, a reined-in wariness . . .

"He's always singling you out," Aiken continued, picking up her thoughts. "Well, not that exactly, but . . . *noticing* you. He watches you all the time, like a hawk. Sometimes he sort of grins."

"He thinks I'm silly and immature. He wrote on my paper on 'Dover Beach' that I'd started out by beginning to understand Matthew Arnold and ended up by drowning him in treacle."

"What's that?"

"It's like Karo syrup, I think."

"Well," Aiken said, "he may write you notes about your mind, but I bet I know where *his* is, and it's not on your head. It's in your pants."

"Aiken!"

Aiken gave her a lazy grin. She was tall and drooping and slender and beautiful; really beautiful, with fine bones and a pure, carved face and misted gray eyes. Her skin was faintly dusted with gold all year long, like a ripening scuppernong, and her clothes were legendary on the campus. Aiken's father was a prominent man in Upper Montclair, said to be very wealthy.

Aiken was an enigma. She was a rebel who paid no penalty. She had come to Randolph because it had a good school of Interior Design, she said, and because the South had always fascinated her. The girls who did not like her—and most did not, even her Pi Beta Phi sisters—were quick to point out that, if she wanted to study design, Pratt and Parsons were right there, or her father could have sent her to any school she chose, even to Europe. The more naïve of her detractors thought she was probably too dumb to get into an eastern or European design school, but this was not true. Aiken had genuine talent and worked long and diligently in her labs; her grades were beyond reproach.

The majority of girls said that she was a nymphomaniac and had to leave Upper Montclair so as not to jeopardize her parents' social position, and that Randolph was as far away and as strict a school as her parents could find. This was not true, either, but it was closer. Aiken slept openly with whomever she chose, and seemed to feel no shame about it. Rather, she enjoyed it.

Maggie had liked her from the moment they met. It did not occur to her that she would be censured for her friendship with Aiken, for the simple reason that Aiken herself seemed to escape censure. She was not liked, but she was not denigrated. Her own sisters and the other sororities on campus did not shy away from her company or warn pledges away from her; the Pi Phis ran her regularly for campus offices and honors and queenships and sponsorships, and she won them regularly. The fraternities did not leer pointedly at her, or pass snickering stories about her at smokers, though they might well have, and did about other coeds who slept around.

The dislike seemed to stem more from the fact that Aiken walked alone or nearly so; her two closest companions were not Pi Phis or even sorority girls, but Independents—one a gruff, mannish, awesomely gifted girl in the School of Fine Arts, who was said to be a lesbian and was the only woman student at Randolph to have a room to herself; and the other a small, shy, painfully homely music major who had the highest IQ ever recorded at Randolph. Aiken dated no one regularly, but was currently sleeping with a fifth-year architecture student in his garage apartment after his afternoon lab, and beginning a liaison with a fortyish bachelor professor of political science. She rarely dated at all, in the accepted sense of the word, but would have coffee with whoever interested her from her classes, or drift with a shoal of architecture students to an after-lab movie or go with them for a beer. When she was hungry for something more exotic than her sorority house was apt to proffer, she would drive to Columbus or Montgomery in her MG and eat alone at a restaurant. The university's rules seemed to pose no threat to her, and she was charming to the housemothers and the Dean of Women, and affable to her roommate and her sorority sisters. Aiken simply did not allow herself to be assimilated.

They slid into a booth, ordered cheeseburgers, lit cigarettes. The Snack Shack at noontime was different territory than at midafternoon or night, when it was largely the province of couples and foursomes celebrating the end of classes, the end of date evenings, the beginning of weekends or allegiances, in the minimal air conditioning. At noon it was given over to the serious business of eating by Randolph students who did not go to sorority or fraternity houses or dining halls or boarding houses. There were many boys, in twos and threes, slide rules slapping against khaki thighs. Some ate alone, books and notes propped against the napkin dispensers, absorbing knowledge as single-mindedly as they did their grilled cheese sandwiches and coffee. Maggie did not know any of them, but Aiken smiled and nodded to several.

Aiken had not finished with the subject of Professor Flournoy.

"He's a very attractive man, I think," she said. "I had dinner over at their house last weekend. Corky took me over there."

Corky was Professor Harold Corcoran, the political science professor. Maggie did not know what to reply. Aiken made no secret of the fact that she was seeing him, or that the relationship had gone beyond that, but she did not flaunt it, either. She made the statement as simply as if she had said she had gone to a fraternity house for Tuesday date-night dinner. Aside from the fact that Aiken could have been expelled for such a relationship, Maggie was impressed with Aiken's unconscious worldliness. She gave the impression, not that she scorned or flouted the tightly circumscribed world of the Randolph undergraduate sorority woman, but that she was accustomed to a wider one and walked there by choice when the spirit moved her, slipping back into the one Maggie inhabited when it was expedient. Maggie felt naïve, outdone, and vaguely envious.

"What's his wife like?" she said.

"Nice. Not very pretty, but awfully interesting. She's a very good painter. Her stuff is all over their walls, and the house is floor-to-ceiling books, and they've got a couple of Bertoia chairs that I swear are the real thing. She's ... Lebanese, or something; she made some little stuffed cabbage-leaf things to go with drinks that were fabulous, and we had a lamb thing that was very good for dinner. And after dinner we talked about the Middle East ... that's her part of the world, you know. Professor Flournoy thinks England and France are being perfect fools over the Suez Canal. He said it was on Egyptian soil, and we owed the British absolutely nothing when it came to that. He said it's an obvious matter of oil, not honor, and we should have more sense than to get involved with it, but, of course, we would."

"Do you think he's a Communist, Aiken?"

"Oh, Maggie, of course not. He's more a devil's advocate. He thinks the whole country is Communist-happy, anyway."

Maggie knew nothing of oil or advocacy, and was embarrassed, so she said, "What else did you do?"

"We listened to records ... all Bach and Handel, wouldn't you know? And before Corky and I left, Kita took me in the kitchen and said she knew it was none of her business, but they were very fond of Corky, and they liked me, and she knew how stuffy the school was about undergraduates seeing faculty members, and she knew a doctor in Columbus who'd fit me with a diaphragm if I wasn't prepared. Prepared; that's exactly what she said. Isn't that quaint? But it was nice of her."

"What did you tell her?"

"I told her I had one. I'd be a fool if I didn't, wouldn't I?"

Maggie flushed and Aiken laughed. Aiken was as open in her speech as she was in other things, and while Maggie admired it, she was also at a loss for words when Aiken's speech strayed over into the frankly sexual, as it often did. In 1956, at Randolph, girls were by no means strictly chaste, but there were rules and manners which governed the matter of who did what with whom, and they were not usually violated.

If, for instance, you were dating a number of men, you might kiss them goodnight on the second or third date with perfect propriety. If you were going fairly steady with someone, you could certainly neck, and might pet . . . above the waist on the outside, if you had not been affiliated long, above the waist on the inside if it looked as though a pin were imminent. Once pinned, girls ceased to talk about what they did, but it was tacitly acknowledged that the field broadened considerably. If a girl was pinned and planned to marry after graduation, it was a foregone conclusion that she had probably gone all the way, but it was not discussed in the late-night behavioral seminars in the sorority houses.

This rule was observed at considerable cost. Girls

who had not crossed the Rubicon might laugh endlessly about it, tell insinuating jokes and sing sly little
songs, talk knowingly of techniques and aberrations,
exchange mots and morsels of sophisticated lore.
But they were, to a woman, consumed with curiosity and steeped in ignorance. One cloistered Kappa
freshman had once asked if one did the Black Act on
top of the sheets or under them; they laughed her
into shamed tears, but no one answered her. Most
of them did not know, and those who did weren't
talking.

If a sorority sister dropped abruptly out of school
to recover from a bout of mononucleosis, that was
not discussed, either.

If a girl went all the way with a man to whom she
was not engaged, pinned, or otherwise attached, she
was not apt to be a sorority girl, and was fair game for
the midnight litanies. If she did it with a number of
men simultaneously, she became a panhellenic joke,
hardly worth expending breath on, and she would
become a new verse in the bawdy songs sung in fraternity party rooms, and be asked out night after
night . . . but not to dinner and formals and house
parties. "She puts out," was the kindest thing one
would hear said about her, and it was a death knell in
Maggie's world at Randolph.

Aiken did all those things and talked about them
with objectivity and a certain connoisseur's relish,
and no knell tolled for her. It was baffling and in-
triguing.

"There was somebody else there I wanted to ask you about," said Aiken, patting Helena Rubinstein powder over her flawless nose. She had large, strong, graceful hands with convex oval nails, bare of polish, and wore an enormous square aquamarine on her right hand. It looked like trapped seawater on her golden finger.

"Who?"

"Charles Tucker. He's an instructor in English, from the North somewhere. He was there by himself. I don't think he's been here very long."

"Why ask me about him?" Maggie was instantly alert. It would not do to have the Randolph faculty talking about the night in Phenix City. She had thought they had escaped undetected; Delia surely had sense enough not to talk about it. Damn Tuck, she thought.

"He said he met you one night before the quarter started."

"Oh, well, yes, we had coffee one night. He's tutoring one of my sorority sisters, Delia Curry. She's . . . "

"A stupid little twat who's going to get herself and probably somebody else in trouble if she keeps parading herself in front of half of Fort Benning at Ma Beechie's. I don't know why the Kappas don't put a stop to that, or that cretin cheerleader she's pinned to. She acts so innocent, but she's just half-whore." Maggie winced at Aiken's language, and then she smiled.

"I know," Aiken smiled back. "The pot calling the kettle. The difference is I'm honest, Maggie. And I don't tease. *Anyway*, this Tuck character is interesting, in a way. He seems so . . . lost, or something. I wondered what you thought about him."

"I think he talks too much," said Maggie in exasperation. "And he drinks too much. And he's so gone on Delia that he can't even function. I'm sure he told you all about that awful scene in Ma Beechie's; did he tell you he didn't lift a finger to get us out of it, that some perfect stranger came and broke up the fight and took us back to the house? He may be interesting and lost, but he surely ought to have more sense than blab that in front of half the faculty. It could get him in just as bad hot water as it could Delia and me."

"Well, Corky and the Flournoys certainly aren't going to talk about it. Ben . . . Professor Flournoy . . . thought it was funny. He said he'd have given a lot to see the Lady of the Lake in the middle of a fight at Ma Beechie's."

"Did he mean me? Oh, God, how can I go back in his class and look him in the face when he knows . . . ?"

"Oh, Maggie, he said it affectionately, sort of. He thinks very highly of you. He said you had untapped reserves of . . . of . . . well, I forget, but it was very complimentary. He said a taste of real life wouldn't hurt you at all, but that Tuck should have had more sense than to take you over there."

"Well, I can take care of myself. I'm all right, I'm right here, aren't I?"

"Thanks to some perfect stranger. Who was he?"

"Oh, some newsman who's doing a story over at Fort Benning. Boots knows him."

"Interesting?"

"No. Rude and opinionated."

"Too bad. You could do a whole lot better than Boots, Maggie. Though he is rather beautiful. I've often thought he'd probably be fabulous in bed, if you didn't have to make conversation with him afterward. Have you . . . ?"

"Aiken, you aren't really interested in Tuck, are you?" Maggie said hastily. Boots and bed were subjects she did not wish to fall under the merciless, pure spotlight of Aiken's attention. "He really is involved with Delia."

"He's got the hots for her, that's all, and thinks it's some kind of tortured spiritual thing. I wonder if a real, whole woman would scare him to death."

"Meaning you?"

"Why not?"

Maggie looked closely at her; she was not boasting.

"I think you just may get into real trouble if you keep on . . . seeing faculty members, Aiken. Sooner or later somebody's going to see you and go straight to Dean Fisher, and then where will you be?"

"Out of this school and into another one, I suppose," said Aiken comfortably. "Maybe Sweden. I've always wanted to go to Sweden and study design. I thought I might, after graduation. Want to go to Sweden with me, Maggie?"

"What on earth would I do in Sweden?"

"Live. Study. Get to know some people who don't think the way you do, or live the way you do. There really is a world out there beyond the Mason-Dixon line. You've got to get into it eventually. I don't care about most of you southerners, but you really are wasting yourself."

"Don't you start on me, Aiken. You're about the fifth person who's jumped on me this summer about the way I . . . think and do things. I don't know what's gotten into everybody; this is starting out to be the queerest summer I ever . . . "

"Good. You listen to them. You think about things. Professor Flournoy was saying the same thing, in so many words. Listen, I've got to get to lab. Where does Tuck usually tutor Delia?"

"At the library, and then they usually go to Mooney's for coffee. *She* says. The Forestry Plot is more like it. Why?"

"I thought I might do a little basic research. The library seems like a logical place for it."

"Aiken, you be careful."

"Of what? What on earth could happen to me at the library?"

She slid out of the booth, waved languidly at Maggie.

"I'm a big girl. Hadn't you heard? I thought the whole campus had."

She grinned and walked out of the Snack Shack. Maggie looked after her for a moment, then gathered up her books and purse and followed her out on the blinding street and turned left toward the green tunnel that dipped off College Street toward Barker Hall, where she had a one o'clock economics class under a crewcut, Teutonic professor named Holger, who always put her to sleep.

8

THE KAPPA ALPHA summer house party was held every year over the long Fourth of July holiday in Destin, Florida, a Mediterranean-looking little jumble of shrimping piers, tourist cottages and motels, and peeling white-board seafood restaurants some forty miles up the Gulf Coast from Panama City. Here, on the west coast of the Florida panhandle, the Gulf of Mexico creamed in warmly, peacock blue and hot, milky green on white beaches, and the sun was savage and golden in the white summer sky. Pensacola to the west and Panama City to the east had gone the way of most Florida coast country; motels and spotlit palms and asphalt beach-front parking lots vied with bars and grills and orange-juice stands and shops that would send coconuts carved into pirates' heads or live baby alligators wherever you wished in the Continental United States. But Destin had somehow escaped, and remained lonely and sunswept and blue-and-white and dune-scalloped.

There was one motel large enough to accommodate the Kappa Alphas and their dates in some propriety, a halfmoon of terra-cotta cottages facing the beach and the Gulf across a sole-searing ribbon of black macadam highway. It was called the Harmony House, and by shoehorning six people into cottages designed, at best, for four, it could at least offer sleeping space to the KA contingent. The brothers occupied the west curve of the half-moon, and the girls the east one. The manager had originally thought to spare his ears, eyes and sensibilities by putting the girls in the section of the semicircle which his own apartments, behind the office, occupied, but he had changed this arrangement after the first house party and put the men there, stationing the girls on the sweep farthest away from him. The boys were all in the women's quarters by midnight, he told his wife, and what he did not see or hear he would not feel compelled to report to the Randolph authorities. The KAs saved the Harmony House from an otherwise barren and impecunious summer season.

At high noon on the Sunday of the summer house party, Maggie lay spread-eagled under the punishing fist of the sun on a beach towel, her collarbones and the tops of her thighs stinging badly, but too stunned with sun and beer and lulled by the rush of the water to move. She would not, she knew, burn; the stinging would redden in the late afternoon after her shower, and thrum in a rhythmic, pleasant hurt under her damp, fresh cotton, but it would be sunk into the even olive tan of her skin by the next day, and she would be burnished and golden and sleek, and look exotic and vivid. She had brought a lot of white things to accent this; her fiercely boned and draped and waist-pinched Rose Marie Reid swimsuit was white, and her short shorts, which she would wear into Panama City in the evening to dance and drink at the Hangout; she would roll them still higher up her mahogany thighs. And her harlequin sunglasses had white frames, dramatic against her bronze, rose-flushed face. Maggie stretched languidly in the sun, loving the heavy lethargy and the damp sweat on her skin, which shone like antique brass with iodine and Johnson's Baby Oil.

Delia, next to her on a pink-and-blue towel, fidgeted peevishly under the sun. The seashore was not kind to her. Her smooth cap of hair, so carefully coaxed into silver-gilt by lemon juice and perox-ide under the gentler spring sun in Alabama, went limp and hung in twin-like hanks in the heavy, hot seawind, and the salt water turned it a faint but un-mistakable chartreuse. She wore a cap of pink rubber flowers to match her swimsuit when she went into the ocean, and swam with her head held high and turtlelike out of the water. A wet head meant an af-ternoon of pin curls under a scarf, which diminished her small face into a blank, dwarf peasant woman's face, something that belonged on a Swiss clock. Jenks hated the scarf, so Delia seldom went into the water. Moreover, she burned quickly and badly, and would peel torturously for weeks, and her Rose Marie Reid, while flattering to her tiny waist, did nothing for her legs. In regrettable point of fact, Delia was pigeon-toed. This gave her a tantalizing, small-girl's gait in her full, mid-calf crinolines and skirts, but was mincing and absurd when she skittered across the hot sand. The sand burned her tender, small feet, and the ocean was full of things that cut or bit her, and Coppertone made her legs break out in a rash where she had shaved them. Delia thought longingly of the night, when she would shine like a Dresden figurine in the smoky murk of the Hangout and could dance.

A shower of sand spumed over them, as if a small mortar shell had hit the beach. Boots and Jenks stood at the towels' edge, shaking seawater from their glistening bodies, like sleek-coated animals. Maggie squinted up at them, her hand shading her eyes against the swimming white explosion of the noon sun. She was struck, as she often was when she saw them together, by their similarity. Jenks Foley was from north Alabama, in the strange, stark hill country that seemed unlike Alabama or any part of the South Maggie knew. His father worked at the Redstone Arsenal in Huntsville, coming home on weekends to his family in the lunar little town where Jenks's mother was postmistress, and where his two younger brothers toiled taciturnly at their high school science and physics books, the more quickly to follow their father out of the town and into outer space. Maggie had met Jenks's family when they had come down for Village Fair weekend the spring past; they were all dark and gnomish and laconic, and awesomely bright. In their darkling ranks, Jenks was as alien as a peacock in a flock of starlings. Even his closest friends in the fraternity—Boots was one of them—had to concede that Jenks was not overly long on brains, but there was a simple sweetness to him, a morning-fresh and dimensionless ingenuousness, that charmed almost everyone who met him. He was physically very like Boots, with a long, graceful body and a thatch of near-white hair only slightly blanched by peroxide, and he wore it brushed close to his head and parted on the side, as did Boots, eschewing the near-universal crew cut. He was long-legged, long-waisted, powerful through the shoulders, and beautiful in motion. The KAs had hoped to have a quarterback in Jenks when they pledged him, but he had been loungingly loath to train, and became Randolph's head cheerleader by a landslide student vote in his sophomore year. He had held this sovereign post ever since. He had a quick white grin and very blue eyes and was unlike Boots temperamentally, which did not affect their friendship. Their talk did not run deep.

He and Delia together looked like a matched set.

"Hey, babe," he said now to Delia. "Come on and get my favorite fanny wet. You been sitting here like a bump on a log all morning. Can't have you getting the body burnt."

"Go on, Jenks, you're dripping on my hair. I don't

want to go in right now. It's too hot. Can't we ride down the beach and get a Coke?"

"Got something better than that up in the room," said Boots, sprawling down beside Maggie on her towel. "Maggie, baby, why don't you and Delia go up and bring down that cooler for us? We made a batch of Purple Jesus fresh first thing this morning. It ought to be just right by now."

"On an empty stomach? No, thanks," said Maggie, turning to baste her back with baby oil and iodine. "I don't feel like moving. Send a pledge. Besides, you drank enough of that stuff to kill a horse last night. You're going to be an alcoholic by the time you're thirty."

"Purple Jesus won't hurt you." He ruffled her hair. "It just makes you piss purple. *You're* going to be a first-rate nag by the time you're thirty. There's no such thing as alcoholics or nagging women on the Delta. Not allowed."

"Tough. I guess I'll just have to get along somewhere besides the famous Delta." Maggie was suddenly cross and hot.

"What's eating you, for Chrissake?"

"Come on, y'all, we're having a party. And it's yardarm time. Speaking of pissing, I'll go get the stuff. I need to take a leak, anyway."

Jenks uncurled himself from Delia's towel and shambled amiably away across the sand toward the road.

"Nothing like a house party to make a guy take a

leak," Boots said, settling back with one of Maggie's cigarettes. "It's not like he didn't have a whole ocean out there."

"My, aren't we *elegant* this morning," Maggie snapped. "And aren't we all of a sudden proper."

"A dose of proper wouldn't hurt you any. I'd give anything to see your folks' faces when you come out with language like that."

"Hell, where do you think I learned it? The old man's got the worst mouth in Mississippi."

"I'll bet your mother just adores it when the two of you start up."

"We don't talk like that in front of Mother. She'd turn us out of the house to sleep with the hands."

"I'm sure of that. In the slave quarters, no doubt."

He scowled at her. "I don't know what's the matter with you this morning, Maggie, but you're about as much fun as a preacher in a whorehouse. What you need is a belt of Purple Jesus and a good ducking. In that order."

Jenks came back, staggering under the weight of the Scotch cooler. He dropped it into the sand and produced paper cups. His purple-ringed grin testified that he had sampled the punch.

"Whooo-ee!" He belched and rubbed his hard brown stomach. "That's good stuff. Here, Boots, Maggie." He doled out Dixie Cups. "Here, sugar, best sunburn remedy in the world."

Boots and Jenks drained their cups and Maggie sipped at hers. Delia rooted hers in the sand and pulled a pink terry-cloth beach jacket over her suit.

"Hey," said Jenks. "It's Sunday morning and here we are boozing it up on the beach. Here's to sin."

"This ain't sin, it's communion," said Boots. "Purple Jesus is just the thing for communion. This is my blood, that I shed for thee . . ."

"Boots, that's sacrilege!"

Maggie shoved at him. The purple liquid went flying out of his cup, coming down in a gaudy shower across Delia.

"Oh, Boots, damn it, just look what you've done," she wailed. "All over my suit and my hair . . . oh, shit, that stuff doesn't come out!"

"Now who's being elegant!"

Jenks rose in a single liquid movement and scooped Delia up and off her towel. "Ladies and gentlemen, Miss Delia June Curry, of Prattville, Alabama, is now about to take the plunge." He ran with her, stumbling, across the beach toward the lackadaisical surf. Delia shrieked and beat at him with her small fists.

"Jenks, I don't want to get my hair wet! Jenks, don't you dare!"

Her shrill voice stopped abruptly as he lost his balance and fell with her into a breaking wave. Both yellow heads disappeared into the beige foam.

"That'll do it for the day," Boots predicted, refilling his cup from the cooler and lying back. "She'll put the freeze on him, and you've got a cob up your ass, and Jenks and I might as well go find us some women somewhere else down the beach."

"Be my guest."

The Purple Jesus and the sun and the morning's cold beer dropped an undulating scrim before Maggie's eyes. The sun stood directly overhead, a physical weight. The beach seemed gauzed with light and silence, though couples on towels and blankets dotted the sand at intervals, and ukuleles plinked, and portable radios squalled thinly and without echo. A knot of KAs and girls was clustered around a portable record player about a hundred yards away. Someone had brought along the party records. They littered the sand, and Maggie could hear the miniature voice of Tom Lehrer, and another small, sly voice, singing "Ship ahoy, sailor boy, don't you get too springy, 'cause the Admiral's daughter lives down by the water, and she wants to steal your dinghy."

Farther down the beach a fat boy named Copeland was playing the guitar, and the brothers were singing "Roll Your Leg Over" and "Mimi, the College Widow" and an exceedingly obscene ballad whose refrain went, "Tingaling, goddamn, get a woman if you can; if you can't get a woman, get a clean old man." Two brothers were tugging at the top of a two-piece bathing suit nominally covering a girl who was shrieking and laughing and pulling away from them; and a tall, thin brother, a Korean veteran who was older than the others, had downed nine martinis in rapid succession on a bet and had gone over in one length, like a Douglas fir, and lay on the sand, thoughtfully shielded by dampened towels. Someone was rigging up a volleyball net. Mother Mac, swaddled like an Arab, sat miserably on a folding chair under an umbrella and played canasta with the other chaperones, a married brother in Electrical Engineering, who yearned obviously to be on the beach with the pack, and his vastly pregnant wife.

"Here we go," Boots muttered as Delia emerged from the water and stalked, stiff-legged with fury, toward her towel. Jenks trotted behind her like a chastened golden retriever.

Delia wet looked sodden and shrunken, like a soaked baby Easter chicken. She was rigid with dignity and Rose Marie Reid boning. Wordlessly, she gathered up her beach bag, jacket, and towel. She started off across the sand, stumbling in her effort to radiate icy hauteur and looking more chickenlike than ever from behind.

"What'd I do? Shit, I thought you came to the beach to go in the water." Jenks flung himself down on Maggie's towel.

"You got her hair wet," said Boots nastily. "There's one thing about women you need to remember, boy. Keep 'em barefooted, and keep 'em pregnant, and keep 'em in the kitchen, and don't mess up their hair. It's an old Delta formula. Never fails." He smiled narrowly at Maggie.

"You aren't funny, Boots," she said. She rose and assembled her own gear and started after Delia.

"Where are you going?"

"To take a nap. It's not the hour, it's the company."

When she got to the door of the cottage she shared with Delia and another Kappa who was dating a KA brother, and three Pi Phis, Maggie looked back down onto the beach. The towel was there, a red flag on the white sand, but they were gone, and so was the Scotch cooler. She picked out their blond heads, finally, down the beach in the crowd around the volleyball net. The cooler was there, too. She sighed. By dinnertime they would both be drunk.

"What are you doing back here? I thought y'all were going to get some lunch."

Delia, emerging naked from the shower, was smooth-faced and placid again, her outrage rinsed away with the Coppertone and salt by the cool water. Delia did not long maintain a passion.

"Oh, they make me sick. They're so damned smug. And they're both going to be knee-walking drunk by five o'clock. I thought I'd take a nap and read awhile. I brought us some hamburgers." Maggie produced a white paper bag from the motel's short-order cafe, and two tepid Coca-Colas in paper cups.

"Thanks. Did you and Boots have a fight, too?"

"Not really. I just didn't feel like staying on the beach any longer. I'm cooked. And I hate Purple Jesus."

"Me too. Was Jenks mad, do you think?"

"You know Jenks is never mad at you. They're too mellow on gin and grape juice to be mad. It's just that Boots is so . . . oh, I don't know, so *sure* of me sometimes. And I get so tired of hearing about the precious Delta. You'd think it was a kingdom, or something."

"Well, it is," said Delia practically, beginning to torture her hair into rows of snail-like pin curls. "Jenks said when he went home with Boots last spring holidays, Boots's daddy rode them around all their land in a jeep, and it went on for miles and miles. They must have fifty hands on the place, and houses for all of them. And he said they had drinks on the veranda that a Negro man in a white coat brought them, and they must have five servants in the house, and a whole slew of yardmen. Jenks said it looked like Tara. It's a plantation, you know, or it was. Boots's granddaddy used to raise racehorses, too."

"Doo-dah, doo-dah," said Maggie around a mouthful of hamburger.

"Maggie, sometimes I think you're crazy. I'd give anything to get married and live in a place like that. You act like it's nothing."

"Well, in the first place, I haven't seen it yet. And in the second place, I haven't said a word about getting married. And in the third place, if I did marry Boots, we certainly wouldn't live with his folks."

"Well, they'll die sooner or later, and you'd be the mistress of Groveland, and have all those servants, and a bunch of beautiful children . . . gee, I don't know if it would be better if they looked like Boots or you. It's just like a dream come true, Maggie. Just think about Jenks and me, raising our kids in Huntsville in some tacky prefab thing." But she did not look sad.

"Delia, is that really what you want to do?"

"Well, sure." Delia looked at her with round indigo eyes. "What else would I do?"

"I don't know. Work, maybe. You'll have a degree in education, after all. Don't you plan to teach, ever?"

"Nope. I had to major in something, and Elementary Education doesn't have any math requirements. Maggie, you know I'd make a rotten teacher. I'll leave the working to people like you and your friend Aiken Reed. Only I bet neither one of you ever works a day in your life."

"Why not?"

"Well, you'll marry Boots in a June wedding with twelve bridesmaids right after you graduate, no matter what you say about advertising agencies and Europe, and Aiken will probably marry old Tuck."

Maggie looked at her. She was cherubic and content in a pink duster, pointing a pistol-like hair dryer at the helmet of pin curls.

"I didn't know you knew about that," she said.

"Oh, sure. The whole campus knows about that. Everybody always knows who Aiken's sleeping with. I don't know how she gets away with it; I'd be pregnant and expelled and I don't know what-all by now. She may be pretty, but she sure is an oddball. I guess that's why Tuck is so crazy about her. He's odd, too. Is she a good friend of yours, Maggie?"

"I haven't known her very long. Oh, I knew who she was, of course, but I didn't get to know her till we had this poetry class together this summer. But I really like her. She's . . . very honest, and she says what she thinks. And she makes me think, too. I get the feeling sometimes that she . . . knows something I don't."

"I bet she knows a whole lot you don't."

"No, I mean something about life that's good and different, and she'd like me to know it, too, but she can't explain it, or won't. Or maybe I don't understand it when she tries to. I think you're wrong about her marrying Tuck, though. I don't think Aiken will get married for a long time, and maybe never."

"Why on earth not?"

"Because she doesn't *want* to, Delia. Aiken will probably have a fabulous career, or whatever she wants. She just doesn't care about doing things just because everybody else is doing them. I admire her for it. I may go to Sweden with her."

"Well, if that doesn't beat anything I ever heard. You have a chance to marry the best-looking, sexiest, richest boy on campus and live on a plantation and you want to go to Sweden with Aiken Reed. Boots won't hear of it."

"Boots *hasn't* heard of it," said Maggie, who had never seriously entertained the idea of Sweden and did not know why she had said it. "And don't you say anything about it, either. Of course I'm not going to Sweden with Aiken. I only meant that I think people ought to do . . . what they really want to do, not what everybody expects them to."

Her own voice sounded strident and alien in her ears, and so she changed the subject.

"Do you care about Aiken and Tuck?"

"God, no. I was just fooling around till Jenks got back to school. I never thought the idiot would get serious about me." She patted the pin curls complacently. "Can you see me taking Tuck home to Prattville to meet Mama and Daddy? Can you *see* him quoting poetry at the country club? No, he's perfect for Aiken, and I hope they live happily ever after . . . in sin or out of it. Listen, Maggie, he's the one who told me about them. He said he'd found a girl who really understood him and that he and I were just some bright, doomed thing. That's what he said, Maggie . . . that was destined to burn out. He said he never meant to hurt me. He told me that the last night he tutored me."

"What did you say?"

"I said he only hurt me when he tried to dance with me."

"Oh, Delia, that was cruel!"

"Why? You know he's spastic on the dance floor."

"Delia, did it ever occur to you that there's more to life than dancing?"

"Well, if there is, I don't want to know about it yet. Speaking of which, I think I'll take a nap before tonight. I can't wait to get to the Hangout. That's the *home* of the Panama City Dirty Bop, you know."

She lowered the blinds against the fiery white outside and turned up the thumping window unit and curled on her side like a kitten and slept. Maggie read a chapter or two of *Not As a Stranger,* and then she, too, fell asleep.

The Hangout was not really a building. It was a pavilion facing the sea on the scabbed fringe of sand that served Panama City as a beach. A blur of neon ran like a river out of sight on either side. To its left was a concrete block seafood restaurant with a cocktail lounge, and to its right was a drive-in hamburger place. The Hangout sold no alcoholic drinks except beer, but it did a brisk business in setups.

Outside the Hangout, the parking lot was filled with cars bearing Kappa Alpha decals, and the shabbier, two-toned chariots of the cruisers and a gleaming Harley-Davidson or two. Inside, the Hangout was dark, lit only by candles in glass hurricanes with fishnet stretched over them, the huge jukebox, and the red-and-green foxfire of neon dancing on the black ocean a few yards away. The Kappa Alphas had occupied a field of tables on the left side of the pavilion. The other tables and the dance floor were the province of swarthy young men in skinlike Levi's, T-shirts with the sleeves rolled high up their biceps, cupping packs of cigarettes, and prowling eyes under slicked-back ducktails and sideburns. Many had baroque tattoos on their upper arms. They were older than the KA brothers, or looked it. The greasers, the cruisers, the rodders, the bikers. Harrison Salisbury had called them the shook-up generation, but they had never heard of Harrison Salisbury. Their girls were wild-haired and closed-faced in painted-on, rolled short shorts and T-shirts or halters. It was nine-thirty in the evening.

Maggie and Boots and Delia and Jenks sat at a table beside the railing that gave onto the beach and ocean. It was stifling hot, even in the tepid sea-wind that blew steadily and monotonously across the dance floor. They had been at the table since seven that evening, when the Gulf was the pink-and-sil-ver of crumpled foil around a chocolate. They had stopped on the way from Destin for fried shrimp, and Maggie and Delia had gorged themselves. Boots and Jenks had drunk gin and Seven-Up. They had brought a bottle of gin from the cache in their cot-tage at the Harmony House and were three-fourths of the way to the bottom of it. Seven-Up bottles lit-tered the table. Delia was giddy and giggling from the alcohol and the amplified thumping of Elvis Pres-ley's electric guitar. Boots was cool-eyed and slurring slightly, sweeping the roomful of alien rodders with his narrow green eyes. They stared back at the KAs and their Jantzened and Capezioed dates silently. Jenks was growing steadily louder; his cheerleader's voice had lost its lilt of enthusiasm and was becom-ing hard-edged and truculent. Maggie had never seen him so drunk or so testy. He and Delia had quarreled steadily all the way from the Harmony House, Delia said. Maggie and Boots had followed them in the Jaguar, and they could see Jenks's white head turned

importuningly toward Delia during the drive, and
Delia's yellow one, staring fixedly ahead.

"What about?" Maggie had asked her in the rest
room of the fried-shrimp place.

"About me dancing with hoods. Jenks doesn't
want me to dance with anybody but KAs. He says the
guys who hang around the Hangout are mean sons of
bitches and don't respect girls, and he won't have me
dancing with them."

"He's probably right. You know what happened
at Ma's."

"That was different. That was Tuck. Who's going
to start anything with a whole fraternity sitting there?
I told him if he couldn't handle a Panama City hood,
he better get out of the ball game. I've been looking
forward to this for three months."

Maggie was restless and bored. She was an accomplished and tireless dancer; she knew that eyes
followed her when she got up to dance with Boots or
one of the brothers. She knew that her white shorts
and shirt shone in the gloom on her polished, tanned
body, and that the candlelight flickered goldenly in
her tilted amber eyes, and that the rodders and cruisers sent messages to one another about her with their
measuring eyes, while their girls drew on thicker
mouths with blood-dark lipstick and sent each other
silent messages of contempt about her, and hated her
shining untouchableness. But she knew that none of
the dusky, oiled young men would cut in. They never
did. She was glad. She thought them feral and fright-

ening and unfathomable. But she wondered why. I guess I just don't project whatever it is Delia does, or Aiken, she thought. I think I probably don't have sex appeal. Maggie did not know whether she was glad or sorry about this.

The smoke and music and the sticky-sweet residue of gin and Seven-Up hurt her head. Maggie found rock-and-roll music more a convenience than a creed. It was necessary in order to dance; she accepted that. But the sound had never exalted or exhilarated her, as it did so many of her contemporaries. She focused, when she danced, on the beat; the near-animal lyrics and the pelvis-grinding gyrations of the performers disturbed her faintly. Elvis Presley both attracted and repelled her, and while she had a number of his singles among her 45s, she had far more of the smoky, bittersweet ballads of June Christy and Chris Connor, and had worn out two copies of *Ella Fitzgerald Sings the Cole Porter Song Book*. The witty, articulate lyrics enchanted her, and the skittering silver virtuosity of Fitzgerald pleased her in the same obscure way poetry did. She also drowsed raptly and for hours over *Jazz Goes to College*; Brubeck and Desmond were cool and soothing and titillating in a way that rock-and-roll never was for her. She had a number of blatantly romantic classical albums too; Rachmaninoff and Tchaikovsky and Rimsky-Korsakoff often battled the Chords and the Platters in the Kappa house, and Sister had taken to awakening her with the finale of the 1812 Overture in retaliation. Mendelssohn's Violin Concerto made her weep.

She looked out over the ocean into the sky, where a full moon sailed high among ragged clouds. The air was thick and sullen, as if a storm might be building. The nape of her neck and the fine gold hair on her forearms crawled slightly, whether with drying perspiration or building electricity, she could not say. She thought the sky looked like the cover of her Rachmaninoff album, and wanted suddenly to walk on the beach, ankle-deep in the black infinity of water. It would be quiet.

"Let's go for a walk," she said to Boots.

"In a minute."

He had become suddenly still and was looking toward the side of the room where the rodders and their girls rose and danced and settled fluidly back into chairs, like a dark flock of birds in perpetual, restless motion. There was a slight but perceptible tightening in their ranks, a thickening current of something, fine wires tautening and thrilling. His eyes followed theirs onto the dance floor, where Jenks and Delia were dancing. They were not alone on the floor, but they might as well have been. Delia *was* alone, in her motion, her eyes closed, her head flung back, her hips moving convulsively to the beat of "Hound Dog," her legs locked stiff, her feet not moving. She looked fluorescent, oddly luminous, as though an invisible spotlight were trained on her. She looked incredibly, viscerally sexual and closed away under a dome of rapt self-awareness. Jenks had stopped dancing; he stood swaying slightly and watching her, his face pared to bone with the coming trouble. He looked like a murderous baby.

Maggie felt the trouble soar as if mercury were running up a thermometer.

"Boots, you better go get Jenks," she began, but the tall boy was already moving out of his crowd and onto the floor, the dark hot-rodder, the candidate for the Mystery of Delia.

He reached for her at the same time Jenks sprang. It was scrabbling and spitting and catlike and incredibly fast. Jenks's indolence went to a lithe dancer's frenzy in an eye-flicker. There was a second's coupled swaying as they grappled in each other's arms, blond grace and bearish, oiled muscle, and then a swarm of Kappa Alphas were behind Jenks, pulling at his shirt, and a corresponding swarm of sun-dark arms were pulling at the rodder. Separated, arms pinioned behind them, chests heaving and breath sobbing through their noses, they stared at each other. No blood ran. The rodders were heavier, older, simpler, but there were fewer of them than KAs. It was a fight nobody wanted, and the antagonists allowed themselves to be jostled and soothed back to their respective tables. Lightning forked greenly into the sea, and thunder cracked, and rain began.

The manager, who had started to reach for the telephone, relaxed back onto his stool behind the candy and cigarette counter. He could read a rumble the way a countryman could read a hard winter in lichens and animal fur. This one was defused. Some prickling alchemy of the building storm had broken the tight wires when it split the sky and sea. He loathed his clientele generally, and their noise and music and brawls and preening jealousies, but on the whole he favored his summer fraternity crowds over his steadier local patrons. They were not, on the whole, trained to violence. But there was always one girl in their ranks, one like the little blonde, who was back at her table, blowing smoke through her nostrils and taunting the blond boy who had jumped the rodder. He truly feared those girls.

Delia knew she was in disfavor with the KAs. After they had thumped Jenks on the back and mollified him back into his chair and put a cigarette and a fresh drink into his hands, they had not lingered to crow and bluster as they usually did after a fight had been averted. They had pointedly ignored Delia and gone back to their own dates, and heads turned toward her and low conversation broke out. The rodders and their dates were talking about her, too; Maggie caught an occasional syllable and bursts of laughter. The rodders' girls were grinning openly at their table. Boots was silent, and Jenks's chin rested on his chest, his eyes on the surface of his drink. The currents of disapproval and malicious amusement were palpable. A KA put a coin into the jukebox, and the arm snaked out and the disc dropped.

The mannerly strains of "Lisbon Antigua" curled out over the floor and out through the thrumming rain over the sea. Maggie knew that a period had been put to the evening's dancing and that, one by one, the couples would drift out of the Hangout and drive back to the Harmony House to continue the drinking in rooms or under the ticking umbrellas on the beach.

"My hero," Delia drawled dangerously into the silence.

Jenks was on his feet in one furious movement. He pinned a long hand around her wrist and threw some crumpled bills on the table with the other. In a mottled white silence, he pulled her out of her chair so abruptly that she stumbled, dropping her straw purse and scattering cigarettes, makeup, and coins onto the floor.

"What do you think you're doing?" Her voice was thin and high.

"I'm taking you home. Back to school. Right now. I'm going to stop at the motel for five minutes flat, and if you're not through packing by then, Maggie can bring what you leave. Come on. Move."

"Jenks, I don't want to go home! The party's not over, you're drunk, and you can't drive like that. . . . "

"SHUT UP!"

It was a voice Maggie had never heard. The room watched as he tugged her, wailing, across the dance floor and out the entrance. A car door slammed, and then another. A motor roared. Except for a low swell of laughter from the other side of the pavilion, there was utter silence. Boots drained his drink and stood up.

"Come on," he said to Maggie, and she gathered up Delia's purse and her own and followed him out to the Jaguar.

"Stupid prick. Poor dumb, stupid prick," he said once on the drive home, but that was all he did say.

They were due to go home the next day anyway, but the spine of the house party was broken, and so most of the cars were loaded early, by noon, and the caravan of sunburns and hangovers started north, through the somnolent, sweetly shabby little towns: De Funiak Springs, Geneva, Bellwood, Eufaula. Jenks had been as good as his word; Delia had been gone when they reached Maggie's room, and the trunk of the Jaguar was now crammed with stray bits of Delia's jetsam: a crinoline, a damp towel, shoes, the hair dryer. Only once on the drive home had Maggie mentioned Jenks and Delia.

"I hope they got home okay. I never saw Jenks so mad. And he *was* pretty drunk."

"Jenks can drive better drunk than most people can sober. But I bet you I know one little tramp that's going to be minus a KA pin next time you see her."

"Oh, Boots, that was just a fight. She *should* have known better, but that's just Delia. You *know* they're crazy about each other. I can't remember a time they weren't going to get married."

"Well, they're not now. And I know. That's over."

"Boots . . ."

"Drop it, Maggie."

And so she did.

They drove for a long while in silence. He drove well, handling the Jaguar as if it were an extension of his long arms and legs. The top was down and the rushing wind made conversation impossible. By the time they were fifty miles from Randolph, Maggie felt burned and whipped and disheveled, and so he stopped and put the top up, and they had a cup of coffee in a stark little drive-in in Society Hill.

"I'm going home in a couple of weekends," Boots said. "Want to come along and meet the folks?"

"I'd like to, but I'll have to ask Mother and Daddy."

He laughed.

"I don't think they'll be any problem. I'll ask my mother to write yours."

"Well, that would be nice."

It was past dusk when the Jaguar pulled into the parking lot of the Kappa house. The sun had gone, but a gray wash of light still lay over the street. Fire-flies winked in the honeysuckle hedge at the end of the lot. The lot was crowded with cars, far more than were usually there in a summer twilight. Lights burned in all the upstairs windows, and in the drawing room downstairs, and from Mama Kidd's rooms. Maggie could see figures outlined in the upstairs windows, gesturing with animation, and more were downstairs, in the drawing room. Another group of girls stood on the veranda.

"What on earth?" said Maggie. They got out of the car. Boots got her luggage and overnight case out of the trunk and slammed it and started up the flagstone path, and Maggie followed him, her arms full of Delia's abandoned belongings.

"Oh, Maggie!" A voice wrenched shrilly from the murmur of softer ones on the veranda, a figure broke from the knot of girls and clattered down the front steps. "Oh, Maggie!" Sister. She was crying.

"Sister. What's the matter?" Maggie's heart dropped sickeningly; a cold hollow replaced it in her chest, where no breath stirred.

"Oh, I thought you'd never get back! It's so *awful*. Oh, Maggie, it's just terrible—"

"Sister, what has happened?"

"It's Delia. They had a wreck, the car went into a telephone pole around Eufaula, and she's hurt *so* bad; oh, Maggie, they took her up to the hospital in Montgomery, and she's still unconscious, the highway patrol called . . . last night, Maggie, in the middle of the night, I heard the phone, and then Mama Kidd just screamed, and screamed, and screamed; I think she's having a nervous breakdown; Dean Fisher's been here all day, and the doctor. . . . "

"What about Jenks?" Boots's voice came out on a very small sigh.

"Oh, dear Jesus! Jenks is dead!"

9

T HE NEWS OF THE ACCIDENT ran through the
summer campus like brush fire. In a student
body of more than seven thousand, there were a few
tragedies each year—automobile accidents mostly,
though these seemed to occur away from Randolph,
between quarters or during vacations. They seemed
flattened and blurred by distance and dissociation as
if by a pane of glass. There had been, a couple of years
before, a multi-car collision among a caravan of Animal Husbandry students, en route to Montgomery for
a seminar, which had left two students dead. But they
had been known only to small circles in their school
and dormitories. An obscure young man had dropped
dead during a long march at the Army ROTC summer maneuvers at Fort Belvoir in 1954; his congeni-
tal heart defect had gone undiagnosed, along with his
personality, until then. Closer to the Randolph collective consciousness, a popular though studious Alpha
Tau Omega had developed a lymphatic malignancy
which had killed him swiftly and, on the main, not so
brutally, but that had been in a Birmingham hospital.
Disaster rarely brushed the truly golden ones.

But now, in one rending predawn moment, Randolph had lost its head cheerleader and, for all practical purposes, one of its legendary beauties. Delia's face, it was reported, was a featureless aspic under the white bandages. Years of plastic surgery, M.A. Appleton wept to the chapter after she and Maggie had visited the hospital in Montgomery. And even then she would not look like Delia, only human. She had not yet regained consciousness at the time of their visit two days after the KA house party had ended. There seemed to be little or no brain damage, though this would not be known until she awakened. She had been thrown clear, but through the windshield. Aside from a broken arm and abrasions from a long slide on the pavement, there seemed to be only nominal injury, except to her face. It was almost as though, the doctors told Delia's parents, she did not wish to wake up. Her parents, numbed, larger and paler models of Delia, had checked into a motel near the hospital and took turns sitting beside their daughter around the clock. They spoke little. The nursing staff considered them no trouble at all.

To the student body, the accident took on an aura of greater clarity, greater luminosity, than other things that happened in their lives. It would later become the thing many of them remembered from their time at Randolph. It divided time. It had about it its own illumination, as though it had happened in the liquid crystal light of a mountain island in a Greece outside time, where the very air was alive with portent; it had little to do with 1956. Theseus and Ariadne were dead. The student body murmured, clung together, looked over their shoulders.

Jenks had been buried in the family plot in the pitted little north Alabama town. The Kappa Alphas had gone en masse, and delegates from the major campus organizations—the Student Government Association, the WSGA, the Interfraternity Council, the R Club. The rest of the cheerleading squad had gone, and the captain of the football team, and the intramural coach. Maggie did not go; but a surprising number of students who had known Jenks only as a gilded figure in orange and blue, leading their Saturday litanies, did. The bare, pocked little cemetery had been crowded with them. Jenks's family, Boots told Maggie when he returned, had stood stonily silent and closed in their darkness, and had not spoken to anyone. "It was just like he was a stranger to them, almost," he told Maggie.

Well, Maggie thought, he was.

The Kappa house was in turmoil. Sister had been correct: Mama Kidd had spent an hour after the fateful telephone call screaming past the hovering faces around her into middle distance, screaming that she had killed Delia. No assurances that Delia was alive seemed to permeate her consciousness. Her screams were short and sharp and piercing, like a mill whistle. Dean Fisher, in a London Fog buttoned up to the neck over her nightgown, had arrived in the thinning darkness, looked narrowly around at the girls in this house where housemothers seemed to go regularly mad, and gone into Mama Kidd's bedroom, where she had shooed out M.A. and the other sobbing Kappas and firmly shut the door. She had walked over to the woman sitting up in bed, regarded her silently for a moment, then slapped her sharply across the face. In the rush of indrawn-breath silence, she had said, "Where do you keep your liquor, Myra?" Mama Kidd had pointed to the Kahlil Gibran in the bookcase, and Dean Fisher had removed it and brought out the pint of Jack Daniel's. It was a new bottle, nearly full. Uncapping it, she handed it to Mrs. Kidd, who drank from the bottle. After that, the piercing screams subsided into a sort of weary, gargling keening, and finally into snores. At 7:00 A.M., she telephoned her own physician.

She passed a day in fitful, drugged sleep, in which deep snoring alternated with wild and incoherent sobbings about guilt and blood and chewing gum and blonde whores and God. That night, the physician, a GP from nearby Opelika, had told the exhausted Dean of Women that Mrs. Kidd would have to have psychiatric care. The Kappa niece, now a golfing matron in Dothan, was located and sullenly agreed to bring her own physician and drive her aunt to a private sanatorium nearby, where she would be boarded for the duration of her treatment. "I certainly can't keep her at home," she had snapped to M.A. Appleton and the exasperated dean, and the tame physician had nodded in agreement. "I know she's got some money somewhere, but God knows how Uncle Cliff left it tied up." And the physician had given Mama Kidd another shot, and the Kappas had packed her a handbag and promised to keep an eye on her belongings until "we know how things are going to turn out," and the niece and the doctor and the stumbling, mumbling woman had driven away to untangle the Judge's money.

Dean Fisher had gathered the girls in the sitting room of the housemother's suite and laid it on the line.

"This is a terrible thing, a terrible tragedy," she said, wishing with all her heart she could borrow a cigarette from one of them with propriety. "But there is nothing to be gained by losing your heads, nor by crying. It cannot help Jenks, and by the grace of God, we may hope Delia will recover. I have asked your house staff to get some supper for you, and it should be ready in the dining room in half an hour or so. My main concern is what to do with you girls for the rest of the summer. I do not think we can realistically expect Mrs. Kidd to resume her duties for some time"—she held up her hand to quell the ground swell of murmuring that rose—"and I cannot very well place this many of you in dormitories. We only have enough open this summer to accommodate the girls who are here. I have two choices. I can move into the house with you myself"—the murmuring rose again, and she smiled inwardly—"or I can leave you to yourselves the rest of the summer and trust you to be the ladies I know you are."

When the babble of ladylike assurance had died, she continued. "All right. For the rest of the summer, you will be on your own. Margaret Anne"—she nodded to M.A., who blinked wetly and palely—"and Virginia Crewes, who is your treasurer, will be responsible for seeing that the house runs just as it has. I have gone through Mrs. Kidd's desk, and I see that you have a simple summer arrangement. It is merely a matter of ordering your food twice a week and giving a week's worth of menus to Estelle every Sunday night. I note that there is enough in your treasury to continue to pay your suppliers and your staff with your summer house fund. Virginia will be in charge of these arrangements, but I suggest that you have a full chapter meeting this evening and work out a schedule for everyone to follow. I anticipate that you will have no trouble, but, of course, you may call on me at any time if you do.

"I need not tell you," she went on, "that I would be open to criticism myself if I did not keep a very careful watch on the Kappa house. I know you are good girls. From now on until we can make some arrangements for supervision, you must avoid any appearance that would suggest otherwise. I do not wish to hear of any lateness, any breaking of curfews and permissions, any young men in the house after their visiting hours, anything at all that is in violation of the rules of this university. If I should hear of any violation, you will understand that I must close the Kappa house immediately and you girls will have to go in as third roommates in assigned rooms in the various dormitories, no matter how uncomfortable that would be for everyone. It is not only I who will be watching you girls, you know. The eyes of the entire campus will be on this house. I hope you will be a credit to the panhellenic tradition at Randolph University."

And so saying, she went home to the gracious apartment in the Administration Building of the Women's Quadrangle and took a bath and wondered tiredly over a glass of sherry which one of them the first trouble would revolve about, and who would report it to her.

In Maggie's room that night, after the solemn meeting had been held and arrangements had been arranged and promises promised and a delegation appointed to drive to Montgomery the next day to comfort Delia's parents and render such service as they could, Maggie and Sister and Cornelia Quin curled up in the path of the electric fan to absorb the devastating twenty-four hours.

"What I never understood was why they left the house party in the middle of the night," said Sister, who was heavily anointed with Esoterica cream across the bridge of her nose, where freckles bloomed each summer. The campaign for the SAE pin was going better, and Sister was taking no chances. "You were there, Maggie. What happened?"

"There was some trouble at the Hangout with a bunch of hoods," said Maggie, unwilling to look into her mind for the ugly scene. "Jenks got mad and drug her out. He said he was going to bring her back here, but I didn't think . . . we didn't think . . . "

"Nobody blames you, Maggie," Cornelia said quickly. "We all know what Delia's like. God, when you think what Jenks puts up with—"

The present tense caught her and her eyes filled.

"Well, she may be my own sorority sister, but she's been asking for trouble ever since we pledged her, and I hope she's happy with what she's done to Jenks." Sister was defiant.

Maggie whirled on her. "Shut up, Sister. Just don't say another word. Think what her life is going to be like now. Just think what she's going to live with the rest of her life . . . if there is any."

But in some place very deep inside her, Maggie was angry with Delia, angry with an anger that she knew would not go away.

"Well," said Sister, too charmed with a new thought to bristle at Maggie's unaccustomed sharpness, "look on the bright side of it. Here we are for the rest of the whole summer with absolutely nobody to check up on us. No bloodhounds, no warden, no bed check. It's the opportunity of a lifetime!"

But the other two were silent. The one of them to whom it was the opportunity of a lifetime lay in a hospital sixty miles away with stiffening gauze for a face and a lifetime that would never be the same again.

10

MAGGIE, HONEY, you go on upstairs now and take a nap. That hellion son of mine has worn you out. You've got circles an inch deep under those pretty eyes. I'll send Vinnie up terreckly with some iced tea."

Coralee Claiborne gave Maggie a small shove-pat, and Maggie, feeling herself dismissed like a child from the presence of an affable but distracted adult, obediently rose from the wrought-iron veranda chair and gathered up her purse and sunglasses. They had come in from a luncheon at the country club "to meet Boots's pretty friend from school"—a blur of bright-flowered silk dresses over big hips and languid, drawling talk and assessing eyes—and dropped into chairs on the dappled veranda for "a little get-acquainted girl talk of our own." After a few ritual sorties—"What do you study at school, honey?" . . . "You're a Kappa, Boots says, that's nice. So many of our Delta girls pledge Kappa, but that's at Ole Miss, of course." . . . "What firm did you say your daddy was with? I wonder if Court knows any of them, I've never heard him say, but of course, Atlanta's *so* far away"—Coralee's talk had lapsed comfortably into the litany of her world: "This big old house, what a white elephant it is," and the problems of help and upkeep, and the two men whose presence seemed to fill the house and the land, even out of sight to the slow river, with their vitality. She talked of both uniformly as though they were children, but feared children, young boy-kings. Maggie had never felt less acquainted with anyone than Boots's mother.

"Well, if you're sure there's nothing I can help you with . . ."

"Oh, shoot, I've got a houseful of help, sorry though it is. Besides, *I'm* not the one that danced until three o'clock last night. And I'd be willing to bet that no-good boy of mine sat up till dawn drinking with his daddy; I haven't laid eyes on him today, have you? I declare, between the two of them . . ."

Her voice fluttered away, implying weary eternities of coping with husband and son of this big white house. She was a small, stout, fiercely girdled woman in peony-printed silk with a deep V that spilled soft, tan-speckled breasts out into the still afternoon, small feet swelling in pointed peony silk shoes, fingers and ears flashing with slightly filmed diamonds. Only her eyes, tiny points of pure, flat green between black lashes, and her perfectly square jaw, blurred with drooping underflesh, spoke of the iron that under-girded her house, her men, and her vast green-and-white world.

"I really enjoyed meeting your friends. They were so nice to me," said Maggie, one foot in the pure yellow sunlight of the veranda and one in the cave-dark of the foyer.

"Well, you're a sweet girl. Run on, now. Boots and his daddy will be back from wherever they went before you know it, and they'll be stomping and hollering for us to come have a drink with them, and you'll be limp as a dishrag if you don't get a little nap. Take off that pretty dress and draw the shutters and lie right down. Would you like Vinnie to rinse out some things for you, or press anything? I'll tell her when she brings your tea . . . "

"Oh, no, really. I don't want to bother her. . . . "

Bother her, Maggie said redly to herself. That's what she's *there* for. Oh, God, it's just so obvious I'm not used to servants. I'm not used to any of this.

She gave Boots's mother a ridiculous, military little flutter of her hand and fled through the foyer and up the dark stairs that curved from the sea of polished floor up into the cool, cavernous upper reaches of Groveland.

In the room allotted to her—a large corner square with the same dark, polished floors as the rest of the house, french doors opening onto a long gallery, and islands of mahogany floating in the rose-flushed dimness—Maggie drew the shutters against the gallery's glare and took off her dress. She hung it carefully in the enormous chifforobe that dwarfed her pale cottons, all neatly buttoned and zipped onto padded, sachet-scented hangers by the impassive Vinnie the afternoon they'd arrived—only yesterday, Maggie thought despairingly. She'd made a flying trip home to Lytton the weekend before to tell Comer and Frances about the visit to the Delta and to wheedle Carrie into getting her clothes ready. Her parents had been delighted. They had met Boots the previous Christmas, when he'd come home with Maggie, and had been charmed by his graceful manners and the lustrous Delta background that lay invisibly but palpably over his shoulders. The diamond pin charmed, too, though it had not been spoken of. "Well, if that's what you want, honey," Comer had said earlier, when Maggie accepted the pin. And Frances had said, "It's not *quite* the same as being engaged, is it?" Maggie had said it was not, quite.

With her parents, Boots had been ingenuous and deferential; care and cherishing for Maggie flashed out of every small attention to Comer, every ritual grace to Frances, every indulgent, teasing word to Maggie and grave courtesy to Carrie. Pictures of Groveland had been offered almost shyly, as if by way of dowry, for Frances's and Comer's inspection.

This is right, she's done well. It was for this, all of it, Frances's eyes had radioed Comer's while they talked of the South and the law and small things, and, Yes, it was for this, Comer's eyes had said back.

So, the Saturday before, there had been a trip into Atlanta, and Frances and Maggie had come home laden with creamy, silky new cottons and shoes and pale, lacy underwear and a puff of a flower-sprigged nylon peignoir for Maggie. "Mama, I'm not getting married," Maggie had laughed, protesting, as the drifts of clothes piled up on her bed, and Frances had replied, "Well, I should hope not, yet," but, Yes you are, my good little girl, my child, had been in her eyes. Her mother and father had hugged her long when she left, the new clothes bannering from the sawed-off broomstick in the back of her car.

"Have a good time. We'll see you in a month or so," they had said, but their arms had said, Goodbye, Maggie, you've done well.

Under the ancestral Claiborne roof, however, in the old chifforobe that sheltered the ghosts of Mississippi lavender and dimity and satins and point d'esprit, the Atlanta cottons looked lost and perfunctory and rawly new, and seemed to hide themselves in shame in the Claiborne gloom.

Maggie washed the careful luncheon makeup off her face in the adjoining bathroom—big, white, dim. Was her house party tan going yellow, were the circles under her eyes as bad as Boots's mother had said? In the thin, greenish light they looked it. She wrapped herself in the flowered peignoir and lay down on the high, canopied bed. I never saw a real canopy bed, she thought. The canopy was a rose-patterned chintz, matching the dust ruffle and the rose of the scatter rugs and heavy curtains. It washed her in a flush that was stifling. Heat and dim rose light were thick in the room.

It was very hot. Outside, from the gallery, green lawns swept away nearly a mile to a fringe of willows and water oaks that shielded the brown curve of the slow river. Darker green magnolias lined the gravel drive that semicircled around the front veranda to the stables in back, which now housed the Claiborne fleet of automobiles and lawn mowers and jeeps. Except for a hectic halfmoon of viciously scarlet roses around a sundial directly beyond the drive's center curve, everything in sight was green, and should have been cool. But Coralee had said at breakfast, fanning herself with a plaited palmetto fan, that the temperature stood then at ninety-two, and by afternoon the heat would be murderous.

"The trees block the breeze off the river," she sighed, "but not the humidity. July's not our best month for visiting. The whole summer is just awful, as a matter of fact. People who aren't born in it just can't stand up to our summers, sometimes."

She had looked greenly at not-born-in-it Maggie.

"Goodness, I'm used to it," Maggie said back. "Atlanta's hot, too, and school is just a steam bath."

"And our mosquitoes, big as starlings. Poor child, you'll meet those critters about dark, I'm afraid. Court has the hands spray along the river once a week during the summer, but I think they thrive on it. Well, I'll send up a floor fan for you. We're used to it, but . . ."

Maggie lay under the exhausted wash of the fan. She wants me not to be able to stand the heat, she

thought. She'd just love me to get out of the kitchen.
Her kitchen. Her house. Correction: her baby's
house. I bet she thinks if I were Boots's wife I'd
come in here the minute she died and air-condition
every damned room in this hotel—and there are fif-
teen that I've counted so far. And I would, too.

Boots's wife. The flower-and-candle barrier of
the Lytton First Methodist Church dissolved and
Maggie saw the country that lay beyond it. Maggie
had a setting for the role now. It was too big and too
hot and oddly dimensionless; it was peopled with
dimmed black ghosts who moved silently through
tall rooms in white coats and aprons, bearing silver
trays and armloads of ironed clothing and brooms
and dustcloths. But it was real. And as slyly, insinu-
atingly alluring as some fatal, enchanted tapestry
landscape, which inexorably drew unwary travelers,
and from which they never returned.

Can a house have Sirens in it, or is that just rocks?
Maggie wondered sleepily. It doesn't matter, because
I don't have to do this if I don't want to. But I do
want to. Don't I? But not now. I don't have to do
anything right now.

She would have liked to shed the damp peignoir
but did not want Vinnie to see her in her too-new,
too-lacy underwear when she came with the iced tea.
She slept.

When she wakened, sweated and stunned and
tattooed on cheek and thigh by the pattern of the
Martha Washington bedspread, some of the light

had gone from the room, though the heat remained. Her iced tea, its ice cubes melting, sat sweating on a silver tray beside the bed. Vinnie was silent of foot as well as face. Maggie stretched and looked at her watch: five-fifteen. A screen door twang-thudded somewhere downstairs; men's feet clattered imperially in the polished foyer, men's voices rang invadingly up the stairs.

"I know two women who better be down here lookin' pretty and drinkin' whiskey in ten minutes flat!" Boots's father.

"Wake up, Maggie, or I'll come up there and haul you out of that bed myself. That ain't no bad thing, either." Boots.

And a low, wordless duet of masculine voices, and laughter.

In the big white bathtub, so old that its porcelain felt gritty to her buttocks, Maggie washed away the heat and the sleep, but an undercurrent of fatigue slowed her arms and legs. She and Boots had both taken cuts in their Friday classes for the six-hour drive from Randolph to Greenville, and had arrived at midafternoon, wind-whipped and beaten from the savage sun. Boots would not put the top up on the Jaguar unless it was raining. There had been hearty greetings and a seemingly endless round of drinks on the veranda, which had worked like a paralytic poison on Maggie's quivering, meet-the-parents nerves. The lush, flat, feverish green of the great river Delta, the heat, the stage-set vastness of Groveland and its horizon-brushing lands, the quiet Negroes, moving as if oiled, Courtney and Coralee Claiborne themselves, all seemed unreal and sketched in with quick brushstrokes of scenery paint. Maggie had nodded, smiled, been hugged and patted, parroted sweet answers, but her only clear, clean thought was, Nobody lives like this, not really. When she'd had a quick bath and changed into just-bought white voile, Boots had whirled her off in the Jaguar to the country club for a dinner dance.

There, to a placid combo whose most contemporary offering was the theme from *Picnic,* Maggie had slow-danced, in a fog of liquor and unreality, with a succession of young men who, though assorted in shape and size, all spoke with Boots's cool, flat drawl and held her too close, getting the feel of the outlander. Their girls, too—in cottons like Maggie's but not quite so dressy, in flat Capezios instead of Maggie's Cuban heels—all spoke alike: a little slower, a little cooler. One of them had been Boots's girl, Maggie knew, but she could not tell which. They did not ignore Maggie; Boots Claiborne's current girl would not be ignored. But their talk, all of Ole Miss and Mississippi summers past and Mississippi people not there, did not include her, either. The girls "loved" her dress in the rest room; the boys nuzzled and flirted; and Maggie, in her stocking feet and her bright, fixed smile, went through her paces for these alien childhood companions of Boots's. But when, at two-thirty in the dark, hot morning, Boots announced that he'd heard the click and had to take this woman home to bed, she was grateful almost to the point of tears. Maggie Deloach was not Queen of anything in the Mississippi Delta. It was another bewildering and fatiguing new insight. Today, spent in the company of Boots's mother, had been no different, and no better.

She slid into the simplest of the new cottons, a yellow sundress, and flats. Tonight they were going to a barbecue at the home of a girl named Snookie, "just down the river a little way," Boots said. Maggie had not caught Snookie's last name, but she had read in Snookie's calm, Disney-piglet face and careless honey pageboy and long, quick hands, never without a Kent, more old cotton money and more white columns and vast lands and another great, wisteria-arcaded veranda. Was she the cast-off girl? Her stomach knotted.

I'll bet they'll all be in Bermudas, she thought, and I didn't bring any. It had seemed almost indecent, packing night before last in her room at the Kappa house, to include shorts. This unknown country of vastness and languor had cried out to her, treacherously, for fullness and grace and rustle.

So she scrubbed Boots's diamond pin with her toothbrush before she pinned it below her Kappa pin—my identification badge, she thought defiantly—and she put on, then removed, the heavy, pink-gold bracelet that had been her Grandmother Elvira's, and she took a deep breath, and went, swiftly and lightly and in dread, down the stairs to the veranda.

Boots in the company of his father was a caricature, both of Boots and of Courtney Claiborne. Gone was the lounging grace and the sleepy cat's demeanor he wore at Randolph; gone, too, were the grave, good child's manners and deference he had shown Comer and Frances in Lytton. What remained of the Randolph Boots, Maggie's Boots, was the slightly sullen complacency that emerged late in the evenings, after many drinks. On his home turf, something raw, male, brawling came into Boots's face and voice, something near primitive, simplistic. Yet ingratiating.

He's acting like an overgrown child, thought Maggie, taking a gin and tonic from the tray held by blank-faced black Cleveland, in a white coat. He's like a child playing grown-up, or what he thinks grown-up is. Imitating his daddy.

Physically, Boots and Courtney Claiborne were much alike. Judge Claiborne, like Boots, was tall, and had been wide-shouldered and slender. The shoulders were rounded and stooped now, more with age and outdoors than the hours he put in in Greenville when court was in session, which were few. There was a small, hard, round potbelly thrusting against his white Sea Island cotton sport shirt. His hair had been the wheat-blond of Boots's but was gone now to a sun-bleached white-yellow. He wore it cut very short, and his tanned scalp showed through. His face

and neck and forearms were very tanned, giving him
the look of a man who should be standing on the
deck of a yacht. In the Delta country, as in her own
South, Maggie had noted, there were tans and tans;
some seemed given by luxurious suns shining caress-
ingly from skies bought by wealth and privilege, the
others seared on by suns beating on fields bought
by sweat and blisters and privation. Courtney Claiborne's tan, though it stopped midway up his upper
arms like the latter, was unmistakably the former. He
was a handsome man, with Boots's high-planed face
and long mouth, but these were blunter in his face,
more savage.

They sat in a circle in the wrought-iron chairs
on the veranda. The sky was yellowing over the trees
along the river, but it was still hot. An occasional
Negro, on a riding mower or pushing a wheelbar-
row, moved slowly across the lawn beyond them and
out of sight toward the stables, nodding and lifting
a straw sun hat as they passed. Courtney and Boots
gave each a wave of the hand, and Coralee nodded as
though she were on a reviewing stand. Maggie found
herself smiling brightly at each, as if she could draw
from the black-to-yellow faces some personal response by sheer force of personality. There was none.

It must be close to eight o'clock, Maggie thought.
They had been drinking since six. The sky would
flare and flame out abruptly, she knew from the
night before, dropping the house and lawn suddenly
into thick, close darkness, and the stabbing mos-

quitoes would start. A smell of something . . . meat cooking? . . . drifted around to the veranda from the kitchen at the back of the house, but no one had mentioned dinner, and none of the servants had appeared except Cleveland. Whose task was it to announce dinner? Vinnie, obviously, was a housemaid, and Maggie had seen a young cleaning girl. There was a cook, she knew, but she had never seen her. Cleveland had served breakfast.

She had not wanted the second gin and tonic; that had been a mistake. Gin and tonic smacked of nightclubs, cities, an ill-worn sophistication assumed by a too-young, alien intruder. This was a whiskey house. Even Coralee drank it; she was on her fourth, and her voice was growing shriller. Boots's and Courtney's roughened.

They had talked of Jenks. "Goddamned awful thing," Courtney Claiborne said. "That was a good boy. Had a straight head on him. Loved this old place, I remember, when Boots brought him home last spring. I rode him all over one morning while this one here was still asleep. For a hill boy he took to the place like he was born here. Beat the shit out of me—'scuse me, Maggie, Mama—at poker, too. Yessirree, he gave this place more attention in one weekend than this boy here does in a year. Boots here don't know any more about cotton than a jackrabbit. Thinks Santy Claus brings it. Got no head for the law, neither. What am I gon' do with him, Maggie?"

He grinned at her, a long, wolf's grin. Maggie shifted uncomfortably in her starched yellow, scratching a mosquito bite on one ankle with the toe of her shoe. "I think he knows a lot about it, Judge Claiborne," she said. "He talks about Groveland all the time. He makes it sound like some kind of... Shangri-la. He loves it. He's always saying Groveland is a real cotton empire... that you built," she added cravenly. Help me, Boots, she said with her eyes. Help yourself.

"Shangri-la, huh? Well, this old place has been good to Boots, that's for sure. Never lifted a finger to learn how to run it, after he was old enough to go to school. Couldn't. He was always in summer school. Drinkin' and chasin' tail, that's all he thinks about. Goddamn, 'scuse me, sugar, I don't mean you. What's gon' happen to this place after I'm gone is anybody's guess."

"Now, Court, that's not so. Boots knows how to run this place; this is his *home*. He's real good with the hands, you know he is. You're gon' have Maggie thinking you don't trust your only child." Coralee smiled the words, but there was iron and ice just behind them.

"Hell, yes, he's good with the hands. Good at huntin' and fishin' and drinkin' my liquor with 'em, and God knows what he's good at with their gals. He don't even know how big this place is. Ten thousand acres, Maggie, of the best goddamn cotton land in the country, what you think about that? Think you can keep this boy from pissin' it all away when I'm gone?"

"Shit, Judge, you'll live to be a hundred and three and they'll have to beat your liver to death with a two-by-four at that," Boots drawled comfortably. He gave his father an ingratiating grin. Courtney laughed, and the thin wire of tension snapped.

"Well, that's God's truth," he said. "One thing this boy did get from me was a good head for liquor. What time did we go to bed this morning, anyway, you remember?"

"I cashed in at five-thirty, Judge. You were still puttin' 'em away when I left. Goddamn, I had a head on me this morning when we left, thought I'd die."

This, Maggie knew, was not true. Boots did not get hangovers. It was a grace note flung to his father.

"Where *did* you all go this morning? Maggie and I missed you," said Coralee, seizing on the slackening of the wire and changing the subject. She was dewed with Bourbon sweat on upper lip and at her faded pink hairline, and her words were beginning to slur.

"Went over to the mill at Stoneville. Tom Cunningham's got his ass in a sling again. Always something." Discontent was crawling back into his voice.

"Maggie met Hoyt Cunningham this summer, Judge," Boots offered hastily. "You remember Hoyt. He's a reporter now, went to Harvard and everything. Maggie was real taken with him." With six words he threw her to the lions.

"Well, hell yes, I remember Hoyt. It was me that

got him that loan to go to school, what you think? Harvard, huh? Well, he's done right well, hasn't he? Bright boy, if I remember right. I always like to hear when a Delta boy does good." He slid a pale dagger of a look side-wise at Boots. "He gon' work on the Greenville paper?"

"Ask Maggie, she's the one that knows," said Boots sullenly, stung as he was meant to be by the side-wise look. Three pairs of Claiborne eyes turned to Maggie.

"Is Hoyt a friend of yours, Maggie? We've known his family . . . oh, for years." Coralee's drawl threw the words away, but they hung in the darkening air as if encircled by chalk on a blackboard.

They've worked for you for years, you mean, Maggie thought. She said, "Oh, no, I just met him at . . . at a place where he was working. He's a reporter for the Associated Press, he works out of Atlanta, but he travels all around covering . . . things, whatever his bureau wants him to cover, in his territory. He mentioned you all very fondly. But no, I don't really know him. . . ."

Then she realized that her words had betrayed her; she knew far more about this son of Courtney Claiborne's mill manager, this boy to whom Court-ney Claiborne's careless largesse had been flung, than she should know about a casual acquaintance. The three Claibornes were silent.

"Of course, Boots has told me a lot about him, too," she said lamely.

"If I recall, you were doing most of the telling, Maggie," Boots said perversely. His father had stabbed him, and his parents, he knew, were not pleased that his girl would fraternize with Hoyt Cunningham. Meet him, maybe. But it could have, should have, been cut off there. This girl does not know where to draw the line, their silence said. In an eye-flicker, Boots had aligned himself with them. Let the bile flow on Maggie now. Spare me, your son.

Oh, no, you won't, Maggie thought in sudden, tight fury.

"Well, we did talk for a long time. I found him fascinating. He has such . . . advanced ideas for a southerner. He believes that the Negroes are on the edge of revolution, that this bus trouble in Montgomery is just the beginning. He says the whole South is going to go up like kindling. He says we've oppressed the Negroes too long. He called it pure, Marxian revolution, with riots and shooting. As a matter of fact, he thought it might begin right here in the Mississippi Delta." Hoyt had not said that, but Maggie, riding on the crest of her own momentum, pushed the spear home. "I guess he would think that, since this is his home and he knows the Delta so well." Silence rang like a bell.

"By God, I didn't arrange for that sonofabitch to go to school to go all over the South talkin' *shit!*" Courtney Claiborne roared. "That motherfucker better not come back around here spreading that shit; I'll run him out of Greenville! After he took my money, after all I done for his folks—Oppressed! Goddamn, there ain't nobody on this river treats his niggers better than me!" He paused to swallow the rest of his drink.

Coralee hissed into the reverberating silence, "*Court!* I will not *have* that kind of language under this roof! Now you hush. What if Cleveland heard you?"

"I don't give a shit! Cleveland knows there ain't nobody that treats . . . Cleveland! Come on out here!"

Oh, dear God, thought Maggie in pain. Please, I don't want to hear this. Please don't do this. She was silent, the flush staining her neck and cheeks. Cleveland materialized in the clotting dusk at Courtney Claiborne's side.

"Yassuh?"

"Cleveland, you heard anything about riots and revolution and shit among the hands?"

"No*suh.*"

"You got any ideas about revoltin' and shootin' and shit?"

"Lawd, God, Mist' Court! Nosuh!"

"No, by God, because I treat you too goddamn good, ain't that right?"

"Yassuh. You treats us all good, Mist' Court. Yassuh."

"Goddamn right I do. All right. You can go, Cleveland."

"Yassuh." The tall black man melted back into the shadow of the veranda roof. The screen door thudded softly. A katydid started its ghostly night-time dissonance off in the trees somewhere. Others followed.

"I hope you're happy, Courtney," Coralee said in a furious whisper. "That scene will go through the help like a shot through a goose."

"Just wanted Miss Maggie here to know how things really stand in Mississippi," he said in a parody of his normal voice. He was breathing heavily. "Jus' want her to know I treat my help good, no matter what Cunningham's snot-nosed kid says."

Maggie realized that he was very, very drunk. Her anger drained away and fear flooded into its place. The world whirled around her head, buzzing and out of control. She must, *must* placate, erase, repair. This whirling world could not be borne; she would die in this chaos of disapproval.

"Boots said you did, Judge Claiborne," she quavered. Tears were threatening to burst past the walnut-sized lump in her throat; they stood trembling in her eyes. "I can tell you do. I think he's crazy, myself, *really* crazy. I didn't mean I *agreed* with him. I can't *stand* him. I'm really sorry if I . . . if you thought . . . " She could talk no more without weeping, so she was silent. I'm sorry, Hoyt, she thought. Two of us got sold down the river tonight. And the thought so surprised her that the tears withdrew. But the terrible fear remained, a fear of things broken past repair.

"Shit, Maggie, the Judge don't mean half he says. He ain't mad at you," Boots said, but he was looking at his father. She had never heard him speak ungrammatically before.

"Of course not, honey; shoot, he's all the time bellowing around here like a bull. Court, you ought to be ashamed of yourself! What on earth is Maggie going to think of us all?" Coralee, too, rushed to smooth and placate, but Maggie did not miss the shoals of satisfaction deep in the words.

"You don't wanna take me too serious, sugar," Courtney Claiborne mumbled. "Not your fault. Sorry. Le's all have another drink."

Boots uncoiled fluidly from his chair. "We got to get on to the Carmichaels', Judge," he said. "We're running late. I'll have a snort with you if you're still up when we get home, though."

He caught Maggie by the hand and pulled her from the veranda toward the stable, where the Jaguar rested in a cave of darkness. He was ever so slightly unsteady on his feet. Courtney and Coralee sat still in the now thick dark, silhouetted against the faint glow from inside the house. The goodbyes they called were hearty and false and blurred. Maggie, crunching over the gravel behind Boots toward the car, felt nothing at all. They would, she knew, have a fight.

11

THEY DIDN'T, THOUGH. Boots was silent until he turned the Jaguar out of the long driveway onto the river road. A mile or so away, under the dead black canopy of the vaulting oaks, he reached over and pulled Maggie against his shoulder. Still profoundly shocked by what she had precipitated, Maggie stiffened. She had expected, at best, a long spell of sullenness and, at worst, a cold, killing, final argument. Boots was not a shouter; his icy, modulated drawl was all that he had ever needed.

He chuckled low in his throat. Boots the lazy big cat was back.

"Damned if you didn't rile the Judge. I haven't seen him so steamed up since he had to come over to Leland and get me and J. C. Morris out of jail in the middle of the night. Goddamn, Maggie, you almost had *me* believing you're some kind of niggerlover. I thank you kindly, ma'am, for getting the old man off my ass."

"Is that why you think I said that?"

"Well, wasn't it? You're sure no radical."

"Boots, I don't think you have any idea what I am, really."

"You're my woman, woman, that's what you are. What else do I need to know about you? Except maybe what you got under all those petticoats. Hell, you may be right, though. I never knew you had that spitfire streak in you. That was really something, Miss Maggie, you chewing out the old man because he was riding me."

"Boots, I'm sorry I said all that. I don't know what got into me, I've *never* done anything like that. It was really awful; Mother and Daddy would die if they knew I . . . but I was just so *mad* at all of you. Your folks don't think I'm good enough for you, and your daddy was sitting there picking you apart, practically, and you just let him, and then you just . . . *turned* on me with all that stuff about Hoyt Cunningham when you know I don't even like him. You were just trying to get on your daddy's good side and make me look like a fool, and you did. I just plain *crawled* in front of your daddy. Oh, God, I wish I hadn't even come." She stopped on a rushing intake of breath and rummaged in her purse for a cigarette.

"Light me one," Boots said. She did, and put it between his lips. He pulled her head down to his shoulder and settled her more comfortably against him. The gearshift bit into her ribs, but she didn't pull away. Obviously, he wasn't going to get angry. Here on the black road he had driven so often, inside the carapace of the sleek car, the unsettling weak princeling was gone and the cool, beautiful, in-control Boots she knew was back. Had he really thought she was defending him, though? Couldn't he feel the currents of Coralee's contempt and Court-ney's sly familiarity in the very air of the veranda? Maybe I'm being way too sensitive, she thought. I don't know what is the matter with me this summer. But the currents, she knew, had been there. They were palpable.

In a rare flash of insight, he picked up her thoughts.

"Don't worry about Mother," he said. "She doesn't think anybody's good enough for her only baby. Hell, she's done her best to bust up everything I've ever had going in the Delta. When she gets it through her head this is different from the others, she'll settle down. I don't ever have any trouble with Mother in the long run. The worst thing you've got against you is that you're not from the Delta, and she'll forget about that before you know it. Now, the old man, he may yell a little, but he likes gumption in a woman. Mother leads him around by the nose, but she's too smart to let him know she does it. He knows damned well you didn't mean any of that nigger shit; he knows you were just sticking up for me. You're going to be just fine on the Delta, baby." He was pleased with the rout of his father.

They had never talked so closely around the subject of marriage. Maybe we won't ever, Mag-gie thought. Maybe it's just a foregone conclusion and there we'll be. World without end, amen. The painted curtain of the church in Lytton parted again, briefly, and Maggie jerked it closed.

"How far is it to Snookie's?" she asked.

"I don't feel like going to Snookie's right yet," he said. "Her old man won't let her have anything but beer at her parties. I'm going to take you downtown to meet Otis, and we'll have a snort with him before he goes on duty. He's always at the Green Lantern about now."

"Who's Otis?" said Maggie, grateful for deliverance from the barbecue, grateful that he was not angry, grateful that, perhaps, she had broken nothing after all. "What kind of duty?"

"Otis Tanner, you know, that friend of mine that's a deputy at the jail. I told you about Otis. Hell, we grew up together. We've raised more hell on this Delta than the James boys. Old Otis never had any money, but he sure can drink liquor and shoot a gun and appreciate a good-looking woman. You'll knock his eyes out. I'll have to defend your honor."

"Where does he go to school?" Maggie asked. She didn't remember him telling her about Otis.

He laughed again. "Otis doesn't go to school. His folks don't have enough money to get his brothers and sisters through high school, much less send Otis to college. There's nine of them, and his folks sharecrop for Colonel Brice Gailliard. Besides, Otis doesn't want to go to school. Hell, he barely got out of high school. He was a senior for two years."

"What will he do, then? Will he farm?"

"Otis isn't about to spend the rest of his life picking somebody else's cotton. He hates that farm. No, he'll be a deputy for a while, probably work his way up. I wouldn't be surprised if he wasn't chief of police one day. Otis is a good lawman. He's tough and just mean enough, and he's the best shot in the county right now. Besides, he's lazy. He'd rather hang around the jail shooting the shit or cruise around in a police car than eat. He used to hang around the jail all the time when he was a kid. His brother was on the force."

Maggie was curious about Otis. Everything about him seemed alien to Boots's world of Groveland and country clubs and veranda parties and Jaguars. In Lytton, the progeny of the town's professionals did not maintain their school acquaintances with the sons and daughters of the town's poor. She thought briefly of the Saturday children of her childhood. She could not imagine being an intimate of any of them.

"Does he come to Groveland? Do you go to see him at his house?"

"He's been out to the place once or twice," Boots said. "To pick me up, mainly. Mother doesn't like him, but the old man does. There's a blackjack game at the jail every weekend; the old man's never once taken any money off Otis, and he can't outdrink him either. I've never been out to the farm. Otis has a room in town that he got when he left school. I usually pick him up there."

"Well, but what do you all do? I mean, does he go with you to the club, or to parties and things?"

"No." He looked at her briefly, the dash lights throwing the high planes of his face into under-lit, faintly Mongol relief. "He doesn't want to go to places like that. We just go have a few drinks or something, usually. Hunt and fish some. Why are you so interested in Otis?"

"It just seems like an—unusual relationship, somehow."

"You mean because he's poor? Otis isn't trash, even if his folks are. Otis is a good old boy."

Maggie was embarrassed. She had sounded like a snob. "I didn't mean him being poor," she said. "I only meant that he doesn't seem to have much in common with you. Not nearly as much as somebody like Hoyt Cunningham, but you aren't friends with Hoyt." Oh, God, why did I have to drag Hoyt up, she thought in panic and confusion.

But he only said, "Hoyt's different. He doesn't think like us. Otis does. You'd have to live over here to understand, Maggie."

That wouldn't help, she thought, rocketing back into despair. It wouldn't help anything at all, my liv-ing over here. I could live here for a hundred years and I wouldn't understand anything or anybody over here. There's something about this place that I don't know . . . no, there's something unknowable about it. Or—and the thought spun itself out in her mind like a skein of spider web—there is something wrong with me. Something has been left out of me.

She was suddenly, floodingly homesick for Randolph, for Lytton, for Comer and Frances and the house on Coleman Street, for simplicity and clarity and structure. I want to talk to Aiken, she thought, and the thought was as clear and self-contained as if she had said it aloud.

12

THE GREENVILLE JAIL STOOD on one of four streets enclosing a shaggy green square, occupied by a two-story white-brick courthouse with four stolid, peeling white columns. In front of the courthouse was a statue of a Confederate officer on a horse; officer and horse were blurred and scrimmed with greenish-white lichens and bird droppings. In the now full dark, they were faintly luminous. Overgrown hydrangeas tangled their top branches in the spreading lower branches of the great oaks. There were a few iron benches beside the paths that bisected the overgrown courthouse lawn, and a stained brass drinking fountain long since arid. Katydids chirred in the trees, fireflies pricked the dark, moths and mosquitoes dove in radiant swarms through the yellow pools of the streetlights.

The jail was a one-story sandstone building that looked, on its facade, like the stores and cafes on either side of it. It had a rusty corrugated-tin awning over the cracked sidewalk, and straightbacked wooden chairs sat in a ragged row on the sidewalk under its windows. It was brightly lit, and men's bod-

ies were silhouetted in the windows, leaning on a
counter or sitting around a table under a hanging,
green-shaded light. Three police Fords and a number of sedans and pickups were parked diagonally
in front. There were no barred windows on its face
to tell a newcomer that this was a cage for men. The
cells, Boots told Maggie as he handed her out of the
Jaguar, were behind the front office, in a long double row that fetched up on a vacant lot and another
street at the rear of the building. The bars were there.
There were twenty cells, he said, generally full, especially on the long, slow-spun weekends of the Delta
summer.

They went into the Green Lantern Cafe, next
door to the jail. Maggie blinked in the sudden white
light. The long, narrow room had booths along its
window wall, looking over the sidewalk and cars at
the curb to the black bulk of the courthouse. A narrow aisle separated the booths from the counter. Behind it, a phalanx of bottles gleamed against a watery
mirror, a scabbed griddle sizzled rankly under a row
of pale hamburgers, and a very fat man in Army fatigue pants and a bursting white T-shirt sat on a stool
behind a cash register. At the far end of the aisle an
open door framed a square of murky darkness, lit by
the unearthly green glow of a big Wurlitzer. Music
blared from the jukebox; smoke hung in still, backlit strata; tables and chairs jammed closely together
were dimly visible. Men's voices and laughter drifted
into the booth-room on the tide of smoke and music.

Men's legs in faded denim or bleached khaki spilled from the booths and tangled in the aisle. Men's eyes turned from each other's faces or lifted from their plates and settled over Maggie. She was the only woman in the Green Lantern.

"Evening, Buddy," Boots said to the fat man. "Otis around?" The rough masculine edge was back in his voice.

"Hey, Boots. Heard you was home. Otis is in the back there."

The fat man, older by two decades than Boots, spoke with the mingled deference and indulgence a powerful minister might accord an adolescent monarch. He looked at Maggie, a long, full look, but he did not speak. Boots did not introduce her.

They threaded their way between booths and counter to the back room. The men in the booths straightened, pulled their legs out of the aisles. Some were eating, hamburgers or fried pies or plates of some fried meat, mashed potatoes, corn and tomatoes, but most were smoking and drinking beer or coffee or RCs and NuGrapes. All were older, closer to the proprietor's age. They wore T-shirts or short-sleeved sport shirts of puckered nylon, and denim or khaki pants. Two wore blue summer policemen's uniforms. Most of them nodded and spoke to Boots as he passed—"How's school?" "How's your daddy, Boots?" "How long you going to be home, Boots?" And he replied—"Hey, C.J., you still beating your wife?" "What's new, Ennis?" "When we going hunting again, Walter?" But he did not introduce Maggie, in her incandescent yellow and bare shoulders, and they did not acknowledge her.

Otis was alone at a table in the corner of the dark room. He had pushed aside a thick, red-rimmed bowl with a spoonful or two of chili in it, and a wrapped packet of saltines. He was drinking Bourbon. His teeth flashed white in the smoky darkness when he saw Boots, and he stood up. Maggie stared. He was the biggest man she had ever seen.

He and Boots knuckled each other on their biceps, grinning. "Goddamn if you ain't still growing, Otis," Boots said. "They going to have to get you a convertible squad car if you don't slow down some."

"And you're still chasin' women, I see," Otis said. He had a rather thin, reedy voice that was disconcerting in one so large. "Got you a real doll, now, ain't you? A genuine, imported Georgia peach, I hear. Them river girls of yours ain't gon' like that, Boots." He gave Maggie a slow, feral, white grimace and looked her ostentatiously up and down. "Yessir," he said. "She's somethin', Boots. You better keep an eye on her."

"This is Maggie Deloach, Otis," Boots said. "Maggie, Otis Tanner. Didn't I tell you he was the worst bird dog on the Delta?"

"How do you do, Otis," Maggie said. "Boots has told me a lot about you."

The words, so integral and proper a part of the grave, semi-flirtatious ritual of meeting back in Lytton, in Randolph, were absurd in this room that smelled of sweat and smoke and maleness, absurd said to this swarthy giant who reeked of them. He had small brown eyes with no depths to them, like shirt buttons; a dark crew cut; a short nose with long, flaring nostrils that gave him the look of a barely tamed predator. He was thick, like a tree trunk, from the widest shoulders Maggie had ever seen to thigh muscles that strained against the blue of his uniform pants. A holster with a police .38 circled his waist. Maggie had seen shotguns and rifles before, often—they were part and parcel of the men's world of Lytton—but she had never been close to a handgun before. It looked dangerous and blunt and ugly, but as much a part of him as a rattle-snake's rattle.

"Well, you just sit right down here, Miss Maggie Deloach, and I'll tell you all about ol' Boots. Maybe when I'm through, you'll shy clean away from him and let me show you around town a little, huh? This boy's been a bad 'un ever since he could walk. Got too goddamn much money and not enough sense. I shore don't know what you see in this boy, Maggie." He laughed hugely and poured himself another drink from the bottle that sat on the table. Boots laughed, too. "Lay off, you sonofabitch," he said. "Give us a drink of that and keep your hands on the table. Maggie's had enough trouble tonight. She's already jumped on the Judge and told him off, and I figure that's enough for one day."

He launched into the retelling of the sad, vicious little scene on the Claiborne veranda, embroidering here, editing there, making a gay and adventurous business of it. He glanced often at Otis as he spoke. The incident would be told and retold, Maggie knew, passed among the ranks of the police station and the cafe until it became legend: How Boots Claiborne brought a little old gal from Atlanta home to Groveland and right off the bat she waded into Courtney Claiborne about niggers and riots and revolution and oppression. The men of the Delta did not like Courtney Claiborne, she realized, though they feared his money and tolerated his sly, sidewise arrogance. Maggie would become, to them, one-dimensional and yet unfathomable, a folk heroine, the girl who challenged Courtney Claiborne on his own home ground. "They're just like Boots," she thought, taking a deep drink of the stinging Bourbon. It will never occur to them I might have been serious. But then I wasn't. Was I? Well, of course I wasn't.

Otis loved the story. He reared his huge frame back in his chair, laughing until tears glittered in the opaque eyes, slapping the table, pummeling Boots's arm, snorting. "Lord God Almighty, Maggie," he gasped. "If you'da hunted a thousand years, you couldn've found nothing that would get next to the Judge so bad. Shit, you got more nerve than any man on the Delta. I'm the biggest sonofabitch and the best shot for a hundred miles, and I'd rassle rattlesnakes before I'd tell the Judge he was . . . oppressin' his niggers. Shit!" He wiped his eyes and poured her another shot of Bourbon.

"I didn't tell him *he* was," Maggie said quickly. "I was just telling him something Hoyt Cunningham— you must know Hoyt, he's from here, I met him this summer—said. And he didn't say Judge Claiborne was, or anybody specifically. He just said he thought there was... revolution coming soon, because the whole South had been oppressing the Negroes for too long. He's a reporter, he goes all over the South, he sees things that maybe we don't see...." Why can't I just leave Hoyt and this whole thing alone? she thought miserably.

"Aw, well, Cunningham," Otis said. "I still think you're mighty spunky, Maggie. Mighty spunky."

"Isn't she?" Boots beamed proudly. Maggie smiled uncomfortably.

"Cunningham, ain't never been like the rest of the old boys over here," Otis observed, passing the bottle to Boots. "It ain't that he ain't *from* the Delta. His folks been here a couple of generations, anyway. And it ain't that he's a queer or a brain, really, though he was shore smart in school. I seen him play some of the best football old Andrew Johnson High ever saw, he's right tough. I don't know what it is, exactly, he just always did kind of treat niggers different from the rest of us. I heard him call ol' Annie Lester that was his mama's washwoman 'ma'am' one day, right on the street. And another time, I remember, he close to tore up Finney Burkehalter over what he done to Mule Coggins. You remember that, Boots?"

"God, yes," said Boots, beginning to laugh. "Tell Maggie, though."

"Mule Coggins is a nigger idiot over here, he's still around here. Had scarlet fever or something when he was a real little kid and never been quite right since. He ain't mean, it's just like he never growed up past six. Goes around haulin' an ol' red wagon behind him just shit full of stuff . . . broken plows, and boxes, and tinfoil and stuff. Everybody knows ol' Mule. Anyway, Mule loves chewin' gum better than anything on earth. Asks everybody he sees if they got any chewin' gum. Most everybody gives him some, when they got it, and some folks carry a pack just for Mule. Well, one day the Feen-a-mint salesman come through town . . . Mule hadn't never seen him, for some reason . . . and he's givin' out samples of Feen-a-mint to folks on the street, see? And Finney Burkehalter—he was about seventeen then, wasn't he, Boots?—he goes up to the salesman and says he'll give him fifty cents if everytime ol' Mule asks him for a pack of chewin' gum, he'll give it to him. And then he tells Mule that there's a fella downtown that's giving out free chewin' gum, all you want. So of course, Mule's right behind him all day, bummin' packs of Feen-a-mint, and he no sooner'n chews up one pack than he's got to go out in a vacant lot or behind a tree and take a crap, but he don't know why, so he just keeps on chewin' and shittin' and chewin' and shittin' all day long . . . Lord, God, that was one sick nigger by sundown. I thought Thomas Kearns at the jail was gon' run him in for public indecency, only me and Finney told him what was up and he didn't. He's a good sport, thought it was real funny."

Maggie looked at him in disbelief and pain. "Was Hoyt in on *that?*" she said finally.

"Oh, naw. He was comin' out of the picture show and Duck Castleberry told him about it, and he went and found Finney and just like to beat the livin' shit out of him. I saw it. I never saw anybody so mad in my life. His eyes got all white-like"—Hoyt's blue, white-ringed eyes flashed again out of the Thunderbird through the darkness of the Kappa lawn in Maggie's mind—"and he was cryin', like, and time he was through with Finney, I thought we was gon' have to take him to the hospital. And he had four inches and twenty pounds on Hoyt."

Boots was wiping his eyes. "I was at Castle Heights that summer," he said. "Jesus Christ, I wish I'd seen that, though. The Judge said Mule almost wore out his britches, taking them up and down."

They drifted off into talk of other summers, and Maggie sat silently, smoking Pall Malls, listening to Hank Williams wail "Your Cheatin' Heart" on the Wurlitzer. There were men in groups at other tables, drinking from bottles; laughter and gruff talk pierced the smoke; a pinball machine against a far wall clanged and pinged regularly. She sat inside a globe of sudden fatigue and abstraction. Not even her instinctive revulsion at the sheer ugliness of the incident penetrated it. I feel like one of those figures in a snowstorm inside a paperweight, she thought tranquilly. None of this... not Mrs. Claiborne, not the Judge, not this big, savage man, not this awful movie-of-a-country with houses too big and too much money and too many servants, none of this, not even Boots, can touch me if I don't want them to. One more night, and then tomorrow we can go back to school, and I can wash my hair and put on my pajamas and read. I can sort this out.

"Well, I got to get on back," said Otis. "Come on, y'all walk over with me. Forrest Seaborn was sayin' he wanted to see you, Boots. And I want to show off Maggie in her yellow dress. I'm gon' tell 'em all you're with me, Maggie."

The fat man named Buddy appeared suddenly in the doorway. He was breathing hard; they could hear his breath laboring in his throat and squealing through his nostrils. The taut T-shirt heaved.

"Otis!" he squalled. "Thomas Kearns said tell you there's been a break!"

The men at the other tables broke off their conversations and stared stilly at the fat man, and then at Otis. He lunged out of his chair, knocking it over, and started for the door. There were nailheads of light in his dark eyes, and his hand went instinctively to the .38 at his waist. Some of the other men half rose, then settled back, murmuring.

He paused beside the fat man. "How many of 'em, Buddy? Which way they gone?"

"'Bout twelve of 'em, Thomas said. All niggers. One of 'em grabbed ol' Forrest when he went back to feed 'em an' took his keys and locked him up an' let as many of 'em as he could out, an' they went out the back, 'crost the vacant lot toward the docks. Thomas said for you to go on back that way; Mooney and Everett done gone back there, too. Thomas said they ain't armed, but they scared, an' for you to look sharp."

Otis brushed past him and was gone. The men in the room stirred like a moving sea; the murmuring grew louder. A small, stringy man pushed his chair back and stood, looking around the room. "I reckon we can look for twelve unarmed niggers as good as the police can," he said into a pulsing void of silence. "Anybody want to give Thomas and the boys some help?" His face was red and full and rapt.

There was a second's more silence. Into it the fat man squealed, "No, now, Vester, Thomas said for me to tell y'all to stay put an' leave it to the *police*. They ain't gon' get far. The boys gone right after 'em. They ain't got no guns."

A balancing hush; it could go either way in an instant. Maggie clutched her purse in her hands, staring at fat Buddy. Her heart skidded high and sickeningly at the base of her throat. Her temples pounded and her face and neck burned. Something witless and primeval and huge walked the room.

"Shit with that. I'm going."

Incredibly, it was Boots's voice. Maggie stared

stupidly. He rose, rocking the bottle and glasses on the table. Another man rose, then another. Other chairs crashed over. In seconds they were all on their feet, moving in an undulating mass toward the door, the murmuring swelling to a dark, heavy weight. Two voices, both shrill, pierced it, the fat man's shrieking, "No, now, y'all, no, now! Y'all stay in here! Thomas don't need you! No, now . . ."

The other was her own. She was on her feet, rooted to the floor, her hands clenched into fists.

"No, Boots, no, no, *no*, Boots, no, no, no . . ."

Is that me, said one part of her mind. What an ugly voice I have. This is really embarrassing, I never scream. I wish that voice would stop. But it didn't, not until the room was empty. Across a motionless plane of smoke, Maggie and the fat man stared at each other.

He broke the stare, turned abruptly, and vanished into the front grillroom. Maggie looked around the room, where only the smoke and the light from the Wurlitzer lived. "What am I supposed to do now?" she said aloud to the room. Her voice sounded flat and thin and querulous.

She walked slowly and stiffly into the front room of the Green Lantern. Her crinoline petticoats rasped in the silence and abraded the calves of her legs. She was aware, dimly, of sweat running from her waist and down her spine. The booths in the grill were empty, too. The street beyond the plate glass window was deserted and yellow in the light from the streetlamps. Fireflies bloomed against the bulk of the courthouse shrubbery. There was no sound from the street or the jailhouse next door, and then there were sounds. Two flat, trivial pops from somewhere outside and behind the cafe, and then another, and then a rapid hiccuping of them, as if Chinese firecrackers in a string had gone off.

Maggie looked at the fat man. He was slumped on the stool behind the cash register. He was intoning, to no one, "Godamighty, oh, Jesus, oh, Lord Godamighty, oh, Jesus Christ . . . " He was staring straight ahead through the door at the empty street and the courthouse square.

Maggie walked up to the counter. "What will happen?" she said simply.

His eyes focused on her and his glistening red face melted into a terrible parody of a smile.

"Clean forgot you was back there, ma'am," he said. "Don't you worry none, it's just a few niggers run off from the jail. The boys gon' have 'em back in two shakes of a sheep's tail. They ain't got guns."

At the word, the shallow pops flowered into significance in Maggie's mind.

"But that was gunfire! It was, wasn't it? Out back just a minute ago? It was! Oh, God, Boots is out there. I've got to call his daddy! Please, your phone, I've got to call Judge Claiborne out at Groveland! You know Judge Claiborne. I'm visiting them, please, I've got to call—"

"No'm!" His voice rose in fear. His fat hand, like a

pink spider, shot out to cover the telephone that sat beside the cash register.

"You don't want to bother the Judge, honey. Boots gon' be all right, the whole force is out there. Them niggers cain't get far, they ain't got no weapons. Ain't no need to get the Judge all worked up. . . ."

"Please! Oh, please—"

Another glissando of pops tore the heavy dark, closer to them, then a man's high shout, and a babel of men's voices and running feet. Maggie stared wordlessly at the fat man, then spun and ran out of the cafe. She could hear his voice, squealing again in terror, reaching after her.

"For sweet Jesus' sake, ma'am, don't go out there!"

Maggie stood still on the sidewalk in the hot, thick emptiness. Her head was roaring with blood. Her heart was jolting her ribs, she could feel every blow, and she could not get her breath. A serene, incredibly sweet odor of honeysuckle, heavier than the air, curled past her nose from the courthouse square. From somewhere out of sight a woman's voice, a radioed voice thick with a vibrato of unshed tears, throbbed: "Oh, the wayward wind . . . is a restless wind . . . a restless wind . . . that yearns to wander. . . ." Staring at the blank front of the empty jail but not seeing, Maggie's lips formed the words, picking them up soundlessly.

"And I was born . . . the next of kin . . . the next of kin . . . to the wayward wind."

There was a sudden, milling explosion of blue

men into the front room of the jail. They had not come through the front door that Maggie was watching. She looked at them with abstract curiosity through the window. They were gesticulating, crowding around the telephone, mouthing soundless words to each other. Some were smiling. Boots was not among them, and Otis was not.

And then a scuffle of feet in the alley on the other side of the jail, coarse breath sobbing, grunts, and a dragging sound as of something heavy, a dead weight, and they were there. They rounded the corner from the alley onto the sidewalk in front of Maggie. Boots and Otis, and between them, arms fastened behind him with handcuffs, stumbling with the force of their dragging arms, a black man in shapeless gray pants and a torn gray shirt, pulled loose from the pants. All three of them stopped.

The Negro was small and squat, shorter by half a head than Boots, a head than Otis. His napped head drooped to his chest, his chest heaved with deep, tearing breaths. He was very black, shining, almost blue-black under the streetlight, running with perspiration. He did not raise his head or move. None of them moved. Boots and Otis stared across the cracked pavement at Maggie, breathing hard. Boots's yellow hair was darkened with sweat, his lips pulled back from his teeth, breath whistling through his nose. Otis wore the wild dog's grin.

"Got the last black sonofabitch," he said.

The Negro raised his head and looked full into

Maggie's face. His face was closed and still, but his eyes were alive. The whites were oddly yellow, veined with red. They held hers. Across six feet of heavy, swimming Delta air, Maggie read pure, naked fear, and dull hate, and something else. She read, as if it were limned on the air, a humble desire to please, to placate, to avoid punishment from the two captors who held him. Please, said the eyes through hate, I will do anything.

In a dome of still, vibrating shock, Maggie thought very clearly and precisely, That's me.

"I didn't know where you were," she said mildly to Boots, and then the gritty, mica-speckled sidewalk swam and surged and slammed up into her cheek.

13

THE NEXT WEEKEND, on a Saturday night, Maggie sat in a canvas butterfly chair on the terrace of Ben Flournoy's house, sipping at a strange, colorless liquid that tasted of licorice and listening to Mozart's *Requiem* and a rhythmic flow of talk. The talk buzzed slightly in her ears, from drinks before dinner and the strange liquid after, and the music boomed, not unpleasantly. Ben Flournoy had poured out her drinks and wine matter-of-factly, as if there were nothing amiss in a faculty member plying a coed with liquor. Indeed, he treated her not as a coed but as any guest who might come to dinner and sit long on his shadowed terrace, listening to his music and sharing his small, exotic house. He had not, as he did in his class, teased her during the evening, but he offered her no careful, grave conversation designed to draw her into the circle of talk, either. His glinting malice was diffused and affable, and it gathered the people on the terrace into a warm and favored coterie who looked with amusement and a faint elevation out into a less favored world. Maggie was charmed.

He sat crouched, chimpanzee-fashion, on the low

brick wall that separated the patio from the small, dark lawn beyond it. His omnipresent cigarette drew red arcs in the moon-shadows as he gestured and stabbed with his dark, nervous hands. Kita Flournoy, small and dark and not pretty but vividly lovely, sat on a canvas hassock at his feet, her head resting against his knees. She was like her paintings, Maggie thought, that glowed from the white walls and leaned haphazardly against low tables and were propped in stacks against the walls of her studio above the garage: gay, rich, with an air of swift authority. If you looked closely at them, you could discern a teeming of detail and minutiae; exquisitely wrought, small, interlocking shapes like mosaic pieces, speaking of the East even though they were abstract. But from a distance, the paintings were bold and radiant, with fluid woman-curves and large masses of pure color. They were unlike the careful, linear, brittle abstracts done by students in the quarterly exhibitions Maggie saw in the Art and Architecture building. She thought they were probably very, very good. Kita did not sell or show them, she said in her shy, precise voice, but she often gave them to friends. "I would not like the pooblic to look so close at them," she said. "They are like, you know, my underwear."

"Kita is still spiritually in the seraglio," Ben Flournoy said, ruffling the glossy black hair out of its French knot, so that it hung in brush and India ink strokes over his wife's cheeks.

"Oh, Ben," she remonstrated. She pronounced

it "Been." She had a pointed smile, like a cat's, or an Etruscan statue's.

Aiken and Tuck sat side by side in canvas sling chairs on the other side of the terrace. Their joined hands swung between them, and Aiken's long, bare foot kneaded Tuck's tennis sock, back and forth, back and forth. She wore khaki Bermuda shorts the color of her polished long legs, and a turquoise T-shirt that turned her eyes and the aquamarine on her finger to blue quartz that shone in the dark.

She was the real reason Maggie was there. Smelling alienation and confusion and a strangeness around Maggie like a vapor when they had met for their poetry class the Monday after Maggie had returned from Mississippi, Aiken had pried the story of the weekend from her over lunch. Both had tacitly agreed to cut their one o'clock classes and talked in the booth of the cafe until nearly three, while the ashtray overflowed and their large Coca-Colas grew pale and tepid. Maggie had been miserable and stunned, and Aiken quiet and noncommittal.

"What happened after that?" she said when Maggie told her she had fainted on the sidewalk in front of the jail.

"Nothing, really," Maggie said. "Boots took me home and Mrs. Claiborne put me to bed. I don't remember much of it. Boots and his daddy went back down to the jail. It must have been four in the morning when I heard them come in. And the next day Boots and his daddy treated me like a china doll or something, bringing me things and making me stay in bed till lunchtime. It was like I was a heroine, somebody right out of *Gone With the Wind.* It was like they . . . *approved* of me fainting on the street like that, in front of the whole damned police force. God, I was so embarrassed, Aiken. I've never fainted in my life."

"Well, the vapors are supposed to be very popular in Mississippi, aren't they?" Aiken was amused.

"It was more than that. It was like they didn't know who or what I was until I pulled that stupid faint. It was like that one thing turned me back into somebody they could, you know, deal with. Or something they could pet, like a dog or a cat. Oh, I don't know, Aiken. I felt so *funny* all weekend, like I was in another country, not even the South. The house is monstrous, I had no idea how big their place was, and all those Negro servants, and so much money . . . and Boots was so different from the way he is here. He was like somebody I never met before. When he wasn't kowtowing to his father, he was strutting like a peacock. I wish you could have seen him after they caught that Negro. You'd think he'd put down an insurrection or something, all by himself. And his daddy was carrying on like Boots had just saved dear old Groveland from the Yankees. But the Negro didn't even have a gun, he was about half as tall as Boots and Otis. You know, I had the funniest feeling when I stood there looking at that Negro. I felt like I was looking at myself."

Aiken gave her a long, pure, gray look. "How do you mean?"

"Well, like ... he was something in a trap and he couldn't get out, and he hated the people who'd trapped him, but at the same time he'd do anything on earth they wanted him to, just so they didn't punish him. And I ... *recognized* that, I knew what he was feeling, I understood that." She gave Aiken an embarrassed smile. "Of course, that's silly, it was just nerves, and I'd had a rotten day. But there's still something wrong and strange about that place. Or"— she laughed uncertainly—"about me."

"I think it *is* you." Aiken stirred her Coca-Cola with her straw. She did not look at Maggie. Maggie felt a deep thrill of cold somewhere in her stomach. Words had been said that should not have been.

"Maybe it is," she said.

"Not wrong the way you think, Maggie." Aiken leaned across the scarred tabletop. Her eyes forced Maggie's to look at her. "But you *are* different. You're different from all your dear Kappa sisters. You're different from any other southern girl I've ever met. You're different from that stupid, hundred-years-ago place over there in Mississippi, and you're sure as hell different from Boots Claiborne. Only you've tried so hard for so long to be just like everybody else, all of them, that you don't even *know* you're different. I don't know who made your rules for you, Maggie, but they're the wrong rules. You're more than all this, you're better. You ought to quit being Miss Maggie

Deloach and go on and be Maggie, do you follow me? Make your own rules. Or find some better ones. It's a fabulous way to live, believe me. I know."

"Aiken, I don't even know how to start." Maggie was near tears. "I know, I guess I realized this weekend that I'm . . . not really like those people over there, that I don't really fit at Groveland, I don't even really know Boots. You know, all the way back home he was crowing about catching that Negro, and how cute and sweet I was with his friends, and how much his folks were going to love me . . . once they get to really know me . . . and all I could think was, I want that house. I want that money. But I don't know if I want you. The boy I'm *pinned* to, Aiken. When I got back to the house, I threw up for an hour. I'm sure Sister thinks I'm pregnant. But it's all so perfect, it's what Mother and Daddy have always . . . " She broke off.

"I'll bet it is," Aiken said.

"Then, if not that, what would I do?"

"Listen, Maggie. I was serious when I said come go home with me after graduation. We'll . . . oh, go to Europe. You said your folks wanted to send you for a graduation present, didn't you? Well, why not go with me instead of some tacky tour out of Birmingham? Or we could go on to graduate school in the East somewhere, surely your parents wouldn't object to that? Or we might get jobs in New York and share an apartment. There are a million fabulous things we could do out in the real world. But I know you've got to get out of here, Maggie. If you stay, the *best* thing that can happen to you is you'll live your whole life in some place that's wrong for you, with some guy who's wrong for you, and you'll never find out who you are, and you'll wonder the rest of your life what went wrong." Aiken's face was flushed and she spoke with a passion Maggie had not known was there.

"What's the worst thing that could happen to me?"

"I don't know," Aiken said slowly. "I don't know."

"Well, but Boots . . . and I have no idea what Mother and Daddy would say if I just . . . left home and went away. I mean, we've never even discussed that. Not since Boots and I got pinned. I just don't think . . . "

"That's right," Aiken snapped. She was close to being angry. "You don't think. And you don't feel. You just walk through your life like something on a track, a toy train. Are you afraid for your reputation if you come with me, Maggie? Do you think I'm immoral?"

"No." Maggie smiled. "I've never thought you were immoral, Aiken." Her smile deepened as she thought about it. "I guess I've always thought you were . . . more moral than the rest of us. If I thought about it at all."

"Well. I've missed half a lab already." Aiken picked up her check and her books and her purse. Some subtle point had been made, some score settled. "Keep it in mind, that's all I ask. You don't have to decide anything for a long time. What you do need is to get away from those featherheaded KAs and that tribe of motherless lambs over at the Kappa house and see some real people for a change. Tuck and I are going over to the Flournoys for dinner this weekend. Why don't you shed Boots for one night and come with us? You'd love Kita Flournoy, and you know Ben adores you."

"I can't do that. You can, because Tuck's faculty, but I don't have any *reason* to be there. And they didn't ask me, Aiken."

But on Wednesday night the phone had rung for Maggie, and Kita Flournoy had said, in her light, melony voice, that Ben had spoken of her often and fondly, and they would be so happy if Maggie would come and have dinner with them. "It will be a lamb dish that is native to my country," she said, and then, when Maggie did not answer, she added, "but perhaps you do not like lamb?"

"I love lamb," Maggie said. "I'd love to come."

Through drinks and dinner, and through half of the curly carafe of wine, the conversation had been vivid but comfortable. The strangeness of being in a professor's house soon dissipated. Ben Flournoy was, Maggie realized, as natural a focus of attention as the sun in the sky. He kept up a running fusillade. He talked of provocative things half-known or unknown to Maggie: of Adlai Stevenson's campaign for the Democratic nomination ("Too good a mind for the country yet; we shrink from men who think"); of John Foster Dulles and his penchant for cliff-hanging ("The man is mad"); of the ominous Middle East ("Kita doesn't mind; Kita is classically apolitical"); mostly of the revolt that had died at birth and in agony the week before in Poland. But there was more of mannerly, stylistic acerbity than heat in the talk, and it required no response. Occasionally he would fling a tantalizing thought to Tuck and wait, head cocked, eyes glinting, for his reply. Tuck seized the morsels eagerly, like a puppy a stick, and worried them and fetched them back to Flournoy's feet. Tuck was exhilarated. This mimosa-smelling patio was not so far away from his book-lined quadrangel room. Aiken, though she brewed him no Earl Grey, was long-boned and fine-faced and cherished Faulkner, if not Gogol, and had a fire in her that he had never even aspired to. They had long since circumvented his landlady. Tuck drank retsina and began, tentatively, to brush the bitter ashes off *Goodbye Mr. Chips.*

    To Maggie and Aiken, Ben Flournoy talked of his days as a student in Paris. Hemingway: "A red post of a man, a brawling bully who thought poetry the province of homosexuals, yet he invariably wrote it when he was drunk, and read it aloud, more's the pity." Gertrude Stein: "A beautiful mind, but she always wanted to be the Pope." "Pound? Mad, of course, but a fine madness, truly." Maggie laughed, she urged, she basked. Something tight and frozen and empty inside her began to thaw and fill, slowly. Kita looked on placidly. With her, Ben Flournoy was gentle; his sim-

ian face, when it turned to her, softened incongru-
ously into sweetness.

Lulled and, for the first time since the weekend
before, not aching and prickle-skinned, Maggie sat in
the quiet dark and listened to the music. She smoked.
She watched silver moths fluttering around the hurricane lamps on the low wrought-iron table. She
closed her eyes. She drifted in a shallow, bright sea
of mimosa and wine and safety and the contentment
that follows exhilaration. Perhaps she slept.

". . . up to the writers of the South to take a stand.
The literary mind is the last voice of conscience crying in the wilderness, in the last analysis, the . . . the
torsh of integration will be caught up by the writers.
The writers'll shtand with th' Negro."

Tuck's voice, slurring badly, reached into Maggie's
cocooned consciousness and nagged her back from
sleep. She opened her eyes, blinking peevishly. Tuck
was sitting far forward, arms on his knees, hands dangling. His hair was damp and spiky and ruffled. He
glowered furrily at Ben Flournoy, who regarded him
brightly from atop the wall. Aiken, curled into the
open palm of the canvas chair, smiled lazily at him.

"Au contraire," said Ben Flournoy, reaching for Maggie's cigarettes. "The voice of conscience crying in
the wilderness is loudly and busily selling the Negro
back down the river. Just last March, I believe, it was
Mr. William Faulkner who told a gentleman from
the London Sunday *Times* that he would have none
of the government's integration policy. He said if he

had to choose between the United States Government and Mississippi, he would choose Mississippi. 'If it came to fighting, I'd fight for Mississippi against the United States, even if it meant going out into the street and shooting Negroes,' is the way I believe he put it. *Time* picked it up."

"Well . . . hell." Tuck gestured with grandiose impatience. "Faulkner isn't in the twentieth century. *Mississippi* isn't in the twentieth century. But the newer southern writers will rally, you watch. It's a beautiful cause, a pure cause."

Maggie's skin wimpled as if in a cold little wind. Hoyt had said essentially the same thing. Pure. Pure revolution. She saw again the Negro's red-veined, yellowed eyes. There had been nothing of cool, rapt purity, nothing of vision there. Only living hate and fear.

"Maggie can tell you about Mississippi," Aiken said. She smiled at Maggie over the rim of her glass. Her drawl was warming but there was something deliberate and implacable in her gray eyes. "Maggie was in an honest-to-God jailbreak over there last weekend. Your Lady of the Lake was all shook up, Ben."

She calls him Ben, Maggie thought irrelevantly. I hadn't noticed that before. And she thought, Oh, Aiken, why are you doing this to me? That was private, that is not for these cool, sure people. You're about to dissect me like a frog and lay out my guts for them to stare at. Don't do this. She gave Aiken an imploring look, but the eyes were shuttered.

"Tell us about the jailbreak, princess." Tuck pounced on her gleefully.

"What happened, Maggie?" Ben Flournoy was looking at her from atop his wall. His hands were still. It was a careful, neutral look, and a waiting one.

"It wasn't anything, it wasn't much of a jailbreak . . . really, it's not even interesting. And it's late. I've really got to get back, it's almost twelve. . . . "

"There's nobody at the Kappa house to check on you, Maggie," Aiken said relentlessly. "And it *is* interesting. I think it may be the most interesting thing that ever happened to you. If you won't tell it, I will."

"Oh, Aiken, *please.*"

"No, Maggie, it's important." And Aiken set her glass down on the flagstones and lit a cigarette and told the story. Her voice was silver like a flute glittering through the still air. She spread it all out for them in the lambent light of her voice: Groveland, the miserable scene on the Claibornes' terrace, Otis, the men in the Green Lantern, the pinioned Negro, Maggie's faint. They were all silent until she had finished, Maggie in mortification and betrayal. They were silent for a moment after.

"Maggie said she saw herself when she looked at the Negro prisoner, Ben," Aiken said lightly. "Maggie had a . . . a moment of truth, wouldn't you say?" Her eyes on Maggie's mute face said, Forgive me. Ben Flournoy did not answer her. He studied Maggie.

"That's barbaric. That's just goddamned barbaric!" Tuck was flushed with indignation and retsina.

"That mob of ... vigilante rednecks probably beat him within an inch of his life when they got him back in that jail. Christ, no wonder the Negroes are mad, no wonder they're ready to fight, no wonder they're taking a stand in Montgomery. . . . "

"Nobody's ready to fight yet, Tucker, except maybe the ignorant white man who hates and fears the idea of integration and the equally ignorant white man who is ready to rush in and abet a noble idea by brute, idiot force," Flournoy said impatiently. He was still looking at Maggie. "The white man capable of truly understanding the ramifications of the whole thing has yet to raise his head and look at it. 'The best lack all conviction, while the worst are full of passionate intensity.'"

"Yeats," said Maggie automatically. He smiled at her.

"Martin Luther King is rallying the Negroes in Montgomery right now," Tuck said sullenly.

"The whole point of the Montgomery boycott is nonviolence," Flournoy said. "This young Dr. King may be as close to a saint in the accepted canonical sense of the word as your placid, Communist-happy generation is likely to see. There seems to me to be a sort of ... you will forgive my excess, but a divine aura about him and his little movement. The early days of Christianity must have been rather like it; he is rather a Christ figure to my mind. He preaches reform by patience, charity, and humility, even though there is a rather terrifying ... inexorability about him. And I think that only charity and humility and patience will see us through this thing that is coming. And reason. On both sides. Lacking it, Armageddon there will be, and soon."

Maggie blinked at him in surprise. All the bright malice was gone. His face in the shadows was somber, almost sorrowful. She had never seen him look like this, never heard him talk like this.

"You think we can avoid violence, then?" Tuck, too, was taken aback.

"Oh, no, there'll be great violence, I'm afraid. There will be violence over this good man's head that he will grieve to see, and I do not think that even he can circumvent it. The white man is his enemy, you see. The so-called liberal white man, with the best intentions in the world, will cry havoc and let loose the dogs of war in the name of right. The white man of reason and decency will not raise his voice until it is too late; he is historically a creature of inaction. And the hard-core white southerner won't have it. King is preaching a deep and permanent change in the fabric and structure of this nation's life; don't think the issue here is the Negro's right to sit at the front of a bus. The southern whites ... most of them ... will go quite mad with fear. They will fight. And sooner or later"—he turned his eyes from Maggie's face to Tuck—"the Negro will fight back. Indeed, yes, the white man is the enemy. Whether or not he wishes to be."

There was a constricted aching in Maggie's chest,

as of tears held back, or breath. The drowsing tightness of the night was gone. She was very much afraid. Something was curling into the half-empty place inside her, forming like smoke into a shape, a substance. Some thing . . . a thought, a feeling, an inevitability . . . was shivering to be born. She did not know what it was.

"Well . . . God, Ben," Tuck said. His voice was chastened, and small. "If we're the enemy no matter how we feel about it, then what is there to do? I mean, we can't just sit back on our asses and watch it happen, we've got to . . . help some way, I mean raise our voices, declare ourselves. Segregation is wrong, integration is right, it's a simple thing, really. . . . "

"The morality of the thing is simple, Tucker," Flournoy said. "Unfortunately, it is men who will, shall we say, debate it."

"Where are you on this? I mean, what will you do? What sort of . . . role will you take, personally?"

"I," said Ben Flournoy lightly and acidly from the wall, "shall continue to teach poetry, in the no doubt futile hope that the essential beauty and truth and ordered passion of my high and noble craft will inspire some young mind to think. And to pick its way through the rampant, rococo emotionality of this thing to some sort of real empathy with the Negro. To get inside his skin, if that is possible, and understand him. To feel what he feels . . . poetry is, after all, a flashlight for the peering into human souls, is it not?" He grinned sardonically. "And *then,* perhaps, to

raise a voice in defense of reason and order and com-
passion."

He flicked flealike from the wall and poured himself another glass of retsina. "Because I do rather
agree with you, Tucker, that men and women of letters just might become the voice of conscience crying
in the wilderness, as you so eloquently put it. Miss
Deloach here might, with a great deal of application,
be such a voice one day. Provided, of course, that she
has truly been gifted with one of those blinding, divine flashes of insight that are the essence of poetry.
A moment of truth, as Aiken has said. I seem to remember one rather promising bit she wrote for the
entirely undeserving newspaper which did not, for
once, deal with the inequities of coeds being forced
to wear raincoats over their bloomers en route to
their physical education classes. How about it, Miss
Deloach? Now that you have seen its fearsome face in
the heart of darkest Mississippi, do you think you're
ready to throw yourself upon the barricades of ra-
cial injustice? Declare yourself? Once more unto the
breach, dear friends?"

He peered glitteringly at Maggie. She stared back.
Through the coiling smoke in her head she saw the
dead white moons of streetlights on an empty Mississippi street, and the tree-trunk bodies of two tall,
grinning young white men, and the powerful, slack
shell of a black man pinned between them. She saw
the open eyes again. I hate, they said. I am afraid,
they said. I will obey, they said.

I know, she said in her own mind.

"I really do have to go back to the house now," she said, rising and setting her glass on the table. "Don't get up, Tuck, I have my car. Dr. Flournoy, Mrs. Flournoy, thank you so much for a wonderful evening. I really enjoyed it. Aiken, I'll see you in class Monday."

In a soft rush of goodbye-come-agains, they saw her to the door. Ben Flournoy stood looking after her as she walked quickly across his moon-dappled front yard to her Plymouth, but he did not speak again. When she had driven away, he turned to Kita Flournoy, who stood beside him, her arm encircling his waist. He rested his chin on the top of her head.

"I'm terribly afraid of being wrong," he said. "I'm terribly afraid of doing a wrong thing."

"You are never wrong, Ben," she said.

They turned and went back out onto the terrace, where Aiken and Tuck lay jumbled together like puppies on a battered old poppy-flowered chaise longue. Both were asleep.

Back at the Kappa house, Maggie let herself in through the sun porch door with the key she had confiscated from Delia and never returned. There was no one to miss it since Mama Kidd had gone; M.A. Appleton concerned herself only with the external evidences of compliance with university rules. If no girls were seen entering the house after curfew, if no young men were observed entering or leaving the house save by the front door and during date hours, she was not going to push things. The key seemed irrelevant to Maggie, its presence both a minor irritant and a convenience. She kept it in her purse.

She removed her shoes and pattered softly up the stairs to her room. Her wing of the hall was darkened; only the hum of electric fans stirred the night air from behind closed doors. Sister was not in their room, but then Sister rarely was these days. The SAE had declared himself penitent for his boorish behavior in the borrowed apartment after Sister had, as she said, "put a freeze on him that only a little old gold pin will thaw." Things were going well. She had borrowed Maggie's sun-porch key and had a copy made and came and went as she pleased within the limits of discretion. Maggie had objected only halfheartedly, and M.A., considering that the imminent pin outweighed the infraction so long as Sister was careful not to be caught breaking curfew, gave up dropping in at eleven to hug her goodnight.

Maggie showered and put on shorty pajamas and the new flower-sprigged nylon robe. In her mirror, in the swimming, underwater light of the moon, the robe looked misty, unreal, a spindrift around her. Her face was pale and her eyes vivid and enormous. I look pretty tonight, she thought. What a waste of pretty this night is.

Shoeless, she padded down to the basement and got a Coke from the humming machine. The basement, the downstairs of the house, the silver lawn behind it, were drenched and soaked in moonlight. Maggie paused restlessly on the moon-whitened landing, then tiptoed back downstairs and through the kitchen and across the back porch to the lawn. A cluster of rusted white metal lawn chairs shone from beneath a fervent arc of honeysuckle, overgrown wildly out of the privet hedge, and she settled into one of them, tucking her feet up under her away from its dew-cold surface. She lit a cigarette and threw her head back until it lolled over the top of the chair, breathing deeply of the yearning honeysuckle and letting the moon wash and gild her cheeks and fore-head and closed eyelids. Her heart squeezed painfully with moon and flowers and being young.

I want, I want, I want . . . something, she thought. What? I want . . . everything to be like this night that is so beautiful that I cannot bear it. I want never to lose this . . . intensity. I want something to happen, *every*thing to happen. I want everything to stay just like this. I want never to lose this night, but I want it to be tomorrow, too. I want. I want! She sat, face upturned, aching with wanting to stop the passage of the moon across the sky, for the space of three Pall Malls. And then yellow lights splashed out over her, over the lawn, and the moon retreated, and squeals and laughter flooded out the crickets and katydids. She slid around in the wet chair and looked up at the lighted windows above her.

"Maggie! Is that you out there? Come up here this minute!"

M.A. Appleton's voice, raised in a girlishness so alien that Maggie stared stupidly at her black silhouette in the window for a moment.

"What's the matter?" she called back.

"Come see!"

Maggie flew through the foyer and up the stairs. The hall in front of her room was thronged with jostling Kappas in pajamas, short robes, bobby pins, Cuticura, and terry-cloth scuffs. Others were crowded into her room. The squeals and laughter rent the night. From the bathroom Maggie could hear the shower roaring full strength, and sounds of scuffling and giggling, and a squeal higher than the rest: "Stop, stop, you'll drown me, my hair, *dammit,* Cornelia, that's *hot!*" M.A., square and pucker-capped, capered clumsily at Maggie and kissed her, missing her cheek and smearing Noxema across her mouth and into her eye. Girls were dancing up and down, hugging each other, surging toward the bathroom door.

"Sister did it! Sister's pinned!" roared M.A. Maggie, scouring Noxema out of her eye with her fist, stared at her.

"Pinned! Sister got the pin!" Even stolid Jean Lochridge was hopping up and down in place. Her pink drip-dry duster was splotched with water, and Persian melon leaked wetly and crazily up her cheeks from her smeared mouth.

"Sister is pinned?" I sound like a parrakeet, Maggie thought. Sis-ter is pin-ned. See the pret-ty pin. Sis-ter is pin-ned.

Sister came bursting out of the bathroom, jostling aside wet Kappas. They had thrown her in fully clothed. Her blue dotted-swiss clung soddenly to her, her crinolines ran runnels of water into her blue flats, the opaque white twin protuberances of the Peter Pan bra shone through her dress. A gold diamond-shaped shield sat dizzily atop the left one, beneath her Kappa pin. Her red hair was pasted in darkened strands over her face. She looked at Maggie through them.

"Maggie?"

"Sister . . ."

"I did it, Maggie."

"Oh, Sister . . ."

"Well, aren't you going to congratulate me?"

A powerful surge of something hurting and splitting and unstoppable began behind Maggie's ribs and burst through her chest and throat. She held out her arms and Sister ran into them.

"Oh, Sister, oh, Sister, oh, Sister," Maggie sobbed. She cried aloud, she wept hard. "Oh, Sister, oh, poor baby!"

She was still crying when they finally left and Sister had changed into pajamas and crawled damply into her bed, and she cried to herself, softly and with a real but unnameable and tidal grief, after Sister had turned off the lights and fallen asleep. She fell asleep still hiccuping, an occasional sob shaking her. The

Kappas, as they left her weeping, had smiled indulgently and fondly at Maggie, crying on her bed. They
thought she wept with joy.

In the morning, Maggie cut her first class. After the
house had emptied of girls, she pulled her birthday
present Royal portable from beneath her bed and
took it out of its case and set it up on the green metal
desk she shared with Sister. She made herself a cup
of viscous tap-water instant coffee and lit a cigarette
and sat down at the typewriter. She stared for a very
long time at nothing at all, and then she began to
type.

"Last weekend, in Mississippi, I met a man I will
never forget," she wrote, "even though I do not know
his name."

She typed steadily for perhaps half an hour,
not stopping to correct mistakes, and then she typed
--30--and pulled the last page out of her typewriter
and put it with the rest and anchored the pages under
her and went into the bathroom to take a shower.

14

THE RANDOLPH STUDENT UNION, along with the new Art and Architecture building and the Small Animal Laboratory, was one of the few air-conditioned havens the campus afforded against the heat. In the evenings, flaccid students could seek surcease in the two movie theaters, and did, often seeing the same movie two and three times. But on a July day of exploding sun and endless stillness, the enervated student body headquartered in the Union, trudging in wet and panting for Coca-Colas and limeades during the fifteen-minute break between classes, sitting long at lunch over sandwiches or flattened hamburgers or tepid salads from the real-lunch counter, cutting afternoon classes and playing ceaseless hands of bridge over carefully nursed cups of coffee. In the midafternoons, when most summer classes were over, the snack bar was jammed with students. The jukebox blared. A fraternity man seeking his steady could find her in the Union, if she was not at her sorority house washing her hair and drying it in the wake of her electric fan, stripped to pants and bra. Uncommitted Greeks could meet and flirt and line up a last-minute date for the evening with far more success than at any other time of year. In the winter, the Union was largely the province of Independent students, who took their meals, studied, watched flickering television in the lounge, began tentative liaisons there. But in the inferno of an Alabama summer, the Student Union went panhellenic, and campus luminaries glittered there in radiant clouds.

By some unspoken summer custom, the tables in the center of the snack bar belonged to them. The fringes of the bland white room were occupied by tables of aspirants, cadets, almost-pretty girls from almost-good sororities, Independent men who nevertheless had captured some minor but interesting campus office, summer freshmen about whom no one knew anything, yet. Some of these freshmen would, the next summer, occupy the tables in the charmed center circle, and knew it, and were content to wait in jostling flocks against the walls, preening for each other and ignoring the measuring eyes of the Olympians. There was a brightdrawn edge to the smiles and posturings of the others, who had, somehow, missed the cut. But there was always hope in the snack bar.

Away from the snack bar there was a long, windowless ell where the cafeteria line was housed. Small tables, which would accommodate two people, lined its opposite wall, and a random peppering of tables edged bravely away from the wall toward the center of the ell. The unchosen, the never to be chosen, sat there, heads buried in books or newspapers. There were no extra chairs drawn up to these tables, no swaggering trips to the big jukebox or the cigarette machine, no forays to the snack bar counter in the main room made from them. Two students at most sat at these tables, often only one. Books and studied oblivion and coffee from a large, filmed metal urn sustained them. No hope was there.

Maggie sat at a large center table in the snack bar that was designed to accommodate eight students and generally, in the summers, harbored twelve or fourteen. It was Randolph's Round Table. Boots and another KA, a pale, puckish boy named Gleason who was president-elect of the student body, sat on her right and left. The editor of the Randolph yearbook, an SAE, lounged back in a chair across from her. He was doing convoy duty for Sister, whose own SAE was imprisoned in a chemistry lab at the far end of the campus. Sister, flushed and giddy with her new status of daughter of the SAE regiment, valiantly bubbled, sparkled, twinkled, teased, dipped her Peter-Panned front into a pool of sunlight that filtered pallidly in through the sliding glass doors from the terrace outside, so that the SAE pin glittered. A pretty girl who was last year's Homecoming Queen was there, and a pretty girl who was this year's Panhellenic chairman, and three other girls who were so startlingly pretty that they did not have to be anything at all. Four of the boys at the far arc of the table had the heavy, carved shoulders and whiplike waists and long, hewn legs of athletes, but they were not. Randolph's athletes were venerated but not assimilated, they did not swim in the mainstream of campus life. They lived and ate and studied, if they did, in a semicircle of wooden cottages around a small amphitheater at the base of Ag Hill, where coaches and trainers could guard their enormous bodies and fragile minds against the onslaughts of coeds and liquor and riotous living. The stockyards, many Randolph students called the complex. Horny Hollow was more common among the coeds.

It was two o'clock in the afternoon of the hottest day they had had yet that summer, the hottest of a searing necklace of days that burned viciously and unbroken in a heat wave that was destined to become campus legend. Maggie and Sister had slept naked for three nights, under towels wrung out in cold water, with the fan trained on their bodies. As a result, Sister's blue-ice eyes were red and dimmed with sinusitis, and her pointed little nose lost its pertness to a slow bloom of pink at its tip. Maggie felt headachy and heavy-eyed and sodden behind her cheekbones. The heat reached into the dim room and sucked the power from the laboring air conditioning, so that the air inside, instead of being stale and glacial, as it usually was, was tepid and oppressive on bare arms and legs. The group was lethargic and short-tempered, yet restive, and the keening moaning of Elvis Presley from the jukebox was whining and debilitating instead of sensual. They had been there, smoking and playing cross, desultory bridge and drinking cold drinks, since noon.

"If this heat doesn't let up, I'm going to come sleep on your sun porch," said Sister to the surrogate SAE, with wilted archness. "Buck naked too. Y'all wouldn't attack me, would you?"

"Lady, it's just too damned hot," he said dispiritedly.

"Hell, this is an April day compared to the Mississippi Delta," said Boots. "It gets so hot on the Delta, you could fry eggs on the streets of Greenville at six o'clock at night. It's why our niggers are so black, they get tanned." Boots's Mississippi stories were a neverfailing source of entertainment to his brothers and others to whom he told them. In his undulating drawl, they took on the quality of folk legends, more vivid than life, and were accepted as such. Unlike the others in the snack bar, he did not seem to mind the heat. He moved his long body slowly, and his sharply drawn face looked carved of golden ice. His green eyes promised cold in their depths. His oxford-cloth shirt, with the sleeves rolled above his elbows, and his chinos were crisp and unwilted. His coolness became him.

"It gets pretty hot over there in a lot of ways, I hear," said Gleason, grinning at Maggie through smoke. "I hear Maggie turned on the heat pretty good under your daddy, Boots. You going to give Gertie Sawyer a run for her money, Maggie?"

The others at the table laughed. Gertrude Sawyer was a shrill, acne-pitted junior in Political Science, whose vague and often quixotic views on Communism, Indochina, Estes Kefauver, Robert Oppenheimer, Kenneth Rexroth, flying saucers, beatniks, and Randolph's oppression of its women students were aired frequently and loudly from the steps of the Student Union or a post beside the main gate, often accompanied by literature run off on the mimeograph machine at the Randolph Independent Organization headquarters. Few students understood Gertrude's skittering soprano litanies, and most would not have known what she was talking about in any case. She had become, comfortably, a campus character, like the gently demented janitor in Semmes Hall, who always had a balloon tied to his wrist, or Pop Haney, the toothless operator of the campus bawdy house and gin mill. "She needs a good lay" was the consensus of the men on campus. No one volunteered.

Maggie shot Boots a swift, savage look. It was too much to hope that he would not tell the KAs about the capture of the Negro prisoner, having been, as it were, the star of the show, but she had hoped the event would overshadow her own fiasco on the Claiborne veranda. Apparently it had not.

He caught her look and gave her a brief, hard hug. "Ol' Maggie here is a real tiger," he said fondly, but he did not elaborate for the waiting eyes. Instead, he stretched long and beautifully, small bones cracking in sequence, and said, "Let's go out to the Bear Trap and tap a keg. Or better still, let's get some cold brew and go out to the lake. I want to get neck-deep in something cool."

"The lake will be just like bath water," said Gleason, but his clever, discontented face smoothed at the thought of the dark pines and brown water.

"Maggie?"

"I can't," said Maggie. "I've got to turn in my column. It's a day overdue now."

"Well, that'll take you about five minutes. Go on upstairs and give it to Bevins. He's always in the *Senator* office. It's air-conditioned is why. I'll wait for you."

"I think I'm going to need to talk to him about it," Maggie said. She had been carrying the column around in her purse since the morning she wrote it. It seemed very heavy there.

"What's it about this week, Maggie? More power to the Girlie Gestapo?" This from one of the very pretty girls across the table, whose prettiness had earned her a fraternity pin her freshman year and considerable hostility from other Randolph coeds. She considered the Women's Student Government Association her natural enemy, rightly.

"No. It's just a column. Nothing you'd be interested in, Sue Ellen. I didn't even know you could read."

The sharpness was unlike Maggie, and they stared at her. She was tumescent and heavy with heat and staleness and a sense of doors closing irreversibly. "I think I will go on up to the *Senator* office, Boots. Go on out to the lake and I'll see you later." She rose. He walked with her out of the snack bar into the hall.

"Don't you want to go with us? It'll be cool," he said. He did not sulk or fling himself off, as he was accustomed to doing when Maggie did not want to do something he did. There was a faintly disturbing difference in her since they had returned from Mississippi, which he had put down to a lingering and proper delicacy after the shock of the jailbreak and her faint. She had been distant and a little quiet, and there had been one Saturday night, the last one, when she had broken their standing date to go somewhere with Aiken Reed. Boots was wary of Aiken, who did not respond to his lowered eyelids and practiced, closed smile. He did not approve of Maggie's sudden and increasingly exclusive friendship with her. He felt shut out. He liked Sister, who tossed her head and chirruped and responded predictably and was a fine and natural foil for Maggie's vivid, ladylike elegance. Maggie *was* a lady, he thought dimly; even her giggles, her flirting, her dancing, had a comforting restraint to them. But he found her new abstraction oddly excessive, in a way real excess would never be to her, and he was disoriented.

"Boots, I just don't feel like being around a bunch of people. Really. I have a headache, and I want to go over this with Terry, and I have a history paper due day after tomorrow that I haven't even started. You go, and maybe we could go get a Coke or something after you come back. Okay?"

"You mad at me about something?"

"No. *No*. Really. I'm just ... hot and fussy." At the slight, petulant, hurt frown that creased his golden forehead, she relented. "I'd love to see you later tonight, Boots. Just us. We haven't been anywhere by ourselves in a long time. Couldn't we do that?"

"Sure, babe." He was, for Boots, sunny again. "Go get on with your career and we'll do ... something by ourselves later on. I got some good ideas. Call you then." He leered showily and dipped back into the snack bar.

Maggie climbed the back stairs to the second floor of the Union building. There, down a long corridor, were the offices and meeting rooms of the various student organizations ... the Student Government Association, the WSGA, the Interfraternity Council, the yearbook, the student newspaper. On this killing day the corridor was dim and most of the offices unlit and closed. But the one at the far end was lit, its door ajar, and a peevish stuttering of typewriter keys came from it. Maggie stood for a long moment outside it, and then went in.

In a small anteroom, at a desk surrounded by metal file cabinets except for a narrow crawl space, an extremely fat boy sat pecking at the typewriter. He was blond, more than blond, bleached. His skin and hair and eyebrows were white-pink. His face looked like taut, shiny, risen dough, as if a fingerprint would remain there. He wore colorless plastic-rimmed glasses. Terry Bevins had been editor of the Randolph *Senator* for two years running, an unprecedented tenure. A Phi Delta Theta legacy from a wealthy Mobile family, he had been pledged only under great alumni pressure which amounted almost to threat of charter revocation. But his elfin wit and firefly mind and natural sweetness had won his brothers in his first quarter as a pledge, and had catapulted him to vast popularity among the student body and into a number of campus offices. At the *Senator* he had found his niche; he was a natural and awesomely gifted editor, and during his time there, the perfunctory little paper took on a layer of glistening advertising fat and a briskly professional look. Maggie was at home with him; and he was with her, recognizing, as Ben Flournoy did, some unmeasured submerged gift, and needling her gently to apply it to weightier matters than she generally did. Like Aiken, he walked often alone and without censure. He was engaged to a sweet-faced brown sparrow of an Independent girl in Home Economics; she wore both his pin and a flinty chip of a diamond engagement ring. He looked up at Maggie and smiled.

"Two days late, Deloach," he said. "Don't tell me there's nothing worth writing about over there in the land of the motherless. How's Delia, by the way?"

"She's better, in one way. M.A. and Cornelia were over at the hospital last week. Her bandages will come off this weekend, and she can probably go home pretty soon after that. The first plastic surgery is scheduled for September. But M.A. says she just lies there. She'd answer questions, but she wouldn't talk to them. Poor Delia ... she was always talking, Terry, always moving. Remember how she used to run on?"

"She was very ... alive, Maggie. Vibrant. I always thought of that word when I thought about Delia. Well, hell, she's not dead. She's going to be all right eventually, isn't she?"

"Physically, I guess. But she'll never look the same. M.A. said the doctor said she could come back to school winter quarter if she wanted to, but her mother says she won't even discuss it. She just ... lies there."

"Misses Jenks, I guess."

Sudden salt flooded the back of Maggie's throat. Jenks's long, bright sweetness.

"We all miss Jenks," she said.

"Well. What you got for me?"

Maggie took the folded sheets of paper from her purse and handed them to him. He tossed them into his overflowing in-basket and swiveled back to his typewriter. Maggie did not move to go.

"Aren't you going to read it?" she asked.

"Maggie, sweets, I got my own editorial to write, and Carter's goddamned sports to rewrite—again." He gestured at the typewriter—"And about ten pounds of this week's galleys to proof before I can leave here today. You'll keep. I don't ever rewrite you.

Only goddamn writer on the staff who can spell and punctuate. Go on off and neck with Boots. Unless you want to hang around and read galleys?"

"I think you'd better read it, Terry."

He looked at her for a moment, then picked up the folded papers and spread them out on the desk in front of him. He read steadily, his lips moving silently. It was a habit Maggie detested, but it did not annoy her when Terry did it. The words, she knew, would be ineradicably recorded in his mind. For a long time there was only the sound of his tiny, popping sibilances, and pages turning. Then he shuffled them and rapped them smartly on the desk, and squared them, and laid them to one side. He looked up at her, holding the look for the space of half a minute.

"Maggie, I can't run that," he said.

"Why not?"

"It's . . . inflammatory. You know as well as I do how the Publications Board feels about this kind of stuff. The *Senator* can't speak out for integration, not publicly, no matter how any of us may feel about it. The Board of Regents would go crazy."

"It's not the *Senator* speaking out, Terry. It's me, just one person, it's just my opinion. And I certainly don't feel like it's inflammatory."

"Not to you, and not to me, and certainly not in the . . . the free press, out in the world. But, Maggie, I got a good bit of shit over that harmless little Autherine Lucy piece you did. Randolph's never had a Negro student. God knows what would happen if a

Negro applied here. It was bad enough over there, and I don't have to tell you this is a ... less sophisticated campus. You can't just come out for integration at Randolph before it even comes up."

"I didn't say that." Maggie did not know why she was so reluctant to drop the subject. He was offering, insisting, to take the matter out of her hands. Relief and an obstinate urgency battled in her. "I'm only urging reason and ... "—Flournoy's shadowed face on the terrace came back to her—"and *empathy* for the Negroes. I only said that to live ... *honorably* ... with them, we have to try to understand them, get into their skins, so that when integration does come, there won't be ... well, violence, shooting and things. I'm really only telling how I sort of ... had a flash of understanding for one Negro myself. Or at least I think I did."

"Well, nobody at Randolph is all that anxious to get inside a Negro's skin, Maggie. Least of all the Publications Board. *Least* of all the Board of Regents. Not on this campus, in one of these dormitories, in one of these dining halls. And everybody's going to interpret this as advocating integration at Randolph, even if you only meant it to be your own little coming of age in Samoa. It's a nice piece of writing, by the way. If it weren't for the subject matter, I'd box it on the front page. This is what I've been trying to get out of you all year. Come on, Maggie, do this for me about the Middle East, or about Communism"— he grimaced wryly—"that's a winner any day, or even about the honor system Randolph does not have."

"I want you to run that column, Terry."

"Maggie, I'd get kicked off the *Senator* staff. And so would you."

"What if you printed a disclaimer saying this was my own personal opinion and the *Senator* wasn't responsible for it?"

"Maggie, does this piece mean that much to you? I mean, are you willing to take the consequences for it? To say it's going to be unpopular is putting it mildly. Have you thought about that? And what about Boots, you're talking about his hometown, his . . . whole way of *life*. Which, I assume, will be yours one day soon. What do you think it would be like for you in Mississippi if this thing ran?"

"Oh, Terry, nobody in Mississippi is going to even *see* the damn piece. About three-fourths of the *campus* won't even read it; you know how it is in the summer. And you let me worry about Boots. And, yes. Yes, this piece *does* mean that much to me." Surprisingly, she realized that it did.

He looked at her again, silently. What a pretty girl she is, he thought. I never knew she had this kind of . . . passion.

"I'll do this," he said slowly. "I'll take it before the Publications Board next Monday night. I'll tell them you're willing for it to run under a disclaimer. That's the best I can do, Maggie."

"Dr. Flournoy's on the Board, isn't he?"

"Yeah. And so is Dean Abernathy, and you know

his politics. He thinks there's a wild-eyed Communist behind every magnolia tree in his backyard. And a wild-eyed nigger behind the Communist."

"Who else?"

"Students. Gary Burton from the yearbook. Isabel Fowler from Pan-hel. Wesley Wingo from the *Farmer*. Me."

"Will you stick up for it, Terry?"

"I honestly don't know, Maggie," he said slowly. "But I'll take it over there."

"Thank you, Terry. You'll let me know?"

"You'll know, Maggie. I guaran-damn-tee you you'll know."

She walked out of the office and down the long green hall. He rose and squeezed himself from behind the crowded desk, grunting, and stood in the doorway watching her go. Her back, in a starched melon sleeveless blouse, was very straight, her waist very slim, her arms glowing dark bronze in the gloom. She held her head level. He thought she looked very thin.

"Watch out, Maggie," he said aloud, but very softly.

15

A T TEN O'CLOCK THAT NIGHT, Boots and Maggie sat in the Jaguar at Stovall's, a starkly unlovely concrete-block cube set back from the Opelika highway in a grove of pines. Many cars were drawn up around it. Stovall's specialized in thick, icy milk shakes and outsized limeades and did a fine business in the heat of the summers. Any Randolph student who had wheels, or knew someone who did, was out of his or her dwelling place this summer night. Most who had headed for the lake or the Forestry Plot to neck had found the torpid heat simply too oppressive for bodily contact. Cologned, powdered, and deodorized skin went wet, then rank, and stuck to other skin, and bare legs adhered stickily to seat covers, and few scores were scored. Most had given up and driven back, tight and steaming and thwarted, to movie theaters and drive-ins.

Maggie and Boots were no exception. Boots had picked her up at eight-thirty, half-lidded from beer and hours of swimming and anticipation, still damp from his shower and smelling of clean, ironed cotton. He felt fine-drawn, prowling, sexy. He had not asked Maggie where she wanted to go but had driven directly to one of the narrow, ribbon-straight roads that bisected the Forestry Plot at precise angles, and pulled off under the canopy of pines. She had not protested. There were other cars crouched a few feet into the prim forest at intervals along the road, but they were silent and darkened and did not intrude.

He switched on the radio: Elvis Presley, inevitably. "Well-lll, since muh baby lef' me, found a new place to dway-ull, *uh!*" "Heartbreak Hotel" had reached number one on the mercurial charts that May and showed no signs of giving ground to any contenders. It ran through the summer like a leitmotif. Maggie disliked it; Elvis Presley's slow, grinding, "serious" ballads intimidated her, vaguely; tugged slyly at some essential, deep-buried sensuality in her that frightened her when it surfaced, as it did rarely but abruptly. The faster, upbeat ones—"Hound Dog," "Blue Suede Shoes," "Don't Be Cruel"—soothed her with their rolling, bawdy jollity. They were surface; they were gay and teasing and did not penetrate.

Boots reached surely for her, turned her face to him, kissed her hard and wetly, moving his mouth slowly and insistently from side to side over hers. Maggie did not feel the sly, small flare of response in her stomach and throat that she usually did when Boots kissed her. She felt smothered, drowned, panicked. The tongue next, she thought. But she did not pull away. Needing to bury the panic in some swift, far, dangerous edge of feeling, she wound her arms

tightly around him, feeling the shirt dampen under
her hands, feeling the smooth slide of muscle. She
heard his breath quicken and roughen, felt his heart
fast and shallow against hers, heard the high, whining
moan that always began in the hollow at the base of
his neck. She pulled him harder against her, but when
his teeth bumped grittily against her own, when his
hand came violently around from her back to her
breast, she jerked her head to the side, away from his
invading mouth, struggling blindly and instinctively
for air as a fish might, drowning in it.

"*Stop,* Boots!" Her voice sounded shrill and thin
in her own ears, a scared child's. For a moment he
pressed her back harder against the leather seat, but
then he released her. He slumped back across the
gearshift into his own seat and struck the steering
wheel with the heel of his palm.

"Jesus *Christ,* Maggie!" It was a ragged moan,
out of the control of his breathing. "Don't start it if
you're not going to finish it! God, you just don't know
what that does to me. I hurt. Shit, I can't take this
much longer!"

It was an old argument, but there was a new urgency in it, a new violence. Secure and complacent
in his acquisition of her, conventional to the core of
his being, he had always been indulgently willing to
wait . . . for the big, dim bedroom off the gallery; for
the roistering, comforting ceremonial sanctions; for
the old, old rites and litanies and initiations. But the
new distance and abstraction in her inflamed him

like an aphrodisiac. Sensing her drawing away into some place he could not fathom, much less follow, he felt a powerful, visceral need to impale her, brand her, mark her. Maggie, in turn, felt fear and a sense of gathering as to leave, and a tearing, conflicting need to cling and be absorbed, and finally a cold and explosive anger. Violation quivered at the kernel of her being like a red toothache. She also felt shamed and guilty. She did not want to be branded a tease. That was for girls who dated around, who had no steady, who were not pinned. This was Boots, this boy would be her husband. Her mouth flinched back, her teeth clenched. No, screamed her knotted stomach. Not yet, not for a while, there's no hurry, said her mind.

He picked up the thought, not as an intuitive person would, but as a well-functioning animal that lived wild might.

"Maggie, let's get married."

"Married."

"Let's go somewhere and get married. Tonight. Nobody has to know. There's nobody at your house to miss you."

"M.A. would miss me; she hugs me goodnight," Maggie said stupidly. "Sister would miss me if I was gone all night. More than that. Don't you have to wait several days?"

"Well, by the time we got back it would be too late to do anything about it, wouldn't it? What's Dean Fisher going to do, campus you? She's got no say-so over married students. We could get an apartment."

"They'd call my parents, Boots. They'd be frantic."

"Hell, you know your parents are wetting their pants for us to get married."

"Yes, but not this way, Boots, not like . . . just running off as though we were ashamed of it, hiding something. Mother would want a . . . you know, a real wedding, at the church at home, a *pretty* wedding, and your folks would too, you know they would. They'd all think I was . . . "

"Pregnant?" He laughed shortly. "Fat chance of that. Anyway, it would be obvious you weren't, pretty soon. They'd get over it, Maggie, once they got used to the idea. We'd have a place, an apartment, the old man would pay for it and for us to finish school. And we'd be—together all the time. We were going to after graduation anyway, you knew that. I just don't think I can wait any longer, Maggie."

"I didn't know we were going to get married after graduation." But you must have known that, said a part of her mind, conversationally, to another part that was wailing in fear.

"Why the hell did you think I gave you my pin? Why did you think I took you home with me?"

"You never said. Not really."

"Well, I'm saying now." Impatiently. "You want a proposal? Will you marry me, Maggie? Will you go with me tonight and get married and be my wife and all that?"

"Boots, I . . . no. Not now. Not tonight, not like this."

"When, then? Next June? Five years from now?"
But some of the congested fire had gone out of him,
some momentum was slowing. He was fidgeting restlessly with the radio dial.

"Boots, do you think maybe we ought to wait
awhile after graduation?" We could just as well be
talking about whether to go get a pizza, she thought.
"I mean, wait until you get established in Greenville,
until I've . . . oh, done something out in the world?"
Aiken said that, she thought. So did Terry. I think
Tuck did, too, and Dr. Flournoy, in so many words.
Am I really all that unworldly? I must be if I said it,
too.

"What do you want to do out in the world?
Greenville is the world, being married is the world."
He was sullen, but without heat.

"I don't know, a job or something, for a little
while. Boots, neither of us has ever done anything but
be in school. I've never *been* anywhere, or *worked*. . . . "

"What do you need to work for? You won't work
after we're married. What kind of work would you
do?"

"Well, I thought maybe writing of some kind."

"Shit, Maggie, you can write all day long after
we're married, if you want to. You want a career? You
could write stuff for the Greenville paper. You write
real good stuff, you could have a column or something. Or you could write poetry and stuff, if you
want to, maybe you could get it printed in a magazine
or something. There's a lady that's a friend of Moth-

er's that writes poetry and they print it in the Memphis *Appeal* right along."

"I mean . . . serious writing, Boots. Writing that makes a difference, changes things. Aiken was talking about going to New York after graduation, and maybe me going and getting an apartment with her. Just for a year or two. You know, till we grow up a little, is what I guess I mean."

"Goddamn it, I might have known it was Aiken!" He was angry with one of his sudden cold, whipping rages. "That's just great, Maggie. Sure, you just go on to New York with Aiken Reed. What are you going to do, hang around some Bohemian dump in the Village and screw her castoffs? Fuck your way right along behind her in a big hotshot advertising agency? Join Aiken Reed and see the world, on your back. Aiken Reed is a high-class *whore,* Maggie. Anybody on campus who wants it can have it. Is that what you want to be when you grow up, Maggie?"

"She is not! You shut up about Aiken, Boots! Aiken is the best friend I've got, you don't know *anything.* She wouldn't *have* you! She . . . sleeps with who she wants to; what you and your precious little brothers think about her couldn't matter less to her. Aiken is . . . the most moral person I've ever known in my life!"

"Well, if that doesn't beat shit! You won't let me near your little white pants because 'it's not right, Boots, oh, no, Boots, I can't do *that,* Boots, you wouldn't *respect* me, Boots,' and then you turn right around and say Aiken Reed is the most moral person you've ever known! What do y'all do on your little private parties, Maggie? Do you take turns laying that asshole Tucker? Do you play fuck the faculty?"

Suddenly and surprisingly, Maggie began to cry. She seldom cried, almost never around Boots. She cried from unknown grief and fatigue and rage and fear; she wept for perfect, broken things.

"Ah, come on, Maggie, I'm sorry." He was relieved and sure again, back in charge. Women cried regularly around Boots. He knew the drill. "I know you're not like that. I didn't mean to say that. Come on, sugar, don't cry. I can't stand you crying. You're tired and upset, you've been upset ever since we went home, and I rushed you too fast. Sure, you want a real wedding, a big, pretty one, and we'll have it. We'll have the goddamnedest wedding that little town of yours ever saw. We'll even wait for a year, if you want to. Just don't talk any more shit about going off with Aiken Reed. . . . I know you didn't mean that, anyway. I just pushed you too hard, and you got upset, and I'm sorry. We'll talk about it later. Come on, fix your makeup and we'll go out to Stovall's and get a Coke."

And they had. Sitting in the open car, waving and calling to people in other cars, watching the ebb and flow of human traffic up to the drive-in window and back, Maggie felt reprieved and weightless and gay, as though she had stepped back from the brink of a spinning void. She looked at the couples in the other cars, head turned to head, an arm draped loosely around a bare shoulder, chiming laughter and music from many car radios, white teeth flashing and sleek ponytails bobbing on tanned necks. The soft weight of honeysuckle, mimosa, and the waning moon lay on the air.

We could all be in a movie, she thought. A movie about college. A musical. I don't care if it's not real. If any of these other people have just been through something like we have, I don't have to know about it. It doesn't show. This is what I thought college would be like when I was in high school, and I'm so glad, so glad that it is, just for right now.

One of the sudden surges of pure joy that she remembered from her childhood, that still caught her occasionally even now, lifted behind her ribs and flung her head back. One day, she thought with abrupt, prescient clarity, when I am forty, I will remember this night, this precise moment, the smells and sounds and textures of it, this sheer youngness . . . and I will know that I can never, ever have this back again.

She laughed aloud with the having of it. "There's Gary and Sister," she said to Boots. "Let's go sit in their car for a little while. I've hardly seen her since they got pinned."

16

O N THE FOLLOWING SUNDAY NIGHT, at nine o'clock, M.A. Appleton neighed up the Kappa stairs, "Maggie, you've got a visitor."

Maggie, in shorty pajamas, surrounded by crumpled, handwritten pages of lined notebook paper, halfway through a faltering paper on Oliver Cromwell, frowned in annoyance at the closed door of her room. M.A. really did have the most irritating voice.

"Who is it?" she called back, not moving from her seat. Boots was the only person who dropped in on her without calling first, and they had agreed that she would not see him that evening. He had said he was going over to the ATO house to work on the Jaguar with a friend who knew about esoteric transmissions.

There was no answer. M.A. had apparently scuttled back into her lair. Maggie got up from the desk, peeling her damp forearms stickily from its surface, jerked open her closet door in exasperation, and pulled her raincoat on over her pajamas. She slid her feet into yellow scuffs and clopped down the stairs to the living room. If that's Boots, I'll wring his neck, she thought crossly.

Aiken Reed stood alone in the dimly lit big room, her back to Maggie. She was examining her face in the dark pool of the old Chinese Chippendale mirror over the console that held the Kappa guest book and a dried arrangement of anonymous, dimmed flowers. The mirror was a legacy from Mama Kidd, who had polished it carefully once a week. In her absence, in the wet, shrouding heat that had not abated, its surface was still and scummed like a stagnant pond. Aiken's face in it was ghostly and drowned, as though she lay under water. Her hands were jammed into the pockets of a khaki London Fog raincoat, and she wore scuffed loafers on her bare feet. She looked attenuated and elegant, like a Dorothy Hood fashion sketch for Lord & Taylor.

"Aiken? Hey," Maggie said, surprised. Aiken had never visited her at the Kappa house, and she had never been to the Pi Phi house to call on Aiken. They met for coffee or lunch or sometimes early suppers at the places Aiken liked, the anonymous cafes or snack shops in town, or they drove in Aiken's MG to drive-ins out the Columbus or Montgomery highways, and had once gone to Montgomery and eaten dinner in a French restaurant. Aiken would have no part of the Union, though she would have qualified automatically for the center tables. The frog pond, she called it.

Aiken turned, giving Maggie her slow smile. "I

thought you might like to drive out to Dairyland and get something cold to drink," she said. "The house is a steam bath tonight, and I knew yours must be too."

"Well, I've got a history paper due in the morning, and I'm not dressed. . . . "

"Go put on some Bermudas. We won't be gone long. I have something to tell you."

"What?"

"It's a surprise."

"A nice surprise?" A sudden thought struck Maggie. "Aiken, is it about you and Tuck?"

"In a way. Will you come?"

"Well, sure. Just let me throw on some shorts."

Maggie ran back upstairs, rummaged a pair of wrinkled, back-buckled Bermuda shorts from her laundry bag, skinned into a red T-shirt. I'll bet they're going to get married, she thought. It shouldn't have surprised her; Aiken and Tuck had been inseparable since early summer. They spent the long, slow afternoons and some evenings at Tuck's apartment, or they went to the Flournoys'. The two couples had become close, Maggie knew. Tuck and Aiken were only apart when he had papers to grade or faculty meetings to attend. Aiken saw Maggie at those times, and though she did not talk about her relationship with Tuck, and Maggie did not ask, she had a rounded, smoothed, filled air about her that Maggie supposed to be the air of a cherished and sexually fulfilled woman. The ripeness of it became Aiken.

The sharp pang of disappointment that stabbed

Maggie at the thought was more of a surprise than the fact. I wonder if I'm jealous, she thought, running a comb through her sweat-dampened hair. We really weren't that close; we never talked about really intimate things, the way Sister and I do. I can't think right offhand what we did talk about, all those hours. But we did. And I wouldn't be losing her, really, because she'd be right here if they got married; she'd have to be. Tuck's job is here. The thought of Aiken as a faculty wife, one of those oddly featureless women Maggie saw in the library or herding small children into their husbands' tiny offices to visit Daddy at his job, or piloting station wagons through the narrow back streets and A&P parking lots of Randolph, was disturbing and ludicrous. But not all faculty wives were like those placid, ponytailed, makeup-less women. Kita Flournoy was not.

I wonder what's wrong with me, she thought. I hadn't really planned to go anywhere with Aiken after graduation. But the thought had been there, she realized, a nebulous comfort. An out.

They got into the MG and drove across the silent campus in the heavy, moonless dark. Maggie looked sharply sidewise at Aiken, but she only smiled enigmatically and switched on the car radio, twirling the dial until she found a faraway station she liked. The cool, gritty voice of Chris Connor spilled out, splashing the poignant words of "All About Ronnie" around their heads. "We'll drink from dry glasses, there's no need for wine, the champagne is Ronnie, and Ronnie is mine." They smoked in silence until they reached Dairyland. It had never attained the popularity of Stovall's, though its milk shakes were just as icy and creamy, and its exterior a bit more attractive, being prettied up with window boxes of stunted geraniums. Some alchemy was lacking. There were only two other cars pulled into its parking lot, and Maggie did not know the people in them.

They ordered limeades, and sat in more silence until a sullen young girl in Dairyland short shorts, with a black bow at the neck of her sleeveless blouse, had slammed the tray onto the lowered window of the MG and stumped away in high heels, her high-rumped behind switching.

"Well, tell," said Maggie, smiling.

"I'm pregnant," Aiken said.

Maggie stared at her. Shock thrummed in the air around her. Aiken might have just said she had murdered someone. Pregnancy had never entered Maggie's mind in connection with Aiken.

"Oh, my goodness," she said, finally.

"Is that all you have to say?" Aiken was smiling at her, the serene, drowsy smile she always smiled.

"I thought you had a diaphragm," Maggie said. She could not think of anything else to say. This could not be happening.

"They don't always work."

"Well . . . God, Aiken." Maggie felt stupid and mildly, clinically aware, as of some grave wound that should and would begin to hurt her badly soon, to bleed, to frighten her mortally. I wonder what I'm supposed to do about this, she thought in peevish detachment.

"What are you going to do?" she said. "I mean, I know y'all will get married, but when will the—the baby . . . how far along are you?"

"Only two months," Aiken said dreamily.

"But that's too early to tell, isn't it? Maybe you've just missed a couple of periods. . . . "

"I know," said Aiken. "I'm sure. I wanted to tell you tonight because I'm leaving school tomorrow. I wanted to say goodbye to you. You've been a good friend to me, Maggie, and I'll miss you very much." Aiken had a way of saying things that were oddly old-fashioned and bare sometimes, things that the cool, flip banter of the campus precluded. In her soft eastern drawl they sounded portentous beyond their actuality.

"Leaving . . . oh, *no,* Aiken, you don't have to *leave!* Tuck will . . . Aiken, has that son of a bitch refused to *marry* you?"

"Tuck doesn't know."

"Well, tell him, for God's sake! Aiken, you can't seriously be afraid to tell Tuck you're pregnant! He's *crazy* about you, he'll marry you . . . *tonight,* if you want him to. You know he will!"

"Maggie, I don't want to marry Tuck." Aiken's narrow, lovely head was thrown far back, resting against the back of the seat. She looked skyward, blowing a thin stream of smoke into the air. She looked like one of the effigies on a crusader's tomb that Maggie had studied in art history, pure, chaste, young, rapt.

"Then what in the world will you do?" It was a wail of pain and bewilderment. "You're not going off and have an abortion, are you?" But she must be. There was nothing left for her to do. The Aikens of the world did not huddle in shapeless cotton smocks in homes for unwed mothers in grimy industrial cities, waiting and frightened and beaten. Maggie had heard of the abortionists. There was one in Tuskegee, a Negro doctor. Boots had hinted of others. The girls who fainted, who left school . . . they came back sometimes . . . she had seen them in later quarters, quiet and cowed and much older somehow, their taut bloom gone. Some of them did not come back. There were stories, told in whispers, of blood and bungling, infection, death. Maggie was terribly afraid.

Aiken turned and looked at her, a level look, but not sad, not frightened. Calm.

"No. I'm not going to have an abortion. I'm going to have my baby. I've always wanted a baby, Maggie, did you know that? It's just that I've never wanted to be married very much. I've never met a man I wanted to . . . be with, for the rest of my life. A lot of men I've wanted to be with for a little while, but not all my life. I've been with Tuck, and I guess you might say I loved him, in a way, but not for the rest of my life. There's something . . . important . . . I don't know what it is . . . that I need to do with my

life. Something . . . somewhere that I haven't found
yet. I'm just starting, Maggie, whatever it is could
be out there anywhere. I could find it any time. But
not here. Not in Randolph in some little house full
of diapers and a mortgage and a set of plastic dishes
and 'The Hit Parade' every Saturday night for the
rest of my life. Maybe what I'm looking for *is* a man,
but not any man I've ever met yet. And I don't think
it's a man anyway. It's more something that I will do
myself. Something sort of . . . great. You know, Maggie, I've always thought that I will be a great woman
one day."

Maggie thought that perhaps Aiken had lost her
senses. She sat there in the fringes of the light from
the drive-in, in a desperate situation, the one situation that terrified them all beyond anything else, with
its inevitability and shame and waste and unimaginable options, and she talked of being a great woman.

"Aiken, I tell you what. Let's go right now, let's
drive over to Tuck's, and let's all three sit down and
talk about this. It's not the end of the world, you'll
see, you don't have to . . . run away. We'll figure out
something, you'll feel a lot better about it after we've
talked. . . ."

Aiken laughed. It was a gay, free, fresh young
sound.

"I haven't flipped, Maggie, if that's what you
think. I don't feel badly about the baby. I just feel
badly about Tuck, because I think I'm going to hurt
him awfully. I'm going to have my baby, Maggie, and

I'm going to keep him and raise him ... or her, it doesn't matter. I'll love that. The baby is a ... part of the great thing. I've always thought I would have children. I'll just be having one now instead of later. It'll be sort of wonderful, I think."

"Well, I think you're *crazy!*" Maggie was beginning to cry without knowing that she was, to clench her fists and shake her head. "You can't just go away from here without telling Tuck. What would you do for money, where would you live, what will your parents say? Please, please, let me help you! Let us help you!"

"You've helped me by just being my friend," said Aiken. She reached over and took Maggie's clenched hands in her long, strong ones. Girls at Randolph did not touch each other, beyond grandiloquent, impulsive hugs at honor-winnings and pinnings and engagements, but Maggie clung to Aiken's hands.

"Listen, Maggie, listen to me. I'm going to New York. I'd wait until the quarter ended, but there doesn't seem to be any sense in that, and I just don't want to have to play out any silly charades with Tuck. Besides, I'll be showing by then, thin as I am. I have money. I have some money that my grandmother left me in trust. I got it when I was twenty-one, in my own account in New Jersey, and I haven't touched a penny of it. There's more than enough until the baby comes, and I'll be working, anyway. My Aunt Deirdre, my mother's youngest sister, has a fabulous job with an interiors firm in the Village; they do just the kind of things I love, real class, real elegance, good

materials, and Deirdre will get me a job there. I've already talked to her. I called her day before yesterday.
They need somebody."

"Oh, Aiken, was she terribly upset?"

"She *loved* it, Maggie. Deirdre is our family rebel,
or was till I came along. She's talented, she's beautiful, and she just doesn't give a damn what anybody
thinks about her. I've always adored her, and she's
always said I was like her own child . . . although
she's just eleven years older than me. Mother never
got along with her; they all think she's . . . oh, I don't
know, bohemian and awful. She's been living with
an artist in the Village for years now, a very talented
man. He's shown all over the world. She could marry
him, I guess, but they just don't want to get married.
She doesn't need the money; she makes a fortune at
her job, and she's sure she can get me on, starting in
September."

"But you'll be four months along then, you'll be
showing!"

"Maggie, they don't care about that in New York.
I'm good enough now, I don't need a degree." There
was no conceit in her voice, only swift, impatient assessment. "I can stay with Deirdre until early spring,
because Paul got a Fulbright to study in Germany till
at least then. I'll be there when the baby comes, and
then Deirdre says she'll help me find an apartment
in the Village, somewhere close. I'll find someone to
stay with the baby, or Deirdre says they have wonderful day care center things in the Village. It's sort

of a new idea, and I'll just ... live and work and raise my baby. It's all worked out, you mustn't worry about me."

"Won't your parents have a fit?"

"Probably. But they certainly won't be surprised. It's what Mother has been predicting for years now. She'll have a marvelous time crying and wailing over all of it to her bridge buddies at the club, and they'll all say what a strong woman she is, and pet her, and she'll adore it. It *will* hurt Daddy." Her voice softened and sobered. "But he'll love his grandchild eventually, no matter what. Mother will, too. It's not like they'd try to ... get the baby away from me or anything. They know I've got Grandmother's money, and they know Deirdre will look after me, no matter what they think of her morals. It's really not going to surprise anybody all that much, Maggie."

"Are you going to tell Tuck at all? I mean, what *are* you going to tell him? You can't just up and leave him without a word, Aiken."

"That's just what I'm going to do, and you must understand why. He'll come to you first thing when he knows I'm gone, and I don't want you to tell him where I am, or that I'm pregnant, or anything. Please, Maggie ... " At a strangled sob from Maggie, she squeezed her hands. "It may sound cruel, but I know better than you about this. I'll call Tuck, once I'm settled, and I'll tell him about the baby ... I owe him that, it's his baby, too, and it could certainly have worse fathers, as far as lineage goes ... but I am not going to tell him where I am. I'll tell you, Maggie, I'll write you, I don't want to lose you, but you mustn't tell Tuck. He'll only come after me if he knows where I am, and, Maggie, *I am not going to marry Tuck. Not ever.* It's better that I break it off clean and finally right now. You know he'd never accept it if I stayed around to talk to him about it. He'd be—wild."

Tuck's face, dark and full of fierce, burning adoration, came back to Maggie.

"I guess he would," she sniffled. Her nose ran.

"Will you promise, then?"

"I . . . oh, all right, I promise. But what will I tell him?"

"Just tell him you don't know where I am, that you didn't even know I was leaving."

"All right, Aiken. But . . . aren't you afraid at all? Just a little?"

"No. I never felt more . . . exhilarated in all my life. I only wish you'd stop crying. There's nothing for you to cry over. I'm *happy*, Maggie. Be happy for me?"

"I'm not crying for you. I'm crying for me. I'll miss you awfully, Aiken, I had no idea how much I'd miss you. I didn't even realize I liked you . . . love you, I guess . . . as much as I do." Maggie was too deeply sunk in grief and betrayal to be embarrassed at her words as she would have been with anyone else, before this. "You were . . . showing me something about myself that I didn't know, I was . . . turning into somebody I think you might have been proud of, somebody you always thought I could be. . . . " She thought of the column she had written, and broke down completely into racking, soundless sobs. Don't leave me, Aiken, she wept inside herself. Everyone is leaving me, one by one, everything is leaving me. Don't you too. She did not know what she meant.

"You can do that by yourself, Maggie. Don't you know that? You don't need me to tell you what to do. But"—Aiken hugged her, hard—"if you ever feel like you do need me, if you decide you do want to . . . cast your lot with the likes of me . . . there'll be room. Any apartment I get, anywhere I am, will have room for you. Deirdre's place is huge, it's like a loft, they've fixed it up so it's *gorgeous,* and mine will have a room for you. It will, Maggie. Always. You and me and the baby in New York . . . how does that sound? Greenwich Village? Wouldn't that be fabulous? Next June? He'll be about four months old, think what fun we could have with him. . . . "

"Oh, Aiken!"

She cried, and Aiken held her. Finally she raised her head and managed a weak, watery smile.

"I should be comforting you."

"Not necessary. But I'll tell you what you *can* do, if you like."

"What?"

"Come over in the morning about eleven and help me load the car. I sent both my trunks with the big stuff on to Deirdre's yesterday . . . you should have seen me. I had to tell Tuck it was four years worth of lab stuff Dean Randall begged me to get out of the Art building basement . . . so there are just some odds and ends. But an old pregnant lady isn't supposed to lift things in her second month. If you came at eleven, everybody would probably be out of the house."

"What will you tell the Pi Phis?"

"Nothing. They'll probably think I'm pregnant and had to leave school." She laughed again. "Do you mind? You'd have to cut Flournoy's class."

"Of course not. But, oh, Aiken . . . " The tears began again. "He'll miss you so much. Would you let me tell him? Just him and Kita? I'm sure they wouldn't tell Tuck if you didn't want them to. But they'd want to know."

Aiken considered, patting Maggie's shoulder absently. "Yes," she said slowly. "I think you can tell Ben and Kita. I really loved them, you know."

"I do know."

"Well, then. Come on, quit crying and let's get back. Christ, Maggie, I never knew you had such leaky waterworks. You're going to have to get over that before next June. I can't have you teaching my baby to be a crybaby. What kind of aunt do you think would do that?"

The next morning Maggie put on shorts and her raincoat and drove the Plymouth over to the Pi Beta Phi house. Aiken was right. It seemed deserted. They made several trips down the stairs from Aiken's room; her roommate was not in summer school, and

she had had the narrow rectangle to herself all summer. Except for a poster extolling the Moulin Rouge, starring Jane Avril, on the wall over one of the chaste little single beds, the room was bare. The beds were stripped down to mattress ticking; the door of an empty closet stood ajar; and Aiken's belongings were piled neatly into the center of one of the naked beds. The room reminded Maggie of Delia's room in the Kappa house, after they'd packed up her things and taken them to her parents in Montgomery. It did not bear thinking about.

"Well. Goodbye, old paint," Aiken said matter-of-factly when they stood in the doorway, their arms laden with the last remaining items. She held a portable drawing board and a short-stemmed T square, a forgotten pair of high-heeled sandals, and a conical pink straw hat bought in Daytona Beach the previous spring holidays. Maggie held folded plaid curtains, a goosenecked student lamp, and Aiken's shabby fan.

"Will you miss it?" Maggie said politely. Aiken had set the tone of the morning when Maggie had arrived, and Maggie refused to violate it.

"Not for a minute. It was hot as hell in the summer and the radiator banged all winter, and there was never enough closet space, and it had the oldest colony of roaches in Alabama. Georgine was always hiding food in here."

"Will you write Georgine?"

"Nope. She was always sneaking off on dates in my sweaters and trying to get in earlier than I did so

I wouldn't know. As if I couldn't smell Emeraude on them for the next eight weeks. Ugh."

They walked out of the room and didn't look back. Halfway down the stairs they met a Pi Phi in black harlequin glasses, drifting sleepily up from the kitchen in a candy-striped robe, carrying a plastic tumbler of orange juice.

"Where on earth are you going with that stuff, Aiken?" she said. "Hey, Maggie."

"Oh, my cousin in Connecticut is getting married, and I thought I'd clean out some of this junk as long as I had to go. I thought I told you all."

"Maybe you did. Well, have a good time and drive carefully. See you in a few days?"

"Sure. 'Bye, Mary Beth. Don't do anything I wouldn't do. Which leaves the field wide open."

The Pi Phi snorted, and they continued on down the stairs and out to Aiken's car. They encountered no one else. Aiken's housemother played bridge and had lunch with a group of housemothers at the faculty club each Monday.

"That will take care of that for a while," Aiken said. "By the time they figure out I've been gone too long for just a wedding, I'll be in New York, and Mother will tell Mrs. Suggs something socially acceptable when she calls to see where I am. Perfect."

They fitted the remaining things into the cramped back seat of the MG. The trunk was already so full it would not close, and they had tied it shut with heavy twine. The neatly rolled and tied sausage of Aiken's shaggy orange rug showed through the gap. Aiken dusted her hands on the seat of her raincoat, then took it off and threw it into the back seat and stood in the sunlight in shorts and shirt. Her long legs gleamed. She looked almost shockingly naked.

"I'll never wear that goddamned thing again as long as I live," she said with satisfaction. "Even if it pours for three years straight in New York, I'm not going to wear another raincoat."

She swung into the car and shut the door. She pulled outsized sunglasses from her purse and put them on, shielding her golden face into blankness. She lit a cigarette.

"'Bye for now, Maggie. I'll write you as soon as I get there. Will you write to me?"

"Of course I will."

"And I'll see you next June." It was not a question.

"I'll . . . write. I'll write to you and we can decide about that later." The muscles around Maggie's mouth were beginning to tremble, and her eyes to fill. She wanted Aiken to go, she wanted to be gone herself.

"Don't wait too long, Maggie."

"Drive carefully."

"I will." She turned the key and put the little car into gear. "Maggie?" she said.

"Yes."

"Thanks for the help this morning."

"You're welcome."

She stood still on the burning sidewalk, feeling sweat begin to trickle down her bare legs under her raincoat. Aiken sat still in the car. They did not look at each other.

"Time to get this show on the road," said Aiken, and she released the clutch and slid the MG out of the Pi Phi driveway into the quiet street. Maggie's hand went out, jerkily and involuntarily, but Aiken did not look back and see her there with her hand outstretched. The MG turned the corner and buzzed out of sight. Maggie stood listening to its cheerful, winding, cricket burr until it faded and was gone. Then she got into the Plymouth and drove back to the Kappa house. It was noon. It would be the first time that summer she had eaten lunch there.

17

Tuck called Maggie late in the afternoon of the same day.

"Where is Aiken?" He had not even said hello. His voice was flat and cold.

"Aiken?" It was thick stupidity on Maggie's part, not evasion. She had eaten lunch with the chattering Kappas in the dim, hot dining room, a perfunctory lunch of cold cuts and asparagus salad, and then had gone up to her room and turned on her fan and fallen into a dead, heavy, dreamless sleep. He had wakened her. For a moment she did not remember.

"She didn't meet me after her lab. She's not at the house. I called and somebody said she'd cleaned out her room and her car was gone. I want to know where the hell she is."

"Tuck, I ... don't know. She did say something about a cousin getting married sometime soon, but I didn't know when it was ... "

"She never told me anything about a cousin. She'd have told me. Didn't you see her in Flournoy's class this morning?"

"I didn't go. I had a history paper due and I had

to finish it. It was on Oliver Cromwell, and I couldn't find any research at the library, somebody else had had the book out for two weeks, so I just didn't . . . " Her voice fell into the telephone like a wounded bird. She knew she was talking too much.

"Oh, God!" It was a treble whimper. Maggie's heart smote her. She began to knot and unknot the curly telephone cord, to prowl at the end of it as the pain and enormity of Aiken seeped back over her.

"Tuck, really, I wouldn't worry. She's probably just . . . oh, gone off for a day or two to see somebody, or maybe it was the wedding, and you just forgot. You know how Aiken is . . . "

"I *do* know how Aiken is. I know better than anybody. She would never go away without telling me. I called her parents, but there was nobody there."

"I think they go to Long Island or New England or somewhere in the late summer," Maggie lied desperately.

"Martha's Vineyard. And not until late August. We were going up there between quarters. Maggie, if you know where she is, for God's sake, *tell* me! I can't stand . . . this is more than I can *stand!*"

"I don't *know,* Tuck! I don't know where she is. Maybe she got a sudden call that somebody at home was sick. . . . "

"She'd have called me, at least. She knows where I am, what classes I have. She wouldn't stop to clean out her room, pack all her clothes, if somebody was sick! She wouldn't drive to New Jersey! She'd get on the first plane."

"Maybe she just didn't want to worry you. She'll call you, Tuck, you'll . . . know where she is as soon as she gets a chance. I'm sure of that."

"Didn't want to worry me! I'm half out of my mind! Maggie, she . . . I love her, Maggie!"

Oh, don't, she moaned silently. Don't, don't, don't.

"She sent two trunks home Saturday," he said tensely. "I just remembered. I helped her. She must have been *planning* this. *Planning* it . . . "

"That was just lab stuff she'd had in the Art building basement. The dean was after her to get it out."

"How do you know that?"

"She told me he was, she said she was going to send it home as soon as she could get it packed up."

There was a long silence in which his breath tore at the air.

"I'm going over and talk to Ben," he said. He was about to cry. "Maybe she was in his class this morning. Or if she wasn't, maybe she called him and gave him . . . some reason. I know she didn't have any more cuts left. Oh, Christ, Maggie, if you hear from her . . . if she calls you . . . please . . . "

"I will, Tuck."

He hung up.

Maggie did not go down to supper that evening. She stayed in her room, listening to Ella Fitzgerald singing Cole Porter. She finished her history paper, blindly and mechanically, and typed it. It was a bad paper, she knew. When Boots called, she told him she had cramps and would see him the next day. She lay on her bed and read *A Passage to India,* which she had had in an English class the year before and had loved. Sister, whirling in to change her clothes before going to Columbus with her SAE for a pizza, was startled.

"What's the matter? Why aren't you with Boots?"

"Cramps."

"God, you just had them. Is anything wrong?"

"No, sometimes they just aren't so regular. It's the heat, I guess. I'm okay, Sister, I'm going to take one of my pills in a minute and go to bed."

"Well, do. You look awfully washed out. You have for a couple of weeks. Do you think you ought to go over to the infirmary in the morning?"

"Oh, lord, no. I've always thought Dr. Weiler was secretly only a veterinarian, not a real doctor. If I'm not back on schedule by next month, I'll see our doctor when I'm home between quarters. Don't *fuss,* Sister, it's just this damned heat. I don't think it's *ever* going to end."

"Well, I hope not. I love it. Fewer clothes to worry about." She grinned wickedly and disappeared into the bathroom and turned on the shower. In half an hour, she was gone.

At eleven, Tuck called her again.

"I finally got her housemother," he said. "She *did* tell somebody she was going to a wedding. Mrs. Suggs is really pissed; she said Aiken didn't tell her about it, and she doesn't have written permission from her parents. Mrs. Suggs had already called her parents, but she didn't get an answer, either."

"Maybe they're all at the wedding," Maggie said. "Doesn't her cousin live in Connecticut?"

"How the hell would I know? I didn't even know she *had* a goddamned cousin. Do you know where in Connecticut?"

"No, I'm sorry. But obviously that's where she is, Tuck. So don't worry. I'll bet she'll call you . . . soon."

"I don't believe she's gone to any wedding. There's something wrong. She just wouldn't leave without telling me. Ben was worried about her, too. Or rather, he thought it was strange."

"What did he say?"

"He said that it didn't seem characteristic of Aiken, but that one of her most sterling characteristics was that she refused to be characterized. He said that to do so would be like trying to parse a butterfly."

"Well, see? He's not really worried. He knows how . . . independent Aiken is. Why don't you just get some sleep now? She'll call you when she can. I . . . promise she will."

"Maggie, I think you know where she is."

"Honest to God, Tuck, I do *not* know where Aiken is." That's true, she thought, I don't. She's somewhere between here and New York, but I don't know how far she would have gotten by now. North Carolina?

Virginia? Maggie thought of Aiken sleeping alone in a white motel bed. Would she be lonely, afraid? No. I would, but I don't think Aiken is.

"If she told somebody she was going to a wedding, then I assume she went to a wedding."

"I'd better not ever find out you knew."

"Well, you won't, so I wish you'd stop *picking* on me. You sound like somebody's hysterical father." Guilt and dull, heavy sorrow made Maggie cross.

"I'm sorry, Maggie. It's just that Aiken is half my heart."

Maggie's throat and nose stung with tears.

"I know. I'm sorry, too. Don't worry, Tuck. Aiken is all right."

The next morning, in her poetry class, Flournoy cocked an avian eye at Maggie. "Miss Reed has apparently decided not to join us again today, I see," he said. "Perhaps Mr. Spender offends her. Or perhaps she has taken a leaf from his book and is traveling toward the sun, leaving the vivid air signed with her honour. What do you think, Miss Deloach?"

Maggie had planned to tell him about Aiken after class. Instead, she looked directly into his face and said, "I think she's gone to a wedding, Dr. Flournoy."

"Ah. A pity. I seem to recall that she has taken all her cuts. I should hate to penalize her for something so plebeian as an Upper Montclair mating rite."

Maggie did not tell him the next day, or the next. She felt, obscurely, that to do so would set some irreversible force in motion, would bring into being some actuality that, kept to herself, might stay ephemeral and abstract and distant. She spent an evening with Boots at the movie theater, watching a rerun of *Brigadoon,* and the next evening they went with a group of KAs and their dates to the lake, to cook hamburgers. They were not alone either evening, and she pleaded studying and he brought her home early both nights. The savage, sullen fire in him seemed banked, momentarily, and he was only amiably, loungingly possessive of her. Flournoy did not mention Aiken again during those two days.

On Friday, at the end of the class, he said, "Miss Deloach, have you a moment to spare? I'd like to see you in my office." The other students looked at Maggie. It seemed inconceivable that her grades were slipping, but you never knew with Maggie Deloach. Maggie kept her face carefully still, but her heart was pounding and the tide of red was flooding up from her chest to her throat, and her cheeks burned.

"Yes, sir," she said.

She walked down the hot, dusty corridor toward the wing of Semmes Hall where the faculty offices were. The floors of Semmes, being nearly a century old, were wide, bare, random boards; the nubbled plaster walls were painted a mourning green. Windows were small and high and arched, so that even on a blinding white noon Semmes was murky and dim, and gave the illusion of coolness. But perspiration beaded her upper lip and hairline, and her interior furnace ran high.

Ben Flournoy sat behind an elephantine, scarred roll-top desk that swam in a surf of papers and dwarfed the small, deep room. Books were everywhere. A jury-rigged shelf over the desk sagged under their weight; they spilled out of a metal bookcase under his window; they sat in drunken, listing piles on the floor and in his one visitor's chair. A photograph of Kita peered blindly out of the morass of papers on his desk, and one of her paintings, a cool, radiant white thing, threw luminous stipples of light into the venetian-blinded dimness. There was a hat rack that held a dusty, rubberized raincoat; a calendar from Mooney's Drugstore that was dated 1955; and a small black iron fan, droning sadly from the windowsill. He motioned her to sit down, then noticed the books piled on the chair.

"Just shove them off," he said. "I thought I'd put them away."

Maggie put the books carefully on the floor beside her, where they toppled over her feet. She sat down. She folded her hands and looked at Ben Flournoy. He looked back, not smiling but glittering.

"The Publications Board met Monday night," he said abruptly. "You knew that, of course." She nodded.

"That young chap from the student newspaper, Bevins . . . a good man, Maggie, incidentally, though I am sad to say I could never interest him in the essential importance of poetry . . . put an extremely interesting item before the board. He did so, I might say, with considerable passion."

He looked at her as if expecting some comment, but she made none. She had thought that he would ask her about Aiken. She had almost forgotten the column, and was momentarily disoriented.

Flournoy made a tent of his hands and considered it with keen interest. "It was quite a remarkable bit of writing, Maggie. I was astounded to find that you had written it. I knew, of course, that you have a . . . felicity for words. I did not know you had courage. It is a moving, open, honest piece of journalism, and I am pleased to tell you that it will appear in the *Senator*."

"It will?"

"Yes. Does this surprise you?"

"Yes, sir. Sort of. It does. Terry didn't think it would pass the board."

"Ah. May I ask why?"

"He thought it was . . . inflammatory. He thought it might get him and me into some trouble. With the faculty, even with the Board of Regents. He said it would sound as though I was advocating integration at Randolph. He thought there might be some sort of . . . outcry about it."

"Mm. Was he concerned for himself, do you think?"

"No, sir. I think he was concerned for me."

"You might be interested to know that Bevins made quite an impassioned plea for your column. He said, among other things, that a sane and eloquent young voice on this campus deserved to be heard no matter what we old fossils thought about what it was saying. He said that a newspaper was an open forum, and that as long as he was the editor of the Randolph *Senator,* such voices would be heard. He said that if we did not accept this column for publication, he was prepared to step down then. At that meeting. He was rather grand."

"Terry said that?"

"He did. We surprised ourselves by giving him a small round of absolutely spontaneous applause."

"But Dean Abernathy . . . "

"George owes me a favor from a long time ago. I have never chosen to allude to it. It seemed a propitious time to do so."

"I'm . . . very grateful to you, Dr. Flournoy."

"Are you, Maggie? I wonder if that gratitude will live beyond the publication of this article. I think you may be surprised at the . . . warmth of reception it is going to get. I wanted you to consider that very carefully now, while there is still time to withhold it. I do not think you will find it a very pleasant experience, Maggie."

"I know that. Terry and I have talked about it. But I really think you all are making too much of it, Dr. Flournoy. Hardly anybody reads the *Senator* in the summer. I never got any comment to speak of about that piece I did on Autherine Lucy. Besides, I wasn't advocating integration; I told Terry that. You only have to read the article to see that. This is a . . . *personal* piece."

"Yes, it is. Intensely so. But it speaks to larger

things, Maggie. Oh, no, you are wrong, this issue of the *Senator* will be read, summer or no. I do not think the reaction will harm you, essentially. It might be quite good for you. But I must know that you are aware that there will be one. I would like you to know, also"—he cleared his throat formally, his face was intent and drained of its customary harlequin piquancy—"that you have a not inconsiderable ally in me. I shall support you all the way in this matter, you have only to call on me. I feel responsible for this piece. Am I not right?"

"Well, yes, sir. I guess you are, for the fact that I wrote it; I mean, when you talked that night about empathy with the Negro, I realized that was really what I'd had in Mississippi . . . empathy. But you're certainly not responsible for *what* I wrote, or for my insisting that Terry run it if he could. That's *my* responsibility. I accept that, totally." Maggie felt exalted, strong, noble. After the guilt of lying to Tuck, the helpless pain of Aiken's leaving, it was a cleansing, scourging feeling. And his approbation warmed her.

"It's a very grave responsibility, Maggie." Flournoy was somber; was it hesitancy, doubt that looked at her out of the dark eyes? "For you and for me."

"I know it is."

"I wonder."

They were silent; he was not looking at her but into middle distance. She sat still for a moment, wondering if there was more, then decided there was not and gathered her purse and books and stood.

"I really do thank you for telling me, Dr. Flournoy. And for . . . sticking up for my column."

He looked back at her. "Maggie, where is Aiken Reed?" he said.

She paused, statue-still, staring back at him, and then she sat down again, and she told him. He was quiet while she talked; he swiveled his desk chair around so that he stared out between the tilted blinds onto the dust-scrimmed grove of trees on the main campus in front of Semmes Hall. He did not move, and he did not smoke. When she was finished, he sat in silence for a while, studying the slatted panorama in front of him. When he turned back to her, he was smiling.

"That is some lady," he said. "That is some lady, indeed."

"I hope you and Mrs. Flournoy won't worry about her. I wanted to tell you, and she wanted you to know, but she didn't want you to worry."

"I'm not worried about Aiken, Maggie. I'm worried about that fool Tucker; of course, he will be devastated. For a while. But I dare say he will get over it, as witness the miraculous recovery from that poor, dim-witted little Curry sparrow. It amuses Tucker to think that he is wise, impassioned, and called to higher than the likes of we"—he flickered evilly at her, to underscore the intentionality of the misuse—"but he is, in fact, exceedingly young and exceedingly malleable. He will wear this cloak of tragedy with great dignity and honor, and in due time, I think,

Aiken will allow him to know his child. By that time, he will, perhaps, be a fit father for Aiken Reed's child. No, I shall worry most about you."

"About me? There's nothing wrong with me. I miss her awfully, of course, but it's not like I'll never hear from her again. We'll write, I'll see her. . . . "

"She was fine ballast for you, Maggie. She would have been fine ballast for you through this storm that is gathering over your unknowing head. Don't frown at me; you really know not what you have done with your little article. Well, no matter. I shall be here, and Kita, and I pray that blond young Adonis of yours may find a shard of grace in his soul to support you. Though I doubt it. Will you really go to Aiken after you graduate, Maggie?"

"Oh, no, that was just talk. . . . "

"You should go, Maggie. You should leave this campus immediately upon receiving your diploma and drive straight there. Never once looking back. That would be a fine life for you, life and air. I don't think there is enough air in the South for you to breathe. And in her own way, Aiken needs you. I would be very happy to know that you were going to Aiken in New York."

He spoke with such intensity that Maggie stared at him.

"Well, I'll certainly think about it, Dr. Flournoy. But that's a long way off yet."

"Not so long as you may think," he said. And with a flutter of nicotine-stained fingers, he waved her off.

"Now begone and consider your singular destiny. I have work to do."

She paused in the doorway. "You won't tell Tuck?"

"No," he said. "Not if that's the way Aiken wants it."

When Maggie got back to the Kappa house, the upstairs phone was ringing. No one was about, so she picked it up.

"Kappa house."

"Is Maggie Deloach there?"

"This is she. Terry?"

"Oh, hi, Maggie. Didn't recognize your voice. Listen, I've just got a second, but I thought you'd like to know your column's going to run. Next Friday. Congratulations, good luck, and batten down for heavy seas."

"I know, Terry. Dr. Flournoy told me. I want to thank you. . . ."

"Shucks, 'tweren't nothing. Bye." He was gone.

Maggie went into her room and shucked off her damp clothes, leaving them in a heap on the floor. She walked naked into the bathroom and turned on the shower. She peered at herself in the mirror. Her tan was yellowing, definitely. There were circles under her eyes, giving her a frail, rapt, intense look.

"Margaret Hamilton Deloach, girl integrationist," she said to her face in the mirror. For the first time since Aiken had left, she laughed aloud.

18

THREE DAYS BEFORE the *Senator* with Maggie's column in it was to come out on campus, Boots's grandfather died in Leland, Mississippi. Boots called her at eight-thirty in the morning.

"I'll have to go home," he said petulantly. "The old bastard was crazy as a coot for five years; he didn't know me from Adam's housecat for two of them, and didn't like me when he did know me. But Mother's carrying on fit to kill, the old man said, and she'll have my hide if I'm not there for the funeral. She's got some idea he's left me some money."

"Did he, do you think?"

"Oh, hell, no. If there was any left he hadn't drunk up or pissed away, he probably left it to his nigger houseman. He'd gotten so he wouldn't let anybody but Roosevelt near him. Anyway, I'm going to leave about ten. I'll be back this weekend. There's a party at the house Saturday night I don't want to miss. It's probably the last one we'll have this summer. We're going to have a combo from Mobile."

"You won't be back by Friday, then?"

"I don't see how, sugar. The funeral won't be till

that morning. And I'll have to sit around with all the relatives talking about what a fine old fart he was. It's apt to get real drunk out. The old man always breaks out his thirty-year-old bonded stuff for funerals. I'll probably drive back Saturday and come straight by there and pick you up for the party. Wear something sexy."

"I wish you could get back Friday."

"What's so special about Friday?"

"Nothing, really. I guess I'll . . . just miss you." There's not going to be anybody here for me when the paper comes out, she thought, and realized she was a little afraid.

He was pleased. "Good. Absence makes the heart grow fonder, they say. Maybe it'll make the bod grow fonder, too. I'll see you Saturday, babe."

The Randolph *Senator* was put into metal boxes around the campus at noon on Fridays. When Maggie left her poetry class on that Friday, her breath was shallow and her heart was beating in her throat. I don't know what I think is going to happen, she thought. Riots on campus when I walk out of here? The National Guard rolling onto the campus in tanks? A firing squad? Flournoy caught her eye and held up two fingers in a V, Churchill-fashion, as she walked out of his classroom, but he did not speak to her. The campus was torpid and slow-moving in the heat when she walked out onto it. Students were drifting apathetically across it, slogging stolidly toward their lunches. Some carried copies of the *Senator,* to read over lunch, and some were reading as they walked, heads down. Many of them spoke to Maggie as she walked back toward the Kappa house, in the shy-cordial manner that they used for campus wheels, and the ones who knew her only waved or offered a thread of wilted banter, as they always did. At lunch, no one mentioned the column. Maggie was relieved, and obscurely disappointed.

After lunch, she did not drift over to the Student Union to see who was there, as she had every afternoon during the heat wave, even when Boots was occupied somewhere else. She went upstairs and washed her hair and began a manicure. She was nerved-up and restless. At two o'clock, M.A. Appleton and Jean Lochridge appeared in her doorway. They were carrying copies of the *Senator,* and they were not smiling.

"Can we talk to you for a minute, Maggie?" Jean said formally. On any other day they would simply have walked in.

She put down her Cutex Natural. "Come on in."

"I guess you know what this is about," said M.A., looking lugubrious. One last cigarette before the firing squad comes, my daughter, Maggie thought in fierce, defensive annoyance. If she says she'll pray for me, I'll spit in her eye.

"I guess I do, indeed, M.A.," she said.

"Maggie, how could you do a thing like this? Didn't it occur to you how this would make us look on campus? Every other sorority is going to just *love* it; they'll probably read it to every rushee that comes through fall rush. We'll be lucky if we get one dog legacy. And as far as pledge swaps go, not even the Zetas will come over here. I could understand if it was somebody like *Delia,* or . . . " M.A., realizing that writing a column would have been as alien to Delia as running for Congress, faltered for an instant, but regained momentum: ". . . somebody who just didn't know better, or was trying to attract attention, but you, Maggie! You are *president* of the *Women's Student Government Association!* What will *they* say? Oh, God, we'll *never* get Cornelia elected Homecoming Queen, and you *know* how bad we needed that! It's been three years since we had a Homecoming Queen. And I *promised* Dean Fisher there wouldn't be any trouble over here, I *promised* her we could run this house ourselves! Now we'll all have to move into dormitories!"

"Oh, *shit,* M.A.!" Maggie was very angry. "I haven't broken any rules! I wasn't even talking about anything but a personal experience I had! You act like I was seven months pregnant and got caught having a drunken orgy in the First Methodist Church! Why the hell should something *I* did reflect on this silly, stupid, precious sorority? None of you care a good goddamn about anything but what a bunch of stupid little . . . *college* boys think about you. You're all a bunch of snobbish, stupid *ostriches* with your heads in the sand. Don't you even *care* what happens to the

Negroes? I mean, after a *century* of being . . . being *oppressed,* they've finally got a chance to . . . "

"NO!" M.A. roared. "I *don't* care about the Negroes. I care about this sorority, I care about our reputation. We're the best sorority on this campus, we always get the best girls, we . . . Maggie, you took a sacred oath to be loyal to this sorority. Doesn't that mean anything to you?"

"You're some Religious Emphasis Week chairman, M.A. Do you think the Kappas are a little bit more equal than anybody else in God's sight? Maybe you think God was a Kappa."

"Maggie!" M.A. was appalled. Her nose twitched; her mouth made a pale, goldfish O.

"Well, you'll probably lose Boots's pin," said Jean Lochridge practically. "A hell of a lot of good that's going to do us."

"If Boots wants his pin back over this little . . . little piece of paper, then I don't want the damned pin," said Maggie. She was frightened at the passion of their disapproval, and honestly surprised, but most of all, deeply and coldly angry.

"We could have to lift your pin for this, Maggie," M.A. said sanctimoniously. "The state alumni chapter is going to have a fit."

"You can have it right now if you want it, M.A."

"I know who's behind this," Jean said. "Aiken Reed. She's trash, she's always been trash, I don't care how many things she's won on this campus. She's goaded you into this just to get at us, and then she's

gone off and left you ... she's a trashy *whore* who'd
rather make trouble than—"

"Get out of this room right now. Right this minute. Both of you, or I'll jerk your hair out." Maggie
was on her feet, her hands curved into claws. There
was a high singing in her ears. Her face must have
been terrible, because they scuttled backward out of
the room. She slammed the door behind them. For
a long time, she stood leaning against the desk, her
heart pounding so heavily in her throat that she could
scarcely breathe. Then she began to cry with sheer
fury and frustration. It helped. In half an hour she
was calm. Round one, she thought. Well, of course,
they'd take it worse than anybody. Silly shits. They
think everybody on this campus just sits around all
day with their breath held and binoculars trained on
the Kappa house. I wonder how Terry's making out
with the Phi Delts?

She started down the hall to call him. Or maybe
I'll call Dr. Flournoy, she thought. He said to, if
things got bad. But then she thought, What's so bad?
Go running to him because of Jean Lochridge and
M.A. Appleton? He said I had courage. Well, by God,
I *do*. Who are Jean Lochridge and M.A. Appleton to
tell me what to do?

So she turned and started back down the hall.
The telephone in the upstairs foyer shrilled. She kept
walking, waiting for Jean or M.A. or another Kappa
to answer it. But doors were shut, and the upstairs

was quiet. Maggie lifted her chin and marched to the telephone.

It was Tippy Sartain from the Dean of Women's office. Maggie liked Tippy, a small, shy, acerbic girl who worked as a secretary to the Dean of Women to help put her large, earnest Veterinary-Medicine-student husband through school. They joked together about the Girlie Gestapo whenever Maggie appeared at the Women's Administration Building for a WSGA meeting. Tippy always called Maggie the leader of the Underground Resistance. Her voice was not merry now. It was low, formal, embarrassed.

"Maggie? Dean Fisher wonders if you could drop over about five."

Maggie went cold and still. "What for, Tippy?"

"I don't know."

"Is it about my column?"

"Really, Maggie, I don't have any idea what it's about. 'Scuse me, my other line's ringing."

Maggie showered and dressed very carefully. She dressed as if she were going to church, in a navy sleeveless dress with a high white collar. She put on white, high-heeled sandals. Half consciously, she left off most of her eye makeup and used only a touch of pale pink lipstick. Then she looked at herself in the mirror and grinned, painfully. St. Margaret facing the lions, she thought. Maybe I should carry my prayer book. But her knees were trembling as she went down the stairs, and her mouth was dry. None of the closed doors opened as she passed them. There was no one downstairs. She got stiffly and carefully into the Plymouth and drove across campus to the Women's Administration Building.

Tippy had gone home when she reached the building, but when she peered into Dean Fisher's reception room, Maggie saw Terry Bevins, sitting alone in a tapestry wing chair. He was staring straight ahead. She walked across the thin-worn, muted Oriental toward him. He turned his head to her and gave her an exaggerated salute.

"*Morituri te salutamus.*"

"Do you think we're about to die?"

"Who knows? Dean Howard's here." Dean Howard was Randolph's Dean of Students. "He's been shut up with Dean Fisher for an hour. What the hell? Bring on the lions. Are you scared, Maggie?"

"No. Well, a little. I didn't think there'd be this much to-do about it."

"Didn't you? I did. Don't worry. You haven't broken any rules, and the Publications Board did pass it. We'll get a stern lecture and probably have to be very contrite, and that'll be the end of it. It was a good article, Maggie. You have nothing to apologize for. Though you might have to eat a little shit. Will you mind?"

"I don't know. I've never eaten any. But what about you, Terry? I feel *awful* about you. I know you did this just for me. . . . "

"Wrong, girl. I did it for me. I agreed with that

article down to the ground. And if you hadn't written it, I probably would never have gotten around to showing my colors. Don't grab all the glory, Maggie."

"Terry, I love you."

"It's my fabulous face," he said modestly. "Or possibly my Rock Hudson physique. I love you, too. Here we go."

The door that led off the reception room into Dean Fisher's private sitting room opened, and Dean Fisher stood in the doorway. She looked tired and, for the first time in Maggie's experience, as old as her years. "Please come in, Maggie, Terry," she said.

It was a painful but rather abstract meeting at the start. Dean Howard, who had a perpetual air of professional camaraderie, as befitted a Dean of Students, looked determinedly at Dean Fisher's pale, creamy Bokhara as he talked. He talked of responsibility, pride in Randolph, his years as a counselor to young people, his tolerance for and empathy with the young. High spirits and youth and vitality, he said, often led to excesses and errors of judgment that were forgivable, if not condonable. He did not mention the column as such, but he tapped his two-toned, air-vented shoes with a rolled copy of the *Senator*. Dean Fisher said nothing, but she studied Maggie thoughtfully. Maggie and Terry were silent while Dean Howard talked, looking attentively at him.

"This little piece of yours, Miss Deloach," he said, looking at her and alluding to it for the first time, "has some very fine sentiments in it. Very fine. I have great sympathy for our colored brothers myself. They have served us faithfully for many years, and there have been . . . inequities. I applaud your sensitivity to the . . . uh, problem. But this has, um . . . ramifications of which I am sure you are not aware. We at Randolph must, first and foremost, have the welfare of this university which we love . . . and which has given its resources to you most generously"—his look took in both Maggie and Terry— "deep in our hearts. We depend heavily upon the gracious offices of some very generous alumni and friends, the good gentlemen of the Board of Regents among them, for our continued well-being. Especially in . . . ah, sensitive times such as these, we must strive to avoid the appearance of . . . er, irresponsible radicalism. Our university was founded and continues to thrive upon sound, solid, conservative principles which must work for the most good for the most people."

Oh, get on with it, thought Maggie. She shot a look at Dean Fisher. She was tapping her shoe restlessly against the leg of her Queen Anne tea table.

"Excuse me, sir," said Terry deferentially. "Have there been any . . . comments from the Board of Regents, or any alumni?"

"No, no, no comments. So far." Dean Howard was impatient at the breaking of his pace. He had been rolling along rather magnificently, he thought. "And with one or two . . . small adjustments, I do not anticipate that there will be any. We can clear up this . . .

unfortunate misunderstanding, I think, with very little trouble. I am mainly concerned with impressing upon you two fine young people . . . and you are, of course, outstanding students and a credit to Randolph"—he smiled, a thin, shark's smile—"the folly of even the best-intentioned actions if they are not . . . um, considered in all their ramifications."

"What adjustments did you have in mind, sir?" Terry's tone was still deferential, still mild.

"Well, in view of Miss Deloach's really outstanding record here at Randolph, and her . . . years of contribution to the life of this campus, I think we can just write off this little incident as an excess of well-meaning high spirits and misplaced idealism, readily forgivable in one so young and gifted and charming"—the shark's teeth flashed at Maggie—"and simply print a little retraction over her name in next week's *Senator*. Now, that's not so bad, is it, Miss Deloach? Now that you are aware of this little . . . potential hornet's nest you have stirred up. Unwittingly, of course."

Maggie was silent, the room was still. The singing was back in her ears. A pane of glass dropped soundlessly and finally between Maggie and the room.

"I don't think I'm willing to do that, Dean Howard," she said. Her voice sounded far away in her own ears.

"Um. Well. I see." There was more silence, while Dean Howard tapped the newspaper against his shoe.

"We cannot, of course, force you to do that. The Publications Board, of course, did review your column before it went into print. Most irresponsibly, I might add. I cannot imagine . . . I have talked with Dr. Bennet Flournoy, who is one of your professors this quarter, I believe, Miss Deloach. He was . . . um, rather outspoken to me on the telephone. But I can understand a professor's . . . warmth, shall we say, for a star and favorite pupil."

You toad, Maggie thought, you slimy toad.

"But I really can't understand Dean Abernathy's decision on this matter. I have been unable to reach him, but . . . "

"I called his house earlier, Irwin, as you asked," Dean Fisher put in unemotionally. "He is . . . not feeling well and cannot be disturbed." There was a flicker of something—it could not possibly be contempt, could it?—in her voice. Just an undertone.

"I see. Well, as I was saying, we cannot force you to retract your sentiments if you do not wish to do so, Miss Deloach. But I must say that your value to the *Senator* must of necessity be . . . questionable, if you do not. I doubt that you would wish to . . . um, continue your association there in that event. You would not, I am sure, wish to harm it in any way."

"Are you asking me to resign, Dean Howard?"

"I'm sure you will see the wisdom of such a course, Miss Deloach."

"No, sir. I'm afraid I don't. And I'm afraid I have to tell you that I will not resign. Terry will have to fire me. Or the SGA Jurisprudence Committee will have to remove me. Since they don't reconvene until fall quarter, and since I haven't broken any rules, I'm not sure that they could do that, sir." Maggie was shaking with the enormity of talking to a dean that way. She was also thrilling with exhilaration like a fine-drawn wire. But distantly, behind glass. Both might have been happening to another person. Aiken was right, she thought dimly. There are other rules.

"In that case, Miss Deloach, I shall ask Mr. Bevins here to terminate your position with the *Senator* at once." He was angry. "It pains me to do so, but you leave me no choice. I will have no more of this ... this inflammatory *drivel* appearing on my campus."

Dean Fisher's eyebrows rose. "Your campus, Irwin?" she asked.

"*Our* campus, Elizabeth, as you must surely see. Bevins, you will see that this is done immediately."

"No."

"*No?*"

"No. *Sir.* Not a chance. Maggie may have written the article, but I'm the editor of the *Senator* and I'm the one responsible for getting it through the Publications Board. I think it's a great piece of writing, and I agree with every word of it, and I will not fire the best feature editor and the *only* one this paper has ever had who is thoughtful and compassionate and ... courageous."

"Then, young man, you will resign your post as editor as of this meeting!" Veins stood out on the concave temples, and a dull red flush crept up from the corded neck.

"No, sir. That's my paper. I won't resign. And since it is an elected position, I frankly think you'll have a hell of a time getting me out of it. Sir."

Howard started from his seat, but Dean Fisher raised a hand. A large, old-fashioned ring of rubies and diamonds flashed on it. She has beautiful hands, Maggie thought irrelevantly. They're like Aiken's. "Wait a minute, Irwin," she said. "I asked you all to come here because, as a woman student, Maggie is under my ultimate jurisdiction. This meeting has gotten out of hand. Maggie"—she turned to Maggie. "You are being exceedingly obstinate, but you are correct when you say you have broken no rules. Irwin, I'm afraid I do think you are, perhaps, over-reacting. Perhaps we can solve this in a manner more acceptable to everyone. Maggie and Terry have virtually unblemished records at Randolph, and I should hate to see unduly severe penalties imposed upon them. What if, Maggie, Terry"—she looked from one to the other almost imploringly—"what if the *Senator* ran just a small line at the bottom of Maggie's next column saying that the *Senator* does not stand sponsor for the opinions of its editorial writers? That way . . ."

"*No!*" It was very nearly a scream from Howard. "I'll have no *more* of this business, Elizabeth! It isn't *you* the president of this university holds responsible for student malarkey, it isn't you every newspaper in the state will call up, it isn't you the Board of Regents will castrate like a . . . "

"*Irwin!*" Elizabeth Fisher's voice cut like an iced lash through his.

"I'm sorry." He rubbed his hand across his narrow face.

"Dean Fisher, I'm afraid I can't accept that, either," Terry said. "That amounts to just leaving Maggie out there by herself, with no support at all, and I *do* support her. All the way. I wish I'd written it myself."

A tired specter of a smile played over Elizabeth Fisher's mouth and was gone, immediately. "What on earth are we to do with you two?" she said.

"There's plenty we can do with them," Irwin Howard said. His voice was under control, but only barely. "This university will not tolerate . . . *anarchy* from its students. I intend to go straight to President Vaughan from this meeting, and you will no longer be editor of this unfortunate newspaper in the morning, Bevins, unless I miss my guess. There are steps that can be taken, some of them quite extreme, and I will not hesitate to take them. You will *not* defy the authorities of this school. I should hate to see you face expulsion, but it has happened before, and can happen again, I kid you not."

"You have no grounds to expel me on!" Terry was on his feet. He was visibly angry for the first time.

"They can be found."

"Irwin, this is nonsense, worse that that! I cannot countenance such statements!" Dean Fisher was angry, too. What a lot of angry people there are in this room, Maggie thought mildly, and then the glass shield snapped. I can't bear this, this is terrible, what is happening? she thought wildly.

"Stop, please *stop!*" Her voice was liquid and tremulous with tears. "I'm sorry, I didn't . . . I resign! I do, Terry! I resign!"

"Maggie, I don't accept your resignation."

"You can't stop me. I won't come into the office any more. I won't turn in my column. You can't stop me."

There was a long, heavy, dull silence, into which the ridiculous, chiming little notes of Dean Fisher's mantel clock dripped like droplets into a pool. One, two, three, four, five, six. Breathing was audible.

"In that case, so do I."

"Oh, no . . . "

"Shut up, Maggie."

There was more silence, and then Dean Howard said, "I regret that this unpleasantness had to happen. How much simpler just to have printed a little retraction. However, we must now put it behind us and get on to more productive matters. Both you young people"—and, insanely, the camaraderie was back—"have more than your share of campus offices and honors. 'The old order passeth,' eh? Forgive me, Elizabeth, but I have things I have to see to . . . a dean's work is never done. . . . " And he scurried out of the sitting room.

Dean Fisher walked with them to her door, in silence. At it, she said, almost wistfully, "A college campus is an ideal place to dispel the cherished old myth that being young is an idyllic state. It keeps me from foolishly lamenting my vanished girlhood. It's really rather dreadful, isn't it, to be young?"

They looked at her in surprise. Deans did not say such things to students. She was not looking at them but out her doorway and, perhaps, far into her own self. But then she did look at Maggie. And incredibly, unbelievably, she winked. And shut her door.

They stood on the steps of the Women's Administration Building in the long twilight, scooped and hollowed. "Want some coffee?" Terry said.

"I don't think so, thanks. Terry, you musn't resign. I couldn't stand it. I couldn't live with that. Please reconsider. I don't really think there's anything he could do to you. . . . "

"It's not that, Maggie. Though that oily bastard could find a way, if he wanted to. It's just that I don't want to be editor any more."

"You love that paper, it's practically your *life!*"

"Do you know the Bible, Maggie?"

"Yes. Pretty well. Why?"

"Remember, 'What doth it profit a man to gain the world if he loseth his soul?' Go on back to the Kappa house and go to bed. You must be beat. So am I. But I think that was the worst of it. There'll be a little flap over our leaving the *Senator,* but in two weeks the whole thing will have died down. Hell, it's summer. The Board of Regents and the alums will have had their pound of flesh, and life will go on. I forget just why."

"Edna St. Vincent Millay."

"Right you are. Go on, now." He kissed her on her forehead and lumbered down the shallow steps toward his car, parked on the semicircular drive. She started for her own. His voice stopped her as she opened the door of the Plymouth.

"Maggie?"

"What?"

"You know what I'd like to do to that bastard?"

"What?"

"Feed him a plaster-of-Paris milk shake."

She began to laugh, and the laughter spiraled, up and up, and it shook her so that it was several minutes before she could start her car.

19

No one mentioned the column to Maggie at dinner that evening. At the far end of the table, M.A. and Jean Lochridge were elaborately involved in a conversation about the procurement of a new housemother. It did not look as though Mrs. Kidd would be well enough to return for the fall quarter, and the Dothan niece had said accusingly on the telephone that the family thought something a bit less demanding would be in her best interests when she left the sanatorium; perhaps being a Gray Lady at a Montgomery hospital. None of the Kappas at summer school seemed anxious to volunteer a family member, or perhaps there were none quite suitable for the post. But, M.A. said, Dean Fisher kept a file of applicants, and they could look over that before the quarter ended. "We'll all be more comfortable with a housemother," she said sweetly, looking obliquely to the left of Maggie under her stubbled white lashes. "Things tend to get a little lax when we're on our own."

Maggie said nothing.

No one mentioned it during the long evening either, except Sister, who dashed in briefly to change into Bermuda shorts. Maggie was deep into *The Age of Innocence,* feeling a bittersweet kinship with the outcast Ellen Olenska and eating peanut-butter crackers. Clouds had massed in from the west while she was in the dean's sitting room, thick and vicious and garishly backlit with the setting sun, but there had been no rain, only sullen flickers of far-off heat lightning. Sister was going with Gary to Columbus to ice skate. "Coolest thing we could think of to do," she said, pulling a T-shirt over her head.

"What on earth got into you to do that piece on the nigras?" she said from depths of pale pink cotton, her arms waving wildly out of the T-shirt's armholes. Her voice was muffled, but unheated. Sister saved her passion for more basic, immediate issues. "Half the house is in M.A.'s room with the door shut, gabbling about it. I hear you had to go see Dean Fisher."

Maggie was endlessly tired, enervated by the heat and the day. The meeting in Dean Fisher's sitting room did not seem as real as the world of Edith Wharton.

"That's right," she said listlessly. "But she was nice about it. It was Dean Howard who was upset. Old fart. You know, I never realized it, but I think he hates students."

Sister's head emerged from the neck of the T-shirt. She looked at Maggie.

"Dean Howard! God, it really did hit the fan, didn't it? What are they going to do to you?"

"Nothing, Sister. I haven't broken any rules. But Terry and I both are resigning from the *Senator*. And *not* because anybody made us do it, either, you might be sure to tell M.A. and that bunch. I'm sure it will make them very happy, though. Fitting retribution."

"Oh, Maggie. What a shame. Well, at least you weren't fired; it won't look all that bad if you just resign. But you know everybody will think you *had* to."

"I don't care what everybody thinks, as long as that... bunch of harpies down there gets off my back. I'm tired of the whole thing."

"They *are* pains in the ass, aren't they? Want me to stop by and tell them you've resigned? Maybe they'll let up on you if I do. Or you can, if you'd rather."

"I don't care. No, I guess it would be good if you would, Sister. I don't feel like talking to any of them any more tonight."

"Well, I will. Wonder what Boots is going to say?"

"I have no idea."

"Nothing, probably. Gary said most of the SAEs thought it was funny. Just one or two of them were kind of... grumbling about it."

"Funny!"

"Well, you know how it is in the summer. Nobody takes anything seriously. Mike Scoville said it was the best thing that had happened all summer; he said he'd give a million dollars to be a fly on the wall over at the KA house when they read it."

"Why should the KAs care particularly?"

"Well, you're one of theirs, or Boots is, and they've got this thing about dear old Robert E. Lee being their spiritual founder and all. You know that, Maggie. Maybe you better lay low for a while."

"I'm going over there for a party tomorrow night with Boots. I'm not scared of the KAs, Sister. They're my friends. Besides, I should think my resigning would calm everybody down. Isn't it just what a lady should do if she's caused a commotion? Bow out gracefully and smooth things over?"

"You *are* mad, aren't you?"

"No. But I'm tired. I think I'll go to bed early. See you in the morning, Sister."

The news of her resignation had, apparently, defused the situation. The other girls were exaggeratedly solicitous of her in the morning, smiling and indulgent as if she had just come back from a long illness. No one mentioned the incident until late morning, as Maggie was preparing to go to the dry cleaners. M.A., returning laden with Toni home-permanent supplies from Mooney's, met her in the parking lot. The day hung gray and motionless and heavy around them. It still had not rained.

"I just wanted to tell you that we're proud of you, Maggie," she said, blinking tremulously. She would have hugged Maggie if her arms had not been full. "We think you did the honorable thing. Jean and I are ready to just forget everything that was said yesterday. I think we all lost our tempers. We know you didn't mean what you said. You proved that when you resigned. I know it must have been hard for you, but it was the right thing to do. I don't think it's going to hurt the chapter much at all, this way."

Maggie stared after her square, retreating back. She opened her mouth to call after her, then closed it again. It did not seem to matter very much if they misunderstood her motive for resigning. Let it go. People who mattered would understand . . . Flournoy would, certainly. But the thought niggled that perhaps he might not, after all. And Boots? He couldn't care less what I write, she thought. He thinks my writing is . . . cute. But her stomach knotted again, faintly, so that she didn't want any lunch. Five hours till he picked her up for the party at the KA house. I'll wear that yellow dress he likes, she thought, the one I had on that night . . . no, I won't either. I'll wear the white one. And I'll tell him about the whole thing when he first gets here, so we can laugh about it and he won't walk into it cold at the house. I can always make him laugh when I put my mind to it.

She drove from the dry cleaners to Mooney's and picked out a new tube of coral lipstick and a bottle of Blue Grass cologne and some bubble bath.

He was drunk when he picked her up that evening, or near it. He had been drinking beer since early afternoon, he said. The heat on the Delta had been murderous, and the drive home had not been any better. He was crumpled and wind-burned; his shirt was stained dark with perspiration and beer. Maggie had never seen him so disheveled. When she had pattered down the stairs, scented and carefully made up and thrumming with nerves, she had found him slumped bonelessly into a corner of a burgundy velvet love seat, flicking ashes onto the rug. Discontent and discomfort dragged his long mouth down at the corners, and there was something honed and dangerous flickering in his green eyes. His dark-golden face and arms were welted with mosquito bites. She could smell the sweet-stale gusts of beer on his breath.

"Bad drive?" she asked when he had hugged her perfunctorily. His arm stuck to her bare shoulders.

"Oh, Christ! It gets longer every time I drive it. And a goddamn highway patrolman followed me all the way in from Wetumpka. I had to crawl, practically. Jesus, it's as hot here as it was in Mississippi. Come on. I want to get over to the house and under a cold shower as fast as I can. If it wasn't for that combo, I swear to God we'd skip this party and just go out to the lake or something."

"I'm sort of looking forward to it," Maggie said. And she realized that she was, looking forward to getting this formal confrontation over, to getting back to that sweet, suspended place in the summer before she had written the column, gone with him to Greenville. Or at least, once the penalties were paid, perhaps this unknowable new sea she was drifting in could be charted. At least that. Obscurely, Maggie knew she could not get back to the before time again.

She knew that his mood was too dark and pre-
carious for just the heat. The funeral, perhaps. She
touched him tentatively on the arm. "Was it bad,
the funeral? I'd like to hear about it, if you want to
tell me."

The skin of his arm wimpled, as an animal's might
when a stinging insect lit on it. She removed her
hand.

"It was just a funeral. It's not like everybody didn't
know the old man was dying for months. Aside from
having to listen to about forty thousand goddamned
relatives I never see till somebody dies, it wasn't so
bad."

"Well, then, what's the matter? Were your folks
really upset?"

He slammed the door of the Jaguar on her side
and stepped over the closed door of the driver's side
into the seat. The top was down. He clashed the automobile viciously into gear.

"Yeah, hell, they were upset all right. Only not
about Granddaddy. Cleveland quit, if you have to
know. And the cook and four of the hands. I thought
the old man was going to bust an artery. I never saw
him so mad. I thought for a minute he was going to
cut me off without a penny."

"You! Why you? Surely they can find another . . .
butler and a cook and some field help? I mean,
I know Cleveland's been there for a long time,
but . . ."

"He quit right after that spell the old man had on

292   Anne Rivers Siddons

the patio when we were over there. And the cook and
the hands left right after he did. They all said they
had folks sick at home, but, hell, Cleveland's got no
folks, he's lived in for ten years, at least. The cook too.
The old man says it's because you got him so worked
up over what Cunningham said that he lost his tem-
per and chewed out Cleveland. And he's blaming *me*
for that!"

"Oh, Boots, no . . . "

"Ah, shit, Maggie, he's just worked up right now.
Taking it out on me. The old man doesn't like to lose
his niggers, and he knows he made a jackass out of
himself. But I wish to Christ you hadn't said that. It'll
take him the rest of the summer to calm down."

You said he liked women with spunk, she said to
herself, but not aloud. She was chilled suddenly, and
frightened in a way she had not been since childhood, when she walked home in the dark after a
Frankenstein movie at the Lytton movie theater and
had to pass through the damp, icy black spot under
the railroad overpass. Something large and unknowable crouched just out of her range.

"Maybe you'd rather not go to the party," she said
in a small voice. "I'd really just as soon go to a movie.
Or out to the lake or something." It was not the time
to tell him about the column, but they were driving
straight toward a confrontation with it.

"Naw. I need a drink and I want to have some fun.
I'm sick as a dog of hearing about niggers."

Oh, God, please don't let anybody mention that column till I can talk to him about it, she prayed. I can fix it in the morning, but please let things just be okay tonight. They drove the rest of the way in silence.

The KA house glimmered and throbbed with the party. Couples stood talking on the pillared portico, drifted on the front lawn with paper cups in their hands, disappeared into the open front door to the drawing room, where, Maggie knew, Mrs. McClesky would be greeting the brothers' dates. The main body of the party had already moved to the back patio and lawn, where the sweating tubs would have been twice replenished. Maggie could hear the combo's percussion through the shrouding Cape jessamine bushes, and laughter. The Japanese lanterns made luminous pools in the trees, carving their leaves into bas-relief in the deepening dusk that came more from the swelling clouds than the setting sun. The air swam against her face. She could feel her heart crashing in her throat and at her temples; she was light-headed with it.

Kip Rossiter, Boots's roommate, and his date were the first people they encountered, on the portico steps. Kip was with Gail French, a small, dark Tri Delt on the cheerleading squad. Frenchy was effervescent and talkative; Maggie had had classes with her and liked her. "Hi, Frenchy," she said. Her throat stuck, and she cleared it. "Hi, Kippie."

"Hey, Maggie," they mumbled in unison. Kip did not look at her, and Frenchy was rummaging absorbedly in her purse for a cigarette.

"Hey, buddy," Kip said to Boots. "You look like ten miles of bad road. How were things at home?"

"So-so. Listen, Kip, y'all take Maggie back and get her a snort of something, will you? I've got to get a shower and change. I'll be right down."

Kip's face flushed dark. He kept it still and made a stagy business of lighting Frenchy's cigarette. "I promised Snake I'd make a run to Opelika," he said. "The goddamn combo drank up the gin before the party got started even. Maybe French . . . "

"I'll come with you. I need some cigarettes." Frenchy hastily closed her purse and gave them both a brilliant smile. "Back in two shakes, y'all," she said. They melted away through the shrubbery toward the parking lot.

"Well . . . Jesus," Boots said, looking after them. "I must really need a shower. Go on back, Maggie, you don't need anybody to go with you, do you? Gleason will look after you till I get down, or Sykes. I see him and Cecy around on the side of the house."

"I'll just go say hello to Mother Mac," Maggie said. Her face was stiff and her ears rang. They were not going to be easy on her. But perhaps they wouldn't actually mention the column to him, surely not, with her right there. And there was probably no one upstairs, in the living quarters, to tell him; everybody would be downstairs by now. He vanished up the central staircase, and she took a deep breath and walked into the drawing room.

Mrs. McClesky stood in front of the fireplace, filled now for the summer with her Boston ferns. Three people stood with her; Maggie recognized Dabney Gleason, the new president-elect of the student body, and Sue Ellen Singer. Her heart sank. Sue Ellen, the pretty one, the startling beauty whose place in this house and at the Round Table in the Student Union was assured by her face, but who had sought and earned no campus honors. She did not need them and thought the girls who had them, like Maggie, were priggish and officious. She looked, with her incandescent pallor and smooth wings of blond hair, like a medieval saint. She had been before the WSGA to be brought to justice for this or that infraction three times while Maggie had been on the judiciary committee. She had dated Boots, though sporadically, before he met Maggie, and was sure that the penalties for her misdemeanors, which she considered excessively punitive, had been the covert work of Maggie. They had not, but the only thinly gauzed animosity struck an answering chord in Maggie, and antagonism crackled whenever the two girls met. Maggie met her slow smile and knew the face of the enemy. The third figure, a male one, had his back to Maggie.

"Hello, Maggie. Where's the boy?" Gleason said, and Sue Ellen smirked silkily, and the figure turned. It was Hoyt Cunningham.

"Come here and meet an old friend of Boots's from home," Gleason said, his gnome's face wearing its perpetual look of knowing. She could not tell if he had read the column or was only being Dabney. "He just got in, looking for a bed for the night. I told him any friend of Boots's was welcome to one, if he could find one that didn't have a drunk passed out in it. This is Maggie Deloach. Hoyt Cunningham, from Greenville, Mississippi. This is Boots's girl, Hoyt."

Maggie stared. She was being rude, she knew, but she was not functioning well. That he should be here in this hostile house was as unimaginable as her mother or father standing before her.

"Well, Maggie, we meet again," he said, grinning at her under the white-ringed eyes. He looked very tan and rumpled, squarer than she remembered, and older. She noticed, sharply, the dark hairs on the backs of his hands, and the dusky mat of hair through his white shirt. He was smoking, with the peculiar, still, intense look that she remembered. His eyes in the dim room were very blue.

"Hey, Hoyt," she said primly. "What on earth are you doing here?"

"I told you I'd drop in on Boots the next time I was in the neighborhood," he said. "I'm on my way over to Montgomery for a couple of weeks, and I thought, well, since it's late and I'm here anyway, I'll go see what this famous KA hospitality is all about."

"And we're delighted," put in Mrs. McClesky gamely. "This is an interesting young man, Maggie.

And he has far better manners than *my* boys. He'll be a good influence, I'm sure."

"I'm sure," Maggie parroted idiotically.

"You all have met, I take it?" Sue Ellen's drawl was tossed silver money in the crackling air. Maggie knew viscerally that Sue Ellen had read the column and would mention it, though not, perhaps, just yet. She would pick her time well.

"Yes," said Maggie and Hoyt together. They looked at each other, and laughed, Maggie stiltedly, he lazily.

"Maggie and I had occasion to share a cup of coffee one evening when I was through here, back at the beginning of the summer," he said. "My old buddy Boots has good taste."

"Surely does," Gleason said. "Maggie keeps things lively around here, doesn't she, Sue Ellen?"

"Doesn't she though? She's quite a writer, Hoyt. Did you know that? Keeps us all on our toes, minding our p's and q's."

He sensed the currents and looked around the circle, sniffing for the source of the subterranean turbulence. He looked at Maggie.

"I heard she was," he said.

"Oh, you'll hear a lot more about Maggie, just you wait," Sue Ellen purred. There was a shimmering silence.

Mrs. McClesky looked from one to another of them, and then said, "If you young people will excuse me, I've got to go check in the kitchen. I de-

clare, with this heat . . . " and she fled through a pair
of swinging doors off the dining room, beyond the
drawing room.

"Well, it's yardarm time," said Dabney Gleason.
"Where *is* Boots, Maggie? Cunningham here ought to
meet some of the guys."

"He's upstairs taking a shower. He'll be down in a
little while."

"Well, in that case, y'all come on out on the patio.
There's brew on draft, but the house specialty is really ripe tonight. I'll get you started around, Hoyt,
and Maggie can take over from there. Maggie's practically our mascot. Everybody's anxious to see you,
Maggie. It's been a while, and you've been a busy lady,
haven't you?"

"*Real* busy. Maggie's been neglecting her friends
for her extracurricular activities." Sue Ellen dimpled.
She took Gleason's arm and floated at his side out the
french doors onto the patio, a poisonous butterfly.

Hoyt studied Maggie for a moment. "You're looking well, ma'am," he said. "As befits a Kappa Alpha
mascot. What's going on with those two? Have you
been indiscreet with a carpetbagger or something?"

"Oh, Sue Ellen's just being her usual charming
self. Nothing's going on. Boots will be glad to see you,
Hoyt. What will you be doing in Montgomery?"

"I'm not sure. There's a rumor that two Negroes
will be enrolling at the Montgomery branch of the
University this fall. We hear things are pretty tense
over there, what with the boycott and all. But nobody

can quite pin things down yet. I'm just going to smell around a little. It ought to be pretty interesting, if it's true."

"I'm getting awfully tired of the Negroes," Maggie flared. A premonitory ripple chased delicately down her spine, like the barely perceptible ruffle a fissure on the ocean's floor might make on its surface. "Every time I turn around this summer, there's another Negro staring me in the face. All of a sudden they're coming out of the woodwork."

"The woodpile, I think you mean," he said. "Can this be the girl who single-handedly took on Courtney Claiborne, the Greenville police force, and the folkways and mores of the sovereign state of Mississippi?"

"How in hell did you know about that?"

"I keep in touch with home," he said briefly. "Well, come on, Maggie. The wayfarer is thirsty. Shall we join your friends for a little libation? Though with friends like that, you sure as hell don't need enemies."

He held out his arm and she laid her fingers on it, lightly. It was warm and rough-skinned and solid. They walked out onto the patio.

Full dark had fallen. The patio was a shifting, sliding, amoebic mass of color and motion and music. The imported combo, transported and pouring sweat, ground out shrieking sound. A tall young man, his head thrown wolfishly up to the sky, howled: "Aw, let it rollllll . . . like a big wheeeeel . . . in a Georgia cotton field!" "Honey, *hush!*" roared the crowd. They picked their way through the writhing fringe of the dancers to one of the tubs. Hoyt ladled them both Dixie Cups of the bobbling mixture and took a long swallow. "God," he choked. "What *is* that stuff?"

"Gin. Grapefruit juice. Vodka. Whatever anybody happens to have around. It gets more exotic as it goes along," Maggie said. She swallowed hers down. "It's better than usual tonight. Get me another, will you, while you can still get to the tub?"

"Are you supposed to be drinking out in public like this? I thought it was against the rules."

Maggie giggled. The punch had hit her hard on her empty stomach. "I helped *make* the rules, didn't you know? Besides, all rules are off."

He squinted whitely at her.

"Are they, Maggie?"

"Yes." She drank down half of her new drink.

The song ended and the combo sat down, mopping sweat from their blinded faces. Someone moved to the portable record player and dropped a record onto it. The quieter, lugubrious chords of Les Baxter's "Unchained Melody" spun out into the night. Some couples slid into slow movement, pasted solemnly together, but most of them moved toward the punch tubs, wiping their faces and holding sodden clothes away from their bodies, and fanning. In a moment, Maggie and Hoyt were swallowed in a jostling sea of steaming bodies.

Not many of them acknowledged Maggie. A few

did, nodding formally to her and giving Hoyt brief, sliding looks of assessment. Maggie stood leaning against the gritty red bricks of the house, sipping steadily, rocking dreamily and watching them. The punch was fiery warm inside her and gave a fine, knife-edged distance to the night. She felt gay, rapt, exhilarated, beyond defiance. She had two more cups of the punch. To those whose eyes she caught, she said clearly and roundly, "This is Hoyt Cunningham, a friend of Boots's and mine from Greenville. Hoyt will be spending the night with you all." And, "Hello, Cunningham"; "Nice to meet you, Cunningham"; "Get you anything, Cunningham? Drink or something?" they all said. And then were busy with their Dixie Cups, their girls, their conversations, or were gone into the crowd. "Hey, Maggie, how've you been?" said their girls. And were gone, too.

Hoyt did not leave Maggie's side. He drank steadily, too, though it did not appear to affect him.

"I feel like a pimp in church," he said, but there was more of amusement and assessment than concern in his voice. He looked very large and dark and massive in Maggie's flaring vision; he seemed to swell and surge and grow. She moved closer to him, leaned against his shoulder. It was hard and did not shift; it gave off warmth against her own. He looked down at her. He isn't as short as I remembered, she thought.

"What about it, Miss Maggie? Has my deodorant failed me?"

"Not Maggie," she giggled, leaning harder. "Mary.

Miss Typhoid Mary. Sweetheart of the . . . the Shquad-
ron. Oh, my. Listen to me. I can't talk."

"What *is* going on around here, Maggie? Listen,
you better lay off that stuff for a while. I don't want
old Boots to think I'm down here getting his girl
drunk. What's everybody pissed off at you about?"

"A prophet is not without honor save in his own
fraternity. *Her* own fraternity, I mean. That can't be
right, can it? Girls don't have fraternities. That's sororities." Maggie chortled. "Only I have managed to
be without honor in my sorority *and* my fraternity.
Now that's got to be a record."

He started to say something else to her, but Boots
was there, suddenly, at her elbow. He was in clean
chinos and a blue oxford cloth shirt, and there were
still the dark stripes of comb marks in his damp hair.
He smelled of soap and Bourbon, new Bourbon, not
stale. It was the smell more than his sudden presence,
which was slightly unreal to Maggie, like an image
on a movie screen, that cut through her own warm
muzziness. He's been drinking upstairs, she thought
clearly, and the wrap of high, distant hilarity fell away
from her.

"Hey, where've you been?" she said. "You've got a
visitor."

"Yeah, Findley said I did," he said, swaying very
slightly. "Hey, Cunningham. I see Maggie's already
fixed you up with a drink. You looking for a bed for
one, or two?" His voice was too soft, and his eyes were
slitted. Has he read the column? Maggie thought. No,

it's not that kind of mad. It's Hoyt. He's heard too much about Hoyt this summer. Hoyt's been right in the middle of everything that's made him mad. Oh, God, what rotten, awful timing. If only he'll pass out before he gets really mean. Before any of these nerds drag up that column. Before Sue Ellen does.

Brightly, she said, "Hoyt's on his way to Montgomery, Boots, to cover a story"—stay away from that, said a crystal voice in her head—"and he stopped by because he's heard so much about the KAs' old-fashioned southern hospitality." Be nice, her eyes beseeched Boots. Be good to me, just for this night. He was not looking at her.

"Well, Maggie here can show you plenty of that," he said. "She's a great fan of yours, Cunningham, did you know that? Talks about you all the time. All over the place. Glad you two got together." He lurched unsteadily toward the tub of punch and dipped a paper cup into it.

"I'm flattered." Hoyt's voice was neutral, but the ring of white around his pupils widened fractionally, and Maggie felt the muscles of his shoulder tense. She moved away hastily. She hadn't realized she was still leaning on him.

"You should be. Maggie's prime goods." Boots tilted his head far back and drained his cup. Droplets of murky purple flowered on his blue shirt.

Couples had begun to move up toward them when Boots had appeared on the patio. They were talking and laughing among themselves as before, but their eyes edged to the three people standing by the punch vat, fell away, edged back. The softer music of the record player still swam behind them, but only a few couples danced. Cigarettes bloomed in the semi-dark. They're like wolves gathered, Maggie thought in sudden panic. Quietly, so you don't notice it till they're there. Hoyt noticed it, too, she could tell, but Boots had not, yet.

The punch seemed to lull him momentarily, and she saw his face gather and clear with the effort to be civil.

"What are you going to Montgomery for, Cunningham?" he said. No, Hoyt, Maggie said under her breath.

"There may be a story about a couple of Negro students enrolling at the University branch over there," Hoyt said. He was being carefully, offhandedly professional. "Not till September, but the bureau thought I might as well go check it out now. Could be some trouble."

"Oh, hell, yes, if there's a way to have some nigger trouble, there'll be nigger trouble," Boots said thickly. "Sick of nigger talk. Just drove three hundred miles to get away from nigger talk. This may be the only place in the goddamn South there *ain't* any nigger talk. Come on, Maggie. I want to dance. Go 'round an' introduce yourself, Cunningham; maybe somebody else'll let you birddog their date for a while." He gestured vaguely at the semicircle of KAs and their dates, and fastened his hand around Maggie's wrist.

"Why, Boots, Randolph is the nigger-talk capital of the *world* now, hadn't you heard? Ask Maggie. She's made us *famous.*" It was Sue Ellen's voice. The silver coins fell into silence at Boots's feet. The inside of Maggie's head went blank and still; the high singing began. There were small intakes of breath, not even sighs. Dabney and Sue Ellen stood at the front and in the middle of the semicircle. Maggie saw Dabney's head bend quickly to Sue Ellen's, saw his lips move and his brows draw together in anger. Sue Ellen jerked away from him and smiled radiantly at Boots.

Boots frowned slightly. "What are you talking about, Sue Ellen?" he said. He looked at Maggie. She looked back, blindly and incandescently.

A soft babble of voices broke then. Someone put on an upbeat record. "Hey, let's light a fire under that combo," somebody said. Kippie. Maggie did not move.

"No, wait a minute." Boots's voice rose above the swelling and shuffling. "What do you mean, Sue Ellen?"

"Oh, nothing." Sue Ellen's voice was still silver, but wavering slightly. Boots's eyes had a supernormally focused look. She dropped her own. "I guess you haven't read it yet. Come on, Dab. Let's dance, for goodness sake, all this standing around . . . "

"Sue Ellen." It was quiet, sibilant. It might have been a roar.

"Oh, for God's sake, Boots, I mean Maggie's column that just came out yesterday in the *Senator*. I think it's a shame and a disgrace on this house, and on this campus, and I think it's awful that nobody would tell you about it. It's about your hometown!" And she turned and flounced into the crowd and was lost.

Boots stood still, rocking, staring at Maggie. The skin around his nose whitened. He turned abruptly and lurched through the French doors and disappeared into the house. The combo struck up then, high and squalling, skidding into a shabby, fractured version of "Heartbreak Hotel." The wolfish young man stood up and began to wail, rotating his scanty pelvis. The KAs scattered gratefully, fluidly, into couples and began to dance.

Hoyt looked at Maggie. "You want to go?" he said.

"No," she said smiling widely at him. "I want to stay. I'm having a good time." She reached for a Dixie Cup and filled it from the tub of tepid punch and drank it down. The singing distance widened, flowed, deepened, warm and Olympian. "I may stay all night. You want to leave, go ahead. I think it might be a good idea."

"Nope." He settled himself back against the bricks of the house. "Think I'll stay for the late show. Looks like a star might be born." His voice was light and level, but he leaned a bit closer to her, propping his arm on the bricks above her head. His fingers dangled very lightly in her hair.

Boots was back before them, a rolled copy of the *Senator* in his hand. His face was distorted, pulled back as with the force of gravity, white and sweating. His eyes were nearly shut. He looked, Maggie thought detachedly, Chinese.

"You just can't keep your mouth shut, can you, Maggie?" he hissed. "Just got to get down there and roll around with the niggers, don't you? Fuck around in the *dirt* with them! This is good, Maggie, oh, yeah, this is real fine stuff, Maggie!" His voice was rising. Couples stopped dancing and stared. Hoyt was still, rigid.

"Boots . . ." Maggie said, mildly.

"Listen, everybody! Listen to what my lady here wrote about my hometown. Isn't this cute?" He scanned the paper, now unrolled, and found his place and read, stumbling: "'Our eyes met and I looked into his. Through them and into another country. It was the country of the human heart. And I knew that I lived there with him. And so do you.'"

He was silent for a moment, his breath heaving and choking and grating. He looked around the circle of white faces. Maggie saw Sue Ellen's, radiant, frightened, like a calla lily. He looked back into Maggie's face. He was blinded. Abruptly, Maggie hiccuped. And giggled. And clapped her hand over her mouth. "Ooops," she said.

His hands shot out and pinioned her shoulders. He shook her violently, like a terrier with a snake. Maggie's head snapped back and forth, back and forth. She could not stop giggling.

"You goddamn little nigger-loving whore!" It

was a high, thin, animal squeal. "You two-bit little Judas—"

Hoyt's fist caught him under his chin and lifted him off his feet. His head snapped back, he stumbled backward and fell sideways against the punch tub. It teetered, tipped, crashed to the flagstones. Purple liquid flooded, blood-dark, out into the circle of dancers, frozen and silent. The combo stumbled to a halt. No one moved.

"Boys! Boys! What is the *meaning* of this . . . ?" Mrs. McClesky stood in the French doors, her hands knotted and writhing, her face crumpled with fright. The white sheep faces turned slowly toward her. "Poor Mother Mac," Maggie said sadly to Hoyt. She slumped against him. "I bet you ruined her party."

He put an arm under her shoulder and around her waist. "Let's get out of here, Maggie," he said, and half carrying, half dragging her, ran her roughly past Mrs. McClesky and through the dining room and drawing room out to the dark street, where she saw, flickering, the dark, carved bulk of his Thunderbird.

"You're always dragging me out of places," she said dreamily, somewhere in mid-drawing room. "Don't you get tired of dragging me out of places?"

"Be quiet. Move your feet!"

On the portico, he stopped to get his breath and shift her weight, and Maggie looked back. She had a clear shot through the house and onto the terrace. Through a radiant scrim pinpricked by tiny lights that bloomed and died and bloomed again, she saw Boots on his hands and knees, vomiting onto the flagstones. Figures were only just uncoiling from the crowd, moving toward him.

"Boots just can't hold his liquor," she said judiciously to Hoyt. And then the lights flared out, and the scrim rushed toward her face, and she slid into darkness like sleep.

20

W HEN SHE WOKE UP, she was looking up into arched darkness, and there was a spattering roar all around her. Her head still spun; she still felt warm and removed and airborne. Giggles floated in her stomach. I feel like the inside of a Coca-Cola bottle that somebody shook, was the first thing she thought. She stretched and encountered resistance with her arms and legs, and turned her head. Hoyt's face swam into view above hers, green-pale in the dash lights of the Thunderbird.

"Hey," she said. "Where we?"

"Hi. You awake? We are at a motel in Lanett. *Outside* a motel in Lanett. I decided to abandon my plans for the evening and find a more congenial place to sleep. And I didn't know what to do with you. You passed out colder than a mackerel. So I brought you along for the ride."

She sat up woozily. She had been lying with her head in his lap in the front seat of the Thunderbird. Rain thrummed on the top of the car and teemed down the windows, blocking vision. A pink-and-green blur of neon swam through it, off at a distance, but no lights were visible near them.

"Yow," she said softly as the car wheeled and rearranged itself around her. "I must still be drunk. You know, I've never been drunk. Look what I've been missing!"

"You don't do anything halfway, do you, Maggie? Sorry I hit your buddy there, but it didn't look like he was going to cool off anytime soon. How come I'm always saving your fanny? You think it's kismet or something?"

"Kismet. You are a *hero,* Hoyt, you know? My hero. And I don't much think Boots is my buddy any more. What do you think?"

"I'd say not, right off hand. Do you care?"

She considered, silent giggles shaking her. "No. I don't think I do. Not with a whimper but a bang. Ol' T. S. was wrong. Bangs are better. Can I have some of that?"

He was drinking from a pint bottle of Jack Daniel's. "Shouldn't I take you back to your house?" he said. "It's almost eleven."

"Noooo-ooobody home," she droned. Really, she thought furrily, I really am drunk. I think I like it. "Got no housemother this summer, Hoyt. Got no diamonds, got no pearls, still I think I'm a lucky girl . . ."

He passed her the bottle and she drank from it, choking and spilling it down her chin.

"I've never been in a motel with a man," she said.

"You're not in one now," he said. "You're outside it. Where you're likely to stay till I decide what to do with you. The question is . . . should I take you somewhere and pour coffee into you, or should we have 'nother little drink or two first?"

"Drinks! You've already bought me coffee this summer. You've never bought me any drinks. I think you're drunk yourself." She peered at him, to focus his face. "You sure look drunk to me."

He chuckled. "I wouldn't be surprised. That was some little scene, Miss Maggie. Didn't know southern gentlemen got that upset. Didn't know Claibornes ever got that upset. Boots isn't going to thank either one of us for that little donnybrook. You think it'll make a stink on campus?"

"No," Maggie said, "because the KAs won't want anybody to know they've got a . . . nigger in their woodpile!" She laughed hilariously. "That's me. I'm a nigger in the KA woodpile!"

He took another swallow from the bottle and passed it back to her. "I read your article," he said.

"My famous, famous article! Where'd you get it?"

"I picked it up when Claiborne dropped it. Wanted to see what it was that made the shit hit the fan."

"What did you think of the great article that started the new civil war?" The car was spinning again. She burrowed her head into Hoyt's shoulder to stop it. He pulled her closer to him.

"I thought it was a silly, emotional, simplistic little

piece of garbage that sounded like a college girl wrote it. But I can see why it pissed Claiborne off. You got him right where he lived, Maggie. There'll be darkness on the Delta for you, sho' nuff, if you ever go back over there."

Maggie sat up and looked at him, widening her eyes to keep him in focus.

"*Silly!* It was *not* silly! It was . . . my poetry professor said it was . . . pro-pro*found,* and *sensitive,* and I was courageous! You just don't know how I've *suffered* for that column, I've been osh . . . ostracized, and . . . "

"Oh, shit. You're no holy martyr, Maggie, just because that idiot Claiborne and his idiot fraternity brothers and their idiot dates jumped on you about a little column in a college newspaper. This column of yours doesn't amount to a drop of piss in a cesspool to what's coming—"

"That's not all! I had to go see the Dean of Women, and the Dean of Students . . . he was so *mean,* Hoyt! Terry Bevins, he's the editor, and I, we *resigned!*" Maudlin sorrow hit her, and she began to sniffle.

"Well, shame on you, then." He fondled her hair, absently. "What did you write the thing for if you're going to turn tail and resign when things get a little hot for you? You might have been in a position to do some real good for the Negro if you'd stuck to your guns . . . you *can* write."

"You don't know anything!" She was suddenly profoundly angry. "You just don't know anything at all! I resigned because Dean Howard was going to get

Terry thrown out of school if he didn't fire me, and he wouldn't fire me, and when I resigned, he did . . . "

"So now Randolph's got two holy martyrs to the cause, and the cause is down the drain. The operation was a success, but the patient died. Maggie, the Negro doesn't need your tears and your tender Junior League sympathy and your . . . your *empathy,* for God's sake." He thumped the newspaper impatiently. "A little college girl's *empathy* for one poor nigger convict in Mississippi isn't going to do this *movement,* this *cause,* any good. Brains, Maggie! Intellect! Discipline, cold, clean *reason*—it's a . . . a . . . movement of history, a giant pendulum swinging, a . . . an inevitable, beautiful *revolution.* I've studied it. I've followed it. I've seen it. It's classic; you only have to look back into history. The Negro won't—"

"The Negro. The Negro!" Maggie was outraged, furious, betrayed. Aloneness wailed in her head. "The capital N Negro! You know what's wrong with you? You know what's the matter with you? Nobody is *real* to you! There's a chunk missing out of you! People don't mean a damned *thing* to you. They're Liberals, or Conservatives, or Good Guys, or Bad Guys, or the Oppressors, or the Oppressed, but they are not *real* to you! They don't sweat, or pick their noses, or itch, or cry; they aren't afraid, they don't *pee.* . . . " She jerked the crumpled newspaper out of his hand and waved it furiously in his face.

"You may be the big expert on the Negro with the capital N, but I met a *man!* I met a *man* in Mississippi!

And it's tearing up my life, and it's ... it's pulling me apart, and that's what's going to happen to you, Hoyt, when you meet a *man!* A *man!* You come back and you talk to me about the Negro when you've met a *man!*"

"Maggie ... Maggie ... "

"Oh, my God, everything is so *awful!* Everybody's gone, I've lost everybody ... "

She began to cry, helplessly at first, the loose, copious tears of drunkenness, and then hard, hurting, shaking sobs that spiraled and soared and tore up from her stomach. He gathered her into his arms and pressed her face into his shoulder. He smoothed her hair, and held her, and let her cry. It was a long time before the awful, uncontrolled crying slowed and she could breathe again. I sure cry a lot, she thought blearily. For somebody who never cries, it's sure been a wet summer.

"Tell me, baby," he said against her hair. "Tell me what's happened to you."

And she did, finally, her mouth still pressed into his shoulder, an occasional sob erupting wetly into his shirt. She told him about Delia and Jenks and Mrs. Kidd; about the visit to the Delta and the jailbreak; about Flournoy and Aiken and Tuck and the column.

"Everything's gone wrong and awful and strange," she finished. "I don't know how all this happened, I don't know how to go back. Everybody I ... *loved* has gone. Boots will be gone. That's over. ... "

"I'm here, baby. Don't cry. I'm here."

"Don't leave me!"

"I won't leave you, Maggie. Ah, I won't . . . "

He kissed her face, softly, her eyes, her hair, her mouth. Blindly, she strained up to him, toward warmth and solidarity and heaviness. He murmured to her, she responded, not knowing what she said, urgency and need swimming over her with his face, which surged in and out of focus. Presently she could not see his face or feel his skin or hear the rain; pure physical sensation was the only thing alive in her. She had never known it could be so powerful. It consumed time and place and dimension; it flooded and drowned her.

She drew back, breath rasping, staring intently to bring his face back into clarity. He stared back, his hands tangled and pulling in her hair, his chest laboring.

"Let me stay with you tonight."

"Maggie, baby, love . . . "

"I want to go with you! Now. Please, please . . . "

"You don't know what you're saying, you don't mean that . . . "

"I do know! I do mean it! I want it! Hoyt, please, *please* don't take me back . . . I want to stay with you!"

He looked at her for a long time. The rain gusted, caroled, shouted.

"Are you sure, Maggie? Are you sure?"

"I'm sure," she moaned, feeling a great, shimmering, nothing-colored void open under her feet. She stepped off into it. "I'm sure."

"Come on, then." He opened the door on his side.

A darkened motel unit loomed out of the flying darkness beyond the door.

"Should you . . . do you have to check in?" It was someone outside and beyond Maggie talking. The distance sang and surged.

"I already did. While you were asleep. Nobody knows you're even here. Come on, love, if you're coming."

"I'm coming."

They dashed through the rain and inside, and shut the door.

21

FOR JUST A MOMENT, for a cool, suspended time when she woke, Maggie thought she was at home in her bedroom in Lytton. She was aware, first, of darkness and coolness . . . deep, deep forest coolness, and a thumping cadence that sounded like the window air-conditioning unit in her upstairs bedroom in the house on Coleman Street. She stretched, long and catlike, and felt soreness in her arms and legs, and an alien sharp pain, and then a throbbing, viselike pain at her temples. I must be sick, she thought. I must have the flu.

And then she was abruptly, coldly, finally awake, and she sat up in bed. She was naked under the rough sheet, and clammily cold. She squinted around the room to stop its sick spinning. It was dim with the gray, underwater light of very early morning. Her clothes lay in a damp heap on a salmon-colored Naugahyde armchair; her crinolines were in a limp drift on the liver-colored carpet. Her strapless Peter Pan bra lay carved and freestanding on the plastic-topped bureau across the room, in a clutter of coins and half-empty motel glasses. Her purse had overturned on the bureau, and cigarettes and lipstick and her compact spilled rowdily out of it.

Hoyt slept in the bed beside her, on his face, one long arm dangling over the side of the bed. The sheet was pulled to his waist. She looked at the whorls of dark hair radiating out from his spine, at a web of faint, inflamed scratches on his back and shoulders.

"Oh, my God," she said softly.

She got out of bed tremulously. Her legs were stiff and rubbery, so that she moved jerkily. There was a fine, nearly imperceptible quivering deep inside her, like the whirring of a hummingbird's wings. Abstractedly, she saw that it shook her hands. "Oh, God, oh, God, oh, God," she whispered to herself over and over, a litany to keep the monstrousness of this at bay. It seemed to help; the frail, lucid, tender superreality of a hangover enveloped her, closing away ordinary reality. She moved gently toward the bathroom, pushing aside heavy air.

She stood under fitful gusts of very hot water, with her eyes closed. With them closed, she could keep awareness safely at a distance. This is not even going to bother me, if I don't let it, she thought, scrubbing dreamily with antiseptic-smelling soap. I can keep this from bothering me indefinitely. It doesn't have to be real, because I don't remember any of it. She didn't, but she did not probe in the whirling inside of her head, either. "The Black Act, the Dirty Deed," she hummed to herself, making a jaunty little cadence of it. She executed a jerky little bump and grind. And I don't even remember it. A thought pierced her with sudden, still, enormous hope. Maybe we didn't. Wouldn't I *know* if we did? She stood motionless in her hope. But then the new pain niggled at her through the hot water, and the hope drained away. But we did, she thought, and the iridescent unreality came flooding back.

Well, what the hell, she thought. So what? I can get him to take me back to the house, and I can get in bed and go to sleep. I can sleep as long as I want to. I don't have to see Boots if I don't want to. I don't have to see him any more. Hoyt either. I don't have to talk to anybody if I don't want to. I don't have to do anything I don't want to do. If I can just get back to the house before this hits. She did not know, exactly, what "this" was, but knew with deep-buried certainty that it would destroy her unless she could keep it at bay, shut it out, keep the bell-like dome of nonfeeling intact around her. Well, I can do that, she thought, and stepped out of the shower and toweled herself and her hair dry, hard and busily. "Wonder what time it is," she said aloud, chattily.

When she came out of the bathroom, wrapped in a towel, he was awake, propped up on their two pillows against the imitation-rattan headboard of the bed. A garish, flat seascape hung tipsily over the bed. "That's an awful painting," Maggie said.

He wiped his hand across his face, his beard making a faint rasping noise. He shook his head from side to side, looking at her. She had a feeling, fleeting and clinical, that for a moment he did not know who she was.

"Hey, lady," he said, and his voice was hoarse in his throat.

"Good morning." She did not look at him, but at her clothes. Busily, she gathered them up and took them into the bathroom. Dressing, she felt vivid, finely focused, totally engaged in the moment. Panties first, then bra, damp with what looked to be a Bourbon stain, then crinolines, then the white voile dress. It was limp and crumpled, but not stained. She ran the zipper expertly up the back. The little hook at the top of the zipper was missing. She smoothed it over her hips. It doesn't look so bad at all, she thought, standing on tiptoe to peer at it in the steamy mirror. He was moving around in the other room; she could hear him bumping, and he must have stumbled over a piece of furniture, because she heard him swear under his breath. She patted her short, wet hair into an orderly cap; ran her powder puff over her face; drew on a bright mouth, with the new coral lipstick. Her eyes looked feverish, glittering, without depth. Somehow they had lost their cola translucence.

When she came back out of the bathroom, he was dressed except for his shoes, standing at the high casement window, the nubbled, lined curtains pulled aside. Pale light limned the room. Maggie saw the empty Jack Daniel's bottle on the floor beside the bed; his shoes, like dead, beached fish, half under it;

his watch lying on top of the coin-operated television set. He turned to her. His face was tentative, naked-looking, his eyes whiter than ever.

"You okay, baby?" he said.

"Fine."

"Maggie?"

"What?"

"I'm . . . are you really okay? Should I be sorry?"

"Good heavens, whatever for? I'm a consenting adult. I expect we were both pretty bombed, weren't we? God, if this is what a hangover is like, I don't plan to have any more of them." She laughed, lightly. Put it off, put it off, don't look, said the crystal voice in her head.

He walked to her, put his hand under her chin, raised her face. "I wasn't drunk," he said. "I mean, that wasn't why . . . "

"Well, I was. Wow. What a merry little old evening, all told." She turned her head away from his fingers, shutting her eyes.

He kissed her lightly on the forehead. "Come on, love," he said. "You're not exactly an old hand at this, are you? It was your first time, wasn't it?"

"There's always a first time for anything," she said. She wanted to be in the car, in the brightening morning, bowling swiftly toward home. She wanted it desperately. Light, normalcy, the house, her bed, a book. She did not want to talk to him any more.

"Maggie? I'm glad it was me. If you're worried that this was . . . a one-night stand or something, don't. I . . . want to see a lot of you from now on. I think I . . . care a lot about you . . . "

"Don't!" The bell lifted, lightning-swift, and anguish flooded in. She closed her eyes, clenched her fists, jerked the bell back into place.

"What do you want me to say? That I love you? That I . . . respect you? I do, that. And maybe I do love you; it's . . . not a way I've felt about anybody before . . . "

"Just don't say anything! I don't want you to say anything! I have to get back to the house now. Goodness knows what everybody's going to think when I come waltzing in . . . what time is it?"

He looked at her for a moment, then reached for his watch and put it on. "It's only six. We'll be back by six-thirty. Nobody will be up this early. It's Sunday."

"So it is. Want to go to church with me, Hoyt?" She giggled again, porcelain breaking.

"Maggie, you're not all right, are you?"

"I'm *fine*. Really. I just . . . want to go."

"We're as good as gone," he said.

They went quietly from the motel unit and got into the car. The morning was still colorless and pearled. Rain stood in puddles on the gravel around the unit. The scattering of cottages, made of concrete block, Maggie saw now, was quiet. All windows were curtained. He started the car, loud and abrupt in the silence. He steered it out of the parking lot.

"Aren't you going to pay the nice man?"

"I paid last night when I registered."

"You think ahead, don't you?"

He reached for her hand; she let it lie limp in his. "This is not a usual thing for me, Maggie, no matter what you think."

"I don't think anything."

They drove in silence for a while, the morning taking on faint color over the woods and fields, the arrow-straight farm roads sheened with pink, like oil slicks, on their black, unlined asphalt surfaces. He reached for the radio, but clicked it off again when a booming, squalling choir announced Sunday morning to east Alabama. Maggie examined the passing land-scape interestedly. She looked over at him, lounging behind the wheel of the car, solid and rumpled and sharply detailed in the morning light, like an Ingres drawing.

"I never really saw you in the daylight," she said.

"Get used to it, then. You'll be seeing a lot of me in all kinds of light. Can you stand it?"

"I don't think so," she said matter-of-factly.

He turned his face to her. The intensity of his eyes swallowed hers. She noticed that he had a peppering of small, pockmarked scars on his right temple.

"What made those scars?" she said.

He touched them. "BBs, one Christmas when I was a kid. You mean that, Maggie? You want me to get lost?"

"I think so, yes."

"Why? Are you ashamed of last night? Or didn't it mean anything to you? You worried about Boots?"

"No. I'm not worried about Boots any more. I just don't think there's anything ... for us to do together."

"There are a million things for us to do together, Maggie."

"Are you kidding? What's left?"

"I'm worried about you, Maggie. You aren't ... acting right. Let's go get some breakfast and talk about this."

"I'm not hungry. Thanks, anyway. How should I act? Are there rules for this?" Rules, rules, sang the crystal voice. Of course there are rules. There are rules for everything. Find the rules and you'll be fine as frog's hair.

"Look, you've had a bad summer. Too much has happened to you. I shouldn't have ... I should have taken you home. But you were the one ... I thought you really ... "

"Don't worry about it, Hoyt. I know I did. I'm not sorry."

"Then why don't you want to see me again? Maggie, it wasn't just a ... *lay*, not to me, anyway. It may have happened too soon, but it would have happened. There's been electricity crackling ever since the first night I saw you. More than electricity. I know you felt it."

"Something, I guess," she said remotely. "I didn't know what it was. All electricity doesn't have to end in bed, Hoyt."

"Well, this doesn't have to end, period. I'm not

going to let it end, Maggie. You're just . . . upset right now. I'll give you some time, but I'm going to call you from Montgomery, every day. And I'm going to come over when you've had time to think about it. Did you really think I'd just lay you and leave you? You don't know me very well if you thought that."

"I don't know you at all. One roll in the hay does not a knowing make."

"Well, it makes a hell of a good start." He grinned over at her, briefly. "We're very good together, Maggie. Very good, wouldn't you say?"

Something very near to terror was scratching on the outside of the bell to be let in. She would not look at it.

"I couldn't say. I don't remember any of it."

"The hell you don't!"

"I don't."

He was silent for another few miles, and then he said, "You will."

She said nothing, absorbed in the horizon. The spires of Semmes Hall wheeled into view over the ruffle of far-off trees. The first rays of full sun, rising above them, pricked the bell tower into sharpness.

The Kappa parking lot was quiet when they pulled into it. Cars were nestled like sleeping chickens between parallel bars of white paint. Windows were curtained and shaded, still dark. Estelle did not come until seven; the kitchen windows were blank. He stopped the Thunderbird under a tangle of hon-

eysuckle-shrouded privet hedge. He stared at his
hands.

"I don't want to leave you," he said.

"I have a lot of studying to do. Test on everybody
up to Yeats. Have you read Yeats?"

" 'And time runs on,' cried she. 'Come out of charity and dance with me in Ireland.' Time runs on, my
pretty Maggie, who thinks she is cool. Come out
of charity and dance with me . . . anywhere. Listen,
should I go by and talk to Boots? I don't want to
leave you with all that shit hanging over your head,
with this column thing up in the air. . . . "

"Don't go talk to Boots!" Another thin chime on
the outside of the bell. "Just leave it alone. I can handle Boots. I don't care about the column, all that's
over now . . . just leave me alone. Please, Hoyt."

"Maggie . . . "

"Please!" She reached for the door handle.

He pulled her back by her left hand, pulled her
close to him and kissed her hairline. "Okay," he said,
releasing her. "I guess you don't want me to walk you
to the door."

The bell slid back into place, and Maggie giggled.
"No. It's locked. And the stable is empty." She slipped
out of the car and shut the door softly. "Goodbye,
Hoyt. Thanks." Thankyou, thankyou, thankyou caroled the voice. Goodbye and amen.

"I'll call you tonight when I get checked in somewhere."

"If you want to." She shrugged.

"I want to. That isn't going to change. Maggie?" She stopped, halfway up the walk. We've done this before, she thought. When I look back, all I'll see is the whites of his eyes. But that was in the dark, that was before . . . she looked back. He was leaning out of his window, and his eyes were not white-rimmed, but blue and shadowed by his dark hair.

"Yes?"

"I guess I love you."

"How about them apples?" Maggie said. She groped the key out of her purse and let herself in the sun porch door. She did not look back. Halfway up the shadowy stairs, her shoes in her hand, she heard the Thunderbird start up, but it did not drive away. She stood for a moment, listening, but by the time she reached her room, glancing at the sleeping mound that was Sister, and drew her curtains aside, the car was gone and the parking lot was still again.

She woke again at two o'clock that afternoon. Jean Lochridge stood in the door of her room, looking cross and unreal in the hot red light coming through Maggie's pulled-down shades. Sister was gone, and the fan sang and hummed. "I thought you were dead," Jean said. "I've been calling you for five minutes. Boots is on the phone."

Maggie leaned on her elbow and stared back at Jean. She was briefly alone on a treeless plain, with pain rushing in on her from the dead, lunar horizons.

Don't look, don't look, chimed the voice clearly. Push it back. The dome descended again.

"Tell him I'll call him later."

"He really wants to talk to you. He says it's urgent."

"Tell him I'm sick. I'll call him back when I feel better." She drew the sheet across her face and slid back toward sleep.

"What's the matter with you? Did y'all have a fight?"

"No," came Maggie's voice through layers of sleep and percale. "I'm just tired. Tell him, will you, Jean?"

"Oh, all right. But it's the third time he's called. I feel like the upstairs maid." And she turned and trudged grumpily down the hall toward the telephone.

Once again, Maggie slept.

22

IN ONE OF HER HIGH SCHOOL biology classes, Maggie and a gangling, acned boy named Bowmar Ferguson had built a terrarium from moss, small plants, earth, and an overturned fishbowl. Maggie had been fascinated by it. The inverted glass sphere had formed its own environment, fed and nurtured the simple plant and animal life they had placed in it by its own alchemy, sustained its miniature territory by its own warm, wet green gases and air. She had watched it endlessly. It was perfect, complete, tranquil, isolated, and thriving away from the stench of formaldehyde and chalk and the clamor of class bells.

She lived now in such a vacuum. She was contained within herself. For the first two or three days after the night in the motel, it had been an effort of sheer will to keep the bright, singing bubble tight around her, but she had managed. Sleeping had helped. So had reading. She had dressed, gone to her classes, come back to her room, read and slept. Anything more lay beyond the translucent perimeters of the bubble and demanded nothing of her.

She would not talk to Boots on the telephone. On Monday, after his last class, he had come by the Kappa house. She heard Virginia Crewes calling her from the drawing room, heard her feet pattering in exasperation up the stairs and down the hall toward her room. She had gone into the bathroom and locked the door, and Virginia finally went away. She had waited until she heard the unmistakable angry growling of the Jaguar fading out of the parking lot, and then she had come out and resumed her reading. She read all of E. M. Forster; finished the *Edith Wharton Reader;* began again on her freshman *Beowulf.* She was fascinated by the new textures and piths she found in the books, which she had missed before, and examined them minutely and with great interest.

The Kappas knew now about the fight at the KA house. She supposed, tranquilly, that most of the campus did. The news of her and Terry Bevins's resignations from the *Senator* staff was all over the campus, too, she knew. She heard little of the usual whispering that would attend such events, because she saw few people. Sister, during those first days, was stricken and solicitous, curling up on the foot of Maggie's bed to talk, to coax, to minister. "I don't think he's mad any more," she said once, peering close into Maggie's face as she lay reading Henry James. "Gary says Kippie says he's really down. You won't talk to him, you won't see him, he's drinking really badly, Maggie. I know he said some things . . . but everybody's forgotten about the silly column by now. He called me, did you know that?"

"Did he?" Maggie turned a page, wishing Sister would be quiet. Were Miss Jessel and Peter Quint real or figments of a repressed governess's hungry imagination? She'd always chosen to think they were real, but now she wasn't so sure. Everything had layers and strata of meaning, endless meaning, if you only took the time to look. . . .

"He wanted me to ask you if you'd see him, just for a minute. I said I would. Maggie, you're *pinned* to him, you've got to *see* him. This is just silly . . . it's not like you to—to punish people."

"I'm not punishing him, Sister. And I'm not pinned to him, either. I'm just tired and I don't feel like talking right now. Okay?"

"Not pinned . . . "

"I mailed it back to him. Sister, I don't want to talk to you any more."

"Well, excuse *me.* I was only trying to help. You lie around here all day, and you read and you sleep and you don't come down to meals, you won't see any of your friends . . . you're getting *queer,* Maggie. Everybody's talking about it. Is it leaving the *Senator,* then? I didn't know you cared that much about . . . "

"I don't. And I wish you'd hush."

"Well, by God, I will, then."

Maggie looked after her as she flounced out of the room, and sighed. She went back to her book. After that, Sister let her alone except for the bare bones of conversation that were required to keep civility alive. She was not in their room often, anyway. The other Kappas, thinking Maggie was grieving for the lost editorship and the lost KA pin, tiptoed solicitously around her when she came downstairs, murmured politely when they passed in the halls, and let her alone. They talked, she knew, at meals, in their rooms, in the Student Union. Many people must be talking. She did not mind.

Hoyt had called that Sunday evening, and every evening for a week. She would not take the calls. The Kappas did not know who he was, only an alien, anonymous voice asking for Maggie, and finally they stopped coming down the hall to her room to tell her the calls had come. They told him she was out, and for a few days he did not call again. Once, after the calls had stopped, she was drifting back from the library at the dinner hour, through the dusky, deserted campus, and saw the Thunderbird cruising slowly down Van Lear Street toward the Kappa house. She saw the back of his dark, rough head. Curiously, she watched the Thunderbird out of sight, wondering if the iridescent skin of the bubble would break. It did not. She changed her course and cut across the campus to one of the movie theaters and went in, to watch *I Was a Teenage Werewolf* with the same judicious interest she had given to *La Strada*.

"There was somebody here to see you," Cornelia Quin said to her when she came back to the house, passing through the drawing room, where a knot of

them were playing bridge. "A guy named Cunningham. He said he came over from Montgomery. We
didn't know where you were."

"I went to a movie."

"Well, he left a telephone number. He said please
call him tonight. He'll wait for your call." She handed
Maggie a scrap of memo pad. Maggie put it carefully
in her purse.

"Thanks, Cornelia."

"Who's he, Maggie? He's interesting. Is he new?"

"He's just a guy I met early this summer. Nobody,
really."

"Maggie . . . "

Maggie looked politely at Cornelia from the first
stair. "Yes?"

"Maggie, what's the matter? We're worried about
you. Everybody is; Terry Bevins has been trying to
reach you, and Dean Fisher asked about you. She
came by not long after the . . . the *Senator* thing, just
to see how we were getting along and bring some
names we could call for a housemother, but I know
it was you she wanted to see. Your door was locked.
You didn't answer. We thought maybe you were sick
or something. Is it . . . is there . . . you know, anything
you want to talk to somebody about?"

"You mean am I pregnant?" Maggie was amused
by the idea, and then she thought, you know, maybe I
am. I could be. The air in the bell sang and swam, but
receded. Wouldn't that be a hoot, she thought.

"No, of *course,* I didn't mean that!"

"Yes, you did. And you know something?"

"What?"

"It's none of your business."

She heard Cornelia's gasp as she went on up the stairs, and she thought, Well, that will keep them busy for a while, anyway. It's as good a reason as any to think I'm strange. They can understand that.

She wasn't, though. Like clockwork, her period came and went. She felt no relief, only a dreamlike wonder at the order and efficiency with which her body went on working when her mind lived in a bell. She missed meals but lost little weight; her skin kept its umber glow and her hair glistened. She smoked a lot, and drank a lot of tapwater coffee, and derived a detached pleasure from asking Sister if she could borrow some Tampax. They'll have to find something else, she thought.

The first week after her resignation from the *Senator,* Flournoy kept Maggie after his class. "I'm very sorry to hear what happened with you and young Bevins, Maggie," he said. "I honestly did not think there would be such a fuss. I have never cared for Howard; he is an egregious ass, but I did not think he had fangs. It must have been quite a painful session for you, and I wish you had called me. I think we might have prevented this, you know."

"It doesn't matter, Dr. Flournoy. We resigned by our own choice."

He looked at her long and somberly. "I'm sorry

you did that. You had allies, you know. You might have accomplished something by staying on."

She started to tell him about the threat to Terry; about the snowballing fury of the meeting; about her own motivations. Then she didn't. I will, later sometime, she thought. Right now it's just too much trouble. The incident seemed eons past; she could not summon up any of the emotions that had erupted from it.

"Well, I've been awfully busy, anyway," she said. "Finals coming up and all. The *Senator* was taking too much of my time as it was. And I've got to go to the library right now."

"I won't keep you, then. You just seemed . . . I thought perhaps you were blaming me for . . . "

"Oh, no. Nothing like that. It's all died down, anyway. Honestly, Dr. Flournoy, I really *don't* care about the *Senator.* And I really *am* busy."

"I should hate to think I have caused you any pain, Maggie."

"Not a single ache." She glittered sunnily at him, got no answering glitter, waved airily, and went out of his class and down the hall and out into the noon sunlight.

Later that week, a letter came from Aiken. "NYC is fabulous, everything I thought it would be," she wrote. "I did get the job; I'm just a draftsman now, but Deirdre thinks I'll be moved up to designer after the baby comes. He's beginning to show a little, a real little bump. They know about him at the office, and they think it's great. Imagine! An unwed mother whose boss worries that she doesn't drink enough milk and fusses like an old mother hen. He's a wonderful man, and the company is stretching things to get me hospitalization and maternity benefits on the insurance. Maggie, it's all just too good to be true, the apartment, and the Village. We go to coffeehouses and listen to poets read their own stuff . . . it's pretty awful, Ben would throw up . . . and Deirdre has all her friends in to meet me. They're interesting, and alive . . . they're doing things. I think about you every time I see them, and how you would love all this. Hurry up, Maggie. Get graduated and come on up here. Write me. Call me." There was an address, and a telephone number. She did not mention Tuck.

"'And time runs on,'" Maggie quoted to herself, hearing Hoyt's voice saying it. "'Come dance with me in Ireland.'"

She put the address and telephone number into her wallet and put the wallet in her purse.

She walked aimlessly into the Student Union one day, during the week before final examinations. She had been avoiding it, not because she would see everyone from that strange, other time but because it had not occurred to her to go there. On this day, she had been walking back from the library, where she spent many hours now, deep into an interior conversation with Daisy Miller. It seemed terribly important to Maggie now to grasp, to understand fully, the motivations of the people she read about in books. "I don't understand why what happened to you was so *inevitable,*" she was saying to Daisy, who peered back at her in perplexity. "It's just that the way I am is not the way they are," Daisy answered her. "There are more of them than me. They outnumber me. *That's* inevitable."

"I don't see why," Maggie said in her head. "Nothing is, really."

"Well, look who's talking," jeered Daisy.

Maggie lifted her head and was in the snack bar of the Union. Her feet had taken her there. She blinked, wondering for a moment what this crowded, smoke-stunned place was. She would have turned and walked out again, but someone was calling her name, and she recognized Terry Bevins. He was sitting with his fiancée at one of the smaller tables on the fringe of the snack bar, and she wondered vaguely if he had been banished from the center ones, but then remembered that Terry and Marie sat there often, that Terry sat where he chose.

He came toward her. "Where in the world have you been? I've been calling you for two weeks. You're never in; I've been worried about you. Nobody's seen you, and Sister said you've gotten queer as a two-dollar bill. You look like you don't even know where you are. What's going on with you, Maggie?"

"Nothing, Terry. Really. I've just let my classes go and I've got a lot of catching up to do. Finals and all."

"I heard you'd broken up with Boots. I heard there was one hell of a stink over at the KA house.

Stupid damned bastard. Is that what's thrown you so, or was it the shit over the column?"

"I'd almost forgotten about the column. And I just . . . Boots and I just really weren't right for each other. We didn't seem to have anything in common. I wonder why I ever thought we did."

"Well, that's the damned truth. Took you long enough to find that out. I hear he's going around with that chick who blew the whistle on you. Sue Ellen Singer. Perfect match, if you ask me."

"Really? How funny." Maggie was interested. "I hadn't heard that. Are they here?" She looked at the center table, the round one. Familiar faces, faces such as she might have recalled out of her childhood, were turned to her, still and waiting. Absently, she waved to the table, and several hands waved back.

"Haven't seen them today. Boots doesn't come in here much any more. Scuttlebutt is he's embarrassed. I can't imagine Boots Claiborne embarrassed. But I guess between that column and the guy who decked him . . . the one you left with . . . who is that guy, anyway, Maggie?"

"Just a friend of Boots's from home. Or an exfriend. Poor Boots. I'm sorry if he's embarrassed. He never could stand that." She was sorry, she realized. Sorry as if recalling something hurtful about someone who had died long ago.

"Is he your new guy, Maggie? Everybody thinks you must have somebody stashed out of town somewhere, nobody ever sees you."

"No. I've only met him twice." And slept with him once, giggled the crystal voice in her head, which had been silent for some time. "He's over at Montgomery covering something . . . oh, something about some Negro students entering the University branch over there this fall. He's with the AP."

"Oh, yeah. A girl named Chryselle Arnold and some guy named Seaton. I've been hearing about that. Nobody knows for sure if they'll show . . . probably pre-register them if they do, by mail, and sneak 'em in the dorms well before fall quarter starts. I hear the town's getting a little ugly about it. King's people are pushing it, they say."

"Something like that. How about you, Terry? Have things been bad for you?"

"Hell, no. I've turned into something of a folk hero, Maggie. You would be, too, if you weren't in hiding. The people on this campus who hate that asshole Howard outnumber the nigger-haters five to one. I guess the whole thing has blown over . . . there wasn't any flack that I know of from the Board of Regents or the alums; our resigning must have done the trick. But I hear Howard got up to make a little talk to the crowd at the Interfraternity Sing the other night—you know the kind of thing, these are my people and the sheep of my pasture—and everybody booed him. He finally had to sit down."

"Really?"

He touched her arm. "Maggie, I wish you'd let me help. You just don't seem . . . in the world, or some-

thing. Come on over to the table and have some coffee with Marie and me. We'll have a long talk, just
like old times."

She gave him a vivid, hasty smile. "Terry, I'm okay.
I'm all right. I've just gotten so far behind...."

He hesitated, then kissed her cheek. "Well, you
call me when you get caught up, and we'll go have a
brew. You're my favorite inflammatory journalist, did
you know that?"

She smiled, a deeper smile. "You're mine, too. I
will. See you later, Terry."

"Take care of yourself, Maggie."

Her parents called that night. M.A. came to call
her to the telephone. "We don't care if you won't
take calls from Boots," she said officiously, "but we do
think you ought to talk to your parents. All we need
is for your parents to call Dean Fisher about you,
when we've gotten this far through the summer without any trouble." She stamped off down the hall, her
duster flaring behind her.

Maggie took the call. "Mama? Daddy?"

Their voices chimed simultaneously. Frances was
on the telephone in the upstairs bedroom, Maggie
knew, and Comer on the extension in his study.

"How are you, baby? We've been worried about
you. You didn't call last week."

"I'm sorry. I've just been so busy... finals are
coming up, you know, and I've just been in such a
whirl...."

"You're not sick, are you? You sound sort of strange."

"Oh, no, I'm just fine. It's just this silly telephone, *you* know. I'm sorry about not calling; I just got so busy . . . I've been out so much, and . . . it's been such a hectic summer."

"I always did say summer school was too much for you, Maggie. You do too much; you need your rest in the summer. Are you keeping up your grades?" Her mother's voice chirred and fussed on the other end of the line. Maggie saw her in her head, drooping and slender in a flowered, long robe, her long hand worrying at a curl of hair over her white forehead.

"Probably out running around every night with that big blond fella," Comer's voice chuckled comfortably. He would be doodling the curly horses' heads he always drew on his desk blotter.

"Oh, well, Boots and I are busy, of course. . . . " Maggie's hand gestured inventively in the air, sketching in dances, swims, picnics, moonlit patios, the props with which her parents, fondly, staged their daughter's world.

"Well, listen. One reason we called, the Mc-Kelveys have offered us their beach house on Sea Island for three weeks in late August and September. They're going to *Europe,* can you imagine, in this heat? And we thought you might like to ask Boots to come with us. We'd planned to leave the day after your

quarter ends, or the day after that, if you need to get
your clothes ready . . . would you like that, honey?"

"Mama, I . . . don't know how I'll be feeling
then. . . ."

"Maggie, you *are* sick, aren't you? I knew you
didn't sound right. Honey, we'll come right down and
get you, when can we, Comer? Tomorrow . . . have
you been to the infirmary? Why didn't you *call* us?"

"Mama, I am *not* sick! The reason I hesitated . . .
the reason I hesitated is that Boots wants me to go
home with him again. We thought we'd drive over
after his last exam is finished . . . his mother wrote
me, but she can write you . . ." Maggie heard her own
voice. It was glib and silver and young. "Mama, we
need to talk about getting married, we have lots to
talk about. I was going to call you . . . you won't mind,
will you, if I spend the holidays with the Claibornes?"
How easy this is, she thought dreamily.

"Why, honey! Well, of course not!" Her mother's
voice was tremulous, thick with triumphant tears.
"But . . . married, Maggie?"

"Well, now, Maggie. Shouldn't our little girl come
on home and talk to us first?" But Comer's voice was
jocular.

"Oh, Mama, Daddy, not till after graduation, of
course. It's just . . . Mrs. Claiborne wants to go over
the house with me, the silver and some of the things
that will . . . you know . . . be ours, that have been in
Boots's family for a long time. . . ." Groveland, vast
and cool and shining with ancestral treasures, spun

out over the wire into the house in Lytton. They were
silent, peopling its emptiness with Maggie's slender,
busy figure. Maggie polishing; Maggie lighting tall
white candles; Maggie greeting guests. How can I?
she said to the crystal voice. Go ahead, you're doing
fine, it said back. They were silent for a moment, and
then Frances said, "Well, darling, you know we're
pleased. You go on and have a good time. We'll call
you from the beach. . . ."

"No, give me the number there. I don't know
where we'll be . . . there are a lot of parties and things
planned. . . ."

"Oh, of course. Well, I've misplaced it, but I'll
send it to you. I have time for another letter before
you leave, don't I? And you write us, too, sugar. Will
you have any time at all to come home before fall
quarter starts? Your clothes . . . "

"Of course, Mama. I'll call you at the beach and
tell you when. You all go on and have a fabulous time,
hear? And I'll see you in . . . oh, early September, I'm
sure. Maybe Boots will come back with me."

"You bring that fella back here with you," Comer
boomed. "We've got a lot to talk about, us two."

"I will, Daddy. And I'll write you. Have a good
time. And Daddy? Mama?"

"Yes, honey."

"I love you."

"We love you, too, sugar. We're real proud of
you."

Maggie went back to her room and locked her

door. She got under the shower and waited for the bubble to break, the skin to split, anguish to come pouring in. She waited to cry. Now, she thought. Now. But it did not. The enormity of the lie tapped and whispered at the round surface outside, but it did not come in. The high, singing silence came, and swelled and roared in her head, and she listened to that until it receded like a weak tide, and then she washed her hair and got into pajamas and opened *The House of Mirth.*

The next morning Maggie cut her classes. She did not go the next day either, or the next. She stayed in her room with her door shut and the fan on, reading. "I really don't feel very well," she said to Sister's guarded face when it looked warily down at her as she woke out of a long afternoon sleep. "I've talked to all my instructors, and they've said I could make up my exams next quarter, if I come back a day or two early. Mama and Daddy are at the beach, or I'd go home, but it's not serious enough to worry them while they're there. I went over to see Dr. Weiler at the infirmary, and he says it's just anemia and I ought to rest. So I think I'll just take it easy till the end of the quarter and do some reading ... I can be doing that, and be all ready for my exams ... and I'll go on home when the folks get back. It will only be a day or two after you all have left." She smiled, radiantly and healthily, at Sister.

"All right," Sister said.

For the rest of the summer, smelling blood, they left her alone.

The day before the quarter ended, Ben Flournoy called her. Totally submerged in *Women in Love,* she padded down the hall when Cornelia's voice called her, and picked up the telephone before she remembered she was taking no calls. But it wouldn't be Boots now, or Hoyt; if they had called her recently, the Kappas had not told her about it. They passed her like ghosts in the house, without substance.

"Hello," she said. Her voice felt rusty and unused.

"I want to know why you have not been in your class this week." He did not say hello. "I want to know what is the matter with you. Kita and I are very concerned."

"Oh, Dr. Flournoy. Well, I've been sick. I have . . . mono, isn't that the *worst?* I thought . . . I thought my roommate called you; I asked her to."

"No one called me, Maggie."

"Well, I'm all right, really, it's just that I'm contagious . . . but I'm keeping up with my reading, I'm all the way through Kenneth Rexroth now. . . . "

"Will you be taking your examination in the morning?"

"I . . . no, I don't guess I can. I'm not supposed to go out. I'll be leaving for home. . . . "

"Miss Deloach, I cannot pass you if you don't take your final examination."

"I understand. That's all right."

"Maggie!" She hardly recognized his voice. There

was agony in it. "Maggie, I have had a letter from Aiken. She has written you several times. You don't answer. She has called; you are not in. A young man named Cunningham has called from Montgomery, twice; he is very, very concerned about you. Why have you cut yourself off this way? *What is the matter with you?*"

"*Nothing*, Dr. Flournoy! Nothing except mononucleosis. You know how that wipes you out; you're tired all the time. . . ."

"Do your parents know you're ill?"

"They're at the beach. I'm not really sick. They'll be home soon, and then I'll go home."

"They should be told. You should not stay alone."

"I'm not that sick!"

He was silent for a moment, and then he said, "Maggie, would you come and stay with Kita and me? Just for a few days, until your parents get home and can come and get you? You should be with someone who can take care of you. . . ."

The bell cracked, crazily, letting shrieking pain in. "Look how you took care of me!" she screamed into the telephone. "Just look how you took care of me! I don't want to stay with you! I don't want to see you!"

There was silence, and then he said, "I thought that must be it. The column. I told Kita that night you were here . . . Maggie, in all the world I have wanted to do one fine thing, one very special thing. I have not been able to do that thing myself, *ergo,*

I teach." There was a pause, singing with pain. He went on, heavily. "I thought perhaps I might help you to do it. The academician's classic achievement, his surrogate immortality. I wish to God that I had died before I caused you pain."

"I'm sorry," she said, crying weakly. The dome snapped back into place and she cried from fatigue. Only fatigue. "I'm sorry. I didn't mean that. It's only that I don't feel good. That's all I meant." Another long pause.

"There is nothing we can do for you, then?"

"No, I'm all right. I'll see you next quarter. I've got you again for Survey of Moderns ... you see, you're not rid of me yet."

"No," he said softly. "I'll never be that."

"See you in September, then."

"Goodbye, Maggie."

The next afternoon, M.A. Appleton, the last Kappa in the house except Maggie, shut the windows and turned off the lights and locked the house and took the key to Dean Fisher. She stood beside her laden car in the parking lot, watching Maggie hang the last of her crinolines and cottons over the broomstick in the back seat of the Plymouth. "You sure you feel like driving all the way home, Maggie?" she said.

"Sure," said Maggie, paying great attention to the snarled clothes hangers. "It's just three hours. Are you off, M.A.?"

"Yes. I'm just going by the Chi O house and pick

up Tish Bennett—thrill, thrill—and then we're off to Gadsden. I . . . hope you feel better by fall. Will you be back for rush, do you think?"

"Oh, sure. Nothing wrong with me that home cooking won't cure. Drive carefully, M.A. Oh, don't kiss me. You don't want mono."

M.A.'s white-lashed eyes flashed her disbelief at mononucleosis, but she did not kiss Maggie and said only, "Well, see you next quarter, then," and got into her brown-and-tan Chevrolet and drove away.

Maggie got into the Plymouth and started it, and drove out of the Kappa parking lot. She drove around the empty copper-colored campus. Only a few cars were left in parking lots at houses and dormitories, waiting for students still fidgeting restlessly in late examinations. The campus looked deflated, bloodless, two-dimensional. The heat seemed to have seeped away with the going of the students, like lifeblood. Maggie drove out to the lake, and then back through Randolph and out to Stovall's. She had a limeade and got two packs of Pall Malls from the machine. She went by the library—the Randolph public library, not the university library—and spent a long time picking out books. She selected *Green Mansions, The Wind in the Willows,* a volume of the Brothers Grimm, *The Jungle Book* and other volumes by Kipling. Then she drove back down College Street and went into the Farmers and Merchants National Bank and cashed a check for fifty dollars. And then she parked the Plymouth in one of the diagonal parking places in front of the little yellow-brick Penn Hotel. She went into the dark cave of the lobby, carrying her overnight case. "I have to stay here between quarters and make up some work," she told the elderly, disinterested desk clerk, who was reading the *Saturday Evening Post* and eating Oreos. "My name is Margaret Hamilton Deloach. Do you have a single room for a week or two?" She was very polite. He slid the stained register toward her and she signed her name, and he handed her a key attached to a brown plastic disc. "Number four, upstairs," he said. "We ain't got nobody to help you with your bags . . . you got bags?"

"Yes, but I'll get them later. My car's locked."

"No visitors, ma'am. It's the rules."

"No visitors."

She climbed the narrow, bare stairs. The stairwell smelled of stale, trapped sun and old carpet. "Ma'am?"

"Yes?"

"TV set takes quarters."

"Thank you."

Maggie put her overnight case down on the metal bureau, painted in brown whorls to resemble wood. She turned on the window air conditioner and drew the faded floral drapes. She slipped out of her skirt and blouse and shoes and lay down on the high, narrow bed. It had a ridge down its middle, like a zebra's neck. She picked up *The Jungle Book* and opened it, skimming pages. "We be of one blood, thou and I," she read. She turned back to the beginning and stuffed a sour pillow behind her neck and began to read. It had been a very long time since she had read it.

23

BETWEEN QUARTERS, the town of Randolph drew back into itself and became a town of aliens. It seemed to Maggie, looking out the window of her room, her elbows propped on the air conditioner, or drifting through the hot streets toward the library or the movie theater or to the smallest of the cafes for her meals, that the people she saw walking on the sidewalks or driving cars along the streets were actors impersonating the townspeople of a small southern town in order to conceal some mysterious inner life from outside eyes. It amused her to think that once the last invader was gone they would come out into the streets in the light of the heavy-hanging, flaccid, late-August moon and practice ancient and unspeakable rites. The middle-aged women in girdles, starched shirtwaists, and sculptured ridges of beauty-parlor curls would put down their grocery bags and become maenads. The middle-aged men in sport shirts and slacks, coming out of the bank or the State Farm office, or drinking Coca-Colas in Mooney's at ten o'clock in the morning, would shed their clothes and put wreaths of crepe myrtle over their balding temples and caper naked in the streets, drinking from wineskins. "They're just waiting for me to leave so they can kill the Corn King," she thought one morning, coming back from the library. She had checked out *The Golden Bough.*

Without the students and their countless small, ironclad rituals, the days were timeless and she went for two or three at a stretch without knowing precisely which day of the week it was. On Wednesdays the noon whistle blew; no mill stood now in Randolph, but one had, once, briefly, and the whistle had somehow never been removed. On Sundays the church bells rang. She remembered one whistle and one morning of caroling bells. A little over a week, then, she thought, and went downstairs and placed a collect call to her parents at the beach house on Sea Island.

"Wonderful time," she told them gaily. "There's so much going on I may stay another two or three days. Is that okay?"

"Of course, baby. It's nice here too, but we miss you. You'll still be home for a day or two before you go back to school?"

"Oh, sure. I'll call again in a few days."

Back upstairs, in the little room that she kept obsessively neat, she lay down on her bed and considered for a moment what she would do next. They would come back to Lytton in another week. I'll have to tell them something, go home or something. I can say we had a fight and we're not going to get married after all. And then I can just come back for fall quarter and go on with everything. That seemed so comfortably remote and unimaginable that she grew sleepy again. You don't have to think about it for another week, said the crystal voice. You don't have to think about anything at all yet. There is time for a long nap, and you have to finish *The Secret Garden* before dinner time. Tonight is chicken potpie. And the picture at the Roxy will have changed. Hurry up. Go to sleep.

She did.

Maggie had not unpacked her car. She brought a fresh outfit and underclothes into the hotel with her every evening when she came back from dinner, and washed the underclothes out in the tiny, brown-stained circular washbasin, and put the used skirts and blouses and dresses in a neat layer over the spare tire in the trunk of the Plymouth each morning when she went for her breakfast. She paid for her room each noon when she left for lunch, with bills from her checking account in the Farmers and Merchants Bank. The elderly clerk did not seem to think it an odd arrangement. He was as incurious as a lizard. He had been there a long time. One morning when she went into the bank to cash another check, the faceless teller said, "Labor Day weekend coming up. You might want to get some extra money out. We'll be closed." September, then, or going to be soon. On impulse, she drew out the balance of the money Comer had sent to be deposited for her. There were three hundred and forty-seven dollars left, and some change. Maybe I'll go somewhere and have a real dinner soon, she thought.

That afternoon, sitting later than usual over lunch in the cafe, her book propped up against the napkin dispenser, she looked up and saw Tuck. He was standing on the street just outside the plate-glass window of the cafe, partially obscured by hand-lettered banners proclaiming air-conditioning and Coca-Cola and the day's dinner special. He stood with two other people, an elderly man who, Maggie knew, taught industrial management, and a young woman in Bermuda shorts and sleeveless blouse, who might have been a faculty wife. The woman wore black-rimmed harlequin glasses and very short, cropped dark hair, and had short, heavy legs, ending in sneakers, but a slender waist. She was not different in perceptible detail from the graduate students and young faculty wives Maggie was accustomed to seeing on the campus, but there was something indisputably eastern about her, which spoke of white steeples and bronze leaves scuttling across New England greens, and stone walls. Tuck had an arm draped around her shoulders and was talking amiably to the elderly professor. It was a comfortable gesture, without ardor. She might have been a sister or a cousin; with their fine dark hair and glasses, they did look alike. I wonder if she's a girlfriend from home, Maggie thought incuriously, staring to see if they were going to come into the cafe. But they strolled on after a moment, back toward the campus and out of sight. I thought he went home or somewhere between quarters. She remembered then that he had said he had planned to go with Aiken to her family's summer place on Martha's Vineyard this holiday, and she thought of Aiken for the first time in a long time. I should write her, she thought. Maybe tell her I saw Tuck and he seemed fine. She'd probably like to know that. I wonder if she's called him, or told him about the baby. He didn't look like a man who's going to be a father. Aiken's fine, pale-gold face swam at the glass of the dome like a face through rain at a window, but did not come in.

A storm broke that evening, just before dinner time, when Maggie had bathed and dressed and was ready to go to the cafe for her dinner. The hot, blanched air of twilight went suddenly eggplant purple, and spears of lightning forked into the earth just to the west of the town; thunder rolled and boomed, rain blew horizontally through the empty street outside the hotel. Maggie pulled aside her curtain and looked at the rain, then sat down in the room's one chair, a sagging, mournful champagne brocade armchair that looked out of place, like a seedy duchess in a grimy ghetto supermarket. She reached for her pile of books, then realized she had read them all and had planned to replenish them at the library next morning. She felt restless and uneasy without a new book. She lit a cigarette and got a drink of metallic tap water, then fished a quarter out of her wallet and pushed it into the slot of the television set. She turned a dial. The set flickered eerily into focus: A street in some city downtown area, obviously, though lined with old trees and parked cars. She saw a stone wall running alongside shapeless, pale big buildings; an iron gate, paved paths leading through grass and trees toward the buildings. There were people running, not fast, dogtrotting and jostling, on the paths and in the streets. They were all heading in the same direction, away from the television camera. Maggie heard automobile horns, and a wordless, high surf of sound as at a football game, and very faint, dry poppings. I've heard that sound somewhere before, she thought vaguely, and got up to turn the volume up. A young excited voice stitched out into the room.

". . . Montgomery campus of the University of Alabama, where violence exploded suddenly tonight when it was learned that two Negro students, Chryselle Arnold, of Russell, Alabama, and Jeffrey Seaton, of Ithaca, New York, have registered for the fall quarter here and are at present in residence in one of the dormitories on the campus. The governor, reached at his office in the state capitol here earlier today, declined to comment on the situation, but said the Alabama National Guard stood ready for mobilization if the tension that has permeated the campus for the past few days should erupt into open violence. Since five o'clock this evening, when it was first learned that the two Negro students were on the campus, the situation has worsened rapidly; mobs of people are gathering on the fringes of the campus and running toward the dormitory where the two students are thought to be barricaded, along with Dean of Women Helena Carr and an unidentified male member of the University faculty, and a Negro minister, also unidentified. From here I can see cars filled with people, shouting and blowing their horns, people running in the streets and onto the campus, hastily summoned Montgomery policemen, trying vainly to contain the crowds. We have reports of rocks and other missiles being thrown at the dormitory where the students are sequestered, and there has been an unconfirmed report of sporadic gunfire. I believe I can hear the gunfire." There was a pause in which she could hear him breathing, and the dry snap of paper. On the screen, watery people still ran through watery trees. "I have just received word that the National Guard *has* been mobilized and will be on the campus shortly," said the young voice. "The governor is en route to the campus, as is President Dorsey, of the University. Newsmen from all over the country are gathered here in Montgomery, and we hope to have live coverage of the situation at the dormitory momentarily. I have been asked by the governor and the Chief of Police to urge viewers *not* to come into the area; there is danger. I repeat, there is danger. . . . "

Maggie stared. Gunfire, she thought wonderingly. That's what that sound was. I should have remembered what it sounded like.

The flickering street changed abruptly to the blank white wall of a building, lit in an unearthly glare. Darkened and shaded windows were visible on two of the building's floors; the other floors were out of sight, off the screen. Under the bottom row of windows, behind a barricade of galvanized steel trash cans, a small knot of men crouched. Figures moved, shadowlike, across the screen, in front of the camera, darting, running low. Puffs of dust exploded inexplicably from the limestone wall behind the crouched, frozen figures. The football noise swelled again, and a louder, staccato stitchery of pops, and a new voice, but again young and high with agitation. Maggie did not hear what he was saying. The camera lurched crazily, suddenly close in on the men behind the garbage cans. One or two held cameras and hand microphones, cords snaking off beyond the screen's range, but most were empty-handed, shrunk and flattened against the building wall, lit monstrously by mercury-vapor lights. One of them was Hoyt.

He was looking directly into the camera. His mouth was open and squared away from his teeth like the mouth of a child crying. The ring of white around the blue eyes shone wildly in the hellish glare of the lights; the pocked scars stood out like craters on the moon. A puff of white erupted from the wall just above the dark head. Dust. He was shouting something, something wild and terrible; Maggie could not hear the words, but his mouth made the same shapes over and over. He looked sightlessly at Maggie through the flaring screen. She looked back, looked for the second time that summer into the eyes of a man blank with terror, a man who would do any-thing, anything at all to avoid harm.

The scene swam sickly back to the campus street, now with the incredible, unimaginable, prehistoric carapace of a tank crawling down it. The crowd had swollen fast. The first young announcer was saying something in a voice on the spilling edge of tears, al-most screaming, but she did not hear it. With a tiny crystal tinkle, the bubble flew apart and was gone.

"Hoyt," Maggie said aloud.

She was well out of Randolph, past the last of the shabby wooden stores and gas stations and driving through dark farm country, punctured only at long intervals with square holes of yellow light, before she realized she had left her room. The rain had stopped. No stars were visible. The low, swollen moon swam in and out of flying clouds. The air was cool and wet; it streamed into the open windows of the car and drove salt tears into the corners of her mouth. Mag-gie was sobbing aloud and mindless with fright. She drove steadily at 80 mph. Voices shouted in her ears, but the singing crystal one was not among them.

"I think I'll stay around for the late show. Looks like a star might be born."

"I helped make the rules, didn't you know? Besides, all rules are off."

"Are they, Maggie?"

"Yes."

"There are a million things for us to do together, Maggie."

"'*Come out of charity and dance with me in Ireland. . . .*'"

"*Don't leave me!*"

"*I won't . . . ah, I won't . . .*"

"*Brains, Maggie! Intellect! Discipline, cold, clean reason . . .*
a movement of history, a giant pendulum swinging, an inevitable,
beautiful revolution . . ."

"*You come back and talk to me when you've met a man!*"

"*I won't . . . ah, I won't leave you. . . .*"

"*. . . talk to me about the Negro when you've met a man! A*
man! A man. . . ."

"*I won't leave you . . . I guess I love you. . . .*"

"*How about them apples?*"

"*A man . . . met a man . . . a man. . . .*"

Maggie had seen the campus in Montgomery before. She and Aiken had driven through it the evening they had dinner there. It was in an old section,
hard downtown, rimmed at its edges with the gentle,
peeling decay of sliding old neighborhoods, but still
lovely and graceful and tree-vaulted inside its walls.
She had thought it a watercolor, something from a
blurred old calendar, prettier than Randolph, dreaming in an enchantment. She drove straight to it.

Downtown Montgomery was oddly deserted;
white streetlights glared on emptied streets, but
two blocks from the campus she began to see the
empty cars, parked crazily along the streets and on
sidewalks, some of their doors left hanging open.
She parked her Plymouth in a darkened filling station, beside the gas pump, got out, began to run.
The parked cars thickened on the side street where

she ran, her heart jolting in her throat, and when she reached an intersection, she saw that from there to the stone wall that marked the beginning of the campus, they were solid and frozen, blocking moving traffic. A sweating young policeman stood alone in the middle of the intersection, whistling at slow-moving streams of traffic spilling in from the four streets, halting them, trying to turn them. He did not notice her. Many of the people in the moving cars obediently turned down other streets, but others emptied out of doors and began to jog-trot along with Maggie, toward the iron gate in the stone wall. They were not college students. Most had the heavy, anonymous faces and bulging, whiplike bodies of men who did physical work at things that honed them hard and paid them little; or they were slack and going to paunch, older, puffing as they jogged along. Maggie ran with them and past them, not seeing them, whimpering with each beat of her shoes against the sidewalk. She had a pebble in one of them.

She ran between the iron gates and onto the campus. The running crowd was thicker now. They made little noise, singlemindedly grunting along toward the hectic glow of light from beyond the shouldering buildings ahead of them. No one tried to stop them as they ran. The atavistic, snarling roar of a crowd came out to meet them, but it was still muffled, as through mountains, and the sporadic popping was as trivial as she remembered. Running together, silently, like some spectral relay team, they broke between two of the dark buildings and into a quadrangle.

The riot was there.

The quadrangle was lit into white, lunar detail by the mercury-vapor spots of the mobile television vans ringing it. Their generators throbbed steadily under the crowd roar like a heartbeat. Lights spun luridly off drifting wisps of something frosty and white. That must be tear gas, Maggie thought. I never saw tear gas.

There must have been two thousand people crowded into the quadrangle. They were a solid wave, a sea, an ocean. The savage noise howled in her ears; no words were audible, but the sound wailed ferally, bouncing off buildings. The popping that cut through it did not sound as though it came from anywhere near her position on the fringe of the crowd; she could not tell where it came from. It sounded high and far away, above and beyond her. She could not see through the crowd to the center of the quadrangle, but she could make out small doll figures in khaki here and there in it, dwarfed and engulfed, futile hands outstretched and flailing at the solid mass of the crowd. The crowd did not seem to be moving much, but it boiled inside itself like a hurricane, surged forward, back, forward again. Maggie dipped into it, elbowing, clawing, shoving. She beat her way blindly through it as through tough sapling undergrowth. No one took notice of her.

She broke through it into an open core of space. She saw the guardsmen then, arms linked in a desperate barrier, backs to the wall of a building. Beyond them, off in the dark where the spotlights did not reach, she made out the bulk of large, grinding machines, tanks or television vans, she did not know which. People darted aimlessly in all directions on the fringe of this inner core; not much seemed to be happening. Spotlights played on the wall of the building, and the crowd seemed to strain toward it like a single mammoth beast. But there was not much real motion, only the sound. It deafened, blinded, choked her. It beat at her face physically, like buffeting wings. She did not see any policemen, only the young, helmeted guardsmen, whose linked, tan arms guarded, ridiculously, the blind face of the building. One of them, she noticed, was crying. There were perhaps twenty of them.

There was another glissando of pops from far behind and above her, and more white dust puffed from the wall, and the line of guardsmen broke and flailed and reassembled, fluidly. She saw then that it was the knot of trapped newsmen behind the garbage cans that they protected. Hoyt was there, crouched on one knee, his arms crossed over his face and above his head. Before the khaki line congealed again, she could see that one of the men beside Hoyt lay on his back, very still, and another leaned over him.

The crowd at her back pressed forward, and then broke and spilled, bellowing wordless resentment.

A red-faced officer in khakis, a huge man, like a tree trunk, stepped a little way into the open space and raised a bullhorn to his mouth. It carried his voice, booming dismally, over the malevolent anthem of the crowd; over the breaking of window glass she had not noticed before; over the chugging of many growling, idling engines.

"You guys bring those newsmen out of there," the man roared metallically. "We've got the sonofabitching snipers pinned down; they're in the bell tower! Move 'em out before we lose 'em again! Come on, you motherfuckers, while you've got cover! Move!"

The guardsmen broke once again, turning toward the little group of men. The crowd sighed, a huge, old ocean sound. Two of the guardsmen shouldered aside the leaning newsman and fumbled at the one who lay flat and still. The other men did not move; Hoyt still crouched behind the trash can, his head covered.

Maggie ran. She ran straight out of the crowd, past the officer with the bullhorn. She ran toward the wavering line of guardsmen. She screamed aloud.

"Hoyt, get up, Hoyt, get up, get up. . . . "

The crowd surged after her, sound exploding over her head, and hard, hurting hands caught at her arms and shoulders. "Get back, get down, you goddamn little fool, you'll get killed. . . . " The big officer.

Hoyt heard her. He shook off the hands of the guardsmen who were pulling at him. He rose unsteadily to his feet, turned a blinded face toward her. She struggled in the officer's pinioning arms. She saw his mouth open, frame her name, bemused, questioning, though she heard no sound.

"Maggie?"

A thin scattering of pops; he spun and sagged, back and down, infinitely slowly, into the ring of jostling khaki and out of her sight. The officer let go of her and lunged forward, cursing monotonously. The crowd surged backward, dragging Maggie with it. The single beast had scented, had seen danger, and turned screaming in flight. Blinded and deafened and smothered, Maggie was drowned in the fleeing crowd and swept back with it.

It threw her up on the darkened fringe of the campus, near the iron gate, against a tree. She leaned against it for a long time, head down like a spent animal, hearing and seeing nothing of the straggling crowd streaming past her off the campus. Her heart and ears were bursting. She felt only the rough bark of the tree against her face and shoulder. Breath returned gradually, and she lifted her head back into the high, singing silence of the glass bell.

She turned and walked with the crowd off the campus. She walked and walked. She walked with the blind, stiff gait of a driven animal. The crowd jostled and pummeled her, but out of the careening night she heard only the banshee wail of sirens coiling in from a distance, the first she had heard.

She walked back to her car, singing in her head with the voice of the bell. Once, she passed an empty car with its radio keening into the quieting night.

"Well, since my baby left me, found a new place to dwell, down at the end of Lonely Street at Heartbreak Hotel. . . . "

Maggie reached in through the open window and turned the radio off.

She reached the Plymouth in the dark filling station and got into it. She drove out of Montgomery and back down the darkened highway into Randolph, and through it, and up through the sleeping mill towns of the Chattahoochee Valley into Georgia. She drove steadily and well. When she reached the house on Coleman Street, in Lytton, it was four o'clock in the morning. For the rest of her life, she remembered none of the drive.

down on the old round oak table, bare now, because, of course, there was no one home. She went into the kitchen and opened the refrigerator. It was bright and bare, too, but there was a blue pottery pitcher covered with waxed paper held down by a rubber band. She took off the paper and sniffed the pitcher. Orange juice. She poured a glassful of it and took it into the breakfast room and sat down and began to write.

She wrote for a long time. First light was beginning to seep in through Frances's candy-striped kitchen curtains over the old double sink when she finished writing. She folded the letter and put it into an envelope, licked the stale, crumbling glue on the flap and sealed it, and propped it against a Chinese bowl on the gatelegged table in the hall entryway.

Then she went upstairs into her room and pulled a slip of paper out of her purse and took it into her parents' room. She sat on the edge of the big mahogany bed with the pineapple finials and drew the bedside telephone to her. She dialed the operator and gave a number.

"Aiken?"

"Maggie? What on earth . . . what's the matter? It's not even light yet."

"I'm sorry. Listen, Aiken. I'm coming."

"Coming . . . here? To New York? That's fabulous, Maggie, but when . . . where are you, anyway?"

"I'm at home now. I'm coming tomorrow, if it's still all right with you."

24

SHE LET HERSELF into the house with the key Comer and Frances had given her when she was a senior in high school. The key was a badge of honor, Comer said, not to be abused. Maggie had not abused it.

She walked through the dark house, room by room—kitchen, downstairs bathroom, back porch. She climbed the stairs. Her parents' room, dim and empty and large. Her mother's sewing room. The big corner guest room at the back of the house. Her own room opposite it, empty, empty. She went into her bathroom and turned on the light and looked at herself in the mirror over the washbasin. White, still face and dark, mirror-water eyes looked back at her. "Still there?" she said experimentally to the crystal voice. It did not answer her. There was nothing around her but an endless, level, lapping calm.

She went into her father's study and rummaged paper and a ballpoint pen out of the top drawer of the old desk that had belonged to his father, her unknown grandfather, the dentist. She took the stationery and pen into the breakfast room and put it

"Tomorrow! ... Well, of course. Sure! I can't wait. But, Maggie, what about graduation? What's going on with you, anyway? I wrote Ben when you didn't answer my letters, but he never wrote back ... and listen, somebody called you here; I don't know how they knew ... "

"I'll tell you all about it when I get there. I'll leave in a couple of hours and I figure I'll be there day after tomorrow. I have no idea how to find you, so I'll call you at work before I start into New York. Will you give me your office number?"

Aiken gave her a number and she wrote it down, carefully.

"Maggie, what did your parents say about all this?"

"I'll tell you about it. I have to go now. Listen, I don't have much money."

"You won't need it. We can find you a job. But, Maggie, listen—"

"See you in a couple of days, Aiken."

"Maggie—"

"What?"

"This guy who called you here, tonight, late. It was really funny. I don't know why he thought you would be here ... "

Maggie's heart swelled and stilled. The crystal voice fluted wordlessly in her ears.

"What guy?"

"I don't know, he wouldn't say, he just said you'd know. And when I said you weren't here, that you'd be in Lytton now, he said, no, you weren't because he'd called there, but that he thought you'd be here soon."

"What else?"

"He said tell you it was just a scratch. And that he'd be seeing you soon. *What* was just a scratch, for God's sake? Who on earth . . . ?"

The crystal voice spiraled up and up, up to a silver crescendo that passed beyond sound into pain and then out of her ears. Clear, cool, liquid silence washed against Maggie's face. Lucidity flooded the bedroom like rain. Lucidity that trembled on the edge of something radiant that could not be looked at, yet.

"Thank you, Aiken," she said.

"Oh, and, Maggie?"

"Yes?"

"He said to tell you he met a man."

The author wishes to thank the following for permission to reprint material in this book:

Anton Publications for lyrics from "All About Ronnie" by Joe Green, copyright 1953 by Anton Publications; subpublishing rights to Francis Day & Hunter; reprinted by permission of the copyright owners.

Bibo Music Publishers, Inc. (a division of T.B. Harms Company) for lyrics appearing on page 184 from "The Wayward Wind" by Herb Newman and Stan Lebowsky, copyright © 1956 by Bibo Music Publishers, Inc. (a division of T.B. Harms Company).

Macmillan Publishing Company, Inc., A.P. Watt & Son, M.B. Yeats, Miss Anne Yeats and Macmillan London for selections from *The Collected Poems of William Butler Yeats:* "The Second Coming," copyright 1924 by Macmillan Publishing Co., Inc., renewed 1952 by Bertha Georgie Yeats; "When You Are Old," copyright 1906 by Macmillan Publishing Co., Inc., renewed 1934 by William Butler Yeats; "I Am of Ireland," copyright 1933 by Macmillan Publishing Co., Inc., renewed 1961 by Bertha Georgie Yeats.

Random House, Inc., for "The Curse" by John M. Synge, from *The Complete Works of John M. Synge*, copyright 1909 by Random House, Inc., renewed 1937 by Edward Synge and Francis Edmund Stephens.

Tree Publishing Co., Inc., for lyrics appearing on pages 33, 45, 226, and 368 from "Heartbreak Hotel," words and music by Mae Boren Axton, Tommy Durden and Elvis Presley; copyright © 1956 by Tree Publishing Co., Inc.

Unichappel Music, Inc., for lyrics appearing on page 299–300 from "Honey Hush" by Lou Willie Turner, copyright © 1954 by Progressive Music Publishing Co., Inc. Copyright and all rights assigned to Unichappel Music, Inc., Belinda Music, Inc., publisher. All Rights Reserved. International Copyright secured.

Any inadvertent omission will be corrected in a future printing if notification in writing is sent to the publisher.